FIVE-MINUTE
MYSTERIES

FIVE-MINUTE
MYSTERIES

MORE THAN 100 CASES OF MURDER
AND MAYHEM FOR YOU TO SOLVE

FIVE-MINUTE MYSTERIES

MORE FIVE-MINUTE MYSTERIES

FURTHER FIVE-MINUTE MYSTERIES

KEN WEBER

QUALITY PAPERBACK BOOK CLUB
NEW YORK

Five-Minute Mysteries
More Than 100 Cases of Murder and Mayhem for You to Solve

*For all the friends who
find themselves in here*

FIVE-MINUTE
MYSTERIES

Contents

1

An Early Morning Murder at 13 Humberview

POLICE CONSTABLE MICHAEL CALEDON PICKED his way gingerly around the piles of gravel and dirt and dust-covered debris strewn about by the road repair crew. Buffing his black shoes to the proper wattage each morning was his least favorite activity and he had no intention of wasting the effort in his first call of the day. He'd parked the patrol car farther away than necessary for the same reason: to keep it clean. When the crew started up at — he looked at his watch — seven o'clock, only nine minutes away, there would be plenty of dirt and noise. He'd seen this bunch move in yesterday to rip up the street.

So complete was his concentration that he found himself on the little flagstone walk at 13 Humberview before he realized it. That surprise, coupled with his sudden awareness that the old lady was sitting on the porch waiting for him, must have showed on his face, for Mrs. Van Nough explained very sweetly:

"I always have my coffee on the porch in this nice weather.

Sometimes I even get out before the sun is over those trees. We'll have to go inside today, though; there's not much point in being out here when they start." She waved at the silent machinery on the street. "What do you take in your coffee, young man?"

Michael used the three short strides up the walk to gather himself.

"Good morning." He held out his hands. "I'm here to get. . . ."

"What do you take in your coffee? I have some muffins too, that my neighbor made."

Michael didn't drink coffee, but how did he say no to such a nice old lady?

"Uh . . . just half a cup, please, and milk, lots of milk." That was how.

"Excuse me, then. I'll be right back." Mrs. Van Nough got up, shuffled over to the screen door and went inside.

Michael was having real trouble controlling his surprise. The lady was not behaving at all like a bereaved widow. Four days earlier, in fact at just this time — his watch now said 6:54 — her husband had been shot in their bed. He was also surprised by how well she spoke. Mrs. Van Nough was deaf, at least according to Sergeant Cosman. Michael had been sent because he was the best on the force at signing. So far, that skill had been entirely superfluous.

His surprise was not diminished in the least when Mrs. Van Nough came back out the door saying:

"No doubt you're wondering how we're able to communicate so easily? Well, I wasn't always deaf. Not until my accident two years ago. Here's your coffee, Constable. I can sign. Are you the one they said would come because you can sign? There's not much need. I'm pretty good at lips. You get good. You have to. Besides, everybody always says the same things to old ladies anyway!"

Her smile grew even sweeter. Michael was so charmed he was almost able to ignore the taste of coffee.

"My other little trick," she lowered her voice conspiratorially, "now don't you tell anybody, Constable." Her smile grew wider and even more irresistible. "My other little trick is, I do all the talking! People don't mind if old ladies prattle on, now do they?

"Now you want to know all about poor Alvin, don't you? I don't know why. I told those other nice policemen everything. Poor Alvin. We were only married three years, you see. He was my third husband."

Without realizing it, Michael bit into a second muffin. He didn't say a word, as Mrs. Van Nough continued.

"It happened when I was having my coffee here, just like this. It was a beautiful day, one of those extra-special summer days. You know, clear, quiet, warm. Of course I couldn't hear the shot, so poor Alvin. . . ."

With a raucous cough, the first of the diesel engines started out on the street, followed by another, then a third, filling the air with a blend of aggressive clatter. The operators held the throttles open, not just to warm up their machines, but also to ensure that everyone in hearing distance would be awake to appreciate their efforts.

Mrs. Van Nough winced. The early morning breeze had brought the exhaust fumes onto the porch.

"Come," she shouted over the din. "We'll go inside. Would you carry the muffins?"

Michael picked up the plate and followed her. How, he thought to himself, how on earth am I going to tell Sergeant Cosman that such a sweet old lady is a liar?

What has tipped Michael Caledon to the realization that Mrs. Van Nough may not be all she pretends?

11

2

The Case of the Slow-Moving Ducks

IT WAS NOT JUST THE SMELL OF lawyers' offices that bothered him, Geoff Dilley decided as he looked around the library. To be honest, there really was no smell anyway; these offices just *seemed* musty because of all those stacks and stacks of law books. What bothered him, Geoff realized, was the overwhelming *importance* of everything.

Starting with the books. That many books simply looked important. Then there were the secretaries. They always seemed so crisply efficient. And important. The furniture was important too: thick and solid and ordered, like the books. Then there were the lawyers themselves.

"They behave like high priests," Geoff muttered aloud.

Geoff Dilley, private investigator, had worked himself up to the point of walking out of the library and chucking the whole thing, when the door swung wide at the urgent bidding of F.V. Douglas Doyle, barrister, solicitor, notary public and senior partner of Doyle, Feldstein and Sperazzini.

Geoff was just beginning to conclude that it was his

imagination which had made the door open more majestically than an ordinary door, when Doyle spoke.

"You're Dilley then, right?" No hello. No greetings. No preliminaries. Just a confirmation of identity. Geoff felt a bit like a hostile witness. Well, two could play that way, and he had been going to leave anyway.

"It was *you* that called *me*. My name is in your appointment book." Geoff felt he'd scored a small point.

Doyle peered over his glasses. "Yes, but it was not my idea. Not at your fee anyway."

"*My* fee!" Geoff almost came out of his seat. He knew he was the most expensive private investigator in town. More than one potential client had had a change of heart after the first discussion of daily rate and expenses. On the other hand, the reputation of Doyle, Feldstein and Sperazzini, although one of excellence, was also one of high fees, and extreme parsimony to boot.

"*My* fee!" Geoff repeated. "Look, if there's going. . . ."

"Gentlemen, please." The soft voice commanded attention. "It was my request to involve you, Mr. Dilley. My name is Ben Paul." From behind F.V. Douglas Doyle, a tall, greying man held out his hand to Geoff. "I'm told you are the best in the field. I asked Mr. Doyle to bring you in."

Doyle took a seat and began talking as though nothing at all had happened. Geoff realized why the man was so good in court.

"Mr. Paul here is being sued. The case is wrong. It's crooked. It's trivial. It should be thrown out." He paused uncomfortably. "We just can't find the weak spot in the other side." He looked at Ben Paul. "As yet."

"I was rear-ended last spring on a country road," Ben Paul explained in his soft voice. "A young man on a motorcycle hit me when I slowed to let a duck lead her little ones across the road. The young man was going very fast. When he hit me, he catapulted right over the top of my car. He was hurt very badly."

"Wait a minute. Wait a minute." Geoff was shaking his head. "First of all, I don't do traffic. Too messy. Too piddly. And everybody lies. Secondly, if he hit you, shouldn't *you* be suing *him*?"

"I've advised my client to countersue," Doyle intervened. "At the very least we can delay the thing a year or more."

Ben Paul continued in his soft voice. "Mr. Dilley, it's not quite that way. You see, I'm being sued for half-a-million dollars over and above my insurance coverage. The young man has two witnesses who will swear that I stopped abruptly and with no reason. That makes me the cause of the accident."

"Well, did you stop that way or not?" Dilley wanted to know.

"Mr. Paul *slowed*," Doyle stated in his court voice. "He slowed because of his laudable commitment to wildlife preservation. He did not stop abruptly."

"The young man is lying," Ben Paul said in his quiet, authoritative voice.

Geoff Dilley saw what a powerful team these two would make in court: Doyle with his declamatory, stentorian style, contrasted with Ben Paul's mellow but earnest sincerity.

"His witnesses are lying too," Ben Paul continued. "They are all family. Cousins by marriage, I think."

"Here's the police report." Doyle handed it to Geoff, who began to skim the summary.

Lake Erie Division — June 10 — 9:05 P.M. —
Concession 9 at Side Road. . . .

"You can read it later," Doyle said. "Everything's there. The problem is simply the witnesses. If we can shake them. . . ." He frowned in thought. "Remember that hot, muggy spell early last summer? You see, they were sitting out front. It happened almost in front of them. I've been there. They have a clear view of the road from their little front yard, but only right in front of the place."

Ben Paul continued. "In fact three seconds earlier, or later, and they would not be able to claim seeing anything, because there's swamp on either side of their farmhouse right up to the road, and big willow trees too."

Geoff pursed his lips. "How come you're so sure they're lying?"

Doyle pulled his glasses farther down his nose and held Geoff Dilley with the look that had withered many a witness. "Because my client is telling the truth." Then he softened. "Besides, their spiel is too pat, too rehearsed. They're lousy actors. Even an amateur can tell they're using a script."

"And you need some way to crack the shell in court?" Geoff added.

"Right," Doyle responded. "Just one simple thing. With amateur liars, you only need a nudge and they'll roll right away." He paused. "Why? You mean you've got something?"

Geoff Dilley smiled. "Yes. Do you want it? At my fee?"

What weakness has Geoff Dilley been able to detect in the witnesses' story?

3

Squash and the Scales of Justice

WHEN THE FOURTEENTH RUN-THROUGH failed as badly as the first, CINCFDSOP yielded to a rare admission of total defeat. CINCFDSOP (Commander-in-Chief: Foreign Dignitaries Security Operations Procedures) was Desmond Malmquist Carver. Junior personnel called him "Mr. Carver, Sir." He'd have preferred "Colonel" but that was officially frowned upon. Agents with seniority called him "Sir." No one addressed him in the familiar, except for Gordon Pape, who called him "Des" — and once "Sink," but that was another story.

An ex-military man like the rest of the FDSOP branch, Carver was accustomed to success, and what he had just been watching did nothing for his — or anyone's — sense of well-being.

"There has to be a way! There just has to be!" He looked at his watch, then slapped the table. "This meeting's over! Go get something to eat. We'll reconvene at 1900 hours. No, 1905. I'll be in my office."

He stood up quickly, too quickly as it turned out, because when the crisis team jumped to their feet with him, they knocked the apparatus flying. Two of them grabbed for the squash balls; another dropped to his knees hurriedly to retrieve the little weights that had fallen onto the floor. Carver paid no attention. He kicked a tiny one-gram weight into the corner and walked out, slamming the door.

Even before the sound faded, he reopened it.

"One of you bring Pape," he commanded.

They nodded in unison.

In the comfort of his office, Desmond Carver took off his tie and dropped into a chair beneath the picture of a young lieutenant grinning beside the burned-out hull of a North Korean tank. He longed for Korea again. It was so simple then, he thought. HQ would say: "Take the hill!" So you shelled it. You led your men up. You took it. Then you led them back down and on to the next one.

"A bit like the Grand Old Duke of York," he said to himself with a grin. "But still a lot better than this crisis nonsense today."

The nonsense today was the general happiness, unfettered comfort, and absolute security of His Esteemed Excellency, Chou Lai Deng, minister of justice, squash enthusiast and most likely successor to the premiership of the People's Republic of China. What made it nonsense to Carver was not the person of Chou Lai Deng, who had proven himself to be urbane, pleasant and cooperative. It was the way in which he had to be protected. Chou had to be looked after — no question about that — but it was never to appear that way. It must never appear to anyone, even Chou, that he required protection, otherwise he would lose face. Yet FDSOP rated the man Category Seven! Even the Queen of England was only Category Five.

The crisis part was tomorrow morning's squash game between Chou and the president. That game, unless FDSOP could prevent it, was going to turn into a diplomatic incident of major consequence.

While the president was a top-flight squash player, there was no doubt that Chou would win — he was world-class. That part was all right, however — in fact, the State Department preferred it so. After all, this was squash, not baseball or golf. As long as the president gave Chou a good run, he didn't have to win. The problem — the crisis — was sabotaged equipment.

An FDSOP agent had obtained incontrovertible evidence that one of the squash balls they were to use was ever so slightly, but quite deliberately, weighted on one side. It would bounce just a bit off center, just a bit off true — and make both the president and Chou look like fools in front of hordes of media.

A jouncing tap on the door startled Carver.

"Gordon Pape, Des!" a cheerful voice announced.

"Not here! The mee. . . ."

The door opened, then closed, and Gordon Pape had taken a seat before Carver was even sure what he had been going to say.

"Heard you needed me," Pape smiled, and proceeded to dangle his leg comfortably over the arm of his chair. He was oblivious to CINCFDSOP's fixation with protocol.

"The squash game?"

Carver willed himself to be calm. Gordon Pape was the only non-military type in the branch. He was irreverent and irrepressible, but simply the best agent they had.

"How thoroughly have you been briefed?" Carver asked, addressing himself to the desk blotter. The dangling leg was too much for him.

"Well, I know all about the game, if that's what you mean," Pape said, "but so does the whole world. The rest of it I'm pretty sketchy on. All that I know is that they might be playing with a wonky ball that would make them both look dumb. I got that from that new kid of yours with the funny haircut."

"That new kid," Carver's glare was focused this time, "is a former marine and the haircut is regulation."

Gordon Pape shifted in his chair so that he could dangle his other leg over the arm as well.

Carver cleared his throat. "The matter, plain and simple, is that we have to replace one bad squash ball with a normal one."

For the first time, Pape sat up straight. "I suppose," he said, "it's not just a simple case of palming the bad one and replacing it, is it?"

"No," Carver replied. "Number one, the squash balls, including the sabotaged one, are being supplied by Chou. Heavy symbolism here. After the game there's going to be a new trade agreement signed. Among other things, China's going to sell us sports equipment."

Pape whistled in appreciation of the situation.

"Number two, they're already on display in Chou's suite. Have been since he arrived. You'd never be allowed to touch them. Besides, there are eight. You could never check that many without being obvious.

"Number three. Our information is that you can't tell the bad one from the good ones by feel or appearance anyway, or even by picking it up."

"So nobody knows which one it is?" Pape was becoming seriously interested.

"All we know," Carver leaned forward, "is that it weighs a few milligrams more than it should."

"I see," Pape murmured. "Is there any good news?"

"There's one piece of sheer luck. Chou is very proud of being minister of justice. Last year the Canadian government gave him a balance scale in twenty-four-karat gold. You know — the Blind Justice statue? It's a real working scale, and he just loves it. Takes it everywhere he goes, and makes sure it's always out where everybody sees it."

Pape was leaning forward now. "That means you've got the equipment right there! Why don't you just send somebody in to do the job?"

For a long time, Desmond Malmquist Carver held his breath. "Maybe," he said, "maybe . . . uh . . . you can help us here." He swallowed. "State has asked for the privilege of carrying the balls from Chou's suite to the court. The Chinese have agreed — they're flattered, in fact. That means I can get one of our people in wearing a gymnasium-attendant's uniform. Even if they frisk him — which I doubt — one squash ball in his pocket is going to look normal enough.

"The problem is time. We've been at it all afternoon with a duplicate of Chou's scales. At the absolute outside, our agent has got time to use the scale for only two weighs. Now, how does he find that ringer using the scale only twice?"

Pape turned to lift his leg over the arm of the chair again, and allowed himself to slip down comfortably.

"You've done a lot of homework, Des," he said with genuine admiration. "Now do you want me to be the attendant tomorrow morning, or have you got someone else in mind?"

Gordon Pape has a solution. What is it?

4

Microwaves on the Freeway?

"GO AHEAD." CONNIE MOUNT SMILED indulgently at her husband and nodded at the CB radio. Frank was itching to turn up the volume and set the tuning a little finer. What they were hearing was too interesting to ignore.

"Do you want to drive?" she added, taking her hands off the steering wheel momentarily.

"No," Frank replied, both hands on the CB dial. "Let me fiddle with this thing."

Frank Mount had left the police force five years earlier, in body but not in spirit. When they had pulled onto the freeway a few seconds ago, on their way to a holiday weekend, the CB had already been set to the police band. But because the adjustment was incorrect, Frank and Connie had heard only intermittent bursts, excited chatter.

". . . semi . . . microwaves . . . ten minutes . . . south . . . Road . . ."

On the repeat, however, they had heard it all.

"Smokey! You got your ears on? This is dispatch at Byron

Transport! I've got a hot load! Semi full of microwaves! Stole it right out of the yard ten minutes ago! Went south down Service Road! You getting this?"

Frank looked up at Connie. "That's Mike Dunn. He's calling right on air. That's smart! It takes too long to phone. Whoever's got that truck, once they're on the freeway they'll be mighty hard to find. Byron puts out over fifty semis all at once this time of the morning. There just isn't enough patrol to check them all! We . . . I mean, they . . . uh, Patrol Center, that is — only has two black-and-whites in both directions anyway!"

"Yes, of course!" Connie was catching the excitement. "And Byron is entirely standardized," she said. "The trucks all look exactly the same, don't they?"

As though to prove her point a pair of identical trucks blasted their air horns at each other as they met in opposite directions. The southbound was immediately followed by two more.

"This is Two-Zero-One Patrol, Byron, I hear you."

Frank relaxed a little. A patrol car had already picked up the call.

"I'm coming right up on the access of Service Road and the freeway. None of your rigs here right now!"

"Two-Zero-One, this is Patrol Center. Set a block. We're sending help."

Frank relaxed even further. "The roadblock will get them," he said. "That was fast."

"What if the truck turns off first?" Connie wanted to know.

"Not off Service," Frank explained. "The only streets are residential — too small for a semi. They'd be trapped."

Connie wasn't satisfied. "But what about that alternate freeway access they put in last year, because of all the traffic jam-ups?"

Mike Dunn's voice came tumbling in on top of hers like an echo. "Byron here. Are you blocking the alternate?"

26

"Patrol Center, Byron. You can't get a semi through that underpass on the alternate."

"Don't be. . . ." Mike Dunn's transmission was lost in a burst of errant static.

"Is that right, Frank?" Connie was as completely involved now as her husband.

Frank seemed less certain than the voice at Patrol Center. "It's supposed to be a cars-only design. Come to think of it, wasn't it a Byron truck that tried it once and got halfway through before it stuck?"

Connie didn't answer. She had pulled into the passing lane and was concentrating on a semitrailer just ahead. The big green-on-white letters proclaimed BYRON TRANSPORT CO. Almost in the same second, she and Frank understood.

"Wow! Clever!" Connie whispered.

"Don't get too close. Just keep them in sight," Frank said hurriedly. He reached for the CB and turned the switch to SEND. "I'll try to raise Patrol Center."

Why do Frank and Connie believe they have located the stolen truckload of microwaves?

5

Double Suicide on Midland Ridge

ESPECIALLY IN THE BRIGHT MORNING sun, the red jeep wagon seemed much too sporty a presence to be a suicide vehicle. It was a very shiny, metallic red, with roof rack and little plastic streamers on the radio aerial, mud flaps behind all four tires and a gleaming chrome trailer hitch. The total effect said sportsperson. Or camper or hiker. Someone in love with life and adventure. Yet some time in the past few hours, the jeep had served an entirely opposite purpose.

From where he stood on a knoll just behind it, Francis Cremer could see one of the bodies slumped over the steering wheel. There was another, he knew; the patrolman had said "a couple." Lovers, probably. Young people often spent the evening hours here on Midland Ridge. It was a popular place to park: private, romantic, and just far enough away from town. Cremer walked down to the jeep, where several policemen were waiting for him. The ambulance attendants, fully aware now that any emergency had long since passed, had turned off their flashing lights and were leaning against their vehicle.

29

"Nothing has been touched, sir." The youngest policeman was speaking to Cremer. "I've been here since we called you."

Cremer nodded. "You've got pictures of this?" He had put his fingers around the piece of vacuum-cleaner hose that ran from the exhaust pipe of the jeep through a hole in the back window.

"Yeah, we got lots of shots, Frank." It was Zerlow, the senior uniformed man present and an acquaintance of Cremer's. "Do you want to know what angles?"

"Not now," Cremer replied. "It looks like a pretty straight-forward suicide. We probably won't even need what you have."

He worked loose a piece of masking tape from the edge of the back window with his thumbnail and peeled off a long strip.

"They must have used a whole roll of this stuff," he commented, mostly to himself, as he ran his fingers over the tape that covered the edges of the hole where the hose fed into the window. All the windows were taped as well; so much had been used where the hose met the exhaust pipe that it appeared as though someone had joined the two with a baseball.

Zerlow spoke again. "Pentland here found them at first light." He nodded at the young policeman. "We called the wagon first." This time he nodded at the ambulance. "But then it was pretty obvious that this was your bailiwick, so you were next. Nothing else has been done yet. Oh, except the license check." He took out a little notepad. "Vehicle's owned by one Owen P. Riggio, 219A First Avenue. That's probably him there."

Francis Cremer made himself look inside the jeep. Almost thirty years as an investigator for the county coroner's office had not hardened him to death even a little. The man slumped over the steering wheel was likely in his mid-thirties, Cremer thought. He forced himself to look closer. Whether or not the man was Owen P. Riggio, he certainly appeared to have died from carbon-monoxide poisoning. The cherry-red lips suggested that. The other body was that of a woman. Cremer could see her light blonde hair, but couldn't see her face or lips because her body had slumped off the passenger seat and partially onto the floor, where it leaned awkwardly against the door. He suspected her lips, too, would be cherry red.

He picked at the end of a strip of masking tape on the driver's door until he had loosened a corner, then began to peel off the strip that covered the crack between the door and the frame.

"Do the tape on the passenger side, please, Zerlow," Francis Cremer said. "But don't open the door, she'll fall out. We'll work from this side."

Zerlow went to do his part; Cremer opened the driver's door very carefully. The silence of the death inside seemed to affect everything on the outside too. No one talked, or even coughed. The birds seemed to have disappeared. A cloud momentarily blocked the sun, making the scene even more tense.

"There's a note beside the gearshift!" Zerlow announced, breaking the spell. All the policemen, the ambulance attendants, and even Cremer began to breathe more slowly. One of the policemen came over for a closer look.

"I didn't see that, sir." The young one again.

"It doesn't matter," Cremer told him. "They were dead anyway." He took a small leather case out of his inside jacket pocket, unzipped it, and extracted a tweezer. He handed the case to the policeman and, holding his breath, reached over the dead man to pull out the note.

"Come here," he said to Zerlow. "Look at this." Zerlow came around to the driver's side, where Cremer had set the note on the fender, and began to read aloud as though for the benefit of the others.

Tell everyone we're sorry, but this is the only way. Jana, you would not agree to a divorce, and Merle and I will not go on without each other.

Owen

31

Zerlow read it a second time, this time in silence.

"Well, that should explain the who and the why," he said to Cremer. With a half-wave at the jeep, he continued, "and we certainly know the how and the where. Now, who gets to tell this Jana her husband has committed suicide along with his lover?"

Francis Cremer gave a long sigh. "I rather think that Jana might know more about this than we do," he said. "In any case we had better talk to her first, before we draw any conclusions about the how of this case. This was not a suicide."

What convinced Francis Cremer to look for something other than suicide as the cause of death?

6

The End of a Mythophile

THE CONTENTS OF THE MANSION of Everett Ashley Woodstock, the *late* Everett Ashley Woodstock, ran the gamut from the exquisite, the tasteful and the rare, to the worst in absolute schlock. Everett Ashley Woodstock had spent a lifetime obsessed with mythology. Not all mythologies, however, nor the meaning of mythology in history, or in art or in literature, but simply a total and exclusive devotion to the stories, characters and artifacts of Greek mythology.

The combination of this passion and his considerable wealth meant that Woodstock's pieces of genuine Greek statuary, particularly those sculpted before 600 BC, were unmatched by all but a few major museums in the world. The same was true of his collection of Minoan pottery. In fact there were some wags in the department of archaeology at the local university who were known to observe that the Minotaur, if he ever came back, would likely feel more at home in Woodstock's solarium than in Crete itself!

But there was another side to the Woodstock experience.

As though to counter the exquisite beauty with which he had surrounded himself, this eccentric old man had dipped into the vulgar and cheap, with a passion that outdid his artistic sense. For every genuine piece of sculpture from the Mediterranean, there were two, three, or even four, huge and ugly plaster-of-Paris statues of the Greek gods or the Greek heroes or the many virgin victims of Zeus. Each delicate vase was overwhelmed on all sides by a gargantuan Ariadne, or a puffy Chloe, or an ample-bosomed but vicious Phaedra.

Chief Inspector Lawrence Darby contemplated this contradiction as he stood in the foyer of the Woodstock mansion, trying to stay clear of the bustle of the homicide unit doing its job around him. The body of old Woodstock, so brutally murdered, had been cleared away and the coroner had left, but the blood, sticky now, still covered the floor, and the photographers and lab technicians continued to comb the place, searching, dusting, photographing. Chief Inspector Lawrence Darby knew they would be here for a long, long time if every piece had to be checked. In the foyer alone, there were seven life-size statues, each representing a principal character in the gruesome story of the House of Atreus, and another set showing Jason and the Argonauts. Over in the archway knelt an obsequious Paris, holding a huge golden apple.

"Must have taken a few tons of plaster for that one," Darby said to the photographer, who had just taken a third shot of Paris' bare bottom.

The photographer looked up quickly. She was embarrassed. "I didn't see you, Chief! Kennedy said to get pictures of everything from every angle, so. . . ."

"Did Kennedy tell you to get some shots of that broken display case over there?" Lawrence Darby wanted to know. "Someone — probably the killer — could not tell junk from class. That vase left behind in the case looks Minoan to me."

Kennedy was Detective Bernard Kennedy, newly promoted, recently assigned, and perpetually and painfully eager. He was out in the solarium trying to begin an inventory of the Woodstock collection.

The photographer was hustling off to shoot the display case when Detective Kennedy suddenly materialized beside a statue of Thyestes that was painted amateurishly in a garish red.

"You should see the stuff in there, Chief!" he blurted as soon as he saw Lawrence Darby. Kennedy always seemed to talk extra loud around his boss. It made Darby feel just a bit older than he was.

"There's all kinds of broken cases!" Detective Kennedy didn't slow down easily once he got excited. "And some of those big statues! I guess they were just too big for the killer to carry. You should see this one . . . uh . . . Damaclis!"

"Dam-o-*cleez*," Darby corrected.

"Yeah, Damocles!" There was no stopping Detective Kennedy. "He's got this giant sword over his head! Hanging from the ceiling yet! And these two guys, Damian and Pith . . . Pi. . . ."

"Pythias," Darby managed to get in.

"Yeah, Pythias!" He smirked. "Wonder what those two guys had going!"

Darby felt weak. "They are a wonderful symbol of true friendship, nothing more."

"Didn't look like that to me!" Kennedy paused for a second to bring a large plastic bag out from behind Thyestes. "Anyways," he continued, "we're gonna have a lot more trouble trackin' down all that pottery than fingerin' the killer. Here's the piece dee resistance."

Darby ignored the pronunciation. "I heard there was a message left by Woodstock. This is it?"

"Yeah. We found it right beside him." Kennedy held up a sheet of newspaper. "See? Lookit! Printed in his own blood. 'VENUS.' With his own finger, too! Must have!"

Darby looked away. He hated the sight of blood.

Kennedy wasn't finished. "And here's your killer!" He held

out an engraved, ebony-handled riding crop. The initials
T.F.W. were very clear. "This is what we found behind the
statue of Venus over there. That's blood on it or I miss my
guess. Bet it's the old man's, too. Anyways, T.F.W. has got to be
Terence Frederick Woodstock. That's the old man's nephew.
Find him, and I'll bet it's case closed!"

Darby paused a moment or two to let his young subordi-
nate wind down. "Detective Kennedy," he said, "I think you're
looking at a frame-up. A clumsy one, too, I might add."

"What do you mean!" Kennedy was indignant. "It's plain
as day! The old guy writes a message in his last seconds. Uses
his own blood. He couldn't possibly. . . ."

"If I may!" Darby raised his voice to Kennedy's decibel level
for the first time. "You, young man, have an obvious gap in
your classical education. Unless it's filled, you're probably
going to arrest the wrong person!"

*What did Lawrence Darby note that Detective Kennedy
seems to have missed?*

7

The Case of the Erring Arsonist

"YOU WERE SURE RIGHT ABOUT that brass company," Ron Forrester said to his wife Jane as he came in the door and stepped carefully around the stacks of files that dotted the floor of their office. Actually, he spoke to his wife's back. She was on her hands and knees, lifting the entire contents of a file-cabinet drawer and turning it into yet another stack. Forrester Investigators Ltd. was planning to renovate.

"Was I? Good. Watch out for the coffeepot. What did you find exactly? Hand me the little vacuum there, please. Is the company as big as we thought?" Jane's concentration on the case was obviously broken by the demands of the renovations.

Ron lifted an empty coffeepot off the seat of a former dining-room chair and sat down gingerly. "What do you want first, the vacuum or the information?"

Jane knelt upright, arched her back, and sighed.

"You're right," she said. "We'd better concentrate on this assignment or we'll never be able to afford the interior decorator." She studied her husband's face for a moment. "Do you really think vertical slat blinds are a good idea? I think they're so cold. And we spend so much time in here. So. . . ."

She stopped abruptly, and then waved hesitantly at all the stacks of papers and files and books. "Sorry. You can see where my head has been for the last hour or two. To be honest, I haven't given a single second to Everything Brass, Inc. What did *you* find?" She walked on her knees to Ron's chair.

"Shift," she said as she smiled at him.

Ron moved over so the two of them could squeeze onto the little chair. He took a single sheet of paper out of his briefcase.

"You were right about Everything Brass, Inc.," he said. "They do make all kinds of little brass stuff all right — ornaments, house letters, small lamps. And they've got quite a custom line too, for the horsy set, mostly harness trappings and customized fittings for carriages. Stuff like that."

Jane frowned slightly. "Shouldn't you be using the past tense? Or do they have another manufacturing plant we don't know about?"

Everything Brass, Inc. had burned to the ground in a spectacular conflagration only three weeks before. The Forresters had been retained by the insurers, Highland Park Fire and Accident Ltd., to look into the causes of the blaze, and to evaluate the validity of the claim entered by Everything Brass.

"No," Ron said, "as near as I can tell so far, the owners have no other property associated with the company. And you're right, maybe I should say *did* instead of *do*. There's no way anything brass is going to come out of that site for a long time. It was one heck of a blaze."

"Then what have you got?" Jane wanted to know.

"Enough to suggest we should look a little deeper into the background of Preston Wendle," Ron replied.

Jane fixed her gaze at a spot on the window frame from which the vertical slat blinds would — might — hang.

"Wendle," she said. "That's the two-thirds owner."

"Indeed," Ron answered. "And the designer, foreman, chief

metallurgist, top-gun salesman, PR man, everything. The other third is owned by his late father-in-law's estate."

"So what is it you've got?" Jane shifted a little and gained a bit more territory on the chair.

"Well, that figure there." He held up the sheet of paper and pointed to a circled number. "The 400,000 dollars. That's their gross income for the past twelve months."

"So?" Jane said. "That's not out of line for a business like theirs."

"But compare that to this," Ron said. He pointed at another figure: 900,000 dollars. "That is what Everything Brass, Inc. is claiming in inventory loss in the fire. Now tell me, how does a company survive when its inventory in the plant is more than double annual sales? As far as I'm concerned, it just doesn't make sense."

"Then you think there's something shady about Preston Wendle?" Jane shifted her gaze now, to the other end of the window frame. She was beginning to convince herself that vertical slat blinds were definitely out of the question.

Ron broke her stare with the piece of paper. "I'm almost positive. But the guy is so clean. He didn't try to hide — even a little bit — that the fire was his fault. He was as up front as could be with the police. And it sure seemed like an accident. Heaven knows his own burns are bad enough!"

"Naphtha," Jane interrupted. "He was cleaning an antique set of brass hame knobs, wasn't he? For a set of tandem harness?"

Ron nodded.

"And he was dipping the hames right into the drum of naphtha," Jane went on.

Ron nodded again. "Right! Now I'll grant you that's an incredibly stupid thing to do, but it's not dishonest. Highland Park may be able to contest his claim because he broke fire regulations. I'm not sure. I don't think you're allowed to open a drum of naphtha like that. I'm not even sure it *can* be done." He paused.

"But he hasn't tried to deny what he was doing. He was perfectly straight about the sparks, too. He accidentally bangs the hame knobs together over the drum. This makes sparks. Poof go the naphtha fumes. Down goes Everything Brass, Inc. And almost takes Preston Wendle along too. Again, it was really stupid. But hardly dishonest."

Jane stood up. "On the contrary," she said. "If Highland Park pays the claim on the basis of *that* story, we'll be out of business. By the way, the vertical slat blinds are completely wrong for that window. This time I'm sure!"

What is the flaw in Preston Wendle's story that Jane Forrester has noticed?

8

The Last Will and Testament of Norville Dobbs, Orthographer

"HAVE YOU GOT LOTS OF TISSUES too?" Amy Clumpus called to her receptionist. "This bunch will fake tears like nothing you have ever seen. Every one of them."

The receptionist had just rolled in the silver coffee service as Amy was arranging seven chairs at precisely equal distances from the big oak desk.

"Come to think of it, bandages wouldn't be a bad idea either," Amy said to herself. "When this will gets read there'll be some wrist slashing for sure."

The last will and testament of Norville Dobbs, Orthographer, was to be read that morning in the office of the senior partner of Clumpus, Clumpus, and Loretto, and Amy was prepared for battle. She knew the contents of the will would not please very many in the family. In fact, she felt that anything short of complete hysterics this morning might be a treat.

The seven chairs were to be occupied shortly by Dobbs' two sisters, Adelaide and Adeline, and his three sons, Lamont,

Telford and Bernard, as well as by Grace, the cook and housekeeper, and Jeurgens, the chauffeur, butler, gardener and jack of all trades. None of them, Amy mused, would be pleasant company even in happy circumstances. The sisters hated their nephews, each other and life. Of the three sons, two were complete dissolutes and the third a greedy and lazy ne'er-do-well. Grace was widely suspected of bringing about the early demise of Norville Dobbs, Orthographer, by means of her cooking. Only Jeurgens, always dull, seemed harmless.

Amy made one last adjustment to the chairs. Such a contrast they were to old Dobbs himself, she thought. Gentle and unselfish, Dobbs had been born with only two passions. One was studiously ignoring the tons of money his father had left him, the other was correct spelling. To the latter, except for a brief pause to marry and father three sons, he had devoted not only his entire life, but also — and here was the crunch, Amy knew — the bulk of his estate.

"They're here!" The receptionist's voice on the speaker made Amy jump, but she recovered herself in time to nod graciously at the seven as they filed in to the carefully positioned chairs. Amy wanted to get it over with.

"Normal procedure," she said, "is for me to read the entire will. If you have any questions, you can ask them when I have read the whole thing. Okay?"

"Well, not quite." It was sharp-eyed Bernard, who held an envelope in his hand. "You don't have the will. We do."

Amy's eyes narrowed.

"Yes," Bernard continued. "We know you have a will there on your desk, but this is a newer one. Father made it out the day before he died. It's witnessed by all of us, even Jeurgens. See? And see the date?"

Amy took it from him but she struggled to keep her hands from shaking. It was a newer will, all right. Bernard went on.

"You recognize that stupid old Underwood of Father's, don't you?"

Amy acknowledged that the typing had certainly been done

44

on Norville's creaky old machine with the raised *e* and the missing crossbar on the *t*.

"And that's his signature. You've seen it often enough."

There was no question that the signature was either Norville Dobbs' or the best forgery Amy had seen in her years as a lawyer. Somehow she felt it wasn't.

"So," Bernard said smugly. "Read. We know what's in it. He told us. But you read it. We want to be legal, you know."

Amy began to read out loud, slowly:

> I, Norville Dobbs, Orthographer, being of sound mind do hereby declare the contents of this will shall supercede all other wills and testaments signed by me before this date, and further declare that the contents of this will shall be read upon my death and that the contents of my estate be distributed as follows:

Amy paused and looked at Bernard, then at the others. "You've all signed this willingly?"

Each of them nodded.

"And you realize that by signing it, you declare that you saw Norville himself sign it?"

Again nods.

"Well, I'm not going to let you get away with it."

What did Amy find to make her suspect fraud?

9

The Case of the
Thieving Welder

MICHAEL STRUAN DROPPED HIMSELF wearily into one of the scratched and creaky chairs at the squad-room lunch table. He was alone, so he sat for a moment waiting for his energy supply to catch up with him. Slowly and very carefully he set out the separate contents of his lunch bag in front of him. Has it come to this? he thought to himself, as he peeked under a flap of the waxed-paper wrapper.

"Don't tell me that looking for surprises in my lunch has become the high point of my day," he said out loud to himself. "Has it really come to this?" He unwrapped the sandwich and tossed the waxed paper in the general direction of the wastebasket.

"Hey! Peanut butter and banana! Maybe life isn't so terrible after all!" His tired face lit up. It was his favorite, especially when the peanut butter was spread so thick it glued his tongue to the roof of his mouth.

Struan leaned back in the chair — carefully, however. The chairs in the squad room had long since given up respon-

sibility for anyone of adult weight. He stretched back to the shelf behind him to reach a shiny portable radio. The sounds of the Grateful Dead had finally worn through to his consciousness. He flicked the FM switch, terminating their noise. Immediately the sounds of the Bruch violin concerto changed the character of the whole room.

"Unbelievable!" Struan whispered. "Bruch, peanut butter and solitude. And I'm going to eat with both elbows on the table too!" He paused. "Maybe it *has* come to this," he added, louder this time.

The door behind him burst open with great force.

"Sarge!" It was Detective Kamsack. "Sarge! I've been looking all over for you!"

Kamsack had been Struan's partner for two weeks last year. He was reassigned when Struan went to the squad leader and requested an immediate transfer to vehicle maintenance. The message had been clearly received.

"Congratulations, Kamsack, now you've found me. It just goes to prove that you should never underestimate the power of coincidence. It's lunch time, and here I am in the lunch room." Struan picked up half of the peanut-butter sandwich. "And don't call me Sarge!"

"Yeah, I found you, Sarge. Figured you might be having lunch." Kamsack was not noted for speed. "We got a citizen out there. She's claimin' robbery. So that's you." Kamsack reached over to the radio and resurrected the Grateful Dead, turning up the volume.

"*Kamsack!*" Struan had squeezed the sandwich so that a dollop of peanut butter now rested on his knee. "Kamsack, do you know what the ancient Siamese did to people who interrupted a meal?"

Kamsack looked confused. "Huh?"

"Never mind, never mind." Struan reached over to the radio again. "If I may," he said, and he restored the Bruch, readjusting the volume. "Can it wait, this robbery?"

"Dunno." Kamsack shook his head. "I think she's something of a VIP. The Captain was sure fallin' over himself."

"Okay," Struan sighed, "show her in. For goodness' sake find a clean chair first."

As Kamsack left, Struan carefully lifted the peanut butter from his trousers with his index finger and licked it. He was sitting there like that, with his finger in his mouth, when Kamsack returned with the robbery victim.

She was elegant, tall, graceful. Her fur coat was full length. The hat she wore would have appeared ridiculous on anyone else, but on her it was all part of a perfect image. She was the kind of woman who made men sit up straight and suck in their waistlines.

And here I am, Struan reflected, in the filthiest squad room in the northern hemisphere, with a sandwich in one hand and my finger in my mouth.

"Uh . . . this is Mrs. Chloris Dean . . . Sergeant Michael Struan." Even Kamsack was elevated to new heights of etiquette.

"Please call me Chloris." She held out her hand. "You like Bruch?"

Struan was now desperately wishing he had not put his finger in his mouth. In a single motion he drew it along his jacket and took her hand. "Just the violin concerto in G minor, really. He uses the cello a little more often than I like in a lot of his other stuff."

Mrs. Chloris Dean was impressed. Her eyebrows said that plainly. Struan immediately felt that he'd restored a bit of balance to the situation.

"Please sit down." Struan waved to the chair that Kamsack had set on the opposite side of the table. "Would you like a sandwich?" Instantly he regretted the question. This lady was definitely crêpes and caviar. Peanut-butter sandwiches, especially thick peanut-butter sandwiches, were hardly her custom.

She showed interest, however, and smiled. "What kind?"

"Peanut," Struan said, "peanut butter and banana."

"No thank you." She continued smiling. "I love peanut butter but not right now."

"Ah, sure. Well. . . ." Struan cleared his throat. "We should get the details here. I'm afraid I know nothing about your situation yet. You don't mind if Detective Kamsack here tape-records our conversation? It's normal procedure."

"Of course not," she replied. "My name, as you know, is Chloris Dean. I live at 417 Wolfe Boulevard. And I've been robbed of my jewelry. Diamonds mostly. I'm certain who did it, too. The insured value is. . . ."

"Excuse me, Mrs. Dean — Chloris," Struan broke in. "Ah, Detective Kamsack, if I may. . . ."

Kamsack was staring slack-jawed at Chloris Dean.

"Kamsack!" Struan finally got his attention. "The tape? Turn on the tape!"

Kamsack immediately reached for the radio, then checked himself and sheepishly turned toward the tape-recorder. "Sorry, Sarge."

Struan offered his most ingratiating smile to Chloris Dean. "Please go on."

She took a breath and waited for Kamsack to discover that he had pushed the rewind button instead of record. Then she began again.

"They're insured for an even million, and normally they're in the safe, but this time. . . . Maybe I'd better back up a bit."

"Okay, okay." Struan was listening carefully. "You're in charge."

Chloris Dean sat a little straighter. "Yesterday morning my husband left on a business trip. He needed his passport and that kind of thing, but he couldn't open the safe. We called the company, and their people couldn't do it either. Finally they had to get someone with a — what is it called — a cutting torch? This man came — a big man — he had a hulking way about him, and he came right into our bedroom with all the tanks and apparatus and cut right through. It took quite a while, but he did it."

51

"So your husband got his passport, but now you don't have a safe — or at least one that's working," Struan said.

"Indeed." Chloris Dean nodded. "And that man — the one with the torch — is the one who robbed me. I'm certain of it."

"How can you know?" Struan asked. "That is a very serious accusation."

"I realize that." Chloris Dean looked up as the concerto ended. "I don't say this idly. This morning at exactly 5:29 — the clock radio is right beside my bed — I woke up and a man was in my room. He had a knife at my throat."

Chloris Dean began to shake just a little. Struan felt there was a hint of tears in her eyes.

"I was terrified. He didn't say anything. And then he sat on me and tied me to the bed. All this time he did not say a word. Oh God, I was so scared." She was crying now — not sobbing but controlled, her cheeks dripping tears. "And then he simply took my diamonds out of the safe, and some cash — it was all right there — and left."

"Hown nid-uh-new-id. . . ." It was Kamsack. He was eating Struan's sandwich! "How'd y'know. . . ." He pushed the mouthful deeper into one cheek. "How did you know it was the welder? Did you see his face?"

Struan was aghast. Chloris Dean simply wiped her eyes, unaffected by Kamsack's social skills.

"He had a mask. One of those ones with eye holes, like a terrorist. But he was big, hulking, the same body shape as the welder. It was him."

Struan reached back and turned off the radio. With part of his mind he had heard the radio host say Hindemith, and that, he felt, would be as bad as the Grateful Dead. "Kamsack here is big and hulking. It was dark, wasn't it? How can you be so sure it was the welder?"

Kamsack smiled awkwardly. There was peanut butter on his chin.

Chloris Dean leaned forward. "The smell. Not a lot. Just a little of that welding smell. You know that gas they use? It must get in their clothes or in their pores or something. I smelled it on him when he came to open the safe. And I smelled it this morning. I tell you, all the time it took me to untie myself this morning, I just knew it was him."

Struan paused for at least a minute before speaking.

"I think, Mrs. Dean, what I'll do is get your statement typed up for you to sign, and then I'll have the welder picked up for questioning. If you don't mind waiting in the outer room, please?"

Detective Kamsack held the door, then closed it after her. He looked at Struan. "You don't seem in an awful hurry to get this guy," he said.

Struan sighed. "I'm not as convinced of his guilt as she would like me to be. We'll pick him up all right. But at the same time, I think we had better go for some background into Mrs. Chloris Dean."

He looked at Kamsack. "Do me a favor?"

"What?"

"Wipe your chin."

What has triggered Struan's suspicions about the elegant Chloris Dean?

10

The Antique Store Shooting

BECAUSE HE WAS A ROOKIE, Cam Lindsey was determined not to make a single mistake. Also because he was a rookie, he had to go by the book, and the book said quite clearly that any felony, indeed, anything that even looked like a felony, meant that the beat cop, or "first officer on the scene" as Captain Tilley liked to put it, had to call in right away for the senior detective on duty.

Cam Lindsey was a beat cop. He had been on daytime foot patrol now for exactly eleven days — his first assignment since graduating from police college. And the scene in front of him said *felony*, all right. It was manslaughter at least, possibly murder, and maybe — likely — robbery as well.

Cam reached for the radio on his belt but then stopped. He'd only been here a few minutes. One or two more would make no difference. Not to the dead man on the floor anyway. Besides, one more check wouldn't hurt. There was no way he was going to make a mistake.

"Well, young man! Are you going to call your whatever

like the other officer said, or are you just going to stand there?"

Bentley Threndyle's voice startled Cam just a bit.

"Or maybe you're just going to stand there and watch poor Morton finish bleeding!"

Cam looked at the body of Morton Threndyle, then turned uneasily back to the man who had just spoken. Bentley's appearance was a counterpoint to the haughtiness of his voice and manner, for he was covered with spilled paint. There was paint in his sandy-grey hair, and on his gold-rimmed glasses, paint all over the expensive tweed jacket and down the right side of his wheelchair. Blobs of it on his knees were still trickling down his pantlegs and filling the creases in his shoes. Even the end of his tie, which stuck out beneath the buttoned jacket, had paint on it. Bentley Threndyle was a random study in Cardona Ivory #2884. Two pails of it. That was one of the things Cam had already noted. He didn't know why, but he felt it might be important later.

The interior of Threndyle Brothers, Inc., Specialists in Furniture and Other Antiques of the Georgian Period, was in the midst of a renovation. The painters had gone on their lunch break before the shooting occurred, and had left opened cans of paint on the scaffold that now stood precariously askew over the whole scene. In the struggle between Morton Threndyle and the intruder — at least according to Bentley — the paint had been knocked over.

Morton too, or rather his body, was covered in paint. In fact he was lying face down in a pool of Cardona Ivory, in which his blood made little patterns and puddles, all interconnected but refusing to blend. A twisting red trail had almost encircled the body from the sandy-grey hair to the almost-white sneakers. Like an incomprehensible modern painting, had been Cam's first thought, very much out of place in this store.

Threndyle Brothers, Inc. was indeed a one-of-a-kind establishment. It was the key business in a street of very trendy, extremely expensive boutiques, although off-the-street business probably represented only a tiny fraction of the Threndyle income. Most of it, according to the rumor on the street, came from international dealings. Morton and his twin brother, Bentley, like their father and grandfather, were among the principal antique dealers on the continent.

Only minutes before, Cam and his partner had heard the shots — two of them — as they were walking down the street past the Threndyle store. Neither had looked in earlier. What with all the antiques covered in canvas sheets, there was nothing to see. The store was closed for the renovation period anyway. They had always made it a point to avoid the Threndyle twins, for neither was very pleasant. In fact, according to the briefing from Captain Tilley eleven days ago, the Threndyle twins were indistinguishable in both appearance and personality, and the only way they could be identified separately was by virtue of the fact that Bentley could not walk.

"Nothing! He's disappeared. Not a trace. I checked the alley both ways. There's no sign of him, but I didn't expect one anyway," Cam's partner said as he came through the back door. "Too bad the paint didn't spill on him too. Maybe he'd have left tracks." He looked at Cam. "Did you call in? I bet Tilley himself will want this one."

"I . . . uh . . . I . . . was just about to." Cam allowed a little twinge of guilt to show in his voice. "Just wanted to make sure we haven't missed anything."

"What's there to miss?" his partner said, somewhat annoyed, while Bentley Threndyle nodded righteous agreement.

"I told you what happened," he said, pushing the wheelchair back so abruptly he almost hit the scaffold. "I told you. The painters weren't gone five minutes when this . . . this . . . this . . . *person* came right through the back door. I know it's supposed to be locked but it wasn't. Morton was going to set out garbage."

Cam almost spoke, then checked himself. When they heard the shots and came running, the front door of the store had been unlocked too. As they burst in to find Morton on the floor and Bentley leaning from the wheelchair holding his brother's wrist, Cam had noted the back door was wide open. He hadn't known about the garbage.

"He came right through the door," Bentley continued, "right up to Morton. I told you all this. He had this gun and he and Morton began to fight. That's why there's paint all over. Then he shot. Twice! Poor Morton. I couldn't help him. By the time you got here he was dead and the man was gone. Look, how much longer do I have to sit here? Can I go? I can't do anything here anyway!"

Cam pulled out his radio. "No," he said, "you'll have to stay, at least until Captain Tilley gets here and until a doctor examines you."

Why does Cam Lindsey want a doctor to examine Bentley Threndyle?

11

Anyone Missing at
the Apiary?

THE GOOD THING ABOUT BEING A one-man police force, Bob Ashby thought, was also the one bad thing. You're it. You're the first, and you're the last. You play first string all the time. But there are no subs on the bench anyway, so it really doesn't matter. When you get an exciting call, there's no one to interfere with you, or give you orders — or steal the glory, if any. But then there's no one to help you either. No one to share your ideas. And most important, no one to back you up.

That's what Bob Ashby did not like about what he was doing right now. He flat did not want to go in to Hoffman Apiaries by himself. It was not that he was so new on the job. Even though he'd been Norberg's entire police force for only a few months now, he was an experienced cop. Police work didn't frighten him.

And although he had been a city cop, he had country smarts. Spending every single summer on his grandparents' farm nearby had taught him a few things. He even knew something about bees. Years ago, in high school, he'd completed a project on bees that earned him the highest mark he'd ever got in science. The bees were not a problem.

The problem was Ed Hoffman. He was downright scary. Not big scary or mean scary, but spooky scary. Bob had only seen him once, but that had been enough. You didn't forget his face, not with those blue eyes, so pale they were almost white. And that funny smell about him. Sweet, like honey. But not really sweet either — Hoffman didn't wash very much. Even his place gave you the willies. It was just off the edge of town, which is natural enough for an apiary, but in a swamp. How many normal people live in a swamp?

Then there was the woman, the one the locals called just that: The Woman. She was short, somewhat dumpy, and never looked at or spoke to anyone, one of those people who seem to go through life without ever communicating.

Bob steered his pickup off the road and onto the rutty laneway that ran through the swamp toward Hoffman's house. For a moment he wished he had his uniform on. Somehow it gave him more confidence. But until he'd heard the gunshot a few minutes ago he really hadn't thought of himself as being on duty. That was another thing about being a one-man police force. You named your own hours, but then the hours never stopped. You were on all the time.

He eased the truck past the last clump of spruce and cedar until his headlights picked out Hoffman's dilapidated shack where it clung to the edge of a small clearing. There was no movement, no sound from the house.

Uneasily, Bob moved the truck as close as he could to what appeared to be the door to the old place. He got out and knocked. Nothing. He knocked again, harder this time, and got a sliver from the old, unpainted boards. He also got results.

"Go 'way!" The voice was outside. It had come from the other side of the house. And it sounded drunk.

"It's Ashby! Police!"

"G'wan! I don't want any police. Whaddaya want here anyway?" The voice was definitely drunk.

Bob followed the voice around the corner until he came upon Hoffman, seated on the ground against the shack with his feet on an overturned washtub. The smell was unmistakable but somehow there was less sweetness this time.

"That shot," Bob said. "I heard a shot and it came from here. No question. Just a few minutes ago."

Hoffman glared with his menacing eyes. "Oh yeah. Yuh must've heard it when it went off." He waved toward the corner of the shack. There was no gun there. "I was cleaning it. No law 'gainst that, is there? It went off. No law 'gainst that neither. It was on account of a bee. I think I got one a' the hives too close ta th' house." He belched wetly. "Made me jump. Flew right inta my face. Confused, I guess. Like cops!" Hoffman snorted at his own joke.

Bob felt embarrassed. Typical overreacting city cop. People in the country have guns. They clean them. If Hoffman is stupid enough to clean it with a shell in the chamber, well that's his business.

"Where's The Wo . . . your wife? The lady?" Bob had to say something.

Hoffman belched again.

"She don't live here. Not my wife anyways. Comes and goes as she pleases."

This is ridiculous, Bob thought. What am I doing here?

"Well for heaven's sake, be more careful with your gun next time," he said.

Hoffman only belched again.

Feeling very awkward, Bob retreated to his pickup, got in and turned it around a little too fast for the space available, and moved down the laneway, trying to put some distance between himself and the smelly old beekeeper. It was only when he got to the road that he stopped cold, thought again, then reversed. Smelly old man or not, Hoffman had some more explaining to do.

What had Hoffman said that made Bob Ashby change his mind?

12

The Return of the Stolen Paintings

FIVE YEARS OF LEGAL WRANGLING over the estate of the late Ms. Freda B. Ogden had almost been resolved when four extremely valuable paintings were stolen from her private gallery. The late Ms. Ogden had been a devotee, not to mention a considerable expert, on the Italian Renaissance. She had also been an ardent feminist, a publicly declared spinster and the last in the direct line of Ogdens, whose fortune had been amassing without pause since The War of 1812.

A perceptive ancestor with a head for chemistry and a nose for marketing had determined the public's desire for a mild blend of whiskey that warmed the stomach without simultaneously blinding the eyes. The result was wealth that, by the turn of the century, was literally beyond counting.

Freda B. Ogden had managed the distilleries, extended the art collection and stamped on opposing points of view with a rigor matched only by the original Ogden himself. When she died five years ago, the distillery business was healthier than it had ever been, all the other enterprises had doubled in value

and, through some exceptionally judicious trading and buying, she had elevated the family's collection of Renaissance paintings to a level that was matched only by a very few international galleries.

The estate was in the hands of Monopoly Trust Inc., and was about to be dispersed among twenty-three squabbling second cousins, when the paintings disappeared.

Monopoly Trust's agent, Wendy Pickell, who, to her considerable surprise, had been dealing quite amicably with twenty-three different lawyers, had suddenly found herself in an impossible imbroglio over the theft. In fact she was slowly becoming convinced that the Ogden estate would never be settled until long after her own was forgotten! Then, as though the case were compounding itself with complete reverses, the paintings turned up again. Only two weeks ago an anonymous telephone call had led the RCMP to an unused barn not far from one of the Ogden mink ranches in northern Alberta. No one was more relieved at their discovery than Wendy.

The first thing she had done was to inspect the paintings herself at the RCMP office in Edmonton. As soon as she arrived, Wendy had noted how carefully the thieves had crated and preserved them. Someone, she had remarked, had shown as much care as Freda B. Ogden would have done. A good thing, for these were priceless works.

Two of the pieces, in fact, were not paintings at all, but sketches, one attributed to Donatello, a preliminary musing for his statue of David; another was a wonderfully fleshy set of nudes in a pastoral scene by Giotto. The latter was especially valuable because the painting, which had eventually followed the sketch, had been lost for several hundred years. The third was an anonymous, early fourteenth-century Garden of Eden scene, with Adam, Eve, God the Father and an incredibly long snake, all gathered together in mild surprise under an apple tree. Its considerable value was due to its age and uniqueness rather than in any artistic or innovative quality. Giorgione's *Rête Champêtre* was the fourth and perhaps the most valuable. It was not even a part of the Ogden collection, but was on exchange from The Louvre at the time of the theft.

Wendy's relief at their undamaged condition was rather sharply modified when she was finally able to take a closer look. Someone—someone with a reasonable degree of artistic ability —had drawn very tiny but quite discernible raisins in the navel of every nude body in all four pieces! The shy maiden in the Giorgione had a lumped cluster of them in hers. Adam and Eve sported very small, black ones, and on the Donatello *David* the artist had arranged them in a small circle.

Vandalism? — perhaps. Mischief? — possibly. A deliberate devaluing of the paintings? A red herring? It was almost certain that the anonymous telephone call to the RCMP about the unused barn had come from someone associated with the raisins. Whatever the motive, Monopoly Trust had been forced to bring in yet another consultant on the Ogden case, causing even further delay. Nothing regarding the disposition of the estate could even be contemplated until an authority had decided whether the paintings could be restored or repaired or whether they had lost value.

It was this authority in the person of one Mark Dexel that Wendy had been patiently watching all morning, as he hunkered before the artworks in the RCMP storage room in Edmonton. Dexel had clumped in carrying two briefcases, a small one from which he emptied several magnifying glasses, some small brushes, an assortment of cloths, two flashlights and a single white glove. The large case — Wendy had to look several times to be sure — was filled with bags of potato chips!

"Don't like the feel of them on my hands," Dexel had said, nodding at the chips as he put on the one white glove. And that had been the extent of his remarks to her. The rest of the time he had spent talking to the paintings and eating the chips with his gloved hand.

Wendy caught pieces of the monologue from where she sat.

"Raisins . . . no imagination . . . never did like the green ones . . . soluble . . . beautiful work, Giotto . . . okay . . . should be . . ."

Through the past two hours, and seven bags of chips, Dexel had peered at, brushed, touched with his finger, sniffed and talked to every navel in the collection. Finally, after what Wendy thought was a somewhat overlong and lascivious stare at the Giotto nudes, Dexel stretched and yawned, came over to where she sat and began to repack his equipment in the smaller case. Very carefully he pressed the empty chip bags flat and laid them in as well.

"Eleven of these and you get a free hamburger," he said to her, very conscious of the importance of this advice. "I can usually get up to two hamburgers by Saturday. Sometimes three! You can get hot dogs too, but not me. Do you know what goes into weiners? The paintings are okay. No trouble getting the ink off. It's water soluble. Took me a while to realize it. I expected more real damage. I'll do it this afternoon if you like. I could do it right away but I've got a euchre game. Beautiful work! The paintings I mean. Even the fake *Garden of Eden*. Nothing like the Renaissance for nudes. Can't understand it though. It just seems so silly."

Wendy Pickell's emotions struggled with shock, relief and developing awareness. She jumped to her feet.

"Of course it's fake! The *Garden*! The *Garden of Eden*! I should have seen that right away!" She felt out of breath. "That explains the raisins too — and the tipoff. The thief has still got the real one!" She sat down and put her head in her hands. Dexel meanwhile put his glove back on and opened the one remaining bag of chips.

"I'm going to be on the Ogden estate forever," Wendy moaned softly.

Mark Dexel was the expert but, even so, he assumed that Wendy would know the anonymous Garden of Eden *was a fake. Why?*

And why does Wendy say that the fake Garden of Eden *explains the raisins and the tipoff?*

13

The Train to Kaministikwia

AT HER POST NEAR THE BACK of the courtroom, Marg Walker waited until the court clerk, Keith Whittaker, took his attention off the papers in front of him. They nodded as their eyes met, and when Marg placed three fingers on the shoulder strap of her bailiff's uniform in a seemingly natural attempt at comfort, Keith's eyes closed to indicate "okay." The bet was still on, but the odds had just been lowered to three to one.

The object of their wager leaned over the bench, his lips set in a thin line. Judge Grant MacDonald was annoyed. His Honor was known as strict, fair, and sensitive, but intolerant to a fault of long-winded witnesses and ill-prepared trial lawyers. He saw both in front of him right now, with emphasis, at present, on the former.

Marg felt it necessary, therefore, to add a little more balance to the bet. Only an hour ago she had offered Keith four to one that Judge MacDonald would lose his temper at least once during the trial of Sherwood Manley. After hearing the first two witnesses and listening to the one in the box right now, she knew she would have to reduce the odds to keep the bet alive. His Honor was on the brink of an explosion and there were several more witnesses to go.

The man in the box was Elias Kohlfuss, conductor-in-chief (retired) of the Kakabeka and Superior Railroad. He was not a man of few words.

"*Mister* Kohlfuss!" His Honor had just interrupted the witness's monologue.

It was the *Mister* to which both Keith and Marg had responded. They had heard that tone before.

"*Mister* Kohlfuss! For heaven's sake, we have already heard from other witnesses that the railroad station is on the extreme western end of Kakabeka Falls. We already know the track runs north and south along the lip of the canyon. We know the dayliner comes up from Thunder Bay. We know that it stops for five minutes in Kakabeka Falls at 7:30 in the morning, and then runs north to Kaministikwia. And we also know that your wonderful railroad company repeats this whole procedure for the people of Kakabeka at 7:30 in the evening.

"What the court would like to know — *all* the court wants to know — is: Did you or did you not punch the ticket of the defendant, Mr. Manley, during the 7:30 morning run to Kaministikwia on September 28 of last year? Surely that is not such a difficult question!"

Elias Kohlfuss was unmoved. Judges, in his opinion, ranked somewhere below conductors-in-chief, if only slightly, so His Honor's spleen was no concern of his.

"Well, you see, Your Honor, the run from Kakabeka Falls to Kaministikwia takes 37 to 39.5 minutes in clear weather. . . ."

"*Mister* Marion!" Judge MacDonald called for the attorney for the defense.

Harvey Marion scurried to the bench. Keith looked up to Marg Walker but she shook her head. She was not prepared to come down to two to one. Not yet.

70

"*Mister* Marion. I have in my hand your Exhibit Four. It is Mr. Manley's ticket dated September 28, one-way from Kakabeka Falls to Kaministikwia. There is a hole in the ticket, Mr. Marion, where your witness may or may not have punched it. And, Mr. Marion, the punched hole takes out part of the 0 in 7:30, and all of the A in A.M.! Now would you please instruct Mr. Kohlfuss to tell the court whether or not it was he who punched that ticket on September 28 of last year!

"Surely I don't need to remind you, Mr. Marion. . . ."

Marg and Keith both tensed. They were sure His Honor was letting go, but he calmed and continued.

". . . to remind you that Mr. Manley's whereabouts at 7:45 A.M. on that morning is crucial to your case. He is on trial for a murder that took place in Kakabeka Falls at almost precisely that time, in — need I emphasize — his motel room!"

"Mr. Kohlfuss . . . Conductor Kohlfuss." Harvey Marion was close to pleading. This was not the first time he had reacted to His Honor's sting.

"Look, young man." Elias Kohlfuss ranked lawyers lower than judges. "I've been a railroad man for forty-seven years. Started in the yards down in Stratford. And I've been punching tickets since before you were born. When you punch, you punch the time. You don't want some other person using the ticket again. Not on the Kakabeka and Superior Railroad. In fact, on our rails we have never once. . . ."

"*Mister* Marion!" Judge MacDonald thundered.

"Yes sir! Yes, Your Honor!" Harvey Marion was literally dancing on the spot. "That will be all, Mr. Kohlfuss. No more questions for now."

Elias Kohlfuss left the witness box. His carriage told the court that his dignity remained unsullied.

"I have other evidence, Your Honor." Harvey Marion was still dancing. "This is a Polaroid photograph. I plan to enter it as an exhibit." He held the picture out to the judge. "That's Mr. Manley in the center of the track behind the train . . . uh

. . . the dayliner. It was taken just before he boarded at 7:30 A.M. His wife took it. She's my next witness."

Judge MacDonald studied the picture with a frown. "And who's that woman beside him, in his shadow? Hard to see her face. She's holding out his fingers. What's that? His wedding band?"

"She's Mr. Manley's sister, Your Honor. He had just been married on September 26. The one on the other side is Manley's brother-in-law. They will both be called.

The judge took off his glasses. Marg Walker leaned forward. The glasses were always a sign. Keith Whittaker half rose in his chair.

"Mr. Marion," His Honor began. "*Mister* Marion! How dare . . . how *dare* you come before this court and. . . ."

He held his breath for a few seconds, released it slowly and put his glasses back on. "This court is adjourned for one hour. I want both counsel in my chambers at once." He stalked out before the courtroom could rise in response.

Keith looked at Marg and shrugged. He knew, as did Marg, that they would never agree now on whether Judge Grant MacDonald's outburst qualified as a loss of temper or not.

They both did agree, however, that His Honor had detected a major flaw in Sherwood Manley's defense. What is it?

14

The Case of the Floral Killer

IN TWENTY-SEVEN YEARS OF conference management, nothing like this had ever happened. Nothing even close in all that time. For twenty-seven consecutive years the annual convention of the International Flower Growers' Association had been held under the watchful eye of its executive director, Jack Atkin. In all that time, Jack reflected, there hadn't been a single mishap. Even five years ago, when some idiot reset the air-conditioning and all the African violets died, his staff had rescued the day. Or the year the Association's chairman overserved himself in the hospitality room and wiped out the potted mums display when he bent over to pinch a bud, Jack had covered in time with extra azaleas. Now this.

He looked at the telegram again.

> URGENT STOP RCMP CONFIRMS PROFESSIONAL HITMAN AT CONVENTION STOP KNOWN TO BE A HEAVY SMOKER STOP ALMOST CERTAINLY ON ASSIGNMENT STOP
>
> MARY B.

Jack set the telegram on one of the marble-topped tables in front of him and stared at the ornate fireplace way down at the other end of the Leamington Room. Normally, the polished oak panelling of this room, and the plush, overstuffed furniture, rich carpet and glittering chandeliers that hung ever so low, never failed to give him a feeling of comfort and warm security. Not this morning. This morning he knew that not only did the convention have a killer, but that he or she most likely had already been at work. Right here in this room. Right there by the fireplace.

Directly in front of the fireplace stood an old and beautiful high-backed love seat. It was one of the pieces of furniture that symbolized the Victorian origins of the Leamington Room, and it had faced the fireplace for more years than anyone could remember. Jack gloomily shifted his gaze from the fireplace to that love seat. From where he stood he could not see the bloodstains on the right side of the love seat, but they were there. The cleaning staff had seen them only a half-hour ago. A pair of matching chairs were on either side of the love seat, and both of these had bloodstains on them as well.

But it was the four missing people — the four missing *strangers* that had Jack so distressed.

"I should have been suspicious right away." He was speaking out loud to himself. "At least I should have watched a bit more closely."

The International Flower Growers' Association was a tightly knit group. Everyone knew everyone else, and they had all known one another for years. Jack was a godfather to no fewer than seventeen kids in six different countries. There simply were no strangers! Yet in the space of one hour, two days ago, four totally new people had registered for the convention: Scollins, Jensen, Hrabosky and Winston. At least, those were the names they had written in the register.

One of them was a geranium grower. No coincidence there, Jack thought. Another was a bulb specialist: tulips, daffodils, that sort of thing. A third was a specialist in cut-flower management. The fourth, Winston, wasn't even a grower, but a botanist. Now they were gone — all four. So were their registration papers.

Last night the four of them had been sitting in the Leamington Room, having sherry in front of this old fireplace. Now there were bloodstains, cigar ashes and possibly the most negative publicity the flower business had ever faced.

"Everything!" Jack had insisted. "I want absolutely everything! All the facts! Anything! We've got some time before the police get here. Don't leave out a single detail. I want you to question every single one of the hotel staff. And scour their rooms. Maybe someone left something. If we can find out which one is the killer before the police do, we might keep the press from blowing this out of proportion."

They had done as he asked, and now it was time to put the facts together. Jack walked through the room to the scene of the crime as his staff began to assemble.

"Let's have it," he commanded. "I don't care how you know what you know — just lay it all out. What we need are some leads, some facts to put together. I'm positive the killer sat right here," he said, pointing to the love seat. "Every other spot had bloodstains."

His secretary spoke first. "The rooms were empty except for this." She held up a tube. It looked like medication. "This was in Hrabosky's room. It's probably for that rash or skin disease — whatever it is — all over his right cheek."

"Had to be!" piped up the morning desk clerk, who had just joined them. "I saw him . . . no, *twice* I saw him rub it on. He sort of sneaks it on — doesn't want anyone to see him do it."

Jack was not overly fond of the morning desk clerk. "You'd be self-conscious too, if your skin was that bad," he said pointedly. He turned back to his secretary. "Anything else?"

"Just this." She held up an earpiece hearing aid. "This was in the room registered to Jensen. He must have been deaf, or at least hard of hearing. And this." She held up a tiny battery. "Guess this is a spare."

"Or a dead one," Jack offered.

Jack's assistant coordinator spoke up. "I'm not sure what good this is, but Scollins and Jensen apparently got a real blast from the botanist about smoking their smelly cigars."

"Well, it might mean something," Jack said, somewhat distractedly. "We know there were cigar ashes under the love seat. And one of the chairs. What we need is something to put all this together."

"I might have it." It was the youngest member of the group, Jack's new accountant. She was attending her first convention. "I spoke to all the hotel staff who were working on this floor. One of the staff distinctly remembers serving Hrabosky in one of the single chairs. It was the rash again. Hard not to remember it. And the botanist was next to Hrabosky. He was the only one drinking dry sherry. That's how she remembers." The accountant took a breath. "But I don't see how all this is going to tell you who the killer is!"

"Don't bet on it!" Jack felt triumphant. "Get me a piece of paper. I'm pretty sure who was sitting in the one place where there were no bloodstains. Scollins had better have a pretty good explanation when the police find him!"

How does Jack Atkin know where Scollins was sitting?

15

A Cash Transfer at the Good Eats Diner

A DIRTY GREEN CHEVROLET SEDAN pulled off the highway into the parking lot of the Good Eats Diner and rolled to a stop in a jetsam of takeout wrappers and emptied ashtrays. The car looked tired. So did the two detectives in the front seat.

The driver's head drooped. His passenger was curled into the corner of the seat, snoring softly.

It was that kind of day. A sudden predawn thaw had turned the crisp winter air into a grey, clammy mist that hung thickly over the copse of evergreens behind the little restaurant. It curled along the snowbanks surrounding the parking lot and left its dampening mark on people, buildings and cars. No one felt up to moving too fast.

Staff Sergeant John W. Ford stared glumly at the Good Eats Diner. The ramshackle little restaurant seemed to stare right back, although any dignity the building might once have had was now subverted by its desperate need for paint, and by the unfortunate malfunction of its neon-tube sign, which announced GOO----TS to anyone more than a few steps away.

As Ford reached to turn off the ignition, his partner reacted in an over-loud voice.

"Not here! What do you think I am, Plastic Man? I can't get the door open!" Bill Seeley was awake and riding a full-blown, early morning mood.

John Ford looked at him uncomprehendingly. He had been listening to Seeley for over twenty years and knew the bark meant nothing. But he couldn't understand what his partner was bothered about.

"The door!" Seeley glared at Ford and jerked his thumb at the passenger window. "The door won't open! We're jammed against a snowbank! I can't get out! Unless you want to question this turkey yourself! Park over there!"

Without a word, or even the slightest sign that the exchange was anything but normal, John Ford moved the gear lever up to reverse, waited patiently for the clunk, and then backed into the spot Bill Seeley had indicated.

"What about some breakfast?" Seeley asked in an entirely pleasant voice. "We're here anyway."

"In there?" It was John Ford's turn to react. "You'd really eat in there?"

"Okay, okay," Seeley backed off. Where to eat and what to eat was something he never pressed with his partner. "At least we can have coffee, can't we? Here, we'll take in our own cups." Seeley opened the glove compartment and took out a pair of plastic spill-proof mugs that looked like they might have come from the Good Eats Diner in the first place.

But John Ford was not listening. He was staring. From the new parking space there was a good view of the Lox Armored Car vehicle that had brought them here on this early-morning visit. Though all the details were not yet available, this robbery was promising to be one of the biggest cases in both their long careers.

Just over six hours before, at 1:10 A.M., Lox had reported its bank service vehicle had failed to respond to the regular fifteen-minute radio check. By 2:00 A.M., it had been confirmed as missing — along with 350,000 dollars in cash. At 2:15 A.M., an all-points bulletin had alerted every police force in the immediate area. Only two hours after that, Ford and Seeley were listening to a highway patrol officer relay the information she had received from the night cook at the Good Eats Diner. It was this man they had come to see.

"That's gotta be the truck," John Ford said, almost in a whisper.

Seeley had forgotten the mugs in his hands. "Look how they parked," he said, "so neat and straight and out of the way. Just like your average law-abiding citizen."

"Yeah," Ford replied, almost to himself. "But then they *are* your average law-abiding citizens. Or at least they were, from what we know so far anyway. Two of them have worked for Lox for over ten years. The woman is an eight-year veteran. Who'd think they would do something like this?"

"Must have been the cash," Seeley offered. "I don't know how long you can drive around with all that dough before being tempted. I wouldn't be surprised if. . . ."

"That's got to be him!" John Ford interrupted.

"Who?" Seeley wanted to know. "Where?"

"Over there." Ford pointed to a very tall, very thin man who had just come out of the restaurant. He had a grey parka pulled over himself, almost hiding a smudged apron that hung below it to his knees.

"He's coming over here too," Ford continued. "Let's get out." He opened the door quickly and stood in the softening snow.

Bill Seeley turned to duplicate the move, then realized he was still holding the mugs. He dropped them on the seat, got out of the car and walked over to the driver's side to stand with his partner.

"You're the cops, right?" The man kept walking toward them and drew back his lips in a fox-like grin, showing teeth that rarely — if ever — had felt toothpaste. His hair was extremely long but only on one side, and from just above his ear it was combed over the top of his head to cover a spreading pate. He needed a shave, and — as though to fill out the picture — his night-long beard and thinning hair had absorbed so many rising clouds from the deep-fryer that even in the dull, foggy air, the greasy shine was impossible to ignore.

Bill Seeley looked at the mugs lying on the front seat and shuddered. He held out his badge with his right hand, precluding any possibility of shaking hands. John Ford did the same.

"I knew it!" The man shook his head and laughed to himself. "I always know cops. You guys stick out. Somehow you always look different from regular people."

Ford and Seeley glanced at each other. After many years of working together, they had learned to communicate with the shift of an eyebrow, the slightest change of expression or even an intake of breath. In the glance, they had agreed to deal with this one as rapidly as possible and get out.

"You're Mr. Hicks, the night cook?" John Ford was being smoothly professional. "And you're the man who saw the three people from Lox Armored Car come into the parking lot this morning?"

The cook nodded. His grin grew wider and he nodded again.

"Right where you see her." He pumped his index finger at the armored car.

Seeley and Ford exchanged another glance. They had both noted the dirt on Hicks' hands. This time it was John Ford who looked at the coffee mugs in the front seat.

"They backed her in, all neat and pretty and straight, right where you see her. Then — just like I told that lady cop — this jeep pulls up. A four-by-four by the look of her. Anyway they gets out, tosses these bags in the back and then off down the highway. Just like I told the lady cop. She said you'd be here. That's how come I was lookin' for yuh. There's another way of recognizin' cops too. Yuh never can tell just once what it is yuh seen. Yuh've always gotta tell it to another cop all over again. Guess that's 'cause you guys all got bad memories, eh?" His voice broke off in a cackle of laughter.

Bill Seeley cut him short. "If you can see that well in the dark, then why don't you know the license number?"

Hicks' jaw twitched as he ground his teeth. The laughter had stopped and the grin was gone.

"I wasn't lookin' for no license number. What do I want to check license numbers for? I'm no cop!"

John Ford leaned on the hood of their Chevrolet hard enough to make the metal pop. It broke the brief tension that had developed.

"What we want to know," he said to Hicks, "is how you could see all this so well at. . . ." He checked his notepad. ". . . at 4:00 A.M. Were you out here in the lot?"

Hicks put his fingers to his ear and then ran them over his head through the strands of hair.

"Yuh see those overhead lights?" he said, pointing a grimy finger. "Mercury vapor. Had 'em put in last year. There's nothin' in this parkin' lot I can't see when they're on. My fryer's sideways to the main window there. When that bunch pulled in this morning, I had four orders of B and E goin'. No time for license numbers." He glared maliciously at Seeley. "But with these lights I can see people *breathin'*. And like I said, this jeep pulls up. They toss in these bags and off they go. Couldn'ta been more'n half a minute."

The glance that passed between Bill Seeley and John Ford was a little longer this time. Both of them even nodded slightly, just before Seeley went to the rear door of their car and opened it.

Ford pointed to the door. "A little ride, Mr. Hicks. Call it a government treat. We're going to go back to the station for a longer visit until you can tell us a better version of this story."

What have John Ford and Bill Seeley ascertained to under-mine Mr. Hicks' credibility?

16

T.A. Jones Strikes Again

THE SIGN ON THE DOOR said:

> Ever Alert Locksmiths Ltd.
> "The unusual is our business!"
> T.A. Jones, Pres.

When Lennie Strachan got no reaction to her knock, she just walked in. On the wall inside, another sign facing her repeated in even larger letters:

> EVER ALERT LOCKSMITHS LTD.
> "THE UNUSUAL IS OUR BUSINESS!"
> T.A. JONES, PRES.

Beneath this sign, in a chair propped against the wall and with his feet on the desk, a man snored peacefully. The name tag on his shirt pocket declared him to be the ever-alert T.A. Jones.

Lennie cleared her throat very obviously. This got no response. Again. Still no response. She dropped her purse on the desk, rattling the pitcher and glasses that took up one corner of it. Finally, the desired effect. T.A. Jones shifted in his chair, smiled lazily and, without opening his eyes, murmured, "Ice. Lots of ice. And water. No soda."

"Sir!" Lennie had lost her patience.

In a single practiced motion, T.A. Jones opened his eyes, dropped his feet, stood up, offered his hand with an ingratiating smile and said, "May I be of service?"

Lennie was so taken aback by the recovery that she almost forgot why she was there.

"Chains," she blurted, "ch-chains. You fix chains, don't you?"

By now, T.A. Jones was fully awake. "That's why we're in business." He had shifted into his most charming manner. "You have a chain to repair?"

"Not . . . well, not exactly. I have this necklace here. . . ." Lennie felt very uneasy.

"Necklace?" Jones was surprised. "I'm a locksmith. The jeweler's down the street. Why don't you just. . . ."

Lennie cut him off. "I've been there." She took a breath. "It's not an ordinary necklace. It's . . . well, here." She put a necklace on Jones' desk. "My husband got it in Germany. It's made of alternating beads — jade, then crystal, jade, crystal and so on. Except for these two — these two crystal ones together."

"Look. You've got two crystal ones together," Jones said.

Lennie turned to judge the distance to the door, but decided on one more try. "The crystals won't come off," she said. "There is no clasp. The chain is continuous platinum wire. If you cut it, that's the end of the necklace."

T.A. Jones picked up the necklace. "There's no clasp," he mumbled. "It's a continuous platinum wire."

Lennie was aghast.

T.A. Jones Strikes Again

"And if you cut it," Jones carried on, "that's the end of the necklace."

Lennie leaned over the desk. "Is there a fee for this analysis?" she wanted to know.

"Not at all, young lady," replied Jones, totally oblivious to her frustration, "but you do want a proper-looking necklace, don't you?" He sat down and began to rummage through the bottom drawer of his desk.

"What are you going to do?" Lennie was anxious now.

"The unusual is our business!" said Jones as he continued to rummage through the drawer. A little smile came over his face. "I'm going to fix your necklace."

What is T.A. Jones planning to do?

17

The Case of the
Attempted Suicide

THE DAY, QUITE SIMPLY, HAD turned into a string of surprises for Doug Nicholson. In the first place, police captains didn't take cases, not on Doug's force anyway. They stayed in the office to oversee things, to administer, to make sure subordinates ran their cases properly. Yet here he was in the elegant library of Berenice Devone, sitting in an uncomfortable chair, waiting for tea — and the opportunity to question the lady.

This was only the first surprise, and it was easy to explain. Doug had to do this investigation himself because his department was understaffed, what with the crime rate and all the time-off requests over the Christmas holiday. Besides, the case was only a wrap-up, a routine report to cover an attempted suicide: Mrs. Devone's husband, Owen, had shot himself three days before and was still in critical condition in hospital.

Doug's second surprise was running into Owen Devone's secretary. Ms. Jasmine Peak was next on the list of those to be questioned. While he was pressing the button to ring the door chimes at the Devone mansion, she had driven up the circular drive and parked behind him. A surprise — but then she worked for the Devones. Why shouldn't she be there?

Their exchange of introductions had been awkward, however. Not his fault, Doug felt. He had identified himself out of a combination of courtesy and old police habit, but Ms. Peak was extraordinarily self-conscious and barely mumbled her name. That had been a third surprise: Owen Devone's firm specialized in worldwide tea and coffee contracts, and one would have expected a secretary who spent part of her day on transoceanic phone calls and another part dealing in international trade to exhibit more confidence. So, another surprise — and it wasn't over yet.

Doug had expected a maid or a butler or some domestic to answer the door. When Berenice Devone herself opened it, he was taken aback.

"You must be Captain Nicholson." Berenice Devone was the last word in graciousness, and apparently not the least bit distressed. "Do come in . . . and you, Miss? . . . oh . . . you must be Miss Peak! I saw you at the hospital, didn't I? That was such an awful time."

Doug had then learned, on the way to the library, that Jasmine Peak had been an employee of the firm for only two weeks when the shooting incident occurred. He had also learned that there were no servants. This latter surprise explained why Berenice Devone had answered the door herself and then left them to make tea. But no servants at all? In a house like this? It just didn't figure.

The answer came without his asking, from the remarkably gracious — and candid — Mrs. Devone.

"I suppose you are aware of Owen's difficulties of late," she said as she came through the French doors with a simple but beautiful Limoges tea service. Her return with the refreshments was a relief to Doug. Jasmine Peak was entirely incapable of small talk. He didn't want to question her here, and the chit-chat about Christmas festivities — the only logical topic — seemed hollow in light of Owen Devone's recent behavior.

"He lost a great deal in Sri Lanka," Berenice Devone said as she poured milk, then tea, into the cup in front of Jasmine Peak. She could talk and serve simultaneously, Doug noted, and do both with polished accomplishment. But there was no surprise in that.

"'Bet on the wrong side.' That's how he put it. You know about the political troubles there. All but one of the plantations with which Owen had contracts simply failed to produce any tea at all." She lifted the lid of the teapot and peered inside professionally.

"Then the frosts in Colombia turned the coffee market into a shambles. Milk or lemon, Captain? Do you know there has never been a frost of that magnitude in Colombia?"

"Uh . . . milk, please." Doug was almost reluctant to interrupt.

"Then with all the pressure for product from his clients . . . I guess poor Owen just caved in."

The monologue stopped for just a moment.

"Of all times . . . on Christmas Eve!" She sighed heavily, then immediately offered round a plate of delicate unsugared wafers.

"Mrs. Devone, I'm going to have to look at the room where he. . . ." Doug had wondered how he was going to bring this up but — another surprise — it seemed so easy. Mrs. Devone's composure had given him courage.

"Of course, Captain. It's a guest bathroom on the second floor. I'll take you there."

The intrusive ring of the telephone made all three of them jump. For the first time, Berenice Devone's control slipped. When she set her teacup down her hand shook, and beneath the ever so correctly applied makeup, her face had paled.

"It's the hospital, I know it's the hospital."

"Let me answer it." Doug rose from his chair and picked up the antique-style receiver. It was his office.

"For me," he whispered to Berenice Devone, tapping his chest with his forefinger, and then he turned to the mouthpiece. "No, I'll be here just a bit longer than I thought. There's been one surprise too many."

What has made Doug Nicholson suspicious?

18

The Lost Mine of Headless Valley

THE LITTLE SINGLE-ENGINE aircraft dipped sharply on its starboard wing, so sharply that Linda Fogolin almost lost her determination to be calm. She said nothing, but couldn't stop herself from grabbing for a handhold on the dash. There was none, of course, and the action made her feel a bit foolish. Her husband, John, was eminently reasonable and easygoing, but there were two things she had learned never to criticize: his judgment of wines and his ability as a pilot. Yet when their Cessna 152 banked even further to follow a loop in the river, she protested.

"Is all this really necessary, John? We're so low I can see the fish down there! Any lower and we can drop a line off the wing!"

John Fogolin's answer was a mischievous grin. He leveled out and trimmed, but not before waggling the control wheel just a bit.

"Linda, we can't take a chance of missing the marker. Von Zeldt said he found the mine entrance on the right bank, about a kilometer above Virginia Falls, and that's where he set out the orange tarpaulin. We've got to follow right along the Nahanni here, and we've got to fly low."

"Okay," Linda responded. "But the falls is not even in sight yet. Do we have to scare the trout? It's bad enough being in the middle of nowhere and dealing with that drunken Von Zeldt. Not to mention all that business about the skeletons with the missing skulls!"

John nodded sympathetically and adjusted the trim wheel again as the plane shuddered in a tiny pocket of turbulence.

"And those people!" Linda continued. "Those people in that town back there where we took off. You can sure tell *they* think we're nuts!"

"Nahanni Butte?" John raised his eyebrows. "The people in Nahanni Butte? Sure they look like they're frightened of this part of the country. What would you feel about a place called Headless Valley? But I think it's just a tourist gimmick. They're no fools."

To undertake this flight, the Fogolins had left a wilderness tour group that was canoeing and camping along the Liard River, having followed the Mackenzie from Great Slave Lake. Like most Canadians, they were vaguely aware of the legend of Headless Valley, of the Macleod brothers and their lost gold mine; how in the early part of this century these two prospectors had gone up the South Nahanni, grubstaked for the season but had never come back. When their bodies were found — their skeletons — a note said they had found gold, a huge deposit. But there was no gold with the skeletons. And no skulls! They had been neatly removed! Since that time several prospectors had died or disappeared in the attempt to find the Macleod brothers' mine.

Now John and Linda had joined the search. They had met Dieter Von Zeldt at the Hudson's Bay post in Fort Simpson. John, with his happy capacity for meeting people with ease, immediately established a nodding acquaintance with almost everyone in the settlement, including Von Zeldt. After a few drinks and some earnest conversation, John had been sufficiently convinced — or at least intrigued — by Von Zeldt's claim to have discovered the mine, that he arranged the rental of a plane out of Nahanni Butte.

Linda was less certain. She agreed that Von Zeldt may indeed have been a trapper. And a prospector. He may even, as he explained to them, have "almost completed" a degree in geology at Washington State before settling in the north. But in her opinion Von Zeldt was a reprobate.

That was why, as she and her husband followed the looping turns of the South Nahanni River in a rented Cessna 152, she was less disposed than he to be excited.

"Look there!" John pointed to the side of a jagged peak. "And there!"

Two groups of Dall sheep interrupted their placid grazing to stare briefly at the noisy intruder. There were over a dozen in each group, and not one of them appeared to be standing on a level support. Their very altitude on the mountain begged the question of how they got there. Linda felt her mood begin to mellow.

"They're beautiful!" she breathed. "And just look where they are! You'd swear that they were painted onto . . . Oh! . . . Oh my gosh! It's incredible! Just look at it!"

"Virginia Falls." John replied with both awe and a bit of tension, for the little aircraft had begun to rock in the turbulent atmosphere created by the magnificent waterfall.

"About twice the height of Niagara," he said as he reached for the throttle. "Imagine putting the *Maid o' the Mist* under there!" He paused for just a second or two to stare at the pounding white water and then pulled more power into the Lycoming 235 engine. "We've got to get over that cloud it's making. I don't want to go through it or around it or we might miss Von Zeldt's marker!"

Linda said nothing. She simply stared at Virginia Falls as the airplane surged higher. Leaving the low altitude now made her feel a bit isolated and lonely.

"Okay, keep a sharp eye now, Linda. It's got to be near here."

As the airplane eased closer to the water surface again, Linda could make out tiny details in the river. She began to feel excitement in spite of herself. The falls, the sheep, the whole adventure — it was all so stimulating. This time when John turned the Cessna on its side as the river bent to the right, Linda did not mind, even though her perspective changed so that she could see straight down through the side window. The river was wide at this point and stretched beneath the plane out of her vision. In fact she strained so hard to see the other bank that she almost missed the tarpaulin right beneath her.

"There, John!" she cried. "Right down there!"

Her husband banked even harder so that out her window he could see the tarpaulin spread out in a rockfall. It was plastic and ratty looking, but orange just as Von Zeldt had said. And more important, it was there. Neither he nor Linda had really expected it to be. John circled around the tarpaulin marker twice before either of them spoke.

Linda was first. "You're thinking what I'm thinking, aren't you?"

John sighed. "You mean just how phony Von Zeldt might be? Yeah, I'm thinking that." He paused and moved the control wheel to make an even tighter circle. "At least we know that near-degree in geology is probably in his imagination."

"No question," Linda nodded. "I'd bet he's no prospector either! But then it's not a complete waste. Let's go back and circle around the falls again, and then see if we can find the sheep once more. I've never seen more beautiful scenery."

Linda and John Fogolin have apparently dismissed the worth of Von Zeldt's claim that he discovered the lost Macleod brothers' mine. Why?

19

Is Something Wrong at the High Commission?

ADRIENNE FINE-FURNEAUX HAD NEVER FELT quite so much on edge. The feeling embarrassed her even though she knew the reasons were genuine. It was her first day on her first summer job after her first year at university. All that, she kept reassuring herself, gave her a right to be nervous.

She pulled the little compact car over to the curb and let it idle while her partner stepped outside to smoke a cigarette. That was one battle, at least, that she did not have to fight. The High Commission security service did not allow smoking on street-patrol duty, and although her partner ignored the rule, fortunately, he didn't smoke in the car, choosing instead to add to the already heavily polluted air of Trafalgar Square.

The engine coughed and missed on the little Austin Mini, startling her. Adrienne revved it a bit and then eased the car forward slightly so that she could catch the last few seconds of the sinking sun in the patch of sky between two buildings.

Driving the car was another cause of anxiety. That was all her partner's fault, however. His name was Vern Brookens and

he was an unmitigated chauvinist pig. To make matters worse, most of the trumps were in his hand. He was a permanent member of the service, he was second in authority and he knew the streets of central London much better than she did.

Vern Brookens had not yet done or said anything overt, but Adrienne knew how he felt and the awareness ate away at her. She knew from the way he looked at her when the D.O. — the duty officer — introduced them: a look of incredulity and animosity.

It was his manner.

"Pleased to meet you, Vern," Adrienne had said with her best smile. Everyone in the security service was on a first-name basis.

"Call me Brookens," he'd said with what was almost but not quite a snarl.

Only an hour ago, at the start of their street patrol, there had been another little incident. As they approached their Mini in the parking lot, Adrienne had held back. All trainees drove on their first day; it was part of the deal. But Adrienne's innate politeness had made her hesitate.

"It's not an automatic," Brookens had pointed out. Nothing more, but it was enough to make her stutter the clutch on the unfamiliar little car.

Adrienne now tried to shake her uneasiness by staring at the solid facade of Canada House. In the gathering darkness she noted that a barely existent breeze was moving the huge Canadian flag ever so slightly. Enough breeze, too, to move the diesel fumes, she mused to herself. Adrienne knew she would never get used to the smell in Trafalgar Square, or in all of central London for that matter.

As though to underline her thoughts, a procession of fuming black Austin taxis clattered by, adding to the thickness of the air. In the right-side mirror she could see another group coming.

"Just like the pigeons here," she said out loud. Adrienne

was no more fond of the pigeons that clustered around the Nelson monument than she was of the diesel fumes.

She looked down the street at the other security car — there were always two street-patrol teams at night now, ever since the terrorist attacks had begun — and then back at Canada House.

"The place is sure lit up." She was still talking out loud. The process made her feel better. "It must be the big NATO meetings next week." Adrienne had already been told she would be detached next week to serve the Belgian delegation.

It was only when Brookens flicked his cigarette butt over the car into the street that the realization struck her.

"Brookens!"

He walked in front of the car to blow his nose with careful, rude deliberation.

"Brookens! For heaven's sake!" Adrienne was beginning to feel very anxious.

He got into the car with the same deliberateness.

"Brookens, there's something wrong. We've got to call the D.O. One of us should go into the High Commission. At least let's check."

Brookens looked over at Canada House very carefully. For a moment she knew he was taking her seriously, but then the near-smirk returned.

"I tell you what," he said. "Why don't you drive over to the newsstand at Charing Cross? Then we'll. . . ."

"Brookens! Look!"

What is it that has Adrienne so upset?

20

The Results of the Eighth Race

"THE RAIL STARTER DID NOT win. Repeat. The number-one dog did not win. Nor did number two. Repeat. Nor did the number two."

Laurie Silverberg took his eyes off the receiver for just a moment to be sure the tape-recorder was working. There were two people taking notes as well, but experience had made him pessimistic.

"Number-three hound finished behind the number two, but not in order. Repeat. The number-three. . . ."

Laurie leaned back in his chair and allowed himself to relax. Everything was in working order. Reception was clear. It should be — the satellite was almost directly overhead. The radio was working, the tape-recorder was working and the notes, he knew, would be accurate.

"Should be a breeze this time," he said to no one in particular, but almost loud enough to distract his wife's attention to the next burst of transmission.

"The five dog ran . . . —ng r —"

The garbled sounds brought Laurie to his feet immediately. On repeat, the sound was no better.

" . . . dog . . . strong. . . ."

"Not again!" Laurie grabbed the dial to change frequencies.

"Wait!" His wife, Sue, put her hand quickly but gently over his. She was one of the note-takers and as familiar with the reception problems at Neewakik Station as anyone. "It's a blip, I'm sure of it!"

The next two seconds were long ones, but it turned out she was right. The interruption was only temporary. When the next sentence came booming from the receiver, it did so with total clarity.

"The four dog was not last and did not finish just before or after the one. Repeat. . . ."

Laurie's look of chagrin and gratitude moved from Sue to Rick Parker, but neither of them noticed. It was Rick's radio in the Department of Northern Affairs office that they were using. He and Sue had their attention fully turned to it.

"The number-two dog closed in the stretch but did not finish next to the number four."

By the time the repeat concluded, Laurie had relaxed again. The rest of the results for the eighth race were obviously going to come in smoothly. He walked over to the coffee-maker in the corner to put some distance between himself and the action. Although he was the mastermind of the network, the things he needed to make it work — the radio, the satellite, the postal system — these were the traitors. Somehow he always felt they worked better, the farther he kept himself from them.

The "network" was a product of Laurie's inventive mind, and a bit of serendipity. The result was legal — or at least not necessarily illegal — off-track betting.

Because of the radio communication these high-flying Anik satellites made possible, the little weather stations and church missions and oil exploration camps of the far north had become a kind of single community in which none of the inhabitants had ever met face to face. Except Laurie. He was a doctor and health officer for an area about the size of France and Germany combined. He traveled throughout the area by plane, boat and snowmobile, and in his spare time monitored the network.

It worked simply. From the South — anything below the 60th parallel was "the South" — every Sunday between 0700 and 1000 GMT, a former patient of Laurie's who was a racetrack fan and an air-traffic controller — in that order — broadcast the results of the second, fifth and eighth races run the previous day at the dog track near his Florida apartment. As well, he gave the entries for the next week.

With the aid of Rick Parker's radio — not to mention his considerable math and computer skills — the participants in Laurie's network generated their own odds and their own betting pool. Within an hour after the results came in, the bettors would hear their results in turn, in a general transmission from Neewakik Station. Winners got their money in the mail.

What kept the authorities at bay was Laurie's rigorous insistence that any profits in the pool go to health care, and the unique method of transmitting the results from Florida. To broadcast, in the clear, which dogs came first, second or third would have been of questionable legality. Hence, the enigmatic messages that were now so fully occupying everyone's attention at Neewakik Station.

A sputter from the coffee-maker startled Laurie for a second, but did not distract him from the final transmission, which was:

"The rail starter did not finish last."

In the brief silence that took over, everyone stretched. Sue Silverberg gathered her notes and began to stick each one onto the bulletin board above her.

"We got it all," she said, "except for the blip in the eighth race."

101

Laurie peered at the notes. "Do you think we can raise Florida for a repeat?" he asked Rick Parker.

"Not necessary, I'd say," Sue put in before Rick could answer. "I think we've got enough."

Sue believes she can determine the results of the eighth race, despite the missing piece. Is this overconfidence or is it possible?

21

Something Fishy at Rustico Farm

MARY RITCHIE SLOWED HER CAR to a stop in the laneway of Rustico Farm and let herself relax. The sleek beauty of thoroughbred racehorses always did that for her, and as she rolled down the window to gaze at the white board fences and the rolling green fields dotted with yearlings and two-year-olds, she felt her tension ease away.

Movement ahead of her and to the right drew her eye to a magnificent bay stallion pacing the fences of his own private paddock. His pattern never altered: along the barn to the swing gate. Stop. Left wheel. Along to the next corner. Left wheel. Stop. Sniff the air. Carry on to the next corner. Left wheel. Back to the barn.

Mary shook her head admiringly. "There he is!" she said to herself. "Heir Apparent. What a beauty! It's almost possible to forget he's worth four million dollars!"

But no one could forget that much money. And no one even dared speculate how much more valuable Heir Apparent might become. He'd already fetched the unheard-of price of two million dollars as a two-year-old. Now, at five years, retired from racing undefeated, with people clamoring to pay his astronomical stud fees, he had just been syndicated for the four million. That's where Mary came in. Her employer, Rothsay Animal Insurers, Inc., was about to take on Heir Apparent as a client. Not only were they going to insure him life and limb, but they were prepared to underwrite his fertility as well. It would be the biggest risk in the company's history, and that's why Mary was tense. She was Rothsay's only investigator and she liked her job. It meant she could spend more time around horses, her lifelong passion. Yet the matter of Heir Apparent made her uneasy.

This was her fourth trip to Rustico Farm, and as she'd said to her boss this morning — also for the fourth time — there was something fishy, something wrong. But when challenged to explain herself, she was helpless.

Although it was not even close to mid-morning, the late August sun was already hot as Mary eased her car toward the office. She carefully avoided the parking space marked Sylvanus Bird, Farm Manager, turned off the motor and got out.

"Over here!" a voice hailed her.

She looked around.

"Here! In the orchard!" It was Sylvanus Bird himself. He was sitting in a lawn chair in a scatter of papers, munching an apple. Mary walked toward him.

"Another interview?" Bird smirked a little. "Well, you people are thorough if nothing else." He leaned to his left and picked an apple off the grass. "Have one. McIntosh. Best apple there is. We had an orchard like this at home when I was a boy. Every tree a McIntosh. That's why I work out here in the morning before the wind comes up. Fond memories."

He stood up and unfolded a chair for Mary, picked another apple off the grass, took a bite and pointed with it.

"Just look at that stallion. Isn't he poetry?" Bird's eyes grew dreamy as he stared at Heir Apparent and continued munching the apple.

"Well have you got the policy? Let's sign and have it done. I've got a big day."

"Yes, I have the papers, Mr. Bird," Mary replied, "but let's not sign this morning. There's one more thing I have to check. And quite frankly, sir," Mary added, struggling to contain her embarrassment, "it's you!"

What made Mary Ritchie suspect Sylvanus Bird of something?

22

Who Hid the Medicine?

"WHEN WE HAVE THE FIRST answer, we'll probably get the second too. Or vice versa." Christian Hawkes passed the transmitter from his left to his right hand and turned his back to the little group at the far end of the conference room. He spoke more softly.

"The thing is, I'm not even sure whether this is attempted murder or just mischief. Well, *stupid* mischief. Anybody who'd hide someone's medication like that is either malicious or bananas. Over."

The two questions to which Corporal Christian Hawkes of the RCMP was seeking answers were: who had hidden Kelly O'Miara's asthma medication in an air duct high in the wall of the Territories Room at the Mountain Lake Conference Centre, and why had he or she done it?

"Are you okay?" The voice on the other end of the conversation wanted to know. "Is everything under control now? Over."

"Yes, everything is fine now," Christian replied. "The road

is not open officially yet but you can see the odd car now without four-wheel drive, and the weather is certainly clear."

Christian had come to the Mountain Lake Centre at dawn two hours before, via snowmobile because the road had been closed and unplowed owing to avalanche warnings. He was the only person at headquarters able to respond when the manager of Mountain Lake had radioed for help just before midnight. What had been needed was medication for Kelly O'Miara, who had been having an asthmatic attack, or, failing that, an ambulance or helicopter to take her to hospital. But weather and the closed road had ruled all that out, so Christian, with his paramedic qualifications and snowmobile expertise, was the next best choice.

"In fact," Christian was still talking, "it was all in hand by the time I got here. The manager found her medication when the cover to the air duct fell off. Whoever stuck it back on did a lousy job. She just got the Ventilin in time apparently, and she is all right now."

He changed the hand holding the transmitter again. "Look. I've got to go. They're getting antsy to leave, and if we've really got a crime here I'm going to have to find out yes or no in the next few minutes. If the road opens send a truck for me and the snowmobile. I'll call you in an hour. Over and out."

Christian set the little transmitter into its cradle and walked to the other end of the long, narrow Territories Room with studied casualness. The customary sensitivity he knew was essential for interrogation was going to be especially important here. The suspect — if there really was a suspect — would be one of the group of handicapped people clustered around the sideboard that took up one wall of the alcove. They were militants the manager had said. "Chewy" was the word he'd used to describe them. "Didn't seem to like anything or anybody."

As he approached them, Christian looked at Perky Hinton sitting calmly in her wheelchair. She seemed confident. And well she might be, he thought. It probably wasn't her; she couldn't reach that high.

Perky, as though she could read his mind, piped up. "It wasn't me. I can't reach up there. Besides what would I want to hurt Kelly for. I didn't even know her till yesterday. I've got nothing against her."

"None of us knew anyone before, you nit." It was Val Horst. He held his white cane well out in front of him. "None of us knew. . . ."

"I don't like this," a voice complained, just a bit wheezily. It was the older man that Christian had noticed before, rocking back and forth slightly on an overstuffed ottoman that was really too low to be comfortable. The man spoke very deliberately. One word at a time. "I don't like this at all. It's just like the institution. Too much arguing. I don't like the arguing."

"It's all right," Christian said. "No one is accusing anyone yet." He turned to the two remaining gentlemen. The manager had made a special point of describing these two when he'd first arrived. Homer and Harry were identical twins, both deaf and so similar in appearance that had not Homer been wearing hearing aids, no one could have possibly distinguished him from Harry.

Christian looked at Homer and simultaneously using sign language, he said out loud:

"Are you the twin with speech?"

"Yes." Homer replied in the slow, careful modulation of the deaf. Like Christian he signed at the same time. "Sometimes I help my brother. He doesn't talk. But that doesn't matter because everybody here can sign. You have to. It's part of the deal."

Harry nodded vigorously and rapidly signed that he was pleased that Christian could sign too.

Perky's voice broke in. "Even if you didn't, officer, it wouldn't matter. Harry can read lips just about better than anyone."

Harry smiled, proud of himself. Then his face grew serious,

and he signed to Christian. "I didn't put the medicine in the air duct. And my brother Homer didn't either. We couldn't have. We were in our room the whole time."

Val Horst snorted. "You were down here yesterday afternoon at five o'clock because you came in when the five o'clock news was on the radio. That is hardly being in your room the whole time."

"I'm afraid that's right, Mr. Hawkes," Perky Hinton added. "That's the time I saw them too. But that doesn't mean they hid the drugs."

"No, it doesn't, Perky," Christian replied. "But it's already obvious that there's someone here who is not being completely truthful. Maybe if we get that cleared up first, we'll get to the bottom of this caper."

Of whom is Christian suspicious, and why?

23

Dead Sea Tour

"THAT WAS THE MOST INTERESTING dinner conversation we've had with anyone on this entire trip," Maureen Bottrell said as she and her husband Harvey entered their stateroom. This was their fourth day on the *Bon Chance*, sailing out of Sedom on the Dead Sea.

"Yes," Harvey answered. "Imagine a highschool physics teacher whose hobby is the Middle East. It just doesn't figure. And Gavin is so knowledgeable too."

"His wife's no slouch either," Maureen pointed out. "Remember this afternoon it was Bea who corrected the tour guide out on the deck when he was giving us all that stuff about the Dead Sea here."

Harvey frowned, trying to recall the incident exactly.

"You're right," he said. "Didn't the guide say the ship is presently at 2,000 feet below sea level, and that we're now anchored in the saltiest water in the world? And then Bea piped up that we're actually — what was it? — 1,302 feet below sea level!"

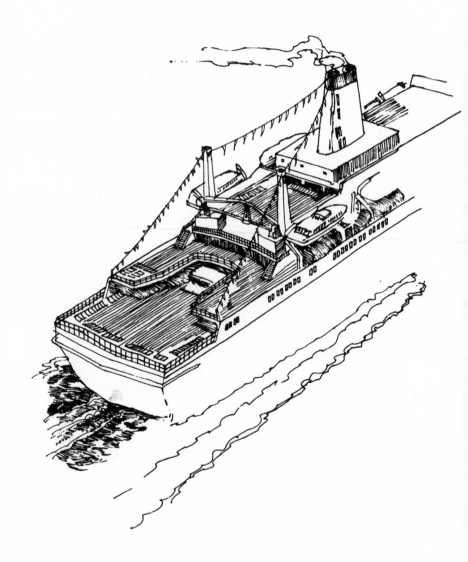

Maureen chuckled softly. "The guide didn't know the stuff about density either. Six times that of fresh water. No wonder the ship slogs along so slowly. But it's the easiest place in the world to swim. You can't even sink! Gavin knew all about that too."

"It's a good thing that Gavin and Bea are with us," Harvey observed. "Or maybe it's even better that the guide is the guide and not the chef. I'd hate to think what our meals would be like under his command!"

A sudden commotion outside their room interrupted their talk. The sound of running feet, first one way, then down the hall in the other direction. Then several voices yelling. Finally, the ship's klaxon sounded its loud alarm.

Maureen and Harvey grabbed their life jackets and ran up to the deck. Their fellow passengers were milling around in confusion, some of them with life jackets, some without. Clinging to the rail at the other end of the deck stood Bea, shaking visibly. Crew members stood around her, looking anxious. The noise of the klaxon was piercing.

Mrs. Feldstein from their neighboring stateroom came puffing up.

"Oh, you don't need those!" she wheezed, pointing to the life jackets. "We're not sinking or anything. It's that nice Gavin. He's dead! He broke his neck!"

Harvey and Maureen were shocked.

"H-how?" Maureen managed to ask.

"His wife—what's her name, Bea—says he dived in. He went for a swim, and he dived in off the deck. And his neck . . . he broke his neck. And his skull. It's awful! I can't believe it!"

Maureen and Harvey looked at each other.

"I don't believe it either, Harvey, do you?" Maureen asked.

Harvey shook his head. "Not for a second. It just doesn't wash. Maybe that Bea isn't so clever after all."

Why do Harvey and Maureen suspect Bea of something?

24

Arranging the Locker Assignments

THE LECTURE HALL OVERFLOWED with bodies. Some of the students had stacked themselves along the stairways on either side. Others had arranged themselves in modest comfort on the window sills. Two individualists at the front had brought camp stools. The class had not yet begun, and the buzz of many separate conversations made any one of them almost inaudible, but the noise level dropped markedly as the professor walked to the front of the room, a thin notepad under one arm, his academic gown trailing from the other. The noise faded altogether as he wrote several numbers on the chalkboard.

47   23

26   18

Carefully, the students transcribed these into fresh new pages of lecture notes.

"The problem here," Professor Lacroix peered over his glasses to be sure the entire class was paying attention, "is fairly straightforward. You must picture yourself standing in the hallway of a school at the beginning of a row of lockers. From there you will determine who — Dinah or Karen — will be assigned the locker farthest from you, and — oh yes — the number of that locker."

The class was indeed listening intently. All but a few were holding their hands and fingers upward in readiness, their attentiveness conveying the message that the opening lecture of Dr. Bill Lacroix's new course in deductive dactylology was being well received.

He went on. "Given that there are a dozen lockers in a row, you have some considerable choice here so, to add interest, besides the two girls, you are also to assign two boys — Luis and Ned — who owing to some peculiar quirk in the administration's view of hall-behavior management, are subject to the regulation that forbids boys to occupy adjacent lockers.

"Now —" He cleared his throat and focussed on a point high on the back wall. " — to mitigate the complexity of the problem, you may assume the preassignation — and therefore the pre-occupation and temporary ownership — of any locker, the number of which is an aliquot of twelve."

Immediately, he checked himself. His students' hands were down and they were scrambling for their dictionaries. Many in the class, he realized, would not be aware that an aliquot is a number which can be divided evenly into another number. To help them, and to slow himself down, he wrote *aliquot* on the chalkboard very carefully, and also *preassignation*. He paused for a second or two, and then with just a suggestion of a gleam in his eye, wrote *infundibuliform* underneath the other two words. It had nothing whatever to do with the problem at hand but Bill enjoyed lexical novelty. He also felt that keeping his students off balance from time to time was a useful pedagogic tactic, and an effective method for changing them from reflexive note-takers into questioners. That was why he also wrote lists of numbers on the board at the beginning of his lectures even though they had no bearing whatever on the topic.

Yet soaring way ahead of his students was a habit he had always had to guard against. In fact Bill Lacroix had spent most of his life waiting for the rest of the world to catch up to him. It was only because he was such a brilliant teacher that his courses at the Academy of Irregular Epistemology were consistently oversubscribed.

He was without a doubt the most popular professor on the campus. Part of this popularity was owing to his extremely individualistic teaching style. But he was also relished as the faculty maverick. Only three years ago, for example, he'd been assigned to supervise an examination in the department of philosophy. The course was existentialism and the examiners, with classic academic smugness and self-congratulation, had set out to astound their students by presenting an exam paper with only one word on it: "Why?"

On entering the examination hall, Bill had exhorted the students to respond with the only truly existentialist answer: "Why not?" Then he took them all off to the campus pub for the rest of the afternoon.

The year after that, having been somewhat ungently moved from the department of philosophy, he was temporarily assigned to the department of human kinetics, where he promptly offered a course in contemplative aerobics — for students who wanted to only think about exercising. It broke the enrollment record at the academy.

Now he was in the department of mathematics, which had accepted him for a one-year appointment on the premise that math was math and even Lacroix could not get around that. He had responded with the first-ever offering of a course in deductive dactylology. It had filled immediately and the waiting list had closed on the first day. Apparently a remarkable number of students at the Academy of Irregular Epistemology were interested in learning the art of thinking with their fingers. The locker problem which Bill had introduced was the first practical exercise of the session.

With the flourish that distinguished his style, Bill clarified any problems with aliquot and proceeded to flesh out the problem.

"You may also assume that one of the boys will occupy locker number ten, that no one's name has the same number of letters as there are in his or her locker number, and that Dinah's locker has a lower number than Ned's. Now that should be enough to help you. Am I going too fast?"

Is Bill Lacroix going too fast? Would you be able to handle the first lecture in deductive dactylology? Who gets the locker farthest from you? And what is its number?

25

The Sinking of
The Alberton Pride

EVEN IN HER RUSH TO GET to the marina, Janice Hancock
could not resist a short, proud pause in the parking lot. It was
the sign at the head of her parking space.

ENSIGN JANICE HANCOCK, CCG

OFFICER COMMANDING

Not bad, she thought. The first woman officer in the Canadian Coast Guard, the first woman *commanding* officer, even
if all she commanded was a pair of small front-line rescue
boats and a radio line to the helicopter service in Dartmouth.
So what! So she did spend most of her time hassling the local
fishermen for setting out with faulty equipment or for ignoring safety regulations. It was *her* command.

A gust of wind almost yanked the car door out of her hand
as she stepped onto the gravel. It was a reminder of why she
was in a hurry, and she began to run across the parking lot.
Only that morning, just offshore, a small pleasure craft had
gone down in a fierce squall. It was the first serious "down"

since Janice had received her posting, and she wanted to get the facts just right.

She'd already got the essentials. *The Alberton Pride* was a thirty-footer, registered in Massachusetts and licensed for pleasure excursions. Built in 1940, *The Alberton Pride* had had three previous owners. The records showed two safety violations issued by the US Coast Guard and she was insured by Lloyds of London.

Now waiting for Janice in the office of Archie's Petrocan Marina, gulping coffee, was the latest owner and skipper: Giacomo Giancarlo Piorelli. She knew he was experienced. He'd held master's papers for fifteen years, and the knowledge made her nervous.

Petty Officer Bowlby half waved and half saluted as she came near.

"He's okay, sir . . . uh, ma'am." Petty Officer Bowlby could not get used to a female commanding. "Just shook up and tired, and awful d —, awful cold."

"Thanks, Bowlby. I'll talk to him," Janice said. "Before you go, get me the precise data on the storm. Wind velocity, amount of precip, that kind of thing. I'll piece it all together after I talk to this skipper."

She stepped into Archie's little office, where Piorelli hunched as forlornly as anyone could. His thinning blond hair was tousled but dry. He was barefoot. One slightly tremulous hand held a huge coffee mug.

"I'm Ensign Hancock, Coast Guard," Janice said. "You're Piorelli, right?"

His reply was a monotone.

"Jim Piorelli. Out of Boston. The Alb . . . The Al. . . ." He stopped. "The *Pride*. It was all I had. Now, nothing." Piorelli did not even look up. He seemed to be talking to Janice's feet.

"Hardly nothing. You're alive," Janice said. "This your jacket?" She picked up a red life jacket with a faded *The Alberton Pride* stencilled across one side. The strings still dripped seawater.

"Yeah. I got it when I saw the *Pride* was breaking up. I guess it's lucky I was this close to shore. No more than a mile to swim." Piorelli just mumbled to Janice's feet.

"It's not the distance so much, it's the temperature," Janice said to him. "If this had happened only a month ago you'd have frozen before you drowned."

"Yeah." Piorelli sighed. "Guess it all balances. The weather's warm for this time of year and I survived. But then if it were normal, like colder I mean, we probably wouldn't have had that freak storm."

Janice moved over to Archie's desk, sat down and put her feet underneath it. Piorelli simply stared at the spot where she had stood.

"What were you doing up here anyway?" Janice asked. "You're a long way from Boston. And why were you crewing a thirty-footer all by yourself?"

For the first time, Piorelli looked up.

"I'm out of Tignish right now. I came up to try summer business here for a change. For the past week I've been doing repairs on the *Pride*, and I only took it out for a test. That's why I stayed inshore." He slumped down again. "Now it's all over the bottom."

Janice stood up slowly, distracted for a moment by the burping sounds of Archie's coffee-maker.

"I'll be back this afternoon," she said. "We'll get you some dry clothes and a place to stay."

As she left the office, she almost walked into Petty Officer Bowlby.

"Are you finished interrogating already, ma'am?" he asked.

"Not by a long shot, Bowlby," she replied. "I'm going to the RCMP office in Dartmouth first. I'd like to see a picture of Giacomo Giancarlo Piorelli before I go any further."

Why does Ensign Hancock want a photograph of Piorelli?

26

The Case of the Scalpel Murder

ANY OTHER TOWN BUT SHORTHORN would have written off old Doc Virgil long ago as an out-and-out, certifiable nut case. Even by the most relaxed standards he was more than just eccentric. For one thing he made house calls, which to some of his colleagues was eccentric in itself. He made them, however, in the company of a pet skunk! The little beast didn't stay out in Doc's big Chrysler either; it accompanied him like a consultant, right into the patient's bedroom.

Another issue was Doc's waiting room. It was a greenhouse. During office hours, patients fought their way through a labyrinth of palm leaves, schefflera and saxifraga sarmentosa to respond to Doc Virgil's shout of "Next!" He did not have a receptionist, officially. Nor a nurse.

Just being able to hear "Next!" was a problem in itself in the greenhouse. Doc loved country music — very loud country music. He had a theory that his plants did too, and that they grew especially well to the sound of fiddles and steel guitars. No one trying to answer the call of "Next!" ever disputed this.

Yet some of Doc's notions had had other effects. He was a fanatic about dietary control of diabetes. Because of his relentless experimentation he had made some breakthroughs, which had been published and reprinted several times in the medical journals.

Perhaps the most serious matter, however, was Doc's drinking. To people outside Shorthorn, and to the few locals who eschewed his ministrations, Doc Virgil was a drunk. To everyone else he simply had a problem, and the villagers adjusted to it in the same way they had adjusted to the greenhouse, to the Ranch Boys at too many decibels and to the skunk.

It was simple. No one in Shorthorn got sick on Thursdays. Thursday was Doc's day off. He faithfully celebrated that weekly recurrence by tying one on, which always culminated in Police Chief Gary Westlake carrying the little man from the back seat of the huge, old Chrysler at about 2:00 A.M., and laying him out in gentle repose in the greenhouse.

Of late, Chief Westlake had been especially careful while tiptoeing in with Doc, for fear of waking Petty. Petty — her real name was Petunia — was Doc's housekeeper or nurse or former mistress or even wife; no one knew for sure. Petty was no shrinking violet and, despite her diabetes, had a bottomless well of energy when it came to expressions of temper. Her battles with Doc were legendary, and she was to be avoided at moments like these. In fact, most of the people in Shorthorn avoided her, period. But without saying so. She was just one more element they were willing to adjust to because of old Doc. No one complained about her — or, indeed about anything regarding Doc Virgil — because every family in the village at one time or another had had reason to be grateful to him. With his unorthodox methods — perhaps because of them — he had touched everyone in Shorthorn. Deeply.

Not least of all, Gary Westlake. That's why he sat so forlornly right now behind the wheel of Doc's car. It was dark out on the Fourth Concession, but the combined red-and-white flashes from his patrol car — Shorthorn's only one — and from the regional ambulance were continuous enough for him to see the bloodstains on the passenger seat. There were even more where Petunia's head had lain on the floor. They were clearly visible amid the unbelievable pile of paper towels, envelopes and empty cat-food packages. With his pen, Gary moved aside a chocolate-bar wrapper and some crumpled tissues to look at the ooze. She had bled a long time.

He was interrupted by Mel Hehn, his partner on Shorthorn's two-man force.

"That forensic fella' from th' region says it's okay t'move the car now." Mel stuck his head almost inside the driver's window. "Says they got ever'thing they need."

Gary had been waiting for that. He reached to find the adjuster under the seat so that he could move it ahead to reach the pedals.

"Where are they taking Petty's body?" he asked Mel. "I want to see it again myself before Doc wakes up."

Doc Virgil was stretched out on the back seat in a Thursday stupor. He was covered with blood too, and in his hand was the scalpel that had finished Petty.

"Hospital, I guess," Mel replied. "I'll ask 'em. Uh . . . where yuh gonna' put Doc?"

"The cell," Gary said. "At least till he wakes up."

Shorthorn had a single cell in the basement of the town hall cum police station and library.

"Tell that fellow from forensic I'll wait in my office. If I don't get this car out of here right now the whole town will be snooping through it."

He turned the ignition key and, along with the motor, everything in the car roared to life: wipers, air conditioner, lights. From the specially mounted rear speakers, the Rolling Stones nearly lifted Gary's hat. It took him a minute to adjust everything.

"Mel!" he called to his partner, who had turned to walk away. "Mel, I've got to arrest old Doc all right. I don't want to, but I have to. Still I don't think he did it. I've got at least three reasons to doubt it. You and I are going to have to dig deeper on this one."

What are the three items that have made Gary Westlake doubtful of Doc Virgil's guilt?

27

Cutting Up the Pierce Arrow

THE OLDEST OF THE THREE men stopped pacing — actually prancing — and planted himself in front of Christopher Watson's desk. He shook an accusing finger at Christopher and harped in a high-pitched voice. "I don't care! I get half! That's all there's to it! And I'm taking half, too! If you don't get that mechanic person over here and start cutting the Pierce Arrow in half then I'm going to do it myself!" He humphed righteously and sat down, and then gripping his knees with his hands and holding his back straight, began tapping his feet on the floor.

"Half!" he repeated. "By four o'clock today!"

His place in front of Christopher's desk was immediately taken by the second man. This one was Willard Glebemount. He was even more strident than his older brother, Chauncey.

"If you dare . . . if you *dare*!" Willard sputtered a lot, and bounced while he talked. "So help me, I'll sue. I'll sue. And you'll never work again. If you let anyone go near any of the cars, I'll . . . I'll. . . ." Willard's threat, whatever it was, got lost

in a combination of chokes and sputters. He sat down to collect himself.

There was a second or two of silence before the third man spoke from a reclining position in his chair. Christopher could not really tell if he had been drinking or not.

"Mr. Watson — Christopher." Alistair Glebemount, the youngest of the three Glebemount heirs, was also the calmest, but then, as Christopher's predecessor had advised him only two days before, no one had ever seen Alistair sober, so it was difficult to conclude that the calm was natural.

"Christopher, why don't you just go ahead and call the man with the cutting torch? It's a simple trade-off. One of my brothers will be apoplectic; the other will be appeased. I, meanwhile," he continued, crossing his legs with a show of languor, "could not care less what you do."

"Not the Pierce Arrow, you good-for-nothing!" Willard had recovered himself, and launched into Alistair. "If you put a scratch on Papa's best-ever car, I'll . . . I'll. . . ."

It seemed to Christopher that whatever Willard intended, he'd never ever be able to tell anyone first.

"Gentlemen!" He had to break the cycle, for out of the corner of his eye, he saw Chauncey had been gathering steam again. "Gentlemen, tea is being served in the library. I will join you there in fifteen minutes with the solution to this dilemma. Could you please . . .?"

Alistair got up and left before Christopher finished. Chauncey and Willard fenced only briefly at the doorway over who would leave first, so Christopher soon had peace in his office.

He sat down wearily, reflecting on the major drawback that accompanied the role of the most junior partner in Alliston, Aubrey & Wickum. A great firm, he thought. He and his classmates had competed vigorously for this position, but on a day like today he wondered whether it was truly worth the big salary and the prestige. Christopher's responsibility, until the next junior was added to the firm, was to administer the vast Glebemount estate. Most of his efforts were devoted to overseeing the whims, jealousies and chronic bickerings of the three Glebemount bachelor brothers.

To compound his bad luck, Christopher had acquired this portfolio at a watershed point. Papa Glebemount's will decreed that by four o'clock this afternoon, his seventeen cars were to be distributed among his four sons, precisely as follows: to the eldest son, Chauncey, one-half of the cars; to the middle son, Willard, one-third of the cars; to Alistair, the youngest, one-ninth.

It hadn't taken any great insight on Christopher's part to deduce just why the Glebemount brothers had turned out as they did. Papa's will was full of this kind of thing. It was guaranteed to keep his boys at one another's throats for life. The division of the seventeen cars into these impossible fractions was just one more thorn in everyone's side.

His office door opened immediately after a short, swift knock. It was the senior assistant to Noel Wickum himself, the unflappable Mrs. Bayles. She was flapped.

"Mr. Watson, the library! They're having an awful row! You must come!"

Christopher ran down the hall after Mrs. Bayles and just missed knocking her over when she came to an abrupt halt well outside the library door. They had arrived in time to hear Alistair tell Willard he wanted the hood ornament and grill of the Pierce Arrow for his one-ninth, and that once he had control of these pieces he was going to spray-paint them in fluorescent yellow. By the time Christopher opened the door, Willard was sputtering and Chauncey was prancing in his chair again.

"Gentlemen!" He was surprised at how readily they gave him their attention. "I have a solution. Please come to the parking lot."

They filed into the elevator, and although Christopher had reason to be tense, nothing more untoward happened than Willard's insistence on facing the wall and, of course, Chauncey's incessant prancing. He pranced them all right out the door and into the parking lot, where the gleaming chrome faces of seventeen classic automobiles seemed to be enjoying the scene in a wicked sort of way.

Christopher had parked them himself the previous night, side by side in the empty lot, relishing the time behind the steering wheel of each one. There were two Packards, a La Salle, a custom-made eight-seater Hudson . . . The list went on.

And of course, there was the Pierce Arrow. Chauncey pranced over to it in double time.

"Mine! mine!" He danced around it and then, with a cackle at his brother, added, "This half!"

"No . . . no . . . Papa's nice . . . I'll. . . ." Willard was beside himself.

Alistair chuckled.

"Gentlemen." Christopher was beginning to feel like an announcer. "My solution. Please wait here. I have a present for Papa Glebemount's estate which, as administrator, I cheerfully accept."

While the three brothers eyed him with silent suspicion, he sprinted across the lot to his somewhat battered but loyal Toyota. He quickly drove it to the end of the Glebemount lineup and parked it there, in sharp contrast to the highly polished 1936 Chrysler Air-Flow that up to now had been car number seventeen. The brothers were unusually still.

"The Glebemount estate cars now number eighteen." For the first time, Christopher felt he had a bit of control over things. "You, Mr. Chauncey, may have your half without any cutting now. That should please you, Mr. Willard; your one-third can even include the Pierce Arrow. It should not make any difference, since only Mr. Alistair drives in any case. And Mr. Alistair, you surely would not want the little Toyota as part of your one-ninth, so since it's left over, I'll continue to use it in my role as administrator. That is, of course, unless one of you would prefer to have it in your share and perhaps leave me a Packard?"

Can you explain Christopher Watson's math? How did he manage to satisfy the Glebemount will without cutting up any of the cars, especially the Pierce Arrow, and still have a car for himself?

28

The Case of the Jewelry
Thieves

THE TWICE-DAILY BUS FROM Lindeville made only two stops
in the straight run due east from Benton. The first was on the
edge of Lindeville itself, right at the point where two used-car
dealerships bracketed the highway, and brought Lindeville to
a close with huge signs that promised fair deals, square deals
and no money down. The second was about five minutes
farther out, in a sparsely populated rural area at the midway
point between the two towns. For years the bus company had
tried to establish several more stops. The highway was too
desolate, it argued, too subject to chilling winds in winter and
overwhelming heat in summer. But the highways department
steadfastly refused. Too disruptive of traffic, the officials
claimed, and precedent setting as well. If it were done for the
stretch from Lindeville to Benton, it would have to be done for
the other three directions too.

So every night the pride of the Lindeville Tour, Transport
and Travel fleet — a former Greyhound Dreamliner, its
dreams long since fulfilled and forgotten — lumbered out to

the car dealerships, where it paused in a ragged symphony of air brakes and diesel coughs to discharge some morose passenger, and then continued on to what locals called the "nowhere stop" before delivering its charges to Benton and points beyond.

The old bus was making the first of these two stops as Steve Fleck of the Lindeville Constabulary pulled around it and accelerated down the highway and out of town. He felt stuffy and uncomfortable in the patrol car; the heater worked properly only on high, and he'd been in the car for two hours now. That afternoon around four o'clock, just before what passed as Lindeville's rush hour, four armed robbers had hit Zonka Jewelry Ltd. in a lightning swoop. Very professional, or at least very experienced, they had stripped the cash register, the display cases and even the small safe where Zonka's kept its Christmas layaway sales. Steve had been in the patrol car when the burglar alarm sounded in the station, but even though he had headed for Zonka's with red light flashing and siren blaring — both of which he hated with a passion — the thieves were well clear by the time he got there.

It had been a carefully planned event. To Steve it appeared almost rehearsed, as it may well have been, for as witnesses described it, the robbers were in and out in only a few minutes, with one man at the door, a second and third gathering the stock and a fourth at the wheel of a car outside. The timing had been precise in every way. There was usually a lull in the store's customer traffic at that point of the day, and the inventory at Zonka's was at its peak, what with Christmas only a week away. The getaway car had bolted into Lindeville's downtown streets just before traffic began to build.

In fact there were really only two things that Steve Fleck could feel good about. One was that he had a good description of the robbers' car: a blue Honda LX, somewhat dirty from the winter roads, with a very obvious dent in the right rear fender. Actually, that part made Steve uneasy. These guys were so professional; yet it almost seemed they wanted their car to be remembered.

The other good thing — Steve felt pretty sure it was a good thing — was that the robbers were still in Lindeville somewhere. They had to be. They may well have been very smooth, but Steve and his colleagues were no slouches themselves. There were only four roads out of town and they had been blocked immediately. Now the roadblocks had been lifted to tempt the robbers out of hiding.

The Lindeville Constabulary was keeping a careful watch on every road, but so far there was no evidence that the getaway car had left town, and a nagging concern was beginning to develop that maybe the enterprising gang had slipped out of town after all.

Steve was quite far ahead of the pride of the Lindeville Tour, Transport and Travel fleet, so he spotted the passenger at the highway stop a minute or so before the bus would arrive. Half on impulse, half deliberately, he pulled over to the rickety old bus shelter.

"I'm going to Benton," he said. "To the outskirts anyway. It's too hot in here, but 'least you don't have to breathe diesel fumes if you ride with me."

The passenger flashed him a warm smile. It was a young woman. "Oh thanks! I was freezing! I'm afraid to hitchhike. There's only been a couple of cars going toward Benton anyway." She got in and immediately began unwrapping the scarf that was drawn tightly over her head.

Steve was very nonchalant. "You didn't happen to, uh . . . notice any of the cars, did you? Like . . . uh . . . new cars or old?" He could hear the bus coming now and glanced in the rearview mirror, to make sure it was stopping, before he pulled onto the highway.

"No." She gave him a warm smile again. "I really don't know much about cars. One was a Japanese car, though, a blue one. They're easier to tell, don't you think? The Japanese cars?" She folded the scarf in her lap. "Anyway, this one had a banged-in fender. That's why I noticed."

Steve slowed and pulled over onto the shoulder of the road. The bus pulled past them, accelerating down the highway in a barrage of noise and noxious fumes.

"What's the matter? What are you doing?" The young lady was frightened. "Why are you stopping? Is this a trick? You're making me miss the bus!" She was almost in tears.

"Miss, we're just going to sit here for a minute," Steve said, "and watch the road until you tell me who you are and where you've been today."

What changed Steve Fleck's mind about taking this would-be bus passenger to Benton?

29

All Applications Treated Seriously

"GIVE ME FIVE MINUTES, and then send in — what's his name? — Halvorsen? Yes, Halvorsen."

MaryPat Neese was speaking to her assistant. Both women were just back from a not very restful lunch. The morning had been far too stimulating.

As executive director of The Unusual Ark, Inc., MaryPat held all responsibilities for personnel, and she had spent the morning interviewing job applicants. In most businesses that was hardly an event to spoil lunch, but for The Unusual Ark, Inc., to have spent the entire morning interviewing applicants was as unusual as the company itself.

Animal behavior management was its field of expertise. The people at Ark were fulltime consultants to a number of well-known zoos. Government clients included the departments of agriculture of Canada, the US, Argentina and Greece. Their ad hoc clientele ranged from circuses and Las Vegas animal acts to canine security companies. It was not a typical corporation.

That's what made it so hard to find employees. The Unusual Ark, Inc., especially since MaryPat had taken over, was not looking to hire run-of-the-mill dog trainers. They were looking for people with real insight into animal psychology. When a single advertisement therefore, generated no less than seven serious applications, MaryPat was beside herself.

The morning had produced one possible winner out of the five people interviewed, and both MaryPat and her assistant agreed this one had the inside track if they could agree on money. Yet Elwood Halvorsen, judging from his résumé, was the most intriguing, and MaryPat was looking forward to meeting him.

She laid out his résumé to look at each section again. Halvorsen's formal education was, if nothing else, episodic: one year of veterinary college, University of Guelph (A average); then a year of employment at Perfect Pets. There was another year at Whipsnade Zoo in London. That looked really interesting to MaryPat, for Whipsnade was Desmond Morris country. However, the résumé did not say what Halvorsen had done there. Back to university again, this time for two semesters at the University of Regina, major in psychology (B average); followed by five months at Blue Bonnet Raceway in charge of hygienic maintenance (whatever that meant!); and then an incomplete semester in marine biology at Memorial University. Finally, coming almost full circle, Elwood Halvorsen had returned to the University of Guelph, this time as an employee (animal management, level 1).

His letters of reference had the usual glow if one read them only once, although MaryPat thought she detected a sardonic note in a Regina professor's comment that "Elwood is invariably stimulated by the challenge of the extraordinary. . . ." The other two letters, one from Perfect Pets, the other a character reference from the Reverend Patch of the Church of the Unbroken Circle — MaryPat read that one twice to be sure — were both full of superlatives.

"All in all, not your run-of-the-mill résumé," she commented to herself, "but then," she acknowledged, "what can you expect when people answer a job ad from The Unusual Ark, Inc?"

She turned to the last piece. This is what had really set Elwood Halvorsen apart. It was a paper he'd written. According to the explanatory note, he'd written it for one of his university courses but had never submitted it. Now he had polished it and included it with his résumé as a prelude to the interview: ". . . to provide Ms. Neese" his note explained, "with some appreciation of my interests and abilities."

The dissertation that followed was entitled, "Group Management of Ruminants: A Proposal for Behavior Modification, Especially of Cattle." In it Halvorsen argued cogently, and with impressive language and logic, that ruminants like cattle could be trained in groups to perform synchronized, ballet-like exercises! Using mild electric shock and associated whistling sounds, he argued, as many as five or even ten cattle in a row could be made to lie down simultaneously at one whistle (by touching the electrified wire to their backs); to stand up again at two whistles (by touching the wire under their throats); or even rise halfway then lie down again at three whistles (by touching one wire at their throats, with another in sequence just over their heads to make them go back down).

The piece went on for several more pages, in which Halvorsen offered some ideas for the commercial application of his proposal, but MaryPat was interrupted by her assistant before she could read them again.

"Five minutes," her assistant said. Then she lowered her voice. "Are you seriously going to interview him? About the cow thing?"

"Sure," MaryPat smiled. "Even if he doesn't know much about his Holsteins, he's at least got his Pavlov down right. Besides — a guy with this much chutzpah, I've just got to see!"

Has MaryPat found a flaw in Elwood Halvorsen's fascinating résumé that suggests he may not have the animal expertise to which he pretends?

30

The Boshkung Mystery Rectangle

AN HOUR AFTER THE BRIEF storm had passed, the boys were still treating the situation as a lark. The fact that the counselor had still not regained consciousness failed to impress them. The younger ones were a bit anxious, but they took their cue from the older, more experienced campers, who had been through this kind of thing before. The older ones knew that every canoe trip at Camp Boshkung had an "incident," and that it was just a matter of time before the counselor would come around.

Only Steve Calumet was a bit worried, though he didn't admit it to the others. Early that morning, when the four canoes had turned right out of Boshkung Lake and into the sun at marker buoy 77, he'd had an uncomfortable feeling. In his six summers — he was the most experienced camper, now fifteen years old — they had never canoed up this way because it was so easy to get lost. There were too many lakes and rivers in this section, and the charts were hard to read accurately because of shifting, swampy areas.

Steve was also the only camper who knew the counselor had broken the rules by not giving the trip plan to at least one other person. All any of the campers knew was that this trip was called the Boshkung Mystery Rectangle. Along the way they would change direction four times. The first three would be called by the counselor. The fourth change would be up to the campers. If they turned in the right direction at the correct marker buoy they would be home for supper. A wrong turn made the trip an overnighter or — at the discretion of the counselor — even longer.

It was a challenge and Steve liked that. But the blatant safety violation bothered him a lot.

Still, until the windstorm the trip had been very smooth and the boys were in a great mood. They had paddled with the current for over two hours, making very good time until the river divided into two looping arcs going in opposite directions. Here the counselor had made them turn at marker buoy 49, and Dinty Scollino had yelled out.

"Hey, 49! That's my grandmother's apartment!"

And for the next ten minutes the boys had chanted:

Number 49, Number 49,
Scollino's old granny
Is in Number 49!

However, the chant petered out when the current strengthened. It took all their concentration to deal with the fast water.

"Exhilarating, what?" Bertie Ludd-Dinsmore had offered after almost an hour of steady, rapid current. Bertie was from England, a first-time camper, but an excellent canoeist.

"Right-o!"

"Pip, pip!"

"Spot on, old chap!"

Bertie could never say anything without inadvertently soliciting a chorus of what all the boys thought were British expressions.

Then the counselor had cut through the catcalls: "Race time! There's another lake just ahead. Turn west at marker 36. There's sand beach dead ahead from that. We'll eat there. Last crew in builds the fire and washes the dishes — go!"

A morning of paddling in strong current had left the boys with plenty of reserve, so that they were well out into the lake when the wind gusts came. The second canoe swamped completely, but they were close to shore and everybody walked in, pulling the equipment after them. The first came in almost without incident, as did the third. The counselor was in that one. The fourth canoe overturned well out, at the marker buoy. Only Steve Calumet and Dinty Scollino knew how close a call that had been. They had gone out with the counselor to bring number four and its crew to shore, and lost the extra paddles, the charts and compass, and two sleeping bags in the struggle.

No one noticed just when the counselor lost consciousness — if indeed he had. He'd carried the fourth canoe the last few steps to shore, and then sat with the boys as they watched the spinning wind devils stirring along the surface until they disappeared on the other side. Then, when they had all caught their breath, the boys were so busy talking out their big scare that no one paid any attention until Arnie Majeski said, "Look, you guys! What's the matter with Hank?"

The counselor lay quietly beside the canoe he had carried in. His face was calm; his arms were folded across his chest.

"He's getting his beauty sleep!" snorted "Mule" Kovacs in the bray that gave him his name. "Too old to cut it anymore!"

"Is he okay?" Jimmy Pitt, the youngest camper, stepped a little closer.

"Naw, it's a gag." Arnie Majeski was no longer concerned.

Dinty Scollino looked at Steve. "This is the big test, I'll bet. He goes to sleep and we have to find the last turn."

Steve shrugged. He felt very uncomfortable.

"He's really okay, isn't he, Steve?" Jimmy had gotten even closer to Hank.

Steve shrugged again.

"Well, he can sleep!" Mule Kovacs announced. "We came here to eat!"

Mule had struck about the only chord that could guarantee agreement and for the next half-hour the boys fell to. Through it all, Hank the counselor did not move. Not until Bertie Ludd-Dinsmore gave voice to the obvious did the boys acknowledge that their counselor's condition might be for real.

"I say, do you not think his color is just a bit off?"

The fact that not a single imitation of his accent rose to mock him, showed they all knew they were in trouble. Panic was not far away.

"We gotta take him in!"

"You mean carry him?"

"Where do we go?"

"Yeah! Where are we?"

"I say we stay here!"

"What if the storm comes back?"

"Let's wait until. . . ."

"Steve!" Dinty Scollino tried to yell over the noise.

"STEVE!" Nobody was louder than Mule Kovacs. "Everybody shut up!"

In the silence which followed, Jimmy Pitt placed the leadership in Steve Calumet's hands.

"What do we do, Steve?"

Steve had been trying to take Hank's pulse, without really knowing what he was looking for.

"I don't know for sure," he said quietly. "But we've got to take him back. He's sick and I don't think we should wait for them to come looking for us."

"So where do we go?" asked Arnie Majeski. "Where's the fourth turn? I've never been way out here before. Has anybody?"

145

Arnie triggered the shouting again and it took Steve a minute, with Mule's help, to regain their attention.

"I think I've got it. Now listen. We stay in this direction until we find marker 18. If I'm right, we go home from there. Let's not waste time. Into the canoes!"

Why does Steve want to find marker buoy 18? And when they do find it, will they turn to the left or to the right to get back to camp?

31

A Letter to Spain

DEIRDRE BRETON FORCED HERSELF to stretch across her desk for the intercom. The blinking light had finally broken through her intense concentration on an ink drawing of the funeral procession of Sir Christopher Hatton, Lord Chancellor to Queen Elizabeth I. It was the original, dated 16 December 1591, and was on loan to the university to support a project of which Deirdre was in charge. Deirdre Breton was an unmitigated Tudorphile and an expert on the subject of Elizabeth.

"Yes?" She spoke gently, knowing the very new and very young department secretary would be upset at having to interrupt her.

She was. "I'm so sorry, Professor Breton. I'm really sorry. I know you did not want to be disturbed. It's just that there's. . . ."

"It's okay, Jeannie." Deirdre tried to be soothing. "Is there a call for me? What line?"

"No, Professor Breton. There's a Miss Philomena Loquor to see you. I told her you —"

From the secretary's office came the sound of several voices talking at once. Jeannie was simply drowned out.

"I'll come out," Deirdre said, and hung up the intercom. She put away the large magnifying lens that she was still holding in her left hand and reached for her glasses, the ones she called her "intimidating glasses." These she wore when talking to the department chairman or when dealing with a recalcitrant student.

Before she could stand up, her door blew open. It was the several voices. They were Miss Philomena Loquor.

"You're Professor Breton? Right? A woman, eh? She didn't tell me you were a woman — no matter, no reason a woman shouldn't know history — now I have something to show you, don't tell me you're busy, I've driven forty-five miles to get here and I'm a taxpayer and I support this institution like everybody else, and don't tell me you've got a class, I just looked at the schedule and you're finished for the day, now look at this. By the way. Loquor. That's my name, Philomena Loquor, my brother was Dirsten Loquor, what do you think?"

All of the above was accomplished in one breath. Deirdre, on the other hand, found herself puffing. In only a few seconds she had completely forgotten Sir Christopher Hatton's funeral and, having done nothing else except listen to Miss Loquor, was completely out of breath.

"Just look at it, what's it worth?" Philomena Loquor was off and running again. She thrust a half-opened package under Deirdre's nose and then set it on her desk. "It was in my brother's collection, my late brother's collection, he's dead, you know. Pneumonia, that's what they said in the hospital. I wonder. Don't trust them for a minute, I'm going to sell it, I'm going to sell all his stuff, what's it worth? That's why I came here, I read about you in the paper. Am I talking too fast? People say I always talk too fast, and who do I sell it to? You're the expert, leastways that's what the paper said."

Deirdre took off her "intimidating glasses." They were quite obviously of no use in any case. Besides, she had glimpsed something in the package that for her was enough to make Philomena Loquor tolerable. Encased between two pieces of thick plate glass she could see faded parchment. A letter, or a document perhaps? But it was the signature, the unmistakable and famous signature, that intrigued her.

She unwrapped the package completely. "Miss Loquor, where did you —"

"It was my brother's, I told you that, I don't know where he got it, it was in his things, he's dead, I told you that too, it's old, isn't it? It's Elizabeth, right? The queen? Good Queen Bess and all that? You're the expert, the paper said you know more about her than anybody alive, I tell you what I thought, I thought you can use it in the showing or whatever it is you're putting on here. For nothing. Free. No charge. But then you tell me what it's worth, tell me where I can sell it, my brother didn't leave much, I even paid his funeral, not that we're poor or anything, what do you think?"

Deirdre had almost, but not quite, tuned out the voluble Philomena Loquor. The parchment was a letter over the signature of Elizabeth. It was written to Philip of Spain, and dated 17 February 1565. Quickly she scanned the florid Latin, translating to herself.

> Elizabeth, by the grace of God, queen of England
> France and Ireland, defender of the faith, to
> Philip of Spain, Sicily . . .

"It's a letter, isn't it?" Miss Loquor was winding up again. "From her to the king of Spain? And it's in Latin? Leastways that's what Lily said, Lily's my girlfriend, she took Latin in highschool, she didn't like my brother much, Dirsten I mean, but that's all right, he didn't like her much either, Lily's smart, she knows her Latin, Lily does, never mind the fancy writing either, she can read it, I trust her, she's my friend, says it's all about the Spaniards keeping English ships and not letting them sail around and do their business, she's smart, Lily is."

Deirdre looked up from the letter and stared at Philomena Loquor, wondering if maybe there was a switch to pull or a button to press, but the lady was in full sail.

"What's that other signature there? Beside Elizabeth's. Lily didn't know that. She said you would though, you're supposed to know everything about Elizabeth she said, so who is that other person? See that one, starts with R, that's the first initial, then the name. Ass-Kam-US." She pronounced it in slow, deliberate syllables, and then paused for the answer. Miss Loquor herself was puffing now.

The seconds of silence were delicious for Deirdre. She sat down and enjoyed them as long as she dared. "That would be Roger Ascham likely — written in Latin, of course. He was Elizabeth's secretary and wrote most of her correspondence."

"Oh."

There was another pause. Deirdre braced herself for the next barrage. It didn't come. Philomena Loquor simply leaned forward a little, and said,

"So. It's over four hundred years old. What's it worth?"

"Miss Loquor, I. . . ." Deirdre wished desperately that she had scheduled a lecture in five minutes. Even a meeting with the department chairman.

"Miss Loquor, I really don't think it's very old at all. Oh, it's good Latin!" She was thinking of Lily now. "And certainly Elizabeth wrote to Philip all the time. On this very topic, too. But not this letter. No, not this letter."

Why did Deirdre Breton suspect that Philomena Loquor's letter was not genuine?

32

The Case of the Walking Sweater

LENA JONES HAD ALREADY concluded for the tenth time that today was not the day to be a store manager, when the head store detective ushered in a very red-faced young man.

"This kid just walked out with this," the detective said, and he threw a crumpled sweater onto Lena's desk. "I got him down the street. He was at least a hundred yards away. And he's admitted it. Open and shut."

"Very well." Lena sighed and looked at the young man. "We'll take your name and address. You realize that the police will be involved too, don't you?" She began to get angry. "What's the matter with you people? Don't you realize that shoplifters are so easy to catch?"

The young man reddened even more, and fought to keep back the tear that was beginning to roll down his cheek.

"It wasn't like that . . . I mean . . . I didn't steal it! Well, no, I stole it, but that's not why I came here. Like I wasn't gonna take it. It just, well . . . sort of . . . like, happened!"

"That's a new one," Lena retorted. "I suppose the sweater

just stuck to you as you walked out of the store. Let's see." She picked up the sweater. "Grey, long sleeved, V-neck, all wool. Yes, they always stick to people." Her comment made the young man wince.

"No!" he almost shouted. "I was like . . . trying it on in the dressing room, and got it on all inside out and back to front. I mean, here it was on wrong, and the tags were inside and all, and I thought nobody would see it was from the store so I just, I mean, I just . . . like walked out! I didn't plan it! Nobody saw it either . . . I mean . . . until this guy stopped me."

Lena looked at the detective. "Who tipped you off?" she asked.

"That's part of the problem," the detective answered. "The security light went on when he went out the door so I just followed him. But the problem is that there are two different clerks claiming the store reward. They both say they saw him leave, and each of them says she turned on the alarm light."

Lena looked at the detective carefully. "This is getting more tiresome by the minute," she said. "Who are they?"

"Borelli's one," he said. "Tina Borelli, the new one in notions. She claims she saw the kid coming toward her and when she saw the label of the sweater, she figured out what he was doing and hit the light as soon as he got to the door."

Lena pondered a moment. "And the other story?"

"That's Singh," the detective replied. "She's a part-timer. Her story is that she saw him stop at the door for a minute and check the street. That's when she saw the sweater label, and she too figured it was a lift and hit the light." The detective leaned on Lena's desk. "Both her and Borelli work right beside the exit door," he offered, "so really, both their stories check."

"In all but one respect," Lena said. "It looks like we've not only got a lifter here, we may have a liar too!"

What made Lena suspicious? And whom does she suspect?

33

The Telegram from Uganda

THE CORNER TABLE AT THE Red Lion was occupied by three journalism students and one of their favorite instructors. Inevitably, the talk had come around to the subject of great foreign correspondents and their greatest stories.

"You mean you actually *knew* Gordon Froggatt?" said one of the students. "Like, more than just to talk to him? You really knew him *well*?"

"Sure," Mark Tully replied. "We worked together at AP for a while; I was his foreign-desk editor once, and then of course our paths crossed a lot when we both freelanced. . . ."

"And is all the stuff true?" another student broke in.

Mark Tully grinned. "Depends what you've heard," he said. "I can vouch for a lot of the stories that go around, but a legend like Gordie Froggatt inevitably attracts material that any good journalist would always double-check first. Don't forget, Gordie was absolutely everywhere. In the sixties and seventies especially. He was simply one heck of a journalist.

There's probably not a single foreign correspondent anywhere who equaled him for finding a story.

"He was trusted, too. So far as I know, he's the only Western reporter that Tass would quote without some kind of propagandish qualification. And certainly nobody — but nobody — ever filed stories quite the way he did."

The third student chimed in. "Is it true he once taught Shakespeare?"

"That's true," Mark Tully nodded. "Right here on this campus, too. Not for long, though. I think it was only for a year; then the Congo thing started in 1960 and he went out there for Reuters."

"I want to know about the Uganda thing!" It was the first student again. "That one's so incredible it has to be true. At least I hope it's true — is it?"

"How much do you know?" Mark Tully asked. "There's a lot went on at that trial. It's the trial — well, so-called trial — you're referring to, I imagine?"

"Yes," the student answered. "The one where Idi Amin himself presided, and where he literally played games with the defendants. Kind of sick, really. It took place in one of the provinces, right? And there were three or four provincial officials up for embezzlement and other things?"

"Three," Mark interjected. "There was the minister of trade; his name was Mombajetta. The TV people had a time with that one! The other two were the minister of justice and the minister of health."

"Why would a guy like Gordon Froggatt be sent to the trial of three provincial cabinet ministers in Uganda?" asked one of the other students.

"Reasonable question," Mark acknowledged. "And it's one I asked myself at the time. You see, I was his editor then." He paused to stroke his moustache. "By 1972, it was becoming pretty clear that Amin was a big problem. A real twentieth-century bad guy. There was reasonable evidence, for example, that he was purging whole tribes like the Lango and the Ancholi. He had become big news."

"This trial was held without lawyers, wasn't it?" offered the third student. "In fact the only lawyer there was one of the defendants — the minister of justice, if I've got the story right."

"That's the way I have it, too," said Mark, "but I think the thing that really grabbed the nose of every foreign-desk editor was Amin's announcement before the trial ever began. He told the press attaché at the French Embassy that if he decided to give the minister of justice and the minister of health the same sentence then, just for variety, he would sentence the minister of trade — uh, Mombajetta — to death."

"No kidding! Some justice system!" The second student was incredulous.

Mark continued. "He didn't stop there, either. Two weeks before the trial he paraded the three of them in the streets of Kampala, and told the minister of justice — the guy was standing there in shackles — that if the other two got the same sentence then he would be stripped of all his property and it would be divided up. All three of the ministers apparently were quite rich. Coffee growers, I think. Then in the same breath he turned to the minister of health, Doctor — uh, Doctor something, I can't remember. Anyway, Amin told *him* that if the other two got different sentences, he would be kicked out of the country forthwith."

"All this before the trial?"

"This is pretty hard to believe!"

"No wonder they wanted somebody like Froggatt there."

The students' reactions were piling in on top of one another — all but that of the one who had first asked about Uganda.

"What I don't understand," he said, "is why Gordon Froggatt became yet more famous at this trial. Wasn't Idi Amin already an international pariah by this time? And an acknowledged maniac? You said he was big news. Everybody else was reporting on him, too."

Mark Tully leaned back in his chair and smiled, enjoying the moment.

"It was the way Gordie filed the story. You see, there really was no trial. No prosecution, no defense. Amin just walked to the bench and announced, 'Uganda has no time for government criminals! Take these three men away! Execute one according to my direction. Exile another. The property of the third is to be divided.'

"Then he simply walked out. The international press was flabbergasted. They had no idea what to report. Oh, mind you, they all rushed to file! But none of them really had a handle on the story."

"Except for Gordon Froggatt," the first student said.

"Except for Gordie Froggatt," Mark repeated. "He got to the telegraph office — the phones never worked in Amin's time — but he had to cover himself from the usual crowd of hangers-on, the bunch that inevitably tried to jump in on his angle to a story, or tried to steal it or whatever. That's when he pulled his real coup. He not only understood Amin's little game right away, he sent it out right under everyone's nose and they didn't know it."

"I heard about that." The second student's voice was getting louder. "He sent a code! What was it . . . 'Jetlear' . . . No, 'Learjet'! Then 'Henry'. . . ."

Mark Tully cleared his throat. "It was:

LEARJET STOP TWO HENRY SIX-FOUR-TWO STOP

DR. ROMEO STOP

For a few seconds the students were entirely silent, trying to interpret the Froggatt message. Then the first one's face lit up.

"So that's how he did it. Not all that mysterious, but really clever!"

"Exactly," Mark said. "It wasn't long before the other press on the scene understood what was happening, but by that time we'd sold the main story to every wire service in the world."

"Clever!" the student repeated. "Absolutely clever!"

How had Gordon Froggatt managed to interpret the sentencing of the three officials? And how had he encoded his conclusions?

34

The Prowler on
Burleigh Court

CODE THREE MEANT HE DID not have to rush, but Sean Dortmund put the red light on the roof anyway. He didn't use the siren, however. There was no need at 3:00 A.M. Code Three meant gunfire with death or injury. It also meant situation over, or well in hand so that officers responding need not endanger themselves or the public getting to the scene. But as inspector, Sean was the active ranking officer at that time of the morning, and since the reports were eventually going to go out over his signature, he wanted to view the scene himself.

The coroner's car, along with two black-and-whites and an ambulance, had already filled the driveway by the time Sean arrived, so he parked on the street. Burleigh Court was a cul-de-sac with only six houses, all of them large and custom-built. There was money here.

He was met on the sidewalk by two of the uniformed men, who took him past the yellow-tape barrier and into the house.

"Everything's in place, Inspector. We got word you were coming." Detective Lalonde was waiting for him in the front

hallway. "Victim is in there." He jerked his thumb toward an open door. "Here's the weapon." Lalonde held up a clear plastic bag with a revolver inside. "Three shots."

Sean could see three shell casings that looked to be .38 calibre.

"And the perp's in that room. We've got the story. Everything's clean. We're just waiting for you to give it a name: murder, manslaughter, self-defense or accident."

"Let's see the body first," Sean said, brushing past Lalonde and through the doorway to where the coroner, Jim Tait, was waiting for him.

"Meet the former Jean-Marc Lavaliere," Tait said grimly. He pulled back the sheet to reveal a very bloody corpse.

Sean leaned closer to compensate for the poor lighting. Lavaliere's body was lying on its back. He appeared to have been in his mid-thirties, athletic and quite handsome. The track suit he wore looked brand-new. Sean crouched down and flicked several shards of glass off Lavaliere's chest for a better look at the wound. The window directly above had been smashed, and pieces of glass were spread all over this part of the room.

"Seems like he came in that way." Tait nodded at the broken window. "Anyway, she must have nailed him right away."

"She?" Sean looked up.

"Yeah," Tait said. "The perp. Ms. Dina White. You haven't spoken to her yet? I didn't realize."

Sean didn't say anything. He was known as a man of very few words so Tait just kept on talking.

"Anyway, they were partners, she and Lavaliere. Advertising business. But according to her, things weren't going so well. Apparently he's a drinker, this guy — or was. They'd been having quite an argument over it for several weeks."

Sean just nodded.

"Anyway, he smashed the window to get in — I suppose we'll never know why. Maybe he was drunk. I'll autopsy that though. We'll know that by tomorrow. Anyway, she thought he was a prowler, and bingo! Three right in the chest. Suppose you can't blame her, really. A woman living alone. Your window gets smashed in at night . . . She must have been awful frightened."

Sean nodded again.

"Anyway, I can't move the remains here till you say so. Are you going to give it a name? Accident? Justifiable homicide?"

There was a long pause when Tait stopped, each man waiting for the other to speak.

"Homicide, yes," said Sean, breaking the silence, but just barely. He shook his head. "But not justifiable. No, I don't think so."

What has led Sean to suspect murder?

35

To Be or Not to Be — Authentic

BOTH SIGNS ON THE LARGE double doors were in elaborate Gothic script. One had been painted a long time ago with painstaking care. It said:

The Crusades Room
Please Enter

Most of the gold flourishes and ligatures had flaked off, and what the original calligrapher would have called majuscules — capital letters, the summit of his craft — had taken on the shabbiness of neglected old age.

The other sign simply hung on the door. It had been born in the crisp whirr of a laser printer, its perfectly shaped and precisely etched letters the product of technology and someone's whimsical choice of typeface for a sign that was only temporary. It said:

Closed To The Public

The ironic contrast was not lost to Glen Crockford as he pulled one of the big doors open, but he said nothing to the young assistant curator who followed him in. Her job, after all, was "artifact systems management and display control." She had an undergraduate degree in archaeology but the museum board had chosen her for her master's in business administration.

When the door closed behind them and their eyes had adjusted to the dimness, her first comment, right on cue, was, "When we reopen next month, the inventory in here will have a 30 percent greater viewer access than before."

Glen suppressed a groan but he couldn't check himself completely; the Crusades Room had always been the board's greatest pride.

"Ms. Sparks. Not *inventory*, please. These pieces. . . ."

She didn't hear him, or else she was not paying attention.

"That's a pretty effective return. As you know, we spent almost seven million of the Lansdorff endowment in here, over half of it on new acquisitions for this beauty!"

She reached under a console, flipped a few switches and one end of the room literally came to life with sounds, backscreen projections and lighting changes. It was the museum board's new pride and joy: a diorama of the seige of Jerusalem in 1099 A.D.

They both took a few steps toward the end of the room and then paused together to absorb the overpowering visual effect of great, thick walls, seige towers and battlements that reached right up to the high, vaulted ceiling. The audio was overpowering too, for as the recording tape turned, sounds of battle grew louder and more intense.

To the right and left sides were lowered drawbridges, each complete with a half-raised portcullis that allowed viewers a stooped entry into the castle itself.

"We're building for predominant traffic flow through the right here." Ms. Sparks was walking toward the drawbridge on the right. "That's why this entrance is closer."

Glen Crockford followed her obediently. He couldn't help but admire what they'd done. Such a difference from the museums we once knew, he thought to himself, although he couldn't help noting the electronic glow in the archway that warned in red: "Young Children May Be Frightened." His cynicism almost disappeared once he went inside, for here the battle raged even more loudly and more realistically. Heating elements in the floor and ceiling meant one could not just see and hear the fire, but actually feel it. There was even smoke — artificial smoke. The fire department and the department of public health had thrown a combined fit when the real stuff had been proposed in the original plans. But the sanitized alternative belched out its approved parts-per-million of hydrocarbon at sixteen-second intervals, and it occurred to Glen that even if it was no more real than the fire, it sure was different from a guided tour.

Except for the walkway, the floors where they now stood were covered in rushes. They were in living quarters, and a scatter of robes, overturned jars and broken furniture suggested that this part of the castle had already been overrun by the invaders. Almost out of the light, a decapitated body lay in the grotesque twist of violent death. Glen tried to make it out through the smoke and gloom. It could have been a woman's body.

"You're obviously not hiding any of the Crusaders' behavior are you?" he said to Ms. Sparks.

"Try this one!" she responded as she led him round a turn where a heavily armored knight held his two-handed sword over a clutch of frightened children. "They were a bloodthirsty bunch, the Crusaders. No point in hiding that fact. Everywhere they went was a slaughterhouse."

Glen was about to ask whether all the bloodthirsty realism was really a museum's proper task when Ms. Sparks took his hand and led him through a low archway.

"It's not all action and gore. This is quieter. See, we have to build in relief every so often. This is the Saladin room. We spent a pot full in here. And in the next one too. That's the Richard the Lion-Heart room. A bit kitchy I guess, but those are two names people know."

It was indeed quieter and Glen felt more at ease. The light was brighter too; in fact the two rooms — adjacent alcoves, really — were almost traditionally museum-like.

He walked slowly, deliberately relaxing the pace. But Ms. Sparks was not in a hurry. Apparently she wanted to spend time here.

"Most of this inventory is from collectors," she said. "We had to pay. In some cases *really* pay! That jewelry was really expensive. Eleventh century. Made in Acre. So was the hookah pipe. The crossbows and scimitars are pretty standard stuff. They're all real but only one of the crossbows is period-authentic. And check this! Here! The Turkish chess set!"

Glen was still staring at the crossbows trying to guess which one was "period-authentic." "We bought this chess set in Venice. It was part of the loot taken from the Turks in the Fourth Crusade by the old Doge. Gorgeous, isn't it? Worth the fortune we paid."

It was strikingly beautiful Glen agreed. And huge. The figures were ivory and black jade. On both sides the king and queen towered over the other figures. The bishops were perfectly matched but had contrasting expressions on their faces. Each pawn was a different tradesman.

Glen was about to pick up a rook to test its heft when Ms. Sparks called out.

"Over here is our problem piece."

Glen looked around. He'd lost her.

"No here. Over here! I'm in the Richard room!"

Reluctantly, Glen left the chess set to join her.

"Watch out for those javelins, Mr. Crockford!"

Glen was tall and the Richard and Saladin rooms were set off from each other by an arch made of two long, pointed spears. He had to duck to get from one alcove to the other.

"You can see," Ms. Sparks was explaining before he got there, "we have a lot more Richard stuff than Saladin."

Glen winced at "stuff" but he could see what she meant. "It's a lot easier to get, isn't it?" he offered.

"Well, nothing's easy in the museum business, but yes, it is. Those bills for example." She pointed to a stack of long-handled spears with hooked blades. "Not all authentic, but that's okay. And spurs, crossbows, swords — that kind of stuff."

Glen wondered if any of it was period-authentic but he didn't ask.

"We have to make scaled-down replicas of some of it, like this mangonel here." She patted a working model of a catapult. "Sometimes authentic doesn't matter all that much if you can show how the technology worked. It's the process then that's authentic. Besides we have *some* real stuff. See the dice? We have twelve pairs that range from mid-eleventh to early fourteenth century. And those candlesticks? They have Sir Hugh Fitzroy's seal!"

She paused for a moment, reflectively. "What we need is a grabber for this room — like the chess set in there." She paused again. "And we have it, but we can't prove it. That's what I mean by our 'problem piece'. There. The bathtub. It's here on spec till next week."

Ms. Sparks led Glen over to a metal tub just large enough to hold a single adult uncomfortably.

"Richard the Lion-Heart's bathtub! Maybe. It comes from Trifels castle in Austria, where Richard was held for ransom," she said. "And we know it's old enough. It's entirely possible Richard used it. But calling it Richard's bathtub — I don't know. It would sure add zip, but I'm really not sure we should pay for something we can't be certain of. You see, bathing is hardly a technology. And really, it's just a tub. Nothing spectacular. But if it were *Richard's* bathtub. . . ."

Glen took a deep breath, held it, then exhaled heavily. He wasn't quite sure Ms. Sparks had stopped.

"Why does this bother you," he asked, "when you already have paid for something whose ancestry is not what you think?"

What is Glen Crockford referring to?

36

Truth and Lies in the Twilight Zone

"THEY WHAT? ARE YOU making this up?" Adam Fewster was shouting into the telephone. "Denticoff! This is the twentieth century. This is the planet Earth!" He was standing now, too. Immediately he regretted the volume of the last comment. Everyone in the squad room was staring at him. Adam didn't shout very much. He wasn't the type.

"Look. . . ." He was calmer now, and even made an effort to sit down. "Look. Just keep a lid on everything. I'll come out myself in —" He looked at his watch. " — twenty minutes."

He hung up the telephone and looked around. The other detectives appeared busy. "It was Denticoff," Adam announced into the unnatural silence. "Not his fault. It's those silver-haired weirdos again." He stood up and reached for his coat and hat. "I'm going out to the Twilight Zone. Just hold my calls." He walked over to the door, stopped and turned around. The two other detectives and the civilian typist were all grinning at him. "Guess I shouldn't have yelled. He's a

169

good kid, that Denticoff." He ducked out before anyone could answer.

Lieutenant Adam Fewster was not the oldest member of the town's small police force. But he was known to be the most understanding and the most patient. That was why the newest recruits — in this case, Denticoff — were always partnered with him. It was also why the majority of the force's oddball calls ended up on his desk.

He'd had a spate of those lately. Like the lady who insisted someone was stealing her front lawn. In pieces. Or the guy who drove his neighbors nuts by playing tapes of jungle noises all night around his swimming pool. A real cracker, that one. They'd finally got him for indecent exposure because he insisted on sitting at the pool with nothing on but a pith helmet.

Nothing, however, was quite like the Twilight Zone. That's what all the detectives called Adventure Villa. It was a retirement community just outside town, but was most emphatically not a shuffleboard-and-gin-rummy rest home. Wealthy retirees came there to live in the beautiful condos and enjoy what the place called its "infinite source of personalized, exotic experience."

Anything the residents of Adventure Villa wanted to do, they could. Adventure Villa had a helicopter which dropped the mountain-climbing club near any summit of its choice. The club's members were too old to do a full climb, but the helicopter made the adventure possible. Also, it was probably the only retirement villa in North America with active skydivers. Adam knew all about them. Two months ago, they had made a mass landing — an illegal mass landing — in a supermarket parking lot. Then there was the Spelunkers' Society, the cave crawlers. Last year they shut down the Santa Claus parade: somehow they had gotten into the town sewer system, and simultaneously popped out of manhole covers right into the middle of the parade. The horses pulling Santa's sleigh had taken off down a side street and delivered a very frightened symbol of the Christmas spirit to a used-car lot instead of the town square. So far none of the nuts from the Twilight Zone had hurt anybody, Adam reminded himself. But the mischief they got into was worse than that done by any bunch of college freshmen. Especially this time. He reviewed the conversation with Denticoff as he forced his car to join the speeders on the express lanes of the freeway. It would be more than twenty minutes, he realized.

Denticoff had been sent to Adventure Villa after a report from a highway patrolman. For a seven-mile stretch on Ridge Parkway every single road marker, every direction sign, even some of the guardrails at Birch Canyon, had been painted black. And on each repainted sign, in the hottest possible fluorescent pink, was stenciled the face of a cartoon-like character with a finger up each nostril.

"Classic public mischief," Adam had said as he sent his young partner out to Adventure Villa. "And if there's any doubt about whether the Twilight Zone is guilty — who else do you know would have the time to do it? Never mind the inclination. This time, let's get some charges. The whole town is getting fed up with this."

It wasn't more than an hour later that Denticoff had phoned with the information that had made Adam Fewster so upset. He slowed as the exit to Ridge Parkway came into view.

"I've got a suspect, Lieutenant," Denticoff had said, the frustration in his voice very plain. "In fact . . . in fact, I've got six! Well, maybe five. Or four perhaps! And not suspects. I've got confessions. At least I think so. Each one says he did it. And the next one says no, *he* did it! And then the *next* one. . . !"

Adam had interrupted him at this stage, trying to slow him down. "Start this again. You've got six confessions? Or five? Or four? But they contradict? Is that what's happening?"

"No, Lieutenant." Denticoff was certainly not in his element. "It's more than that."

171

This was when Adam had lost his composure. Denticoff had gone on to describe another incredible corner of the Twilight Zone. "I'm calling from the Hall of Ambivalence, Lieutenant. And I'm not making this up! It's a lodge here at the villa. It's where these two clubs meet: one's the Fraternal Society of Prevaricators; the other — Lieutenant, believe me! — is the Veracity Society. The steward here says they're really serious. One group always lies, even about the time of day. The other always tells the truth. And nobody knows who belongs to what club! It's a big secret. That's the reason for the Hall of Ambivalence!"

Adam felt a twinge of embarrassment again as he followed the signs through the Adventure Villa gates to the Hall of Ambivalence. He noted that none of these had been painted over. Denticoff was waiting for him in the parking lot.

"They're inside, sir. All six. It's sherry time." He added the last comment in a tone that suggested that to him, sherry time was as improbable as the whole situation.

"You've got names, at least?" Adam asked. "Addresses I guess would all be the same, wouldn't they?"

Denticoff reddened. "Uh . . . so are the names, Lieutenant."

"What do you mean?"

"Their names . . . uh . . . they're all named Tantalus."

"You mean they're brothers?"

"Two of them are women, sir. No. They all give the same last name — Tantalus."

"You asked for I.D.? What about the steward? Can he shed any light?"

"It's like this, sir. I came in and they were all sitting at this long table. Not around it, but side by side. Like ducks. And the first old guy says, 'I'm B.B. Tantalus and I'm the one you want.' And then he gets this big grin and says, 'I'm quite a sign painter, no?'"

Adam realized they were both still standing in the parking lot with the car door open. His ignition warning buzzer was announcing, to no avail, that he was about to lock his keys inside. Denticoff carried on.

"But then the next one — one of the women — says, 'No, *I'm* B.B. Tantalus, and *I'm* the one you want.' And then they *all* say it. All but the last one. And *he* says, 'I'm B.B. Tantalus, but I'm an elective mute.' That's when the steward came in. He's the one who told me all about the Fraternal Society of Prevaricators and the Veracity Society."

Denticoff was talking so fast now that Adam felt obliged to do something to interrupt him, so he slammed the car door with a bang. His young partner jumped. The keys were locked in.

"Maybe there's a lead in these societies," Adam offered, taking advantage of the break. "These two clubs. If we find out who belongs to what, then we should at least know who's lying and who's not. Maybe they're all lying. They're certainly all nuts."

Denticoff shook his head. "I tried, Lieutenant. After we talked on the phone, I went in to ask them just that. I said, 'Look, this is police business now. The fun and games are over. Now which club does each of you belong to?' I was really firm. Then there was this long silence and the first guy — the first B.B. Tantalus — made this terribly prissy face before he answered me. I know he answered, but I didn't hear exactly what he said because number six — the elective mute — knocked over a whole tray of glasses. I only heard the word *society*. Then the second one said — really loud, too — 'He said he's a prevaricator! I always thought so. Well I'm not. I'm for truth!'"

The young detective paused to take a deep breath. "And then it happened again!" he said. "Number three and number four and number five, *each* said the same as number two. All except number six — he said nothing."

"Well don't feel bad." Adam patted his partner on the shoulder. "At least now we know who tells the truth and who doesn't. It's a place to start, anyway. And I'll bet when we sort out the liars, we'll find the painter, too. "

How does Adam know who belongs to the Fraternal Society of Prevaricators and who belongs to the Veracity Society?

37

Blowing Up the
Reviewing Stand

FOR JUST A MOMENT, Vin Murray let his nervousness take over completely. He allowed his breathing rate to increase and let the sweat come out and sit on his forehead. He felt a spasm of fear begin at his knees and roll up through his body, leaving a vague sickness in his stomach. Then, just as quickly, he suppressed it all. With deep breaths he willed his pulse rate back to normal. He wiped his forehead with the back of his hand and held out his fingers. They were steady. With deliberate calm he curled them into a fist and rapped on the door. No coded knock. No special sequence of taps. Just an ordinary rap on the door. The IRA does not play games.

"Yes. Now!" The voice that came from inside seemed to Vin to be a bit distracted, as though its owner were preoccupied with other tasks.

Vin stepped inside, glad to be free of the pungent smells of cabbage and urine and mold that permeated the hallway of the tenement. The room was dark but the hall had been poorly lit so it took only a few seconds for his eyes to adjust to the gloom. Almost immediately, he picked out the black drape that was strung across one corner.

From behind it, the voice said, "Talk."

Vin almost let the nervousness come back. Although he had been Scotland Yard's most successful undercover agent ever, this was the first time in three and a half years he had been in the same room with "K."

"Well?" K was waiting.

"It's all set," Vin said in his lowest and calmest voice. "Tomorrow afternoon somewhere between 1500 and 1505 hours."

"I've heard that kind of assurance before." K was not impressed.

"We've gone over this a hundred times," Vin was quick to answer. "Have you seen the films?" He checked himself. "Of course you have. Sorry." He took a slow, deliberate breath. "She always starts off left foot first. Never varies. It happens every time she reviews the troops. Prince Philip always starts out the same way, but one pace behind her. Then any others always string out in single file behind the two of them."

K moved in his chair behind the black drape. "You're boring me," he said.

Vin's lips compressed, more in anger than fear. "This time they walk together. Side by side. It's his regiment, so it's his right. Now the switch is pressure sensitive. It will be set out on a sheet of thin plastic near the far end of the first rank. Under the red carpet, so nobody will know about it except the two privates who roll it out. And they're ours.

"They'll activate it, too. We know she always takes three steps to his two. By the time they reach the switch area, their right feet will come down together. That's enough weight to complete the circuit, and . . . *boom!*"

"How do you know she won't stop to talk to some corporal or. . . ." For the first time, K seemed involved.

"She never has with these," Vin answered. "Remember, it's *his* regiment. And he won't talk if she's there."

Behind the drape, K was obviously intrigued.

"And the explosive?" he wanted to know.

"Plastic," Vin answered. "It'll look just like all of the other wires running around the reviewing stand. That's why we can't set it off by remote."

"Good." For the first time, K betrayed some emotion. "And you're sure she and the Duke will be clear? She's not the target, you know. Just the brass on the reviewing stand."

"Only the stand," Vin said confidently. "We'll get them all, but she'll be safe."

"Good! Good work. Now go." K was already into other business.

Vin Murray stepped through the door back into the smelly hallway. He winced at the sound of a domestic battle from one of the small rooms just above and walked as fast as he could toward the exit. He had a new identity to assume and a plane to catch. His days as a plant in the IRA were over, but a major terrorist plot had been foiled.

What's the flaw in the bombing plot which Vin has described, but which K has not picked up?

SOLUTIONS

1
An Early Morning Murder at 13 Humberview

A deaf person would not react to ambient noise by raising her voice to compensate for it. Quite likely, Mrs. Van Nough can hear, and if so, would find it difficult to explain why she did not hear the gunshot that killed poor Alvin while she was supposedly on the porch.

2
The Case of the Slow-Moving Ducks

In the country around Lake Erie, in fact in most of North America, no one would be able to sit out in their front yard in June, at dusk, during warm weather, if they lived anywhere near a swamp. They would simply be "eaten alive" by mosquitoes. The witnesses, with swamp on both sides of their front yard, were certainly not likely to have been where they say they were.

3
Squash and the Scales of Justice

Gordon Pape has recognized that by balancing six balls in the first use of the scale — three on either side — the FDSOP agent will need only one more use to find the heavy ball. If in the first weighing, it is one of the six, then the side it's on will come down. The agent will then know it's one of the three on that side. For the second weigh, he balances two of the three. If they are equal, the sabotaged one is the third one; if the bad one is one of these two, that side will come down.

If in the first weighing of six, the two sides balance, then the bad ball is one of the remaining two.

4
Microwaves on the Freeway?

The stolen truckload did not get onto the freeway at the normal access because of the roadblock. Therefore it must have used the alternate. To get through the underpass, the thieves let enough air out of the tires to lower the overall height of the truck. Connie and Frank have noticed the flatter tires on this one Byron truck.

5
Double Suicide on Midland Ridge

If the crack between the jeep door and the frame was covered by masking tape, then the victims were either already asphyxiated by carbon monoxide, or at least unconscious, when they were put in the jeep. They could not have taped the door in this way if they had been inside.

Jana, if she is the murderer, has unwittingly implicated herself with the note. Even if she is not guilty, she's an obvious suspect.

6
The End of a Mythophile

Everett Ashley Woodstock's devotion to Greek mythology was exclusive and total. Chief Inspector Lawrence Darby might have been suspicious, in any case, of such a clumsy frame-up; the fact that the message said VENUS and not APHRODITE convinced him. Woodstock would never have used the Roman substitute for the Greek name.

7
The Case of the Erring Arsonist

Despite her preoccupation with the vertical slat blinds, Jane Forrester noted the flaw in Preston Wendle's story. Brass does not spark, so banging the hame knobs together would not have caused the naphtha fumes to ignite.

8
The Last Will and Testament of Norville Dobbs, Orthographer

Amy was acutely aware of Norville Dobbs' obsession with accurate spelling. He would never have signed a document that spelled *supersede* incorrectly.

9
The Case of the Thieving Welder

The elegant Mrs. Chloris Dean likely noted the odor of acetylene on the welder when he cut open the safe, since it does permeate and linger. Michael Struan is willing to acknowledge that someone with intelligence and a sharp sense of smell would certainly be able to recognize the smell and make the connection. However, he was made uneasy by the fact that Chloris Dean, who so readily recognized acetylene, was apparently unable to detect that the sandwich he offered was peanut butter and banana, despite the fact that she was interested. Both peanut butter and banana give off strong fragrance. Anybody who could recognize acetylene in a high-stress situation would surely recognize the odor of peanut butter, especially if it's a favorite.

10
The Antique Store Shooting

Cam Lindsey suspects Bentley Threndyle may really be Morton Threndyle. Although they are identical twins, or at least sufficiently identical to fool all but the most careful examination, it is Bentley who cannot walk and must use a wheelchair. Yet Cam saw the paint dripping from Bentley's (or Morton's) pantlegs into the creases in his shoes. Someone who does not walk, would not have creases in his shoes.

11
Anyone Missing at the Apiary?

Having had experience in an apiary, Bob Ashby realized that bees do not fly at night. He also knew that Hoffman would know that too. An errant bee, then, could not have been the reason for the gunshot.

12
The Return of the Stolen Paintings

It is apparent to Wendy Pickell that the thieves intended to steal only the anonymous *Garden of Eden* and set up a number of red herrings to throw off, and then stop, the subsequent investigation. They stole four paintings and presumably returned them all, having engaged only in what appeared to be a serious but harmless joke: namely painting raisins into the navels of nudes, as though it were all a freshman prank.

The discovery, or re-discovery, of the paintings was a relief to Monopoly Trust and Wendy Pickell, but the vandalism was an entirely new matter. And the thieves must have intended that Wendy and Monopoly Trust be further relieved to learn that the damage was easily remediable. All this distraction was designed to let the fake *Garden of Eden* slip in undetected.

Mark Dexel, and then Wendy, however, knew that paintings of Adam and Eve in the Renaissance, especially the early Renaissance, usually depicted those characters without navels. The artist who produced the fake had to give them navels to make the distraction work. It almost succeeded.

185

13
The Train to Kaministikwia

It is difficult to establish from the testimony of Elias Kohlfuss whether or not Sherwood Manley took the 7:30 morning train or the 7:30 evening train, although clearly he had a ticket, dated September 28, one-way from Kakabeka Falls to Kaministikwia.

The photograph upsets Judge Grant MacDonald because he foresees perjury. Manley's wife, sister and brother-in-law will testify that the photograph was taken just before boarding in the morning. Yet the photo was taken in the evening — probably the night before.

The dayliner was facing north. Manley and the others, therefore, had to be facing south for the picture. If the sister was in a shadow (she would have had to be on his left to hold up his wedding-band finger) then the sun had to be in the lower western sky, indicative of evening, not morning.

14
The Case of the Floral Killer

To understand Jack Atkin's deductions, it may be useful to get a piece of paper and do as he likely did — make a diagram. The furniture at the end of the Leamington Room, where the killer and victims were sitting, looked like this:

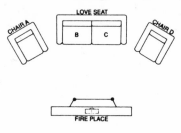

A love seat holds two adults. If Winston, the botanist, sat next to Hrabosky, who sat in one of the single chairs, it's almost certain that Winston was in position B and Hrabosky in chair A. Hrabosky was self-conscious about the skin on the right side of his face, and would have placed himself so that the offending characteristic was away from the social situation.

This puts Scollins and Jensen in C and D, but not necessarily respectively. Cigar ashes suggest at least one of them was in a chair, and at least one in the love seat. It's very likely, however, that Jensen was in chair D. If he was deaf or hard of hearing, with or without his hearing aid he would have placed himself for an optimal visual scan of the social situation.

Since there was blood on both chairs and on the right side of the love seat, then position C, where Scollins likely was sitting, becomes very suspicious. It's not definitive, but Jack is right in believing that Scollins is a prime suspect.

15
A Cash Transfer at the Good Eats Diner

John Ford and Bill Seeley were directly involved in this robbery case from at least 4:00 A.M., probably earlier, and were aware that before the sudden predawn thaw, the winter air had been very cold and crisp.

At the time the passengers and cash were supposedly transferred from the armored vehicle into the jeep in the parking lot of the Good Eats Diner, Mr. Hicks was at his fryer, inside the restaurant. From this vantage point he could see into the parking lot quite easily, especially with the mercury-vapor lighting system. However, with the outside ambient temperature below the freezing point, and the inside temperature of the diner well above, the windows would have been entirely covered in frost and condensation, especially in a place like the Good Eats Diner. Mr. Hicks' claim to have seen into the parking lot from his vantage point at the fryer is certainly suspect.

16
T.A. Jones Strikes Again

The resourceful T.A. Jones is looking for a hammer in the bottom drawer of his desk. To repair the necklace, that is, to restore the pattern of alternating beads without cutting the platinum wire, he is going to smash one of the crystal beads.

17
The Case of the Attempted Suicide

Berenice Devone is unquestionably a sophisticated and experienced hostess who, while pouring tea, is in her element. Yet she had committed an unpardonable social gaffe by pouring tea for Jasmine Peak without first asking her how she would like it served. She would only do this if the two knew one another or had been together for tea before. Yet they supposedly, except for a stressful encounter at the hospital, had never met!

18
The Lost Mine of Headless Valley

The Macleod brothers really were prospectors and they really did go up the South Nahanni in the early part of this century in search of gold and never returned. A dispute continues, however, as to whether the skeletons found later were really the Macleods and whether they really found gold, *and* whether the skulls of the skeletons were really missing. Nevertheless, the legend prevails. The valley where the bones were found is known as Headless Valley. Several prospectors, indeed, have died in the same general area since that time, some of them in circumstances hard to explain. (There have been twenty-five reported deaths and disappearances since 1920.) And many of the local people continue to insist the area is haunted.

John and Linda Fogolin are likely much safer in a Cessna 152 than in a canoe or dugout, but they have properly dismissed Von Zeldt's claims of geological or prospecting knowledge.

They are flying *up* the South Nahanni, as can be deduced from the fact that they had to gain altitude to get over Virginia Falls. John is flying the plane and although a Cessna 152 has dual controls, pilots always sit on the left. Linda, sitting beside him, is, therefore, looking out at the *left* bank of the river where she saw the marker. The left bank of a river is always the bank on the left going downstream. If Von Zeldt were either a former geology student or a prospector, he would surely have known this. Yet he told the Fogolins that the marker tarpaulin was on the right bank.

19
Is Something Wrong at the High Commission?

Proper flag etiquette dictates that flags be flown at night only at sea. On land, they are to be taken down at sunset, with or without ceremony. An important high commission like Canada House would observe this ritual carefully. When Adrienne saw that the flag still flew in the darkness, she knew that something was amiss.

20
The Results of the Eighth Race

The garbled transmission told Sue that there were five dogs in the race. Of these, numbers one and two did not finish first. Nor did number three, which cannot be second or third either, since it finished behind two but not in order. For the same reason, number two cannot be fourth or fifth.

Dog number four cannot be first or last. Nor can it be third because that would put it next to the two, which would have to be second. It cannot be fourth either because that would put two in second and one in third. It cannot be second because that would put two in third.

The first-place dog then is number four, which would put number two in third and make number three fifth. That would make the number-one dog fourth, and the elusive number five, second.

21
Something Fishy at Rustico Farm

Anyone raised near an orchard, Mary realized, would know enough to be very careful eating any apple picked off the ground. An apple that falls on the ground is likely to have a worm or a fungus or be overripe, any of which could cause it to fall. For some reason, Sylvanus Bird does not seem to be entirely truthful about his upbringing.

22
Who Hid the Medicine?

Val Horst carries a white cane signaling to the rest of the world that he is blind. Yet Christian noted that Val Horst knew what Harry the twin had communicated in sign, about being in his room with his brother all the time. Christian, quite rightly, wants to find out why Val Horst is pretending to be blind. In that may lie the answer to the hidden medication.

23
Dead Sea Tour

Gavin was sufficiently knowledgeable about the Dead Sea to realize that one would never dive into water with density six times the density of fresh water. As a physics teacher he'd have known the danger. Bea apparently has a reason for lying.

24
Arranging the Locker Assignments

There are four students — Luis, Ned, Dinah and Karen — each to be assigned a locker in a row of twelve. Since aliquots of twelve have been preassigned, this eliminates lockers number one, two, three, four, six and twelve. Of the ones remaining, namely numbers five, seven, eight, nine, ten and eleven, Luis gets number ten. (It can't be Ned because his name has three letters. So does the number ten.) Since two boys cannot be assigned adjacent lockers, Ned can't go into number nine or eleven, and since Dinah's locker number is lower than Ned's, and she cannot be seven or eight (five letters in *Dinah* and five in *seven* and *eight*) she must be in number five. Karen cannot be in seven or eight either, so she is in number eleven, the last available locker in the row.

25
The Sinking of *The Alberton Pride*

Ensign Hancock might have pondered, briefly, the coincidence that the skipper, with such a very Italian name, had blond hair. But this would not be enough to cause suspicion by itself. Ensign Hancock has reacted to the fact that someone holding master's papers referred to his ship as "it." Any experienced sea-going type would never use "it," but rather "her" or "she" when talking about the ship.

192

26
The Case of the Scalpel Murder

Although the initial evidence may suggest that Doc Virgil killed Petty in the car while he was drunk and then crawled into the back seat to sleep, Gary is suspicious of the obviousness of this.

It is likely that Gary believes someone else killed Petty while Doc was passed out, and then drove the car containing her body and Doc, to the spot on the Fourth Concession where it was found.

His first suspicion is the chocolate-bar wrapper. Is Doc, with his obsessive nature and his concerns for diet, going to eat a candy bar? Petty was not likely to, since she was a diabetic.

Secondly, Doc Virgil was a little man; yet Gary had to move the front seat ahead to reach the pedals.

Finally, when the car had been turned off, the radio was not tuned to an all-country station.

27
Cutting Up the Pierce Arrow

It appears that Christopher Watson will not be a junior partner for long. By adding his own car to the total of eighteen, he was able to give half (nine) to Chauncey, one-third (six) to Willard and one-ninth (two) to Alistair, making a total of seventeen. There is one left over, presumably the Toyota, for himself.

28
The Case of the Jewelry Thieves

When Steve Fleck picked up the young lady at the bus stop, it was at least 6:00 PM. He had been in the car for two hours, since the robbery at 4:00 PM. In what is obviously a northern-hemisphere climate one week before Christmas, darkness would have fallen at least an hour before; therefore, the young lady could not have seen that the passing Japanese car was blue; even noting a dented fender was unlikely. Steve suspects she is a plant, to convince him that the thieves have headed east out of Lindeville.

29
All Applications Treated Seriously

Ruminants, especially cattle, get up from a reclining position back end first. Touching their throats with mild shock to make them get up would not be effective, or at least not effective enough to make as many as five or ten cattle move simultaneously. Touching them at the *back* end would be far more effective. Halvorsen seems to have experience with animals, yet his paper contradicts this.

30
The Boshkung Mystery Rectangle

Steve has noticed a mathematical sequence in the marker buoys. At marker 77 they turned right and went east (into the early morning sun). At marker 49 (7×7) they turned again (north or south). At marker 36 (4 × 9) they turned west. Steve is looking for marker 18 (3 × 6). Once there, they will complete the rectangle. They will turn left (south) but only if they turned left (north) at marker 49. If they turned right (south) at marker 49, then their turn at marker 18 will be right (north) to get back to camp.

31
A Letter to Spain

Had Philomena Loquor bothered to think for a minute, she would not have needed to bother Professor Deirdre Breton. Elizabeth I was queen of England from 1558 to 1603, and Philip II was king of Spain from 1556 to 1598. But Elizabeth was never known as "the First" until 1952, when Elizabeth II ascended the English throne. Elizabeth never signed her name "Elizabeth I," but only "Elizabeth R." (for Regina). (For that matter, Elizabeth II does not sign "Elizabeth II," but either "Elizabeth" or "Elizabeth R.," just like her predecessor.)

32
The Case of the Walking Sweater

If the young man put on the sweater inside out and back to front, the label would have been on the outside front. Singh would not have been able to see it because she saw the young man's back as he checked the street.

33
The Telegram from Uganda

Mark Tully must have been a bit of a Shakespeare buff himself to interpret Gordie Froggatt's telegram quickly. From it he understood that the minister of trade, Mr. Mombajetta, would be stripped of his property and that it would be divided up. (The king in Shakespeare's *King Lear* divides his property — his kingdom — while he is still alive.)

The minister of justice, the only lawyer, would be executed. (In Act Four, scene two, of Shakespeare's *Henry VI, Part Two*, Dick the Butcher presents the famous line: "The first thing we do, let's kill all the lawyers.")

The doctor, the minister of health, was to be exiled, as Romeo was in *Romeo and Juliet*.

Froggatt deduced all this from Amin's public statements. The three ministers each got a different sentence. That meant the minister of trade (Mombajetta) would not be executed. It also meant that the minister of justice would not be exiled, but that the minister of health would be. Since the sentences were to be *different* for each, and the minister of health got exile, the minister of justice therefore faced execution because the property option could not apply. Mr. Mombajetta lost his property.

34
The Prowler on Burleigh Court

Inspector Sean Dortmund may well have been unconvinced by Dina White's story because of several small things: Why *three* shots all in the chest if she was so frightened? And how did she get to Lavaliere so quickly? Apparently he was shot right at the window where he came in. The strongest suspicion for Sean, however, is the glass. If Lavaliere had smashed the window and then climbed through, there would not be pieces of glass on *top* of his body. Sean likely believes he was shot first, then the window above his body was broken.

35
To Be or Not to Be — Authentic

The Turkish chess set, for which Ms. Sparks says the museum paid a fortune, is not Turkish. Turkish and Arabic chess sets — especially in the time of the Crusades, but even today — admitted no women onto their chess boards, so there would be no queens. (They use the vizier for that piece.) Also, there certainly would be no bishops. (These are represented on the Saracenic board by elephants.) It may indeed have come from Venice. The Fourth Crusade set out from there in 1198 under the eighty-year-old, partially blind Doge, Enrico Dandolo, and ended up plundering its own eastern allies. But the chess set that came back with the loot was Christian.

Richard the Lion-Heart, incidentally, could well have used the bathtub — if it was in Trifels castle in 1193-94. Although the upper classes of his day vigorously eschewed bathing, the Crusaders learned of its benefits from the infidels and had taken up the practice, along with chess, quite enthusiastically.

36
Truth and Lies in the Twilight Zone

Adam has placed B.B. Tantalus number 6 in the Fraternal Order of Prevaricators. He said he was an elective mute; yet he spoke at least once, so cannot be trusted to be truthful.

Numbers two through five are all liars too, because number one's answer, which Denticoff did not hear, could only have been ". . . in the Veracity Society." If he were a liar he would say he was in the truth group, and if he were in the truth group he'd tell the truth. The only answer he could have given was that he is in the Veracity Society. All the others said he was in the Prevaricators' group, which makes them liars.

Since all six confessed, and only number one speaks the truth, he is B.B. Tantalus, and he's also the mystery painter.

37
Blowing Up the Reviewing Stand

When two people set out side by side with left feet first, and one takes three steps to the other's two, their right feet will never come down together if they walk at the same basic pace such as would be chosen for reviewing troops. Thus, there will not be enough combined weight on the pressure-sensitive switch to complete the circuit that would set off the explosives arranged around the reviewing stand.

MORE
FIVE-MINUTE
MYSTERIES

To Beau,
who was there for all the words

Contents

1

A Clean Place to Make
an End of It

WHAT INTRIGUED BOB GIBSON — BOTHERED him, actually — was how *clean* the inside of the car was. Someone, quite possibly the dead woman herself, had vacuumed the interior rugs with special care. There wasn't a speck of dust anywhere on the dash, either, or along the steering column; even the short stalks behind the knobs on the radio had been wiped. The leather cover over the gearshift box had been cleaned of the dust and grit that always collect in the creases. That had taken a wet cloth or a chamois, Bob realized. So the cleaning was not just a casual, spontaneous effort.

It wasn't a new car. From where he was leaning into it, with both fists pressed into the driver's seat, Bob peered a little closer at the odometer. The light wasn't all that good in the little garage, and the car had been backed in so that the waning winter daylight from the open garage door came through the windshield directly into his face. Still, he could make out the figures: 47,583. No, not a new car at all. But one in great shape.

Bob leaned across the seat and, with the tip of his index finger, ticked the switch on the armrest to lower the passenger window just a bit. He checked to see if the earnest young policeman at the door had noticed, but he hadn't. If he had, and objected, Bob would have argued. The smell in the car was nauseating, and he needed to relieve it by letting a bit of draft through.

It was a smell he'd encountered before. Not so often as to be familiar with it. Maybe a half-dozen times or so in the past thirty years, but after the first time he'd never forgotten. It was the smell of a body in the early stages of decomposition: a hint of sweet and a hint of foul. Sickening.

The smell clung, too. The garage door had been open for several hours, ever since the body had been discovered earlier, around noon. But the whole building was still filled with the odor, and Bob knew it would be a long time before the fabric in the car would be free of it.

Inside the car, of course, it was worse. The doors had been open only long enough for the photographer to do her grisly job, and then again when the coroner removed the body. Bob was here to tow away the car to the police pound.

Over his years as owner of Palgrave Motors, Bob had come to know the police very well and he was the one they invariably called in situations like this. Therefore it was not, as he had reflected only seconds before, the first time he had been called to the scene of a suicide. Nevertheless, although all he had to do was take away the car, the whole business gave him the creeps.

According to the coroner, the woman — Bob didn't know her name — had backed the car into the little garage some forty to fifty hours ago, closed the door and simply sat there with the motor running until the inevitable happened. The body had gone unnoticed for almost two days, the coroner estimated.

"You didn't touch anything, did you?"

2

It was Officer Shaw. Bob hadn't heard him come in. The young policeman had been left behind by the investigating detective with specific and stern instructions that nothing was to be disturbed. Shaw took the order seriously.

Bob looked at him, uncertain just how to put his suspicions. He pointed to the two-way radio in Shaw's belt.

"Can you call your sergeant on that?"

Shaw didn't answer; he just looked at Bob curiously.

"'Cause I think he'll want to take another look at all this," the older man said. "Missed something, I think."

Why has Bob Gibson drawn this conclusion?

2

Chasing the Bank
Robbers

KAY FIRST HEARD THE POWERFUL engine as she topped the rise that bumped up at the crest of the long hill. Muscle car, she could tell. Trans Am probably. Or a customized pickup with all kinds of soup. Speeding, too, she knew. Well, it was going to have to slow down pretty sharply when it caught up to her, because there was a stop sign where the Twentieth Side Road met the Tenth Line in a T just ahead. In the past, more than one car had gone roaring through into the field beyond. She should know, too. Kay MacDuffee was number two in Caledon Traffic Section.

"Not today, I'm not!" Kay said out loud. Loud enough to catch the attention of the dog pacing along beside her. His tongue was lolling out after the walk up the big hill.

"Today I'm on vacation," she said, patting the head of the big red setter. "Sorry. *We're* on vacation. Right, old pal? And we don't care how fast they're blasting up the hill. It's not our problem. Today, anyway!"

The car was fast, all right. It whooshed past her with a

tremendous ululation from the decelerating engine, signal light blinking, then brake lights flashing in a cloud of choking exhaust. It didn't stop at the sign but slid into a bit of a fishtail as it turned left and tore hard up the Tenth.

It *was* a Trans Am. Black. License...

Kay gritted her teeth.

"I'm on vacation!" she shouted, and willed herself not to see the license number.

The shout was drowned in an engine clatter she hadn't even heard; it came so close upon the heels of the first car. Another Trans Am! Just as noisy and, if anything, faster than the first!

Kay braced herself for the whoosh and the foulness of the exhaust of this second one. She was an inveterate walker — the steep long hill at the end of the Twentieth was a favorite route — and she knew muscle cars not only sounded uncivilized, they smelled worse.

This one fishtailed even more than the first as it hit the gravel, for the Tenth was not paved to the south. Like the first car it was black, and it had roared to the corner with brake lights flashing, although this driver didn't bother with signals.

The roar of the two cars gradually fading in opposite directions accentuated the silence that began to gather around Kay once more. She shook her head. One thing she liked about her vacation time was that she could walk after nine in the morning when the traffic was almost nonexistent. Nothing quiet about today!

She crossed the road at the stop sign to walk back down the hill on the other side. Then she heard the third car and, almost immediately, saw it pop over the rise. The red light was flashing. No siren, though. It screeched to a stop beside her as the policeman in the passenger seat rolled down his window.

"Pardon me, ma'am. We... Sergeant MacDuffee! What... oh yeah, you live out here, don't you? Listen. This is heavy. National Trust was held up back in town about ten, fifteen minutes ago. We just got the call. Getaway's a black Trans Am. The license has a seven and a five. Don't have anything more except they had to be local. Car disappeared in a subdivision, seemed to know exactly where to go, then apparently headed this way. A lady in her garden back at the Eighth says she's sure she saw a black car tear up this way only a minute ago. You see it?"

"Have you got a backup?" Kay asked.

"No. We're alone."

"Darn."

Kay MacDuffee has to send the patrol car after one of the two Trans Ams. Which is her most likely choice?

3

The Power
of Chance

AFTER THIRTY-SEVEN YEARS ON the bench, Tom Houghton
had developed a pretty dim view of the role of chance in human
affairs. He was by nature a logical person, and tended to view
the world that way. Chance, in his opinion, was an explanatory
last resort for those who didn't have the brains or the will to
think things through. But after what had happened yesterday
afternoon, he knew he just might have to revise that point of
view.

The chain of events — chances — began in his court late
yesterday morning in a break-and-enter case: two teenage boys
and a girl, all three well past the young offender stage. The
third prosecution witness had just raised his right hand, and
the "I swear" had come out with a bellow. Tom wasn't sure
whether the man was being defiant or just loud. Whichever it
was, with only those two words, he'd made everyone in the
court look up sharply.

The witness was a big man, maybe fifty, fifty-five, Tom
thought, with a huge distended beer belly. His belt was slung

so low it looked more like a truss than something to hold up his pants. The belly and the loud "I swear" triggered recall of a paragraph in the pretrial report. This must be Walter Hope, Tom realized, the one they called Whispering Hope — no wonder! He was the construction worker who claimed to have overheard the kids trying to deal goods on the patio of the Lagoon Saloon.

Tom tried to catch the eye of the young prosecuting attorney before she got started. Not only was she young, she was new, and this could turn into a lengthy examination. Sometime later, Tom was to acknowledge to himself that it was at this very point that "chance" might have taken over.

A double shot of chance, actually. The first unusual occurrence was that the Yankees played the Blue Jays that afternoon, one of those rare midweek 1:30 starts. The second was that Tom had tickets, and it really wasn't his turn for them. He and four others had a pair of seasons. They called themselves the Twenty Percent Club, for at the beginning of the schedule each year they divided the tickets five ways. Tom's Yankee game for this series would normally have been the next night, but weeks ago he'd made a trade. Chance?

Whatever the chain of circumstance, there was no way he was going to miss the first pitch no matter how slowly the wheels of justice might grind as a result, and so, very unobtrusively, he gave the high sign to Maurice Marchand standing at the back.

"Just a minute, Ms. Dankert." Tom caught the prosecutor before she stood up.

Maurice, the bailiff, saw the signal and walked urgently to the bench. Just as urgently, he whispered in Tom's ear, making very definitive movements with both hands. It was an old ploy that Tom Houghton rarely used, but, well, a Yankees game was a Yankees game.

"I'm afraid it will be necessary to adjourn," Tom announced to the court.

Maurice Marchand, meanwhile, had turned to face the courtroom and stood impassively with his arms folded.

"We will reconvene — how about an early start? Nine a.m. tomorrow?"

There were no objections.

Forty-five minutes later, His Honor was locking his car at a parking lot by the Skydome. Another dollop of chance? Well, maybe: it was the *last* space in the lot! Tom wasn't all that keen about leaving his car there. Just across the fence lay the remains of rubble from a demolished building. The workmen clearing it were on lunch. It meant dust and dirt, but to find another spot to park would also mean missing the first inning. Tom opted for dust and dirt.

Two hours later he saw the consequence of his decision, but another helping of chance made it a minor issue. It had been a dull game and Tom had left in the bottom of the eighth to beat the rush. After unlocking his car — actually, it wasn't *too* dirty — he straightened to take off his windbreaker, and there, not more than half a dozen paces away on the other side of the fence, was Whispering Hope! Any other time Tom would have paid little attention, but there was no ignoring or mistaking that huge gut.

Hope was standing by the wheel of a backhoe with two other men. The three were having one of those shouted conversations so typical of construction sites where the equipment noise makes communication difficult. Unlike Hope, his two companions — a lot younger, Tom noticed — wore ear protectors, but they were pushed up above their ears. Walter Hope's hands were cupped behind his. His hard hat was white, too, Tom noticed, while the others' were yellow.

Whatever the subject of the conversation — it appeared to be a joke, for all three guffawed when it ended — the two younger men turned away to pick up shovels. Tom watched Hope hitch his hands under his mighty belly and swing up into the seat of the backhoe. The cover flap of the exhaust pipe, which had been barely vibrating before, now clattered away like a flag gone mad as the big man drove up the revs and poised the bucket to scoop some rubble. This was a man who loved to wrestle his machine.

Tom opened his car door finally, and sat in. He was depressed. Not only a lousy game, he thought, but — was it chance? — I've run into a witness.

"Now what do I do?" He was talking to the steering wheel without seeing it. "Do I speak to Ms. Dankert in chambers tomorrow? Talk to the kids' counsel too? Well, before anything, I'm going back to read that pretrial report again. If I go right now, it'll take me till just after the evening rush."

He started the car and waited patiently for the engine to warm. From the driver's seat he could see the car was dirtier than he'd first thought.

What will Tom Houghton be looking for in the pretrial report? What is bothering him that he feels he may have to bring up with the two attorneys?

4

On Flight 701 from Hong Kong

IN ONE SENSE IT WAS just an afterthought, but it earned Ralph Ransom a commendation and enhanced his reputation considerably in the branch. Immediately after his brief acceptance speech at the annual awards dinner, Ralph was commended yet again — this time by the director personally — for the tactful and diplomatic way he had explained the reasoning that had led him to assign two teams to the airport for the arrival of the suspected smuggler. Others would have sent just one.

Essentially, it was his experience as head of the west coast section of Canada Customs Investigations Branch that had taught him — the hard way — that a flight from Hong Kong on a weekend invariably brought out large groups of welcomers, with a resulting level of bustle and activity that often confused surveillance teams. That's why he'd pressed the intercom on that wet Saturday morning last November after the call had come from the DEA in Seattle, and asked his secretary to call out the Cummings team.

11

And then he'd pressed it again immediately and said, "The Kavanagh team, too!"

Right away both teams wanted to know how the DEA (the American Drug Enforcement Agency) had gotten involved in a diamond-smuggling case. Ralph had to reply that he didn't know. He'd find out, but for the moment there was the more urgent business of acting on the tip and meeting Cathay Pacific's Flight 701, due in at Vancouver's International Airport from Hong Kong at 1320 hours PST.

For more than a year, the Investigations Branch, along with the RCMP, the Hong Kong police and Interpol had been gathering evidence on a diamond-smuggling ring whose operations started in Durban, passed through Singapore to Hong Kong, and then moved into North America via Vancouver. Ralph couldn't be absolutely sure that this tip was related to the ring. But he also couldn't take the chance of ignoring it.

All he had been able to get out of the rather surly informant in Seattle was "You and the Mounties got a live one on your diamond thing on the Cathay Pacific 701." There was no name and no photo. There couldn't even be an explanation of who or what or why. Ralph suspected — and he certainly had no intention of sharing this with the surveillance teams — that the reason for the surliness, not to mention the sparse information, could be traced back to the sloppiness of the DEA unit in Hong Kong. The Seattle man was sure ticked off. Ralph's reading of the situation was that the DEA had been running a sting in Hong Kong and it had turned sour. The tip, if it really turned out to be a tip, was probably an attempt to salvage something. In any case, all Ralph had on the "live one" was a physical description, and he knew he wouldn't even have gotten that if it hadn't been for the fact that the Seattle man owed him a few large favors.

He'd sent the Cummings and the Kavanagh teams out then, to identify and follow a "male, Chinese, maybe forty years old, about five foot seven, hair parted left, thick glasses — Coke

12

bottles! — khaki suit two-piece, white shirt, no tie" who would be disembarking at 1320 hours from Cathay Pacific Flight 701.

On the way out, Iggie Kavanagh had stopped in the doorway to ask if they were supposed to watch for a drop or a pass or anything specific. Ralph didn't know whether to be sheepish and admit he didn't know, or pull rank and make Iggie wish he'd kept his big mouth shut.

He did neither and only said, "Just monitor in detail. Keep me current. I'll decide later what to do about him. *If anything,*" he added under his breath.

Shortly after that the first field call had come in, and it made Ralph sit up straight. *There were two subjects!* The point man of the Cummings team, dressed in the white coveralls of the clean-up crew, had picked up the subject immediately and handed him off at the gate to the number two. Then, as he headed for the lockers to strip off the coveralls and get to the luggage area, he almost gave everything away by staring in astonishment. Suzy Hammill, the point for Iggie Kavanagh's team was following *another* Chinese man who fitted the description perfectly! Suddenly the two-team decision by Ralph Ransom looked very good. But before Ralph could permit any self-satisfaction he still had to decide whether either subject was "a live one."

He was able to make that decision about an hour later when both Kavanagh and Cummings called in. Kavanagh was first.

"He went through young Turpin's counter," Iggie reported, referring to the newest uniformed customs officer they had at the airport. "The kid was good. Stamped him through. No fuss, but we got all the basics off the passport. What we've got is Won Lee of Kowloon... let's see... forty-five years old, purpose of visit business, speaks English. No North American stamps and he says this is his first visit here."

"Okay. Then?" Ralph was listening closely.

"He went straight to The Thomas Cook Foreign Exchange. Used his American Express for $300 Canadian. Then he bought a Vancouver city map at W. H. Smith. I think maybe he's a chocolate freak. Bought two Mars bars at the stand across from Thomas Cook's. Cabbed to the Bayshore... ah... used Checker seven-six-four. Then before he checked in he bought another Mars bar at the smoke shop in the lobby. And after he got his key he went back and got *two more*! Mars bars, I mean.

"He's in room 1014. An ordinary single... Oh, one thing. The guy's as hyper as can be. He sort of flits more than walks. In the Cook's lineup and again at the hotel his feet were tapping away all the time. He doesn't like waiting. Each time he bought the chocolate bars he just pumped out the change at the people on the register. It only takes him seconds to buy anything. Oh, yes. Almost forgot. Manager says he used American Express to check in. Staying two nights."

"I assume your team's in place if he leaves the room?" Ralph asked. "You need any help? Anybody compromised?"

"Yes, no and no." Iggie replied. "But he's been on the phone almost from the second he went into his room."

"Good work," Ralph said. "Stay on the line if you can. I've got Andy on four."

Andy Cummings' account was somewhat similar. The gate officer checking the passport, Jean Lajoie, identified one Huan Lee of Hong Kong, forty-one years old, in Canada for business reasons, very frequent traveler in the Orient — stamps on top of stamps in the passport. Never been to Canada or the U.S.

"Speaks good English, too," Andy said. "Least accordin' to the teller at th' Royal Bank. Cashed four hunnert bucks in traveler's checks... uh... uh... Thomas Cook, if that matters. Uh... they'll hold 'em till tumorruh 'f we want prints."

"I'll think that one over for a bit. We have time," Ralph said. He hesitated to press Andy for more. Andy Cummings' habit of overly casual speech was strictly a telephone phenomenon. He didn't talk that way in person and the inconsistency had always intrigued Ralph.

Andy didn't wait for a prompt, however. "Lessee... no more

stops at th' airport. Checker two-one-two to th' Hotel Van. Oh, yeah! Made a phone call from the lobby! Afore checkin' in. Strange, huh? Room's covered by traveler's check. He's in 414. Thassa suite. Booked fer two nights."

Andy paused, as though deciding whether to add more, and then did. "Funny thing. 'E's only got one small suitcase. Suzy checked with Cathay P. 'Tsall he checked on."

"You saw something wrong with that?" Ralph wanted to know.

"Naw... well... kinda skimpy for a guy 'n a *suite!*"

It was Ralph's turn to pause now. "Could be. Has he used the phone in his room yet?" he asked.

"Nope. We gonna tap?"

Ralph paused yet again.

"Andy?"

"Yeah?"

"Stay on the line, will you? I've got Iggie here, too."

"'Kay." Andy replied.

"I think," Ralph said, "we've got at least *one* live one!"

Ralph Ransom has a suspicion about one of the two men. Which one? And what has made him suspicious?

5

Trying to Find
Headquarters

WITH THE FOG SO THICK that visibility was limited to about
the length of a pair of outstretched arms, it was a real surprise
that Corporal Fogolin had found a road sign. Not that finding
it was going to do much good. The sign, like all the others in
the area, had been broken off and tossed away by the retreating
German forces. This one, however, had ended up in the ditch
instead of way off in a field somewhere, and Fogolin had
almost stumbled over it. His discovery gave the little group a
chance to rest for a moment while Captain Doyle moved up to
take a look at the thing for himself.

When Doug Doyle saw it, his heart missed a beat. It was —
or rather it had been — one of those overloaded signs the
French are so fond of using on rural roads. Short pieces of wood
with one end shaped like an arrow, nailed to the four sides of a
square post and pointing to every nearby city, hamlet, church
and place of geographical interest that could give the sponsoring community some importance. Lying there in the ditch, the
sign no longer appeared to have any value to anyone, least of

all a group of soldiers utterly lost in dense fog.

Some of the pieces were still attached. ST-AUBERT, where they were trying to go, was stuck straight into the ground as though to get there it would be necessary to dig straight down. On a broken piece under a clump of grass, Doug could see the letters CA. Must be Caen, he surmised. The sign to Vire lay on the ground, too, broken in half with the two parts still clinging together. The same was true for Flers. The one for Falaise — wherever that was — was unscathed. Bayeux was intact, too, as was Saint-Luc-Sud, but the one nailed perpendicular to it, Saint-Luc... something, was partly broken off. Someone had scribbled over the sign to Lisieux: "KÖLN 600 km". It had never occurred to Doug before that German soldiers might get homesick, too.

"What now, sir?" Corporal Fogolin broke in with precisely the question that Captain Doyle kept pushing away to the edges of his consciousness.

"Ah... ah... we take five minutes to rest" was Doug's hesitant reply. "You tell the others."

"Okay, sir."

"And no cigarettes! Even if we don't know where we are, there's no sense announcing ourselves to a sniper."

"Sir!" Corporal Fogolin backed up and in two steps was enveloped by the mist.

Doug sat down wearily. He held his wristwatch close to his face, moving his arm back and forth slowly. Although he'd had no night training, it hadn't taken him long to learn that in pitch blackness it was easier to read his timepiece that way.

Fifteen minutes past midnight. A new day, he realized — 19 July 1944. Only a week ago — *one week ago!* — he had been sitting at the Errant Piper on the outskirts of Leicester, trying to get a cute little American bird to understand that there was nothing at all quaint or unusual about English place names. She'd giggled almost uncontrollably when she'd learned he had been born in Stow-on-the-Wold but, to his irritation, didn't see anything the least bit unusual about the name of her own hometown, Cheektowaga, in the state of New York.

And he couldn't get her to see either that whether a car had a "boot" or a "trunk" it was all the same, or that having an "ice" wasn't any more or less civilized than having "ice cream."

Now he could show her! If only she were here now, so she could see how much better a word "cock-up" was for the mess they were in than any word the Americans had.

A right proper cock-up, too. In the first place he had no business leading men in a combat area. He was a captain, all right, and these American infantrymen had a real respect for him. Or at least wariness; they certainly weren't as casual as they had been with their own major.

But I'm a cryptographer! What do I know about combat? Doug Doyle kept having to push down the fear that thought produced.

The only reason he was even here was to link up with Montgomery's headquarters staff. They wanted decoding expertise.

This whole affair, however, had been a cock-up from the beginning. He'd left Leicester on six hours' notice for Portsmouth in order to be ferried over to Juno Beach. There the Canadians were to move him up to Monty's headquarters. But his ship diverted first to Southampton and then landed at Sword Beach! No one there, of course, knew or cared who he was, and that took even more time to straighten out.

Yesterday — no, the day before yesterday now — he'd finally been shifted to Utah Beach to join an American infantry major who was being posted to Montgomery's headquarters as liaison. That's when the cock-up changed from ordinary to extraordinary. He and the major and three others overloaded a jeep and set out at dawn yesterday from what Doug now realized was the relative security of Utah Beach. The plan was to make Monty's headquarters by noon. At Bayeux they were held up by MPs but had a ringside seat for an aerial bombardment that made Doug's few nights in London during the Blitz seem pretty mild.

When they were free to leave, by late afternoon, they could hear but not see the battle in the far distance. Ironically, several thousand miles away, people listening to their radios knew more than they did: that along the River Orne that morning, General Montgomery had launched a major tank offensive. It was intended to move the Germans off the heights to clear the way to Paris, and Monty planned to accomplish that by evening. Unfortunately the Germans had other ideas, and the biggest tank force the western Allies had put together thus far in the war was stopped dead in its tracks. Vaguely aware that something big was going on, yet uneasily shut out of all this history in the making, was Captain Douglas Doyle, cryptographer.

At dusk the fog had rolled in, and with it came tragedy. After about two hours of crawling along the road with the jeep in first gear, the major had called a halt to cool the engine and give everyone a chance for roadside relief. He was the last one out and stepped on a land mine. He died instantly. By diving instinctively for the ditches the others saved themselves, because the jeep went up two seconds later.

The cock-up was then total. They had no idea where they were, the maps had burned, the radio was gone, the fog was if anything getting thicker, and Doug Doyle whispered to himself in disbelief, "Good God! I'm in command!"

That was about 10 P.M. Since then, they had walked along the ditch, Doug's first order. The Jerries might have mined the road, he reasoned, but the ditches... well, odds are they didn't have the time or the inclination. Now, with Corporal Fogolin finding the road sign, the cock-up had reached a turning point.

Doug scrambled up to the road on his hands and knees. "Up here, chaps!" he called softly. "We can walk the road now, I think."

Immediately they gathered around.

Doug continued, "Single file again. I'll lead. We turn down this road."

Corporal Fogolin stepped closer to peer through the fog at Doug's face. "Turn, sir? Here, sir?"

He got a reassuring nod from Doug. "Yes, here." He paused. "Don't worry, Corporal. What's the expression? 'No sweat'?" To himself he added, "Peculiar way to talk."

Captain Doug Doyle has apparently been able to determine where the group should go. How has he done this?

6

The Case of the Disappearing Credit Card

OTHER THAN THEIR MOTHER, JULIE Iseler was probably the only person who knew how to tell the Saint twins apart. Their father apparently couldn't, and certainly no one else could — except maybe Tammy Hayward, for like Julie she'd cut their hair from time to time. The clue was that Peter Saint had a double crown, a double "cowlick" it was sometimes called, but his brother, Paul, had only a single one.

Both boys' crowns made their hair exceptionally difficult to style. Cut too short, the hair at the top of their heads stuck out every which way. If it was left long, the cowlicks tended to dictate what happened to the rest of the head. That, in any case, was academic. The Saints, Peter and Paul, had short hair. It was one of the few battles — perhaps the only one — their mother regularly won.

However, the problems associated with periodically realigning the Saint boys' mops were not the only considerations that weighed on Julie's mind this morning as she looked over the day's appointments. (The twins were down for just before noon.)

21

Yes, their hair was hard to cut, but, well, Tammy could do one and she the other. What made the day ahead seem so long — she looked up at the clock; it was only 8:50 A.M. — was that a visit from the Saints was just not the kind of thing to brighten one's day.

"Hell on Reeboks," one of Julie's regulars had dubbed them, and that may well have been a mild view, for these two did everything possible to give the lie to their surname. They were only nine years old, duplicates of each other even down to their ample sprays of freckles, and they had already established a reputation for themselves that guaranteed a shudder at the news of their imminent arrival.

They were well known at Hair Apparent, and regarded with wariness. Not without cause, either. One of them had pinched Julie last spring as she'd bent to retrieve a pair of scissors. That's how she'd found out that, unlike his brother, Paul was left-handed. During the same visit Peter had almost baked Mrs. Horschak by surreptitiously turning the big bell dryer to MAX and resetting the timer. "Double trouble" was far too mild a metaphor for Peter and Paul Saint. No one used it anymore.

The front door to Hair Apparent opened and the movement of air shook the hanging wall dividers. It was Tammy.

"Sorry." Tammy had an embarrassed smile. "My car."

Working for Julie was Tammy's first full-time job. She was also the proud owner of a first car, which unless its record changed was soon to become a former car.

"No problem, Tammy." Julie returned the smile. The two of them got along especially well, and just seeing her walk in was bringing back Julie's innate good cheer. She held the smile and watched Tammy hang up her nylon shell jacket, then bump her arm on the nearest wall divider.

The smile turned into a laugh. "You can't get used to those things, either," Julie said. "Don't feel bad. I've already walked into the one by the cash this morning. You'll be happy to know the people from TBS are coming this afternoon to turn them around the right way."

TBS stood for Tasteful but Secure, a decorating service that Julie had hired for the first major renovation of her salon. Neither she nor Tammy was particularly pleased with the result. Before the change, Julie could work at her chair — the center one of three — and, in any of the big mirrors these chairs faced, monitor the entrance door, the waiting area, the cash register, even the two sinks and spare chair, which in that sequence took up the wall to her left.

The new hanging dividers changed all that. Suspended by chains from the ceiling, these huge pieces of Lucite formed a more-or-less wall between the working area and the waiting area. The idea, Julie granted, made some sense. The panels created two rooms, in a way, out of one big one. They permitted flow-through — in theory at least — for by turning sideways you could slip between panels and "walk through the wall." And the real bonus, supposedly, was that the panels were specially treated to permit a kind of translucent see-through from one side, while the other side reflected. The purpose was to give Julie and Tammy's patrons a sense of privacy in the chairs, while permitting the two stylists to see through to the entrance and waiting areas.

Fine. Except that the workers had hung the panels the wrong way. Customers in the waiting room could see into the work area, but the only way Julie could see them from her center chair, short of backing up a few steps and sticking her head through the wall, was via her mirror and then the mirror in front of the spare chair on the side wall. Not terribly secure. And neither Julie nor Tammy was sure it was all that tasteful, either.

"You've got Mrs. Goodman in a few minutes, Tammy." It was time for business. "Perm. And there's a whole lineup of kids. Not surprising. It's back-to-school time."

"Oh, yeah!" Tammy's eyes widened. "It's going to be so strange watching everyone else go, without going, too!"

Julie hadn't heard her. She was absorbed in the appointment book. "George from the bank... Either one of us can do him.

Wash and cut. He'll be in a hurry as usual. Mrs. Morelli, the Saint twins, then…"

Tammy lit up at that. "Did you *hear* what those kids did on that Vacation Bible School bus? They took the bolts out of the driver's seat. While she was driving! I don't know how they managed it. Anyway, the first time she braked she went right under the steering wheel! It's a wonder —"

The wall dividers swung in sympathy to the opening door. Mrs. Goodman had arrived for her perm. Julie and Tammy both went to greet her. Thoughts of the Saint twins faded, for Mrs. Goodman was their favorite senior. To both of them, she was "just a doll."

"Oh, my! You've changed things," the old lady said in her sweet, ingenuous way. She really *was* a doll. "Well, it doesn't matter, dear." She had turned her attention to Tammy. "You're still here, and that's all that matters. Shall we get started?"

Tammy led Mrs. Goodman to her chair, to the right of Julie's. The door opened again. The dividers shook. It was a mother with three very small children. For a moment, Julie was perplexed. Only one of them was school age. Oh, yes, the Beaumonts. First one off to kindergarten. This was going to be an important haircut.

That was the last opportunity for contemplation, because things then got very busy. By the time George from the bank came "to be squeezed in," both Julie and Tammy were a full appointment behind.

And the Saints were on time.

Julie slipped quickly through the wall to explain that things were running just a bit behind. Maybe fifteen minutes.

"Oh… oh… now… oh…" Mrs. Saint lived perpetually on the edge of crisis, and Julie's news threatened to push her over.

"Oh… goodness. Now… oh… okay… okay… This is what we'll do."

Mrs. Saint spoke only in the first person plural — or the

24

royal *we* — Julie could never figure out which. She also had a habit of swaying from the waist in a kind of oval bobbing pattern not unlike the mating ritual of some large water bird. The bobbing began to float her toward the door.

"We have one more errand, so we can do that. Now, boys, we won't leave those chairs, right?" To Julie she added, "Fifteen minutes? We'll be right back."

Julie backed up a few steps. The boys were paying no attention whatsoever to their mother's admonitions. One of them was busily but carefully engaged with a red felt-tipped marker, outlining a "tattoo" of a dragon that had been dyed onto the crook of his elbow. Every few seconds he'd check the one on his brother's arm to be sure his duplication was precise. The Saints had apparently visited Unter's Variety Store on the way, for the tattoo was the stick-on type that comes in packs of gum. Despite her mild concern over what else the twins might do with the red marker, Julie couldn't help noting the similarity in the two boys' artwork.

She turned back to resume the final trim on George, and promptly walked into one of the panels. The resulting *thunk* startled everyone except Peter and Paul Saint. They had gotten up and moved to different chairs the instant their mother left. With an empty chair between them to serve as working surface they began to unwrap what looked like enough chocolate bars to zit an entire junior high class for life…

None of this bothered Julie for the moment. She had George to finish and things were getting even further behind. With all the activity she was just a few breaths shy of being frazzled *and now the telephone rang!*

One thing TBS had put in that was going to stay for sure was the roam phone receiver on the back of Julie's chair. This innovation meant she could answer calls without leaving her customer; because of the big mirror, she didn't even have to lose eye contact.

She gave George an I-know-this-is-taking-longer-than-it-should look, as she picked up the receiver and balanced it on her shoulder to talk. Now she had both hands free to continue with him.

"Is this Julie or Tammy?" It was the easily recognizable, inviting voice of Mrs. Goodman. "I can never tell you young girls apart on the telephone."

"It's Julie, Mrs. Goodman. How can I help you?"

"Oh, thank you, dear. I think I left my credit card at your place. It wasn't in my purse when I got home. I think when I..."

Automatically Julie looked up to take in the cash register first. Right there! A VISA card right on the cash drawer ledge below the keys. Funny they hadn't seen it before.

"Yes, it's here, Mrs. Goodman. I'm sure it's yours. Just hang on a sec and I'll — Mrs. Goodman! I'll call you right back!"

"Tammy!" Julie set the roam phone on the shelf below the mirror and picked up the blow dryer. She didn't want George to hear, so she turned it on near his ear.

"Those Saint kids!" she said to Tammy. "Paul. The single crown? He just took Mrs. Goodman's VISA off the cash. I saw him in the mirror. We're going to go over quietly and get it from them before their mother comes back, or she'll have a stroke! We'll both go. You just stand in front of Peter. I'll get the card from Paul."

Tammy's voice was urgent. "How do you know it's Paul? Did he turn his head?"

"No!" Julie replied. "It was the tattoo!"

They slipped through the wall, Tammy leading.

"But they *both* have a tattoo!" Her whisper was very loud.

Julie was calm but determined. "It's Paul," she said.

How can Julie be so confident in her identification?

26

7

A Badly Planned
Saturday?

THE SCENE, WERE IT NOT for the sad story associated with it, would have been idyllic. One of those nature segments that appears at least once a night on public television. Or a piece from a commercial by a conservation group.

It's the birds, Jeff Baldwin concluded, that make one sensitive to just how peaceful it is up here. The only sound, except for the occasional click/whirr of his camera, came from the birds. There was also, now that he paid attention to it, the steady rush of the wind, but it, too, was peaceful as it sieved through the pines. More a background than anything else. A background for the birds.

From where he sat on the carpet of pine needles, Jeff could see six — no, seven; no, *eight!* — different species: jays; chickadees, of course; finches; a pair of woodpeckers. He could hear a cardinal even if he couldn't see it. Nuthatches: two varieties of them —

Suddenly his cataloging was interrupted by the mildest and most silent and simple change. It put a chill on things. A cloud

27

had slid over the sun, and what had been so warm and inviting only seconds before — a perfect example of nature's grace — seemed to become gloomy and ominous. Even the birds quietened, in sympathy with the mood. Or did their silence create the mood?

Whatever. It reminded Jeff of why he was here. He picked up his camera to check the settings. There was sand on the edge of the lens cover and some pine needles stuck in the buckle of the carrying strap. As he lifted the camera to his eye, a tiny insect added to his unease by settling on his ear. He brushed at it. No effect. Again. It wouldn't go away. Then he realized it was only a thin curl of bark from the top of the stump that formed his backrest.

In the brief moment when all that was happening, the sun came back, just as suddenly as it had disappeared. The cardinal began to sing again and the wind softened. But Jeff's good feeling was gone now. His sense of peace had been exchanged for one of unrest and the press of duty. He was here to do a job.

Jeff Baldwin was a reporter, and he was way up here at this elevation to do a follow-up on the Turner-Burnside rescue. Two hours ago he had left a rented 4 x 4 at the end of an abandoned logging road and scrambled on foot up a very rough hiker's path to this — well, call it a clearing, he thought. Actually, it wasn't a natural clearing; it was really a growth of young pine, regenerating after a fire that had cleared out the area more than thirty years ago.

What made it a clearing was that about twenty or twenty-five of the young trees had been cut. All of them like the one Jeff was sitting against. Neatly, with a crosscut saw.

The trees had been used to make the Turners and the Burnsides a crude shelter. Jeff couldn't see it from where he was sitting now, but he knew it was only a few steps away, around the knoll to the left. He had photographed it only a couple of minutes ago, taking particular care to get the light setting right. He wanted all the dead pine needles on the trees to show. This would be the big spread picture. It would help the story.

The Turners and the Burnsides were snowmobilers. Last January they had set out on their machines for a Saturday of "trailing." It was an excursion marked by disaster: disaster of their own making, reinforced by bad luck.

To begin with, they had not told anyone — least of all the forest service — where they were going, or even that they were going at all! They weren't reported missing therefore until the following Monday afternoon, and the search hadn't begun until Wednesday because of the bad weather. No one even knew where to look until a helicopter crew spotted the Burnsides' jeep at the foot of Ebbett's Pass. The Pass had been closed since November.

Even so, things might have turned out all right for the two couples, but a combination of circumstance piled up on them like the snow that had begun to fall that Saturday afternoon. First the drive belt broke on Jeannie Burnside's Citation. That should not have been a particular problem, since all snowmobilers carry an extra drive belt. It's automatic. Like a spare tire. Except Jeannie didn't have one, and hers was the only Citation. The others each drove a V-Max.

Then the storm hit. Naturally, since the two couples hadn't told the forest service they were going up (or asked permission: the proper procedure) it follows that they hadn't bothered to check with the weather service, either. By the time they got here, to what was now a clearing, a storm had dumped mounds of fresh snow on top of what was already a record winter's snowfall. Dan Turner later described the fresh snow as over his head in spots: too much even for snowmobiles. That's when they built the shelter. Mark Burnside had a mountain pack — hence the saw — and they holed up to wait out the storm.

At first there was no reason to worry. Jeannie Burnside might not have carried an extra drive belt, but she was notorious for packing way too much food on all these trips, and this time was no exception. For a short period, according to Dan, it was almost fun. Neither couple had children or any immediate have-to-get-home responsibility. There was food and shelter. Three snowmobiles worked, and they weren't lost.

But Marie Turner got sick. Food poisoning, the autopsy said later. By Sunday night she was dehydrated and delirious. Her pulse was thready and she was drifting in and out of consciousness. So on Monday morning as soon as there was light, Mark Burnside set out on foot down the mountain, using snowshoes he had fashioned from pine branches and vinyl strips cut from the snowmobile seats.

His body was found when the snow melted, about two months ago, at the bottom of a long straight drop. His neck was broken and so was his left arm. Dan Turner speculated that with the poor visibility in the storm, Mark must have walked right out into air. It was too bad he hadn't waited. Only a few hours after the Burnsides' jeep was spotted, a helicopter was hovering over the clearing and winching out Dan Turner and Jeannie Burnside. A quick second trip was necessary to recover Marie Turner's body. By that time she had been dead almost thirty-six hours.

Jeff Baldwin had been the only reporter to get near the scene. He'd talked his way onto the 'copter that came back for Marie's body, and his story and pictures had been picked up by every wire service in North America and two or three in Europe. In fact it occurred to Jeff that by coming up here to get a feel for his follow-up story (there was going to be a big magazine spread this time) he was also one of the first people, if not the very first, to visit the spot since the week of the rescue.

He patted his vest to be sure he still had the extra film. He'd need it. But what concerned him most right now was whether he should go to the police first when he got back down. If he told his editor first what he had learned up here, she would insist on running the story, and nuts to the police.

But publishing the story first could easily condemn Dan Turner or Jeannie Burnside or both. And what he had, Jeff knew, wasn't *absolute* proof. Fishy, though. Very fishy. He wondered what Dan and Jeannie meant to each other, what kind of relationship they had. The answer to that might help with his decision.

What has Jeff Baldwin learned at this mountain scene that is making him debate whether to go first to the police with the information, or to his editor?

8

From *Sine Timore*
(The official newsletter of the National Association of Security Services)

WINNER OF THIS MONTH'S TROJAN Horse Award is Stephen James, vice president and general manager of Vigil Security in Niagara. Stephen proved the aptness of his company name by breaking an industrial theft ring at a principal client: Category Tool & Die Makers in Monmouth.

Category, as readers of *Sine Timore* will be well aware, has been plagued by a rash of product theft, particularly of precision cold-rolled steel parts. The situation in this company has been aggravated, too, by what are possibly the worst employee-management relations in the Dakota Industrial Basin. A record three wildcat strikes last year followed what was supposed to be the resolution of a six-month legal walkout. The spark in the case of each walkout was shop steward Horace Cater's contention that Category management was union-baiting in its attempts to stop the thefts.

Before Stephen and Vigil Security were brought in, as agreed to by both union and management, Category Tool & Die had been using the random search method, which, in seven attempts, had turned up only one uncertain suspect.

Stephen's first step when his company accepted the contract was to halt the random searches, then establish an inventory control marking system. Hand counts of inventory, compared with computer printouts, confirmed the company's belief that the theft was taking place principally at the close of shifts. Certain workers on the floor were apparently walking out with the heavy parts concealed on their persons or in carryons.

Since the company had already tried a security X-ray scanning system (which triggered two of the wildcat walkouts) it was obvious to Stephen that this method was not ideal. The third walkout had occurred when management initiated a hand search system of the duffle bags that all shop floor employees carry from their work stations to the change-and-shower room or directly out to the parking lot, as they choose.

Every single employee responded in the next shift by carrying his or her personal items — and, management alleged, stolen parts — in cardboard boxes sealed with tape. Cater acknowledged that this was his idea, and that the union had supplied the cartons. As Stephen James explained to *Sine Timore*, breaking the taped seal on these bread-box-sized cartons constituted violation of privacy in the eyes of the union — a grievable action — and justified the "collective response" (which is what Cater prefers to call the walkouts). These were the conditions when Vigil Security took over at Category, but Stephen James was able to crack the situation to the satisfaction of both management and union.

His solution involved some minor reconstruction in the exit area where employees punched out their time cards. Before Vigil's involvement, Category workers at the end of a shift would walk through a pair of electronically responsive doors into a lobby, then through another pair of doors to the change-and-shower room. Before passing through the first pair of doors, workers would pull their personal time cards from a wall rack, insert them into the time clock to be stamped, then return them to a rack on the other side of the clock.

Stephen's strategy was to move the time clock and the second rack to the lobby. On only the third day of this system, Stephen was sufficiently certain of the culprits to detain them and open their sealed boxes in the presence of steward Horace Cater.

The success was total. Two of the guilty workers independently identified key members of the theft ring to Stephen in the presence of both management and union. The guilty parties are facing prosecution, and Category Tool & Die no longer has a theft problem.

Sine Timore congratulates Stephen James and Vigil Security, winners of the T.H.A. (No photos are published at request of Mr. James.)

How was Stephen James able to pick out the workers who were stealing parts?

9

"Could Be the Biggest Thing Since Tutankhamen"

"WHERE?"

Thomas Arthur Jones had not intended to shout into the telephone, but the conversation that up to now had occupied only half his attention suddenly engaged him completely.

He had been deeply engrossed in a final proofreading of his paper on the Olduvai Gorge skeletons. (Jones felt the Leakeys had seriously misinterpreted the significance of these remains; this was to be his third published contribution to the debate, which he himself had begun with his presentation six years ago at the annual meeting of the Learned Society.)

"Where?" He repeated. "Say that again!"

The amount of interest in his voice was a full turnabout from the desultory "Jones" with which he'd first answered. That was his standard opening: polite but uninviting, a response he'd perfected over his past two years as Professor of the Schliemann Chair of Archaeology at the Smithsonian. By sounding preoccupied, he could filter out and quickly dismiss the calls he didn't want. That was just about all of them.

This particular one had begun terminally, for to "Jones" the caller at the other end had said, confidently, "Tom Jones? T. A. Jones?"

There was a chilly pause before Jones replied, "This is *Dr. Jones, yes.* Thomas Arthur Jones."

The voice changed immediately from confident to supplicant. "Dr. Jones. Of course. Dr. Thomas Jones, ah... ah... 'Impact of Andean Orogeny on Fossil Distribution in the Oligocene Era.' *That* Dr. Jones, right?"

This citing of one of his early papers had kept the eminent Dr. Jones on the line, yet the substance of the call immediately reversed things again, for Jones was convinced he was being sucked into a joke. Thomas Arthur Jones had little time for jokes.

The voice identified itself as Jimmy Strachan, associate editor of one of the country's largest newsmagazines, and then proceeded to announce that a hiker — a rock climber, actually — had come to him with a tale of discovering a Stone Age tribe, or what appeared to be a Stone Age tribe. For Jones, that was the tip-off: he knew this was definitely a joke. Until Strachan told him where the discovery had been made. That's when Prof. Jones shouted into the receiver.

He did it once more.

"*Where?*"

"Staten Island." Strachan risked a rude response by repeating phonetically, "Stat-en I-land."

"I am not a simpleton, Mr. Strachan. Nor am I hearing-impaired." Jones spoke very deliberately. "We *are* talking about Isla de Los Estados, are we not? You wouldn't have the temerity to pretend that in New York harbor..."

"Dr. Jones, *please.*" This time it was Jimmy Strachan's turn for a little one-upmanship. That he'd scored a point or two was evident in Jones's grudging but apologetic reply.

"All right. But you understand that as a government-sponsored institution we have just about anyone calling here and I simply don't... well... I'm sure you understand."

"We get them, too, Dr. Jones." Strachan's tone had moved to the now-we-share-a-bond level. "And that's exactly how I first treated this man's proposal. I felt — you know — Stone Age tribe, indeed! But you should see his photographs! That's what kept me from tossing him out. You see, I don't know much about the Stone Age. Fact is, the only real reference point I've got is that movie — you know, ah — *Quest for Fire?*"

Thomas Arthur Jones just grunted.

"Anyway, his pictures will sell you, I'm sure." Strachan was speaking more confidently and confidentially. He knew he had Jones's interest now. "This guy, he's into archaeology in an amateur kind of way, but what he wants is money. Sorry. I'm getting ahead of myself. The guy — never mind his name for right now — he's a Brit. He's been going to the Falkland Islands ever since the war there. Something to do with compensation for the sheep farmers because of the war. Anyway, he's a rock climber, and while he was there on one of his trips he popped over to Tierra del Fuego."

"Quite a pop." Jones interrupted. "That's got to be over five hundred miles."

"Yes... ah —" Strachan was thrown a bit off stride — "ah... I understand Fuego's supposed to be a real score if you're a climber. Anyway, to make a long story short, he got himself over to Staten Island... ah... Isla de las Es-es."

"*Los* Estados," Jones filled in. "It's almost spot on the intersection of the fortieth parallel and sixty-five degrees."

There was a pause. Advantage Jones.

"Okay. Right. Anyway, the island's where he discovered the Stone Age tribe — ah... the *alleged* tribe." His voice wound up again. "But you've gotta see the pictures! Anyway, what he wants is $100,000 for an exclusive."

Thomas Arthur Jones reflected for a second or two on the $1,500 that had accompanied the Arthur Evans Prize he was awarded last year.

"... and what we would like you to do, Tom — *Dr. Jones!* — is verify the discovery for us before we spend those kind of bucks." There was a tiny break before he picked up again, his voice just ever so much less assertive. "We... ah... we'd need to know your fee first, Dr. Jones. Of course expenses are covered."

Thomas Jones looked at his paper on the Leakeys. He'd only been to South America once. A month at Iguassu Falls had come to nothing that time because the Paraguayans and the Argentines had had a falling out over the project. This island was a good two-thousand-plus miles south of that. It would be three or four days' travel — one way. A week at the site. And the publications! The question was... what kind of fee would a news-magazine pay?

Strachan ventured tentatively, "We're asking you, Dr. Jones, because... well... you're the real expert on anything post-Pleistocene, aren't you?"

Whether it was his intent or not, associate editor Strachan had played a very high trump. He'd said the one thing that Thomas Arthur Jones, B.Sc., M.A.(Oxon.), Ph.D., F.R.S.C., could not set aside. And he'd cut the fee in half.

"I must say, Mr. Strachan, it certainly does sound intriguing. I guess I could do it. Now, my fee is really incidental. I'll accept a per diem of, say, $300? But you must understand, I only fly first class." That was a quick addition. Jones congratulated himself. "I imagine I'll have to go through Rio and Buenos Aires."

The delight in his caller's voice told Jones he could have nailed down a much higher per diem.

"Excellent, Dr. Jones. I'll have one of our people in Washington come to you today if that's all right, and I'll courier the photographs. They'll be there tomorrow morning."

The conversation ended a few minutes later with various pleasantries and expressions of mutual respect. Just in time, too; Jones had a meeting down the hall. He walked as quickly as he could — Thomas Arthur Jones did not run — thinking how timely that call had been. The meeting was a regular department affair to discuss what success the faculty was having in the never-ending search for grants and awards. This Staten Island thing could become big.

The following morning, however, Jones's absorption in the Olduvai Gorge paper shifted the Stone Age tribe to the back of his mind — until the photographs arrived. He was bent over his drafting table when the department secretary came in with a package that soon took up the whole of the working surface.

"Gorgeous. Excellent!" Jones muttered when he pulled the pictures out of the slit in the side of the package. Most of them were blowups, in black-and-white.

The first several shots were of the inhabitants. They certainly appeared Stone Age: short stature, very wrinkled skin on the older ones — backs and stomachs, especially. That was good. So were the stooped shoulders. There were missing teeth. One of the younger ones had a broken arm that hadn't healed correctly. The skin was very black, almost Australian aboriginal, Jones thought. He didn't know quite what to make of that. Many of them had that furtive, uncertain, trapped-small-animal look he'd seen so often in the faces of primitive people who encounter something — especially technology — that is beyond their comprehension or frame of reference.

Shots of the living area had been taken with several different lenses. A fisheye had been used to produce an all-encompassing view of a very large-mouthed but shallow cave on the — Jones turned the photograph forty-five degrees — it would have to be the north side of a solitary mountain. Hill, really. A fire-pit took up most of the floor area at the arch of the cave mouth. Leading away from the entrance, the ground was level and well swept. In two subsequent shots, a larger view of this area showed children playing a game that appeared not unlike soccer. He couldn't see a ball, though.

Interior shots suggested the group had been here a long time, and planned to stay. Food hung from slings tied to stalactites, well out of reach of the dogs and children Jones saw in the pictures. There was a lot of it: drying meat, what looked like onions, a kind of rutabaga, some other vegetation — spices? medications? — but more meat than anything else. They were certainly successful hunters. That would also account for the skins they wore.

The floor was remarkably clean. Space seemed to have been divided into living areas with tiny walls of smooth stones. The walls were symbolic, for none of them were more than ankle height. One of the most interesting features was a pool, apparently fed from an underground stream. It drained away through a crack at the rear of the cave. Clearly, the pool was an important reason for the choice of the cave.

The rock climber had used a strong flash for these shots, for there was no rear entrance/exit to provide light back there. On several shots the flash had reflected off shiny objects arranged in geometric patterns. Bones, perhaps? Flint would reflect. Maybe something of religious significance to them.

The final set was presumably of the entire population. They looked ludicrously similar to school class photos, the kind of shot of the third grade in which one of the girls in the front row inevitably forgets to put her knees together. Or a boy in the back row discovers for the first time in three years that the building has a roof and he turns to give it a full scientific examination just as the photographer presses the button. These shots were taken outside the cave, to the left of the entrance. Behind the inhabitants, the surface was again level and clear, just like the area out front, as far as the camera could see.

An aerial shot confirmed that this was true all the way around the cave. The tribe had evidently opted for security over protection from the elements; they wanted to be able to see a good distance in every direction. Still, Jones acknowledged, the whole terrain was like that as far as he knew. Too cold by far for dense vegetation in any case.

Thomas Arthur Jones sighed. It would have been an interesting trip. He looked through the entire lot of pictures again and then went to his desk to find Jimmy Strachan's telephone number. Fascinating, in fact. But Jones's sense of ethics wouldn't let him go any further without telling his potential client that this was very unlikely to be a Stone Age tribe, that indeed it was far more likely to be a flat-out fraud.

"Oh, well —" he picked up the receiver "— at least I get to give the Leakey paper in Edinburgh. Maybe I can find a couple of interesting malts."

Why is Dr. Jones quite certain that the rock climber has not discovered a Stone Age tribe?

10

A Report on Conditions at Scutari

IN FORTY-TWO YEARS OF bearing witness to the follies of humankind, Bill Lacroix had never felt so totally, utterly, helpless and frustrated. The immediate cause — of several — was that the soldier in front of him was dying, and he could do nothing at all about it. Septicemia from an untreated bayonet wound had taken over the young fusilier's entire body and was about to win the lad's final battle. No more than eighteen, Bill thought, if that. He doesn't deserve to die here. Not in this filth.

Bill bent over the soldier and put his hand on the boy's forehead. It was burning hot with the fever that tore away at the body. The irony of it all — the terrible, dreadful irony — was that the wound hadn't even come from the enemy. No Russian had caused this.

The soldier was a private in the 90th Light Infantry. He still wore the uniform; there had been no attempt to take it off or to change it as his condition had worsened over the past few days. In the boredom of the trenches outside Sebastopol, he and several others had been fooling with their bayonets. It wasn't much of a cut, but here in Scutari, in this warehouse that passed for a hospital, or across the Black Sea in Crimea, a scratch could be as fatal as a musket ball in the gut. Already, death from disease was taking away British soldiers four times as fast as the fight-ing. That was the deeper cause of Bill Lacroix's anger.

"This un's gone, guv'."

Bill turned to look at the orderly standing in the aisle. The man was almost completely covered from shoulders to knees by a huge apron. It seemed to be more appropriate for a tannery than a hospital. But then, it was easier to wipe blood and bits of flesh from leather than from cotton, and this orderly had come from the surgery in the next building. He was serving a two-week punishment for drunkenness. A burly fellow, Bill noted. Good thing, probably. His job was to kneel on the wounded and hold them down as the surgeons extracted bullets and shrapnel, or amputated, or as often as not, simply hacked.

The orderly stood there, tapping the forehead of the soldier in the cot behind Bill. "'E's gone," the man repeated, pushing the dead one's eyelids closed with two blood-encrusted fingers.

Several hours before, an officer had reluctantly instructed the orderly to escort Bill around the hospital. Although he was non-military, Bill represented the *Times* Fund, and potentially he had clout. The high command here in Turkey was beginning to appreciate the power of public opinion.

Bill forced himself to look at the dead soldier in the bed behind him. This man too still wore his tunic, unbuttoned and lying open, and Bill could see the mulberry rash that covered the skin. Typhus. He shuddered. There was no end to the awfulness here.

A rumble of thunder drew his attention back to the soldier with the bayonet wound. There were no walls in shed no. 14, and the young lad's head lay right under the edge of the roofline.

Bill walked to the foot of the bed. "Help me pull this into the aisle a bit," he said to the orderly. "At least he can die without rain in his face."

"Right, guv'." The orderly helped Bill pull the bed into the aisle a few inches.

"Let's do all of them like his," Bill said. "If that storm is anything like the one yesterday..." He didn't bother to finish.

The two of them worked together, pulling alternate beds into the aisle, eight on one side, the same on the other. The orderly was quite willing. This was better duty than the agony and screaming in the surgery.

"You th' Russell chap, guv'?" he wanted to know. William Howard Russell had been the *Times'* special correspondent whose reports from the field had ignited public opinion in London, and had even attracted the attention of Queen Victoria. His accounts of the dreadful conditions and overcrowding at the huge Barracks Hospital in Scutari had triggered two immediate results: the arrival in Turkey of a group of women under the charge of a nurse the military command referred to as "that dreadful Nightingale woman"; and the establishment of the *Times* Fund for the benefit of wounded soldiers.

"No. My name's Lacroix." Bill bent over to pick a soiled dressing off the floor of the aisle, then straightened immediately. He hadn't realized how foul the smell was at bed level. At that height, the smell of gangrene and suppurating wounds was overlain by the stench of men lying in their own soil.

"Be ye with t'other chap, then?" The orderly had that curious insouciance of the street.

"What other chap?" Bill was instantly on guard. He had thought he was the only civilian inspecting here.

"The one this mornin'. The toff. 'Ad t'show 'im round, too. Right proper one, 'im. All fancy like." The orderly knuckled his dirty finger against a nostril and blew with great vigor. "Didn't bother 'im none in 'ere, it didn't." He paused to clear the other side in the same way. "Sat there b'th'door. Wrote nigh an hour 'e did. 'Im 'n' 'is fancy ink pots 'n' all." He repeated the expurgation at the first nostril. "'Spect 'e's comin' back. Left it all 'ere when old Rags 'imself come by. Mus' be friends, 'im 'n' the toff."

"Rags" was Lord Raglan, the one-armed commander-in-chief of the British army in the Crimea. Bill's antennae were pulsing now. What was Raglan doing here? He never went near the wounded if he could help it.

"'E sat 'ere," the orderly said, "over 'ere," he added, wiping his hands on the tannery apron with more than the usual effort as he walked toward a portable mahogany writing table at the entranceway. Bill wondered why he hadn't noticed it before; its pristine elegance stood out so in this crowded ward of dirt and death.

With great care the orderly nudged a sheet of cream linen writing paper. "'Spect ye c'n read, guv'."

It wasn't meant sarcastically. The orderly was just as curious as Bill to know what was written there.

Bill leaned over the table, then bent very close. In spite of the fact that Shed 14 had no walls, the light was very dim. Before him lay the first page of a letter — no, a report! It was written in a careful, deliberate script.

29 January 1855
The Barracks Hospital, Scutari

Sidney Herbert, Esq.,
My dear Sidney,

I sit, as I write, in Ward Number Fourteen, where our brave soldiers recover from their wounds. Regrettably, not all will do so for such are the fortunes of war. Nevertheless, all is done that can be done. Indeed, there are those here, whose station in life has been such that the accoutrements available to them, at the point of their extremity, represent an experience of considerable novelty.

From my vantage, I can observe the care of our stout fellows. They recline in two rows in this ward, embracing a passageway from which the ministrations of the attendants are delivered. It is quite orderly. In each row, eight heads point outward; eight pairs of feet point in. Very like the parade square at Lockham, which I am sure you remember, as I do, with fondness.

Barracks Hospital here in Scutari, contrary to ill-founded, and I suspect, ill-intended rumour...

"Right fancy writin', i'n't, guv'?" The orderly's presence — and his breath — broke in over Bill's shoulder, but neither penetrated the fury. Bill was outraged! The death, the dirt, the gross incompetence, the distortion of truth, and now what appeared to be a deliberate attempt to deceive the Secretary of State for War.

"'S'matter, guv? Smell got yuh? This 'ere shed's one o' th' better ones. Them what's got walls is worse."

There is much in the condition of Shed Fourteen to anger Bill Lacroix. But what has triggered his conviction that there is collusion to deceive Sidney Herbert?

11

At the Scene of
the Accident

IT WAS THE KIND OF day that Sue Silverberg knew from experience was only going to get worse. The only thing she *wasn't* sure of was just how bad it was going to get, and how soon. This combination of certainty and uncertainty was responsible for her foul mood, and the mood accounted in turn for what she was doing at that moment to a long string of southbound traffic. Highway 50 was one of those busy two-lane thoroughfares that should have been upgraded to four years ago, but never seemed to make the cut whenever budgets got sent back for review.

Sue was driving the big white patrol car at just below the speed limit: too fast to test the courage of drivers behind her; too slow for the anxious heavy-footers who made Highway 50 such a dangerous road.

She looked in the rearview mirror at the growing line of angry drivers. "Serves them right," she grumped to no one in particular, but in saying it, woke up her partner.

Sully Nod was a tribute to his name. He could drop off so

fast in the partner seat that every single member of the force who had ever paired with him swore that he had never actually worked a full shift in his twelve-year career.

"Yeah — aa-*humph*!" Sully had allergies. "Who knows? Maybe with all his lawyers he'll get it put off for another six months."

Sully could wake up as fast as he could fall asleep, but this reply belonged to a conversation that ended five minutes before. It made Sue smile in spite of herself. She even nudged the accelerator a bit. The line behind was getting too long and sooner or later someone was going to try something stupid. One thing about riding with Sully, she thought, it kept you off base, and that went a long way toward healing a lousy mood.

"Maybe," Sue replied, quite willing to revert to the topic that Sully thought was current. It was going to be current with Sue, anyway, for some time, for only a few hours ago she had learned that her upcoming vacation was going to be put on hold by the also-upcoming trial of Charles Xavier Borino, reputed philanthropist and alleged con artist. The case had come forward and been put back at least three times, as Borino's lawyers swarmed at every possible loophole. Sue was a key witness.

Sully was still awake.

"You were going to Vancouver, weren't you," he said. A statement, not a question. There was very little hidden information in Sue's watch.

"Uh-huh." Sue didn't really want to talk about it.

She checked her side mirror and eased into a left turn lane as she slowed for a traffic light at Cedar Mills Blvd.

"Let's get off and go down here a bit," she said. "Let them crank up for a while."

Sully didn't answer. He was asleep again.

The abrupt news of the changed trial date had come on the heels of a transfer notice that really made Sue burn. Of the six people on her regular watch, only Sully and Sindar Mohan were experienced. Now Mohan was being moved, and his replacement was another rookie. Not that rookies are bad in themselves, Sue knew. They have to start somewhere, and traffic is the traditional launch pad. But rookies always seemed to cause so much paperwork. They screwed up more often. Like yesterday. That's why she was on the road with Sully. The kid who was supposed to be behind the wheel today was on sick leave. He'd neglected proper procedure while bringing in a drunk and paid for it with a car door slammed on his fingers.

That meant more paperwork for Sue. Not just the incident itself but all the paper that was piling up on her desk while she was out here doing the kid's job!

That thought stirred up the blackness in her again, but not for long. A snore from Sully crossed a burst of static from the radio.

Sully got to the switch before she did. That happened invariably and it never failed to impress her.

"Aa-*humph*. Twenty-one. Go ahead."

Another burst of static. Sue speeded up to reach a hill for they seemed to be in a reception trough.

"Yeah. Twenty-one. Aa-*humph*. Aa-HUMPH!"

There was a pause at the other end and then a very tentative "Twenty-one? Ah — is your — are you — do you read?"

Sully looked a bit sheepish. "Yes. You've got us. Shoot."

"Okay, twenty-one. We have a call from two-niner-two. Could be a fatality. Cedar Mills Blvd. just west of Number 50. Thought Sergeant Silverberg would want to know."

Sue spoke up. "Thank you, Central. We are only five minutes away."

Sully signed off as Sue made a leaning U-turn to take them back toward and across Highway 50. Two-niner-two was Peterson, the very newest of the rookies. Because the light was green in their favor they made the scene in three minutes.

Sue pulled over to the edge of the road. "I think we need some pictures before anything else" was her first comment.

Sully waved the camera and gave her an I'm-already-there

shake of his head as he got out of the car.

The tableau seemed simple, yet it threw up questions. In fact, it looked like the kind of setup the staff at the police college were so fond of.

On the verge in front of a very well-kept cemetery, facing away from the patrol car, sat a large Mercedes-Benz sedan. It was new — or at least it looked new to Sue. In any case, it was one of those machines that would never have to explain itself.

On the opposite side of the road sat an extremely well-dressed Corvette. Another very noticeable car. And just to make sure, it had a rear bumper sticker that said CATCH ME! One of those machines that got speeding tickets just sitting in the driveway.

What drew the most attention from both of them, however, was the body that had been moved — dragged — from the middle of the road to the cemetery side. It was a dog! Sue looked around the area to make sure she wasn't missing another body — the *real* fatality. Nothing. It was just the dog. One of those strange-looking things that no kid ever has for a pet. Sue had no idea what kind of dog it was, but she could tell you didn't get this one free from the pound.

She went back to the car to turn off the flashers. No sense in attracting gawkers. She did the same for Peterson's patrol car, parked perpendicular to the roadway in the cemetery drive.

Peterson! Where was he, anyway?

Sully apparently had the same thought for he called quietly, "Sue!" and pointed.

At the back of the cemetery, almost out of sight behind a phalanx of headstones, Peterson was bent over, laboriously copying into his notebook.

"Peterson!"

Sue knew she shouldn't have shouted in that tone, but this was too much. There's no way that...

"You! *You!*" Sue was not the only player here with a loud voice. "*You! Policeperson!* You're in charge here, aren't you."

It was a statement. Sue felt that today everybody was making statements to her.

"You'd better be prepared to do something!" The lady was not finished making statements. "Have you any idea what my Fritzie is worth?"

Ah, Sue couldn't help thinking, a question! Even if she didn't have the answer. And somehow she knew she didn't want to know the answer, either. Fritzie had to be the dead dog.

"He's an Entelbucher Sunnehund." The lady was getting louder. "And his real name is Prince's Violet Centaur. Does that mean anything to you?"

Another nonquestion. Sue looked at Sully. What is this today!

"I didn't think it would! It means priceless. That's what it means. Now you…"

Sue tuned out. She was tired of statements. Against her inclination she studied the lady instead of listening. She was of indeterminate age. Could be forty. Could be sixty. Hefty. Hair drawn back. No makeup. Leads with her chin, too, Sue concluded. Probably talks this way even when she isn't upset.

She looked around for skid marks, but couldn't see any. What she did see was Sully, unnecessarily far from the scene, but apparently busy with the camera.

Meanwhile the lady's monologue was interrupted by the hasty arrival of Peterson. He shouted over the lady. "Sergeant Silverberg! Sorry I made Central think it was a fatality, but this lady, she…"

"I said to this young man, now you get…"

"Madam… ma… *madam!*" Sue hated to shout, especially in front of Peterson, but she just had to prevent an instant replay. "Madam, the officer over there will be in charge of this investigation." She pointed at Sully, who was getting farther and farther away. "Constable Nod. Give your statement to him. And, madam, make sure you give him all the details. Now, Peterson…"

Sue turned and took the young policeman with her before

51

the lady could wind up again. "Now, Peterson," she repeated.

"I just came on the scene, Sergeant. I'm patroling Cedar Mills going east, see..."

Sue had a sinking feeling; yet she kept silent. Somehow this case was taking on the odor of complication — and paperwork. If she was careful there might be a way around that.

"... and I saw this body — well, the dog — in the road. And the big one, the MB, was here, see, and over there was the 'Vette."

For the first time, Marv glanced at the drivers. The man in the Mercedes was sitting in the front seat, looking studiously bored. The Corvette driver was leaning on the fender of her vehicle. She was very young. A kid, really. She was trying to look bored.

"This was how long ago?" Sue asked.

Peterson looked at his watch. "Thirty-four minutes now." He added proudly, "I arrived on the scene at 8:56."

"Okay. Okay. Then what?"

"Anyway, I saw it was only a dog, but I got some pictures."

Sue was pleased at that.

"And I pulled the dog to the side. No point in blocking traffic, right? But here's the fix."

Peterson had his notepad out and held up in front of him almost as though he were testifying.

"The kid, the girl with the 'Vette — it's hers, by the way — she says she's been in the cemetery for nearly an hour. Got a local history project in school so she's in the back there getting names and dates off the stones. See? I wrote down the ones she said. Now, the girl says she heard tires, not real loud, then a *thunk*. She looked up and saw the guy in the MB stopped in the middle of the road and then pulled over. When the kid got to the road she saw the dog. It twitched a bit, then stopped.

"Now, I got here only a few minutes later, and the story I got — I talked to the MB guy first — is that he, the MB guy, and the kid were coming down the road toward each other and *the kid hit the dog!* Then the kid did a U-ey. Like she was going to run? But then she changed her mind and pulled over.

"And then this lady! What a stirfry! Anyway, it's her dog. A champion of something. Did you know it's a —" Peterson read from his notes "En — tell-buck-er-sen."

"Yeah, I got that, Peterson." Sue didn't want the rookie making statements, too. "What did you do then?"

"Well, I told the drivers to go to their cars. Got to get everyone away from this lady. Then I called Central. First I checked the front of the cars. Both bumpers are clean — you can see for yourself. Meantime, the lady took off to call her lawyer. So the only thing I think I've got to do till you get here is check the kid's story. That's why I was back there when you came."

Sue knew for sure now that the day was already worse. In point of fact, it was now a matter of whether the whole year was going to go sour. This case seemed likely to turn into a lawsuit. She took a breath very slowly and held it.

"What *else* did you do then, Peterson?"

"Why... nothing. What else is there?"

Sue Silverberg just groaned.

Someone has finally asked Sue Silverberg a question, a clear question, but it makes her groan. What has the rookie Peterson neglected to do that would go a long way to resolving the opposing stories of the two drivers?

12

The Midterm Exam: Which Way Is Up?

THE SUDDEN APPEARANCE OF AN image on the huge drop screen reduced the buzz of conversation in the auditorium to whispers as soon as Professor Sean Hennigar turned on the overhead projector. Latecomers rushed for the few remaining seats near the front. A few of them despaired of finding an empty chair, and simply hunched on the floor of the center aisle.

"As you were told in the opening lecture of the course —" Sean began. The silence now was absolute; he never spoke very loud at any time and the opening sentences of his lectures were especially soft; it was his technique for filling the front rows and getting instant attention when he started, "— for a passing grade, you will be required to interpret a representation, or 'map.' The 'map' is what you now see before you on the screen."

A single tardy student clumping in through the upper rear doors was scowled into a tiptoeing crouch when the entire back row of students turned simultaneously. In today's class there was no time for nonsense or interruption. This was the midterm

54

exam. It was one of the two occasions each term (the other being the final exam) when attendance was perfect and attention was absolute for the once-a-week lecture in Adventures in Archaeology 333.

The reality was that not many students took "AA-cubed," as they called it, very seriously at first, for neither Sean nor his co-instructor, Professor Swift, had illusions that the course was anything but a science course specifically designed and modified for nonscience students. "Bird science" was the generic title given courses like this one, a title that did not have the slightest connection with ornithology.

Years before, the Senate of the university had earnestly decreed the necessity of science for arts students and required therefore that all "artsies" pass a minimum of one such course in order to graduate. Junior faculty invariably were stuck with these students, few of whom could tell a quadratic equation from a test tube, or even, as the chair of Physical Sciences once put it, use a calculator right side up. The result was courses like "Amazing Physics," "Tabletop Chemistry" and the surprisingly popular "Adventures in Archaeology," taught by Sean and Dr. MaryPat Swift. One of the reasons for its popularity was the style of examination the two instructors dreamed up each year: bizarre on the surface, and certainly in the mode of *Raiders of the Lost Ark*, these exams were nevertheless a serious challenge in thinking, and a breath of fresh air to students accustomed to the tedium of instructors who saw science only as SCIENCE.

"Your challenge," Sean said, continuing his explanation, "is to choose the proper *aspect* by which to interpret this representation."

He took a pen from somewhere in the folds of his tattered poncho, which instead of an academic gown was his regular and constant lecturing attire. (Whether he actually wore a shirt underneath it was a subject of considerable discussion in the campus pub.)

"You have no doubt noticed on the screen," he said, tracing

the outline of the figure on the transparency with the pen's sharp point, "what appears to be a large letter H."

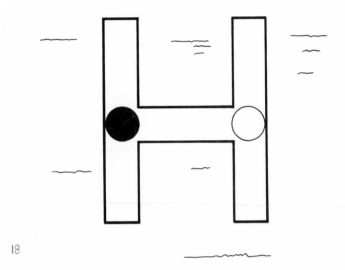

18

Indeed, the image did look like a large H outlined in black. Both vertical bars and the horizontal bar were drawn faithfully straight and in the proportions of the Western alphabet's eighth letter. The three bars were only about the width of Sean's thumb on the transparency, but projected on the screen, they appeared much wider.

In every way the image looked just like an ordinary letter H, except that from where the students sat, the outline of a circle filled the intersection of the horizontal bar and the right vertical. An identical circle, but solid — shaded in — filled the intersection on the opposite side. In the lower left corner, somewhat fainter than the rest of the diagram, was the number 18. At several intermittent points, below, on and above the H, were even fainter marks, indistinguishable, but clearly in a regular horizontal pattern.

"Your assumptions are as follows." Sean looked out at the

class. "One, that this is an *old map* locating an object of supreme religious significance to a distant, somewhat primitive mountain culture, probably the Salubrian, or it could be the Egregian. That won't be an important difference until your final exam with Dr. Swift. For now, all you need to deal with is that the map is from one culture or the other."

At the mention of MaryPat Swift, there was a general rustle, and grins. Professor Swift was an acknowledged rebel on the faculty. A full professor, tenured because of her extensive publications, she was unlike senior staff in that she deliberately taught at least one bird science course a term. Part of student lore on the campus was her alleged practice of taking a bag of birdseed, not to her lectures, but to meetings of the science department! MaryPat shared the teaching of "AA-cubed" with Sean.

" *Two*" — Sean tapped the transparency with his pen "— the map was recently found in a book that has been in storage at the British Museum for the past hundred and fifty years or so. And *three*, the parallel bars represent vertical shafts dug in the earth. If you dig down one of them, you will locate this treasured religious object. It is represented by the shaded-in circle. The other circle — the one in outline — is a highly sensitive and destructive booby trap. Obviously you don't want to dig into that one.

"For a passing grade then, you must choose the proper aspect of this map. That is, identify the *top* and bottom so that you'll dig — theoretically, of course — down the correct shaft. There are four possible views. One is correct. Don't forget to explain your reasoning. Remember that no respectable archaeologist would take a chance on being only half certain, because of the booby trap. Those of you who wish to come forward and examine either the screen or the transparency more closely may do so.

"May I remind you that this question constitutes one-half of your grade. The other half may be earned in the final examination, which Dr. Swift will present in the last class. Are there any questions?"

Would you get a passing grade? What are the four possible views of this map and which is the correct one? (For the other half of your mark, go to Dr. Swift's exam next, in The Final Exam: Digging in the Right Place.)

13

The Final Exam: Digging in the Right Place*

FINAL EXAMINATION
Adventures in Archaeology 333

27 April, A.M.   Lecture Hall A/B/C
Examiner: MaryPat Swift, B.A., Dip.C.S.,
M.Sc., LL.D. (Paris)

NOTE: Candidates are reminded that results of this examination constitute one-half of their total grade. Those candidates who did not achieve a passing grade in the midterm examination are nevertheless eligible to sit for this final.

M.P.S.

You have been given a map, which shows a buried object of supreme religious signifcance to a culture that you have determined to be either Salubrian or Egregian. The distinction may eventually be important since in the Salubrian culture all religious ceremonies are performed with the participants

*Before attempting this five-minute mystery, be sure to solve the previous one: *The Midterm Exam: Which Way Is Up?*

59

facing south, whereas the Egregians do the exact opposite.

The map is in the form of a letter H. One vertical arm represents a shaft dug in the earth to bury this object. The other leads to a sensitive booby trap. If you have determined which shaft is the safe and which the dangerous one (by completing the midterm examination successfully) you are ready for the excavation. Your task now involves decisions about this excavation.

Here are the details:

Having received a sizable research grant, you have been able to travel to the upper reaches of Salubria (actually, of what you *think* is Salubria; it's very poorly charted) to do a trial excavation. Regrettably, travel being what it is in that part of the world, you and your somewhat unreliable guide have had a difficult time. By car, muleback and finally on foot, through tunnels and over badly mapped mountain passes, you have come to what you believe is the Salubrian plain, on the border of Egregia.

During this arduous trek, you are aware that you crossed and recrossed the border of the two countries several times, and suspect that you crossed it several more times without knowing it. You don't know with any certainty whether you are in Salubria now or just outside it in Egregia.

Moments ago, you emerged from yet another tunnel to see before you the clear evidence of two shafts dug in the earth, some eight to ten meters apart, just as your "map" shows. Between them stands an adult Salubrian. At least, it *may* be a Salubrian; it could just as easily be an Egregian, because there is nothing in their appearance that would enable you to tell them apart.

To complicate your situation, an exact duplication of this scene can be detected off in the distance. There, just out of range of a shout, is another pair of shafts, eight to ten meters apart, with an Egregian — or is it a Salubrian? — standing between them.

Precisely at midpoint between the two sites is a tall pole. You can see it from where you stand, bisecting the setting sun. Hanging limply at the top in the windless dusk are both a Salubrian and an Egregian flag. You are on the border, all right, but which country is which?

One good result has come from your advance research. You know that in the Salubrian culture, truth is the primary value of daily life and the essential element for redemption, so that Salubrians can always be counted on to tell the truth. Egregians are exactly the opposite. Lying is, for them, the ultimate art form and spiritual realization.

There are three requirements for the successful completion of this examination: One, *you must approach* either *but* not both *of the two subjects you see.* Two, *you may then ask the Salubrian or the Egregian, as the case may be, a* single *question to find out where you are.* Three, *you must then describe in a short paragraph what your digging strategy will be.*

Could you pass this examination?

14

A Double Assassination at "The Falls"

OUT OF HABIT, VINCE MORO reached up to clean a finger-print off the rearview mirror, before adjusting it down a bit so he could see out the back. Then he picked up the envelope that was balled up and stuffed behind the gearshift in the center console, and put it in the glove compartment.

Don't know why I'm doing this, Vince thought as he reached over to pick up a pair of cigarette butts from the floor on the passenger side. "I really don't know why." This time he said it out loud, while throwing the two butts out the passenger side window — or what was left of it.

The fact was, Vince was compulsively neat, and nothing bothered him more than a messy car. It was a point of personal pride that no vehicle left Vince's Auto Body dirty. Not ever, no matter how tiny or insignificant the repair.

But this car? There was surely no point in cleaning it. Certainly no point in trying to repair it. The thing was a write-off, and Vince was simply here to tow it away to the wrecking yard. The front and back of the car were okay. In fact, the dash had that spotless, uncluttered look Vince always liked in cars that had just left a rental agency. And the shelf beneath the back window was pleasantly free of the invariable accumulation of clutter and junk.

The front seats, however, and the front windows, the center post, even the roof above the front seat: they were a different matter. The killers had sprayed so many bullets over these areas that the headrest on the passenger seat had been chewed right off, leaving a frothy stump of stuffing, its original whiteness now covered in drying blood. A few minutes ago Vince had overheard one of the investigators — he was sure it was one of the CIA guys — say that both victims had taken over twenty rounds in the upper torso.

"You the guy from Hertz?"

The voice in Vince's ear startled him, but he strove not to show it. His hearing more than his sight told him it was the sergeant from the highway patrol. Although the two men had met before, more than once, the sergeant never, ever recognized Vince. Or pretended not to. Vince didn't like him.

"I have been *retained* by Hertz," Vince said, getting out of the car with deliberate slowness. "I'm here to take the car. It's cleared to go?"

He folded his arms and leaned against the car. It was the same sergeant all right. A tall fellow, at least a head taller than Vince. And he had the annoying habit of standing so close when he talked that the other person had to lean back to look up, or else step backward. That's why Vince leaned against the car.

"Not yet," the sergeant replied as he took off his hat and wiped his forehead with his sleeve. Vince was sure he was actually moving closer.

"Not yet," the policeman said again. "There has to be some —"

"Okay, Sergeant, if you will, please! The photographer can use you now."

Vince whipped around quickly. It was not a voice he'd

heard before, today or at any time. The accent was British, and as the speaker approached, Vince knew he was a complete stranger. That was not surprising; the place was crawling with investigators. The CIA was here; Vince knew that for sure. And the RCMP. Two of them had come from Ottawa in a Lear jet. And the whole scene had been shut down while they waited for two more people to come up from Buffalo. No one had told Vince directly, but he could tell they were in charge. Now who the British guy was, Vince had no idea at all, but certainly he was connected with the affair.

Just before dawn, two diplomats from the French consulate in Buffalo, New York, had crossed into Canada over the Rainbow Bridge at Niagara Falls. Not more than a few minutes later, while stopped at a traffic light, they were shot down in an absolute storm of machine-gun bullets. Then their bodies had been dragged out of the car and, as though to send a message, laid side by side in front of the car and sprayed with bullets again. The assassins had escaped.

"Excuse me, sir." The British accent was very polite. A great deal more polite than the sergeant. "Who are... oh, yes. Forgive me!"

The man peered closer at the badge that dangled from Vince's shirt pocket and proclaimed CLEARANCE – SITE ONLY.

"You're the gentleman here to tow away the vehicle, aren't you? If you don't mind waiting just a few minutes more. Some photos we need. It would be convenient if you didn't drive over the outlines there."

He pointed to the chalk outlines on the pavement in front of the car, which marked where the bodies of the diplomats had lain. The sergeant was now lying down beside the longer one. It was clear his dignity was wounded and Vince was just beginning to enjoy that when the accent said, "There's one more thing, actually. It's frightfully awkward, I know, but you... uh... you are just about the size of one of the victims. Do you... uh... would you mind awfully lying down there like the sergeant? I'm sorry, I can't really explain why, but it will help us. A reconstruct-the-scene sort of thing, you see."

For an instant, but only an instant, Vince wondered if maybe he wasn't being had. But the sergeant was already lying on the pavement, and the situation was hardly one for humor, macabre or otherwise. He nodded and went to the front of the car, glad now that he'd left on his coveralls to drive out here, and lay down beside the other outline.

"A bit embarrassing, this," Vince muttered to the sergeant. There was no response. The sergeant was definitely embarrassed and had no wish to discuss the fact. "All in the interests of justice," Vince continued, determined to make it known that he could make light of the indignity. "By the way," he said, "would it help if you knew which one of them was driving when they were shot?"

The sergeant sat bolt upright so suddenly that the photographer yelled. "How do you know?" the policeman asked.

How does Vince Moro know who was driving?

15

They Come in Threes, Don't They?

THE DOOR TO THE INNER office opened quietly, but Mike Dunn didn't pay much attention. He and his wife, Dale, had run Dunn & Dunn Insurance Brokers together for so long now that they could interpret each other's purpose much of the time without exchanging a word. In this particular instance Mike's subconscious told him that the way the door had opened signaled no more than "errand: no communication necessary." Dale had something to pick up or look up or enter in a file: something that couldn't be done in her own office.

Nevertheless, this errand got his attention. Dale had the morning paper and on her way to the file cabinet quietly set it on the corner of Mike's desk.

The headline announced
CASTRO SCOOPS UP REST OF SUGAR INDUSTRY.

Mike stared at it for a long time, unwilling to look directly at his wife. When he finally did, she was smiling at him gently. After the briefest of pauses, he smiled back and said,

66

"Thanks. It would have been easy to say 'I told you so.'"

Dale just shrugged. "No milk was spilt," she said, then changed the subject immediately to show she meant it. "Have you looked at the applications that came in this morning?" she asked.

"Right here," Mike replied, glad for the shift away from anything to do with Cuba. "Go through them yourself. See what you think. I like the guy from New Denmark. He's even got — now where is it? — ah, here! His résumé is the only one with a title page. Lends a little class, I thought."

He handed the résumé to Dale. It was in an acetate folder and the front page read:

R. David Sloan
12 Colonial Street
New Denmark, Ontario

Tel. No.,
Quaker 4 - 7124

D.O.B.,
31 May 1932

Present Employer,
Islington Insurance Agency

"Looks organized, doesn't he?" Mike enthused. "At least from the appearance of that. And if we are going to have an office way out in Rexdale, one of the first things we need is someone who is organized, don't you agree? By the way, you don't think Islington would say we stole him, do you? I wouldn't want —"

The ring of the telephone stopped him short. That was another part of the accustomed practice between him and Dale. It was a given in the office that most of the time, a telephone call meant a client call, and that took immediate precedence. At home it was always a contest to see who could outwait the other in picking up the receiver, but not here.

"Dunn and Dunn," Mike said into the receiver.

"Mikey boy!" the caller began. Mike Dunn knew instantly who it was. With a curl of distaste on his lips he looked up at Dale and mouthed, "Mac, at the service station." With his free hand he made a revolver sign at the telephone and pulled the trigger.

"Hello, Mac. What did you find?"

"Mikey! You feedin' this thing Purina maybe, 'stead of Texaco? Don't blame yuh! Yuh've gotta feed dog food to a dog!" He burst into a loud cackle at his own joke, as Mike's heart sank.

"Just how bad is it?" he asked.

"Well, Mikey, I got the fuel pump fixed. Stopped the leak, anyways. And the hood's unstuck now. But those automatic transmission buttons. I mean — it's nuts puttin' them in the center of the steering wheel! Look, I gotta take the steering column right out — the *whole steering column*! You're looking at another six, maybe eight hours' labor."

Mike sat silently, his forehead now cupped in the revolver hand.

"Hey, Mikey! You still there, boy?"

"That's *two!*" Mike said.

"What? Two what? What're yuh talkin' about?"

"Nothing." Mike sat up straight and cleared his throat. "Mac, don't touch the thing till I call you back, okay? I've got to think about this. I just may write it off."

"Your car, Mikey boy. Whatever you say. But listen, I gotta bill yuh for…"

"I know, I know." Mike cut him off. "Of course you do. I'll call you back before noon," he said, and hung up.

For a moment, silence hung heavy in the office, until Dale asked, "What *is* 'two,' anyway?"

There was silence for still another moment as Mike teetered on the edge of anger and self-recrimination, but gradually his innate good humor took over.

"You're the two," he said to his wife. "Number *one* is, you said not to buy one of those new Edsels last year. And how right you were! Mac practically owns us now. *Two* is right here." He pointed at the morning paper. "You said to sell our shares in Bowman Sugar when that fellow Castro took over in Cuba this summer, because he'd nationalize everything. I didn't agree but... thank heavens we did!"

Dale frowned just a little. "I'm not completely with you here. So we won one and lost one. We sold the sugar stock and we bought an Edsel. Maybe we should keep it. The thing's so bad it could be valuable someday! What I don't get is the *one, two*!"

Mike looked up at her. "*Threes*, Dale," he said. "Everything comes in threes, doesn't it? Now, you've been bang on twice already this morning. I'm just wondering what the third is going to be!"

Dale opened her mouth then closed it again, but not before Mike reacted. "Oh, no!" he said. "The third?"

Dale just nodded, then said, "Here. R. David Sloan."

What about R. David Sloan troubles Dale?

69

16

Witness to a Hit-and-Run

DIANE VAN HOOF GLANCED AT her watch. Five more minutes. That's when the mysterious caller — she'd called herself "Betty" — said she'd be here.

"I seen d'car what hit 'er," she'd said in that pinched-lip style that Diane had now become so used to hearing. "I'll tell yuz what I seen." (*H'oil tell yuz whud hoi seen.*) "But not on d'phone. D'Two Seasons. In d'café dere."

They had agreed on a time, and that's why Diane now sat on one of the hard wooden chairs in the lobby café of the Two Seasons Motor Hotel. The name of the place was typical of the ironic humor one encountered here in Labrador, particularly in the northern part, where humor was almost the only defence against the bleakness and — for anybody from "The South" — the overpowering sense of isolation.

Diane was from "The South," a local expression that, for all practical purposes, meant the rest of the world. There was no "north"; *they were the north!* And if there was an "east" or a "west," Diane hadn't heard of them yet. Only The South.

70

She nodded gratefully at the young waiter as he adjusted the blinds, having noticed that the sun was shining directly into her face. At the same time she couldn't help being a cop, and made careful note of how out of place the young man looked in this plaid-shirt, macho mining town, with his sallow, indoors complexion setting off the hair tied back in a ponytail.

Diane wanted to tell him to turn down the thermostat too. That was another thing she'd noticed right away, as soon as the RCMP had transferred her to Labrador. All the buildings were overheated. It was as though the idea was to cook away winter, which was by far the longer of Labrador's "two seasons."

At the training college in Regina, there'd been only one lecture on acclimatization, the art of adjusting to a new post. This was Diane's second full-time assignment in her seven-year career. She'd now had enough experience to confirm for her that more than one lecture was needed to prepare police officers for the little things.

Her first assignment had been with the drug squad in Windsor, and although she'd been well trained for the antidrug detail, no one had really warned her about the impact of working across the river from crime-ridden Detroit. Now Labrador. She'd been ready for the cold and for the isolation, but nobody had told her she'd have to oversee the spray-painting of giant snowbanks along the runways at the airport, so that pilots without radar could find it on sunny days when reflection made them blind.

And no one had told her how meaningless the restaurant menus would be by midwinter. Most of their food came from "The South," and if the fall stockup was miscalculated or the weather was bad enough to preclude air-freighted fresh food (at shocking prices), then the only certainty was caribou: caribou steak, caribou stew, caribou burger... One of the latter was sitting heavily in her stomach right now, the only item on the luncheon menu that the kitchen could fill.

"You be's d'new constable d'en?"

Diane started. For an instant, the memory of another lecture flashed across her mind: the one about the danger of daydreaming in uniform in a public place.

She stood up, embarrassed, and offered her hand. "You're Betty? Constable Diane Van Hoof." Betty was confused for a moment, then took the offered hand limply.

"Please sit down," Diane said. "Would you like some coffee? Tea?"

Betty nodded. "Sure. (*Shore.*) D'tea." She sat down opposite Diane. In her enormous parka, which was still tightly zipped, she overflowed the chair like a bundle of freight on a loading dock.

"I seen 'im 'it 'er. Blue Jimmy. Jus' like ours." (*Arz.*) "I can't stay long. Me 'usband'll be 'ome soon. 'E's in d'mine." (*D'moine.*) "Likes 'is meal quick when 'e gits 'ome. 'E said to phone yuz."

All this came out in a rapid burst that entirely belied Betty's behavior. She seemed slow, lethargic. Her appearance suggested that, and on the telephone her voice had, too. But now she seemed tense, very hyper.

The issue was a hit-and-run accident two days earlier that had the town in an uproar. A native child had been struck down on the road not far from the community school. The driver and the vehicle had disappeared. There were absolutely no clues, and until now, no witnesses. The child had been airlifted south and now hovered between life and death in a Montreal hospital. Diane knew that if the little girl died, the racial tensions that regularly simmered beneath the surface here could well blow up into a major problem. As it was, the potential for trouble was high no matter what the outcome.

"We lives near d'school." Betty was obviously not given to small talk or long preambles. "I'm settin' out d'supper and I hears a bump 'n' I looks out 'n' dere's d'kid lyin' dere. And she's a blue Jimmy drivin' away."

Despite the excitement of a possible breakthrough on this hit-and-run case, Diane couldn't suppress her fascination at how, by pinching her mouth forward at both edges, Betty could talk almost without moving her lips.

"Me 'usband said to tell yuz. 'E said to tell yuz, too, we don't want nothin' t'do with no court. 'Specially now he works d'swing fer a while startin' next week. But see, we's got one a' dem Jimmys, too. She's black. 'F anybody else seen it — d'kid, I mean — we don't want no mixup, me 'usband said."

Betty had unzipped her coat finally to take out a package of cigarettes. For the first time, Diane noticed the tobacco stains on the woman's fingers, then in a few seconds understood why. As soon as Betty lit up, she began reflexively flicking the filtered end with her thumb, holding the coal more or less over the ash tray.

Diane really wasn't sure how to approach the next stage. It was obvious Betty's message was complete, for she sat in silence, sipping tea with one hand and flicking the cigarette with the other, alternating sips with drags.

She decided on the direct approach. "It's very good of you to come forward. Now, of course, I'm going to have to talk to your husband, too. Then I'll have to see your Jimmy." She took out her notebook. "We're talking about a General Motors vehicle, right? The Jimmy? Does your husband drive it to work regularly?"

For an instant — only an instant — the teacup stopped en route to Betty's lips while she flicked furiously on the cigarette end. It wasn't much, but it was the confirmation Diane was looking for. She knew now she'd have to push even harder.

Specifically, what makes Diane Van Hoof suspicious of Betty's account of the hit-and-run accident?

73

17

The Plot at the Rockface

ON THE EASTERN FACE OF the mountain, up very, very high, the six men toiled numbly, side by side. Had he bothered to go to the extreme southeastern corner of the compound and look up (which he never did), the commandant would have been able to just make out the six tiny figures with their guard. He would not have been able to see exactly what it was they were working at, but, then, he didn't need to. He knew.

The labor was backbreaking. As each man heaved and swung his sledgehammer he would grunt, as though a hammer could never connect with the rockface unless pushed there by the expulsion of air through the larynx. The men's bodies shuddered with each blow on the unyielding rock. *Thunk! thunk thunk thunk! thunk-a-thunk! Thunk!* There was no rhythm. Just lift. Then smash. Try to lift again. *Thunk!* Hang on till the next break. There would be water to drink. Then the tongues that felt like dead tree branches would cool, and shrink enough for easier breathing.

Most of the time the hammers just bounced off the rock.

Then every once in a while a crack would appear, a hairline. More pounding. The crack would open and become a fissure. Still more pounding. Finally a piece would break off and fall to the narrow platform at their feet. When there were enough of these, the guard would tap the barrel of his rifle against the water bucket: the signal to load the wheelbarrows and wrestle them down along the narrow winding ledge to dump the pieces into the gorge below so that more men could pound these pieces into smaller pieces. From there the pieces went into dilapidated coal cars and were freighted — no one really knew where. Down to the coast, that much the prisoners knew. Probably all the way to Dubrovnik.

Negotiating the wheelbarrows down the twisting ledge was easier than the pounding, but much more dangerous. A wrong step and it was over the edge, straight down to certain death. Even if only the wheelbarrow slipped over, it was the end for whoever had been pushing it. The barrow could not be retrieved, so the Romanian guards simply stood the prisoner on the spot where it had gone over and gave him a choice: jump or be pushed.

Just yesterday it had happened again, and the prisoner had jumped. He even gave the guards the finger first, but no one from the work party on the rockface believed the guards understood the gesture. They were too stupid.

Certainly the one they called Igor was. A foul-smelling brute with a lower lip that drooped so far it obscured most of his chin. He had an incredibly hairy face, which even the fanatical SS officer assigned to the camp could never get the man to shave. None of the prisoners had the faintest idea what Igor's real name might be. No one wanted to know. A name personalizes. Makes connections that in turn make it harder to hate. Or kill.

Igor tapped the bucket. The six men dropped their hammers and moved to the wheelbarrows with the stooped, robotlike movement that humans acquire when their lives are being crushed by mindless, exhausting labor. Except for one very tall man. He walked a little straighter — but not too much straighter. He was very careful not to draw unnecessary attention to himself. But clearly he was not as deadened as the rest.

That's because he had joined the group only this morning to bring the complement back up to six. The Romanian guards and their SS adviser knew him as Vlad Kljuc (number 475216), a partisan and a Communist from somewhere here in the republic of Montenegro. His real name was Trevor Hawkes, and he was formerly a machinist from Bristol, and now a member of His Majesty's Special Air Service, the SAS. Just prior to his "capture," he had graduated from the Allies' mysterious Camp X outside Toronto, in Canada.

Trevor Hawkes was here for one purpose only: to free and bring to Dubrovnik, by any means possible, one Peter Nova, the man now walking just ahead of him toward the wheelbarrows. Nova, Trevor knew (and it was all he knew), was a Slovene from Ljubljanca, who had a reputation in the Yugoslavian resistance as the one Communist leader who wanted to bring Communist and royalist factions together peacefully. He had been teaching at the University of Zagreb until 1941, when the Nazis had moved into Yugoslavia. Two years later they scooped up all the known Communists at the university and brought them up here to the camp on Kuk. Now the Allies wanted Nova badly. Trevor Hawkes had no idea why, but that was the least of his concerns right now. Right now he was simply following Peter Nova, waiting for an opportunity to do more talking.

The trip with the wheelbarrows was free of incident, and when Igor brought them all back to the rockface he signaled a rest, waiting in slow-witted anticipation for what he'd seen happen every single time before. It happened again.

The six men who had worked side by side with the hammers on the narrow and dangerous little ledge, and who followed one another carefully and silently to the dumping site, now sat three against three like adversaries. Which, indeed, is what they were.

The SS adviser — no fool — insisted that every work party must number six: three Communists, followers of the partisan Josip Tito, and three royalists, Draza Mihajlovic's men. Left alone and rested, they were as likely to set on one another as on their Axis captors.

Until three months ago the two sides, royalist and Communist, had put aside their differences, albeit uneasily, to face the common enemy. But now, in spite of the efforts of leaders like Peter Nova, their civil war was open and vicious, with their respective forces often trying to go around the Axis occupiers to get at one another. This kind of passion, properly used, made camp control a lot easier. Facing Trevor and Nova, therefore, were three Serbian royalists — two farmers and a civil servant from Belgrade.

"So just *how* do you propose to accomplish this dramatic scheme?" Nova looked straight ahead as he spit the words at Trevor.

For the big SAS man the question was a breakthrough, despite the acrimony in the tone. Until this morning Nova had had no idea who Trevor was, and certainly didn't know that his capture was really a deliberate insertion. But the question meant Trevor had been accepted now, however warily. What had tipped the balance was Trevor's having mentioned, during the previous rest, some very private, personal facts that had been supplied by Nova's sister. So far so good. Now he had to get the wiry little man to agree to an escape attempt.

"The basket," Trevor replied, leaning forward to massage his ankles.

"The basket? Go out in the basket? You're a fool!" Nova hissed loudly, then realized he had attracted Igor's attention. His face turned very serious. He pointed to the wheelbarrows and spoke to Igor in Serb.

"Your wife has just given birth to pigs again."

The royalists were suddenly alert. None of them looked up, but one smiled a little. As for Igor, it was obvious he couldn't follow. He looked back and forth from Nova to the wheelbarrows as a string of drool slipped over the edge of his ponderous lower lip, heading for his waist. He waved the rifle barrel in a dismissive gesture. It broke the string.

"Either you're an idiot or you think I am." Nova was talking to Trevor again. "It won't work in the first place, because you need *two* men to get the basket across. One can't pull it up. It won't hold three and I won't leave *him!*" Nova pointed with his eyes at the man on his right, the third of the Communist trio, then added, in an almost defeated way, "Those three over there will cut his throat the instant they've got him alone."

Trevor's reply unnerved Nova. "I know," he said.

With a jerk of his head, Igor seemed to remember why they were there and tapped the water bucket. Rest was over. So was dialogue. At the next break, their rations were brought up by two other guards. In their presence no one dared to break the rule of silence, for these two had a leg up on Igor, and it wasn't until after the first trip down the ledge with the wheelbarrows that Trevor could continue.

"We all go. The royals, too. All six of us," he said.

"*In the basket?*" Nova still didn't believe Trevor. "*All* of us? I suppose two at a time and your real name is Noah!"

The "basket" was a means of transport across the deep valley that local inhabitants had devised, who knows how many years before. It was a rope-and-pulley affair, with one terminus just up the path from the rockface where the six men were working. Its power was human strength. Two adults — all it would hold — were needed to pull it across to the other side because of the upward angle. At that terminus, another narrow pathway snaked up for a short distance to a pass and then disappeared. The return to this side needed only one person. The basket rolled back most of the way, but its weight caused the rope to sag so that from about fifty feet out, it needed a passenger to pull it in the rest of the way.

The SS officer had ordered it cut down, but because he never came up here, and because the Romanian guards were mountain people and liked to amuse themselves with it, the basket still hung there, a tantalizing sight to those prisoners who dared glance up the path to look at it. Even so, there had never been a single escape from the camp, via the basket or by any other method, because of the trackless mountain wilderness, sure death to anyone who didn't know where — or how — to go.

Trevor was unruffled by Nova's objections. "I have a way," he said.

Nova was silent for a minute. "What about Igor? I suppose you're going to —"

His sentence stopped there as he followed Trevor's gaze to the hammers. But now his tone changed from one of petulant objection to simple skepticism.

"The royalists," he continued, raising his chin at the three, who were, as usual, ranged opposite. "What if they don't want to go? Or if they want to go some other way?"

Trevor looked straight at Nova for the first time. "Do you think they'd want to stay and explain what happened to Igor? And there's only one other way out if they stay on this side, and that's back down through camp. Unless they're mountain climbers, and they don't look like it to me."

Now Nova was really interested.

"When would we go?" he wanted to know.

"First time there's fog. My guess is tomorrow morning. We should have gone today! It would have been perfect!"

"But then…"

Nova's next objection was anticipated. "I know the way." Trevor said. "That's why I'm here. We go to Dubrovnik. You'll be met there. It's tricky, but I've been a climber for years. I can get us down if you do what I say. All that's needed now is for you to explain to them."

Peter Nova stared at the ground for just a moment. His nostrils flared slightly as he took a deep breath. Then he began to speak to Igor in Serb, all the while pointing to his shoes, then pulling up his pantleg and flapping it in a demonstration for the puzzled guard.

"You three," he said. "Listen to me. We're getting out. Escaping. All of us. The new one here... *don't look at me! Look at the guard!* Now hear me out."

Igor's gaze followed Nova's pointing from shoe to pantleg and back again. However he interpreted it, he didn't like it, and tapped the water bucket.

Nova concluded with "I'll say more next rest period."

Had Igor been any brighter he might have noticed a new animation in the step of his work party as they filed back to the rockface. Even the third Communist, who had not been able to hear all of Trevor's presentation and who could not speak Serb, seemed to be infected by a sense that something was up.

The mood almost cracked at the next and last break. There was another problem.

"It still won't work," Nova said to Trevor. "Even if the royalists cooperate, we just can't let ourselves be outnumbered. Either this side or over there. Feelings are too deep. They'll slit our throats."

Trevor's calm never shifted. "I've thought of that, too," he said.

What is Trevor Hawkes's plan for getting the two sets of enemies across the deep valley, given all the problems Peter Nova has brought up?

18

Regina Versus Kirk

12 March

Memo to Wm. Seeley,
      c/o Seeley, Leeballoux, & Trace

From Nat Neffer Transcription Services

Regarding **Regina Versus Kirk**

Bill,

Attached is a copy of the transcript from Day 2, as you requested (minus pages 18 through 20). I have not included Judge Benoit's opening caution to the jury because it's word for word, as on Day 1.

    I apologize again for the missing pages at the end. That's when the machine broke, as I told you on the phone. It should be up and running tomorrow and I'll fax the rest to you ASAP.

Gloria

BENOÎT: Call your next witness, Mr. Ford.

FORD: The Crown calls Dr. Finlay J. Quinn.

(Quinn sworn in)

FORD: Please state your name and occupation for the record.

QUINN: Finlay J. Quinn, doctor of forensic pathology in private practice.

FORD: Dr. Quinn, did you attend at the death of Thorvald Heintzmann, on request of the Bayview Homicide Division?

QUINN: Yes.

FORD: Is this your report of findings?

QUINN: Yes.

FORD: Your Honor, the Crown wishes to enter Dr. Quinn's pathology report as an exhibit.

(Report entered as Exhibit A)

FORD: Now, Dr. Quinn, could you tell the court what you established as the time and cause of death?

QUINN: Using accepted forensic procedures, and given that I was able to attend fairly shortly after the shooting, I was able to determine that death occurred between 4:45 and 5:15 P.M. on July 14 of last year. The victim died of three gunshot wounds to the chest. They were fired from a .25 caliber weapon, and all three bullets passed through the body. The spent bullets lay on the floor by the south wall of the room.

FORD: They didn't lodge in the wall?

QUINN: No. It's not likely that shells of that caliber would have enough remaining force to do so after passing through an adult chest.

FORD: For the bullets to pass through the body then, the person shooting would have to be standing fairly close?

QUINN: Within six or seven feet, in my opinion.

FORD: Was death instant?

QUINN: Within one to three minutes in my opinion.

FORD: That's all I have, Your Honor.

BENOÎT: Mr. Seeley?

SEELEY: Dr. Quinn, these three gunshot wounds, were they grouped on Mr. Heintzmann's chest?

QUINN: Grouped?

SEELEY: Close together.

QUINN: One shot went in directly below the sternum. Brushed it. Another was about five inches to the left and up forty-five degrees. The third was three inches below that... sort of at seven o'clock from the second wound. The precise measurements are in my report. There's a diagram, too.

SEELEY: Is it possible to tell which one was the most effective killing shot?

QUINN: Yes. The third one I mentioned. It did the most damage to the heart.

SEELEY: And it was the third one fired?

QUINN: That's not possible to tell for certain.

SEELEY: So that particular shot could have been the second or even the first one fired.

QUINN: Yes.

SEELEY: Thank you. No more.

BENOÎT: If there's no redirect, Mr. Ford, then call your next witness.

FORD: Thank you, Your Honor. The Crown calls Chief Inspector Jack Regan.

(Regan sworn in)

FORD: Please state your full name and occupation for the record.

REGAN: Chief Inspector John Anthony Regan, Bayview Homicide Division.

FORD: It is correct that you are the chief investigating officer in the murder of Thorvald Heintzmann?

REGAN: That's right.

FORD: Would you give us a summary of your initial involvement?

REGAN: I'm going to refer to my notes, okay?

BENOÎT: Any objection, Mr. Seeley?

SEELEY: None.

BENOÎT: Very well, proceed, Inspector Regan.

REGAN: On the evening of Saturday, 14 July of last year, I took a telephone call at 6:00 P.M. citing an emergency at 267 Thornbay Avenue. The caller identified herself as Royal Orchard.

BENOÎT: Excuse me, Inspector. That's a person?

REGAN: The housekeeper in the residence. Royal is her first name. The surname is Orchard.

BENOÎT: Carry on.

REGAN: I attended at the address at 6:10 P.M., where I found the body of Thorvald Heintzmann.

FORD: Was the victim dead when —

SEELEY: Objection. Victim.

FORD: Your Honor, it's clear that Thorvald Heintzmann died by violent means. To refer to him therefore as a victim is certainly not out of order.

BENOÎT: Gentlemen. I acknowledge that there may well be some uncertainties in this case, but the fact that the deceased was slain by a hand other than his own is not in doubt. I don't think there's anything wrong with "victim" Mr. Seeley. Overruled.

FORD: Was Thorvald Heintzmann dead when you arrived?

REGAN: I could not find a pulse and he was not breathing.

FORD: Before you describe the scene I have here photographs of the scene, which I would like to enter as exhibits. My friend here has copies.

BENOÎT: Any problem, Mr. Seeley?

(Seeley shakes his head)

BENOÎT: For the record, Mr. Seeley.

SEELEY: No objection.

BENOÎT: Very well, the clerk will enter a series of nine — *ten* — photographs. These will be Exhibits B-1 through B-10. Carry on.

FORD: Inspector Regan, as the members of the jury examine

the photographs, perhaps you could tell us where the body was when you came in?

REGAN: The body was in a study. This is at the end of a straight entrance hallway leading from the front door. The study is the last room on the right. The body was inside the room, approximately in the middle, lying face down in a north-south aspect, with the feet toward the door at the north. The body was about ten feet from the door and ten feet from the opposite wall, and lying almost against a desk on the west wall.

FORD: So the victim was shot by someone standing in the doorway to the room or just inside?

REGAN: It would be hard to conclude otherwise.

FORD: Chief Inspector, from your considerable experience in investigations of this nature, and given that you have already heard Dr. Quinn testify that Thorvald Heintzmann died one to three minutes after being shot, is it your opinion that he died where he fell?

REGAN: No, not quite. As you can see on the photographs, there is a patch of blood on the floor to the victim's left. Level with his torso. It's my conclusion that he fell onto his back first, but then rolled over.

FORD: You mean in the agony of violent death?

REGAN: I don't think so. It's pretty clear he had a purpose in mind.

FORD: A purpose?

REGAN: I believe the victim was trying to write a message. He had a pen in his hand, as the photograph shows — one of those big felt marker pens — and a piece of stationery was under the hand. There was more stationery of exactly the same type on top of the desk. It was disorderly, as though a hand or something had pulled across the pile.

FORD: So you feel that Mr. Heintzmann rolled over and tried to pull down a piece of paper and a pen from the desk so he could write a message.

REGAN: Yes.

FORD: But he died before he could write anything?

REGAN: Not quite. The letter K was written on the sheet on the floor.

FORD: The letter K? That's the same letter that starts the name of Kirk.

SEELEY: Objection.

BENOÎT: Mr. Ford, you know better than that.

FORD: Apologize, Your Honor.

(Sheet of paper and pen entered as exhibits C and D)

FORD: Inspector Regan, I have a certificate here. Excuse me, Your Honor, I neglected to mention this exhibit.

BENOÎT: Thank you. The clerk will enter Exhibit E, Firearm Registration Certificate.

FORD: Would you please tell the court, Inspector, what name appears on this certificate?

REGAN: Devon Kirk.

FORD: And what is the weapon registered?

REGAN: A Remington .25 caliber five-shot revolver.

FORD: I have two more exhibits at this point, Your Honor.

(Exhibits F and G entered)

FORD: Would you describe Exhibit F to the jury, Inspector?

REGAN: It's a book of matches. The front cover says Olde Thornhill Bar, written in three lines. On the back is a telephone number. Inside, the name of the bar is repeated on the upper flap. There are two matches removed under the Ls. On the striking band there is —

FORD: That's fine, Inspector. Where did you find this book of matches?

REGAN: On the desk near the stationery.

FORD: And would you tell the jury what Exhibit G is, Inspector, and where you found it?

REGAN: It's a gold ring. What appears to be a man's wedding ring. It was on Mr. Heintzmann's desk, under the stationery.

FORD: Would you read the name inscribed on the inside of the ring?

REGAN: Devon Kirk.

FORD: Thank you. No more questions.

BENOÎT: Mr. Seeley?

SEELEY: Inspector Regan, what was revealed in the fingerprint analysis of this ring?

REGAN: It wouldn't have been possible to get prints off the ring. It's got an etched surface and —

SEELEY: Then what of the book of matches and the stationery?

REGAN: Only the victim's prints on the stationery. On the matches, his again and another print. From a Mr. Mellish.

BENOÎT: Just a minute.

FORD: If I may, Your Honor, Mr. Mellish is our next witness.

BENOÎT: Very well.

SEELEY: And in the room? Fingerprints?

REGAN: Again, Thorvald Heintzmann's, and those of Royal Orchard.

SEELEY: No other prints of any kind?

REGAN: No.

SEELEY: By the way. The ring. The stationery was piled on top of it?

REGAN: No, not quite. When the stationery was disordered — sort of pulled over — those pulled-over sheets covered up the ring.

SEELEY: I see. Inspector Regan, I have here a report.

FORD: Objection. Is counsel entering new evidence?

SEELEY: Your Honor, I intend to submit this as an exhibit.

BENOÎT: A bit unusual, Mr. Seeley, to enter exhibits in cross-examination.

SEELEY: My friend here established the issue of the murder weapon. This is a related matter, and the police officer is the ideal corroborating witness. Unless you'll permit me to call him as my witness, too?

87

BENOÎT: You know that's not possible. Okay. Go ahead. But it had better be relevant.

(Exhibit H entered)

SEELEY: Would you describe this report for the court, Inspector?

REGAN: It's a police department Form 517B. Theft under $500.

SEELEY: Go on.

REGAN: It reports the theft of a Remington .25 caliber hand-gun from the home of Devon Kirk.

SEELEY: And what is the date of that report?

REGAN: April 9 of last year.

SEELEY: I see. April 9. Now, Inspector Regan, was there anything else in the room we have been talking about, or on Mr. Heintzmann's person?

REGAN: Just the ordinary things. His wallet, a pack of cigarettes, some change. That kind of thing.

SEELEY: So the only really unusual things are the ring and the so-called attempted message.

FORD: Objection. Counsel is leading.

BENOÎT: Sustained.

SEELEY: With regard to Exhibit C, the... uh... message, what letter follows the letter K?

REGAN: Why... no letter. There's just a K.

SEELEY: A capital K or a small K?

REGAN: You can't really tell.

SEELEY: I see. You can't tell. Your Honor, I have no other questions at this time, but I reserve the right to recall this witness for further cross.

BENOÎT: Mr. Ford?

FORD: No objection,.

BENOÎT: I think perhaps we should adjourn for lunch at this point.

FORD: Your Honor, my next witness should be brief. He's employed and has to work this afternoon. With the court's indulgence...

BENOÎT: All right.

FORD: Crown calls Mr. Muggs Mellish.

BENOÎT: Muggs?

FORD: That's what I have, Your Honor.

(Mellish is sworn)

BENOÎT: Just a minute, Mr. Mellish. Is Muggs a correct first name?

MELLISH: It's how I'm known, sir. My given name is Montmorency.

BENOÎT: I think I understand. Carry on, Mr. Ford.

FORD: Mr. Mellish, you are a bartender at the Olde Thornhill Bar?

MELLISH: Yeah. Yes.

FORD: And were you at work on Saturday, July 14, last year?

MELLISH: I worked the noon to 8:00 P.M.

FORD: Did you see the accused, Devon Kirk, on that day?

MELLISH: Yeah, he's a regular. Was in about two o'clock that day. Stayed maybe an hour.

FORD: That's all, thank you.

BENOÎT: Will you be brief, Mr. Seeley?

SEELEY: Just two questions, Your Honor. Mr. Mellish, how is it you remember Mr. Kirk being in the bar that day?

MELLISH: Well, like I said, he's a regular. And he had his base-ball uniform on that day. Kinda stood out.

SEELEY: Did Mr. Heintzmann ever visit the bar?

MELLISH: Yeah, he was a regular, too. But if he was in that day I never seen him.

SEELEY: Thank you.

(Noon recess)

BENOÎT: Mr. Ford.

FORD: I have one more witness. Ms. Royal Orchard.

(Orchard sworn)

FORD: You are the housekeeper for the Heintzmann family?

ORCHARD: Yes.

89

FORD: Prior to the mur — the death of Thorvald Heintzmann, how long had you been employed there?

ORCHARD: Three months.

FORD: Your statement says you discovered the body. Tell us how.

ORCHARD: Saturday's my day off every second week. Other week's Thursday. I was off, but I came back to get a jacket and my smokes. Me and Vern — that's my boyfriend — we were going to go to the drive-in.

FORD: What time was this?

ORCHARD: Just before six.

FORD: Who else was in the house at this time?

ORCHARD: Nobody as far as I know.

FORD: And when you discovered the body of Mr. Heintzmann, you called the police?

ORCHARD: Yeah.

FORD: From the phone in the study?

ORCHARD: I never went in there. I ran to the kitchen and phoned.

FORD: Where was your boyfriend all this time?

ORCHARD: He was waiting in the car.

FORD: Thank you. Your witness.

SEELEY: Did you come in the front door that Saturday, Ms. Orchard?

ORCHARD: Yes. I… I don't normally, but I thought there was no one home, see, and so… Anyway, I didn't think it would matter.

SEELEY: Do you live in the residence?

ORCHARD: No, actually, I live in the annex, sort of next door.

SEELEY: Sort of next door. I see. Well, what were you doing in the main house then?

ORCHARD: My jacket. I was pretty sure it was in the kitchen.

SEELEY: The kitchen is near the study?

ORCHARD: Not really.

SEELEY: Then why did you go that way?

ORCHARD: Well, there's two ways to get there from the front. I just went that way, that's all.

SEELEY: Um-hmm. That is all. Oh. Was the front door locked?

ORCHARD: Yes. It's always locked.

SEELEY: You have a key?

ORCHARD: Yes.

SEELEY: Is the back door always locked?

ORCHARD: Not usually.

SEELEY: Was it on that day?

ORCHARD: I don't know. I doubt it — everybody came in that way.

SEELEY: Ms. Orchard, are you right- or left-handed?

ORCHARD: It's funny. I'm both, sort of. One of those am-am-

SEELEY: Ambidextrous?

ORCHARD: Yeah. That's it.

SEELEY: No more questions.

FORD: That's the last Crown witness, Your Honor.

BENOÎT: Mr. Seeley, you indicate only one witness on your pretrial advisory?

SEELEY: Yes, Your Honor. The accused, Mr. Devon Kirk.

(Accused sworn and identified)

SEELEY: Mr. Kirk, how long had you known Thorvald Heintzmann?

KIRK: Over twenty years.

SEELEY: Know him well?

KIRK: I was the best man at his second wedding — also a witness at the subsequent divorce. We played softball every Saturday in the summer. Fishing trip once a year. Belonged to the same gun club. Yes, I knew him well.

SEELEY: Tell us about the gun club.

KIRK: We both are... *were* members of the York Targets. It's a club for competitive target shooting. Handguns. Thorry and I both qualified at marksman level two years ago.

SEELEY: And did you play softball together on July 14 last year?

KIRK: Yes. Our game was at noon. Thorry played first base. I pitched, same as always. A lot of people saw that.

SEELEY: How is it that your wedding ring was in Mr. Heintzmann's study that afternoon?

KIRK: The umpire wouldn't let me pitch with my wedding ring on. This was kind of a delicate game. Bit of a grudge match. So Thorry kept it for me. I'd left my equipment bag in my car. I guess I forgot to ask for it back and he forgot to give it to me.

SEELEY: Mr. Kirk. Did you shoot Thorvald Heintzmann?

KIRK: Absolutely not. He was my best friend. I had no reason to.

SEELEY: Thank you, that's all. My friend likely has questions.

FORD: Yes, I do. Mr. Kirk, where were you at 5:00 P.M. on the afternoon of 14 July last year?

KIRK: I was at home asleep.

FORD: And is there anyone who can corroborate that?

KIRK: No... no.

FORD: Mr. Kirk, you smoke, don't you?

KIRK: Yes, I do.

        Bill,
            Machine broke down here. You're missing
        the rest of Ford's cross- and both your
        summations to the jury.
        G.

Although there are a number of incriminating details that John Ford will no doubt emphasize in his summation, Bill Seeley should be able to raise reasonable doubt over a number of issues. Which did you notice?

19

Danger at the Border

WHEN FRANK MOUNT CRAWLED OUT from underneath the van with a grim look on his face and shook his head, Gene Fewster was tempted to make a crack about repairing "magic wagons" with incantations instead of spare parts. He didn't, though. Wisecracks weren't his style, even when things were going well. And right now they were going very badly. Besides, his wife, Ann, for whose benefit he'd have said it, was totally preoccupied at the moment. She was down the road a bit with Connie Mount. They were watching their portly companion, Juan Tomas, emerge from the jungle growth into which the road disappeared.

"*Norte,*" Gene Fewster heard him say, jerking a hitchhiker style thumb toward the roadway on his right.

"*Norte, norte,*" Juan Tomas said twice more.

That clearly upset Bluebeard. He was a recently acquired traveling companion and Ann had chosen his name. No one had any illusions whatever about there being humor in it. None was intended; the man wasn't any more amusing than their predicament. Bluebeard was Bluebeard because of the eyepatch that crowned an unbelievably repulsive scar across his hairy left cheek. The ridge on the scar spoke plainly that this wound had known neither stitches nor surgical clamps, perhaps not even disinfectant. The process of healing had not been easy.

Yet the scar was completely upstaged by something that gave the name "Bluebeard" a discomforting credibility. It was his machete. Huge, like a cutlass, it was bigger than anything they'd seen in Honduras or here in Guatemala. He carried it not in his belt or in a sheath, but in his right hand, with the flat of the wicked blade resting in the crook of his arm. Like Bluebeard's sword.

No sooner had Juan Tomas spoken than Bluebeard unleashed a string of angry Spanish that no one understood except, of course, the intended receiver. The chubby Juan was entirely unintimidated; his toothy, good-natured smile never changed. But then, it never had since he'd joined them. Ann was convinced he had once been an extra in a B movie. Connie was sure he even slept with the smile on his face. Frank had actually tiptoed around the campfire last night to look.

"*Norte*," Juan Tomas said once more, and waved Frank and Gene toward him with one hand, Connie and Ann with the other.

"*Señores. Señoras.*" Juan Tomas was going to hold a conference. Bluebeard did not appear to be invited. The little group gathered around Juan. B-movie type or not, Gene thought, the little guy was sure likable. And he didn't carry a machete, either!

"*Señores,*" Juan Tomas began, and then as though he suddenly remembered he was addressing *norteamericanos* with their strange notions, he quickly added, "*Señoras.*"

"*Norte*... safe. Good, eh? Up..." He pointed back up the road from which he'd come. "Up de road. I see... *gafas.*" He put his fists to his eyes and swung his head left, then right.

"*¡Sí!*" Juan Tomas's grin got wider. "*¡Sí, binoculares!*"

He turned right around and in his hitchhiker thumb style

pointed to a spot up the road where the valley walls began to get very high.

"*I see de son… De son go on…*"

Again Ann was the first to understand. "Reflection! He saw the sun reflect off the lenses of the binoculars!"

The others were right with her.

"Soldiers?" Gene asked.

For the first time, Juan Tomas's grin slipped ever so little.

"*¿Soldados?*" He shrugged. "*¿Bandidos?*" The grin dissipated even further. "Much gonnes, *señores. Gonnes.*"

Gene's breakfast lurched in his stomach. They had gotten so close — so close to the border and safety! Now this.

Two months ago, the Fewsters and the Mounts had begun a once-in-a-decade vacation. That they were in Guatemala was a compromise that for the most part had turned out to be a splendid success. Frank and Gene were avid Enduro bikers and they had wanted to traverse Panama, Atlantic to Pacific, on their off-road machines. Connie and Ann were equally avid about birding. They wanted to join a guided birding tour of Costa Rica. The compromise was an off-roading/birding/camping circuit of Honduras and Guatemala in a Toyota Land Cruiser. What had begun with grave misgivings on everyone's part turned out to be the most original, the most exciting, the most rewarding vacation any of them could possibly have imagined. Until three days ago.

On the outskirts of Antigua, on their way back to Guatemala City for the plane home, they were stopped by soldiers of the Guerilla Army of the Poor. In flawless English the leader told them there was fighting in Guatemala City and that the airport was closed. With perfect politeness he told them that to go anywhere near the city would be far too dangerous. He also took the Land Cruiser.

In Antigua they managed to rent a battered Chrysler Magic Wagon. Their plan — which they did not share with the renters — was to travel north on highway 1 to San Marcos, then across the Mexican border to Tapachula, a city large enough to have flights to Mexico City.

The plan had worked smoothly. In fact, the only unusual thing that happened was acquiring Juan Tomas on the next day. He appeared in a little village just as they were paying for gasoline at what passed for the local service station. After remonstrating with the dealer in very loud Spanish, he held out his hand to receive from that worthy a generous number of *quetzals,* which he promptly handed to Frank. It was obvious that he had saved them from being cheated. During the subsequent attempt at thanks and conversation, accomplished through an amalgam of Spanish, broken English, much pointing and hand-waving, Juan Tomas heard Ann say "San Marcos." At that point, the smile began, and he simply got into the back seat of the van. Both Juan and the smile had been there ever since.

Whether or not he made the Mounts and the Fewsters uncomfortable was soon irrelevant, for it was an hour or two later that soldiers appeared again. The first group was a truck convoy that barreled by them going south down the highway. They paid the van no attention at all.

Shortly after, they were stopped by four soldiers at a roadblock. There was no question that something was heating up. However, Juan Tomas seemed to charm this group, bestowing his smile and a string of Spanish on each in turn, and before long they were under way again.

"No... no... no..." Juan couldn't find the word he wanted so he smiled and said, "I feex."

And he had guaranteed his seat in the van.

Yet at the next roadblock, even Juan's charm had no power. There were only two soldiers at this stop, but there was no question that this time there was trouble. One of them was drunk; the other — in everyone's opinion, he might as well have been. They were ordered out of the van, and Juan was told, in language that made them all wince even without translation, to shut up. He did. And the smile disappeared, too. But then, as though there were some providence in charge, an officer suddenly appeared in a pickup truck and motioned the two into the back. Just as quickly and without a word, the three tore off down the road. The vacationers were safe again for the time being, but the incident scared them off the highway. They were beginning to feel more like refugees than tourists.

They went on, but by dusk they were utterly lost. They had taken so many turns and reversed so often, and had followed so many little dirt trails, that they no longer had any idea where they were. Only a vague trust in Juan Tomas kept their spirits up, for his smile came back to stay, and every time they took a turn more or less north he would shake his head and say,

"¡Sí, San Marcos!"

It was when they turned off the road to make camp that things really began to fall apart. Beginning with the van. Frank was driving and he didn't see the hole. However, they all heard and felt the result. A broken axle.

Connie was first to pick up the next concern. For some time the group had seen that to continue their press northward they were going to have to drive through a valley ahead. Now Connie saw in the gathering darkness that just inside the head of the valley the road forked.

"San Marcos?" she said to Juan, pointing first to one road, then the other.

"Sí, San Marcos," he replied, pointing to the left fork. And then he repeated "San Marcos" while pointing to the other!

"You mean they *both* go to San Marcos?" Frank asked him.

Whether Juan Tomas understood, or even whether he answered, was lost in Ann's scream. Bluebeard appeared. Silently and entirely without warning right behind her! It was a scream of fright, and Bluebeard must have realized this for he held up his left hand in the universal "okay… okay" gesture and backed up a few steps. He tried to smile, but the scar made him grotesque. No one could remember later whether Juan Tomas had spoken.

After Bluebeard made eating motions, saying "*Por favor*" a couple of times, the anxiety level dropped a bit, although the meal was eaten in the darkness and in complete and uneasy silence. When it became apparent that Bluebeard had no intention of leaving, the uneasiness turned to outright discomfort. Frank offered the consideration that Bluebeard was probably a good guy who just looked bad, but there were no seconders. They spent the night sleeping in shifts.

At the first appearance of the morning sun, Bluebeard was front and center for breakfast, which again did nothing for comfort or conversation, especially since Juan Tomas had left. He'd stuffed a tortilla in his mouth and said, "I… ah… look, eh? San Marcos. I look." Then he disappeared up the right fork.

It was just under a half-hour later that he re-emerged with his advice to take the other road — the left fork: advice that had so stirred up Bluebeard.

Gene stared briefly at the two men, Bluebeard glaring and Juan Tomas smiling, then looked at the fork. "I think," he said almost absently to Frank, "we'd better opt for beast over beauty. I'm for taking the right fork."

Frank tried to peer through the jungle at first one road, then the other. "I agree," he said finally.

Do you agree? Is there any reason for Frank and Connie and Ann and Gene to disregard and act counter to Juan Tomas's advice?

20

The Case of the Strange
Hieroglyphs

DESPITE THE FACT SHE'D LIVED more than half her life in
North America, Deirdre Breton steadfastly refused to use
Canadian or American idiom when the opportunity arose
for the British style. Especially if the British choice was just a
bit arcane. That's why she told Robin Karmo to shine his
"electric torch" to the "off" side. It confused Karmo for a few
seconds, and that gave her just a touch of satisfaction. Karmo
might be a brilliant archaeologist, but he was also an obnoxious know-it-all, and Deirdre, along with everyone else on the
dig, was tacitly committed to chipping away at his ebullient
self-confidence.

"The *off* side," she repeated, then deliberately allowed just a
touch of weariness to shade her voice — somewhat like an
impatient tutor. "Your *right* side. The hand that's holding it."

"I know." Karmo didn't miss a beat. "The switch is stuck.
Who requisitioned these *flashlights*, anyway? It sure wasn't me!"

Deirdre bit off her response. Karmo was clearly a no-win
case. Instead she focused her light beam on the hieroglyph, or

what appeared to be a hieroglyph — the symbol over the archway that had started this little exchange in the first place. It was the third unusual marking they'd seen since entering the newly discovered maze of tunnels early this morning. All three of them over archways.

They both peered at it in deep concentration, their progressively unsubtle rivalry temporarily set aside in its mystery. Karmo's light now overlapped Deirdre's so that they could see the stonemason's work very clearly.

"Except for those opposing directionals at the bottom," Karmo said, as much to himself as to Deirdre, "there's no resemblance at all to the first two."

"Mmm… not in concept, anyway," Deirdre replied. "But I'll wager it's the work of the same tradesman. That's his mark on the bottom, I'm sure. The opposing arrows."

Deirdre turned off her flashlight. Her electric torch. So did Karmo. The only light now came from the miner's hats they were wearing.

"But you have to agree…" she went on. Her tone was no longer combative. The argument, for the present, anyway, was over; now there was simply dialogue between two scholars with a mutual interest. "You agree, surely, that these are direction signs. Code. They're clues to the route we should take — whatever's at the end."

Karmo made a face. Agreement under any circumstances never came easily for him. "Well, I doubt they have religious significance," he said, "although I'm surprised we haven't encountered anything with a burial or afterlife sense by now. But, then, probably these tunnels — this part, anyway — were all robbed clean centuries ago."

Deirdre waited patiently for him to finish speculating, and trained her helmet light onto the floor. "The first one," she said, getting back to her point, "the one we thought might be a crude type of crown..." She bent over and in the dust traced the symbol in the patch of light.

"Definitely not Phoenician," Karmo said with authority.

He was more expert than Deirdre on the Phoenicians, and she thought he brought them up far more often than necessary, but she ignored the implicit offer of further explanation and returned doggedly to her argument. "This... uh... hieroglyph was over the first archway we came to. The first point where the tunnel divided into two."

The light from Karmo's hat bobbed up and down just a bit. Agreement.

"And we took the one to the right," she continued. "Your idea."

The bobbing was more vigorous this time.

She went on. "Now, the passage from that point was straight except for two very definite turns, the first ninety degrees, the second about half that. First left, then acute right. And definite turns. Nothing gradual."

Karmo took up the retracing. "Yes, then we came to the second archway, where it divided in two again."

This time Deirdre's hat beam was bobbing. Karmo didn't seem to notice. "And that arch," he said, "had this one." He drew another figure on the floor beside the one Deirdre had traced.

"And... well... I've got to say this one does look more European than the others." He paused. "In any case we took the tunnel to the right again." He shone his flashlight up to the arch in front of them. "This time —" he stopped completely for emphasis "— this time, I think we should fork to the left. And here's why."

Deirdre was glad the darkness prevented Karmo from seeing her expression. She disagreed entirely, and her body language would only have made him intransigent. She kept silence to let him have his say; there had been too many arguments on this dig already.

Excavation had begun formally only ten days ago, after three years of difficult preparation. They were based just outside Acre in modern-day Israel. (Deirdre kept calling it St-Jean-d'Acre, its name under the occupation by the Crusaders.) The digging was on a "tell," or very large mound, where preliminary investigations had practically guaranteed activity of historical significance, possibly Phoenician, from the seventh or sixth century B.C.E.(Karmo's inclination) or twelfth- and-thirteenth-century activity under the Crusaders (Deirdre's prediction). Maybe even both!

Neither Deirdre Breton nor Robin Karmo disputed the history of the place. Acre had once been known as Ptolemais, a city of Phoenicia, but since then had been occupied by Arabs, by the Seljuk Turks, twice by the Crusaders, by the famous Saladin, and by many more — including Napoleon — until it became part of Israel in 1948.

The tension between the two archaeologists had almost become an open split when a member of the work crew, a graduate student from Cambridge, fell through a hole one afternoon into what turned out to be the entrance to a maze of tunnels that burrowed deep down under the tell. All digging had stopped then until the maze could be explored and mapped by the dig's two leaders. That was assuming they could get along well enough to accomplish the task. Deirdre Breton was simply not prepared to back down in the face of Karmo's monumental ego, especially now that the stakes, potentially, were huge. Although everyone took great care to avoid making the comparison out loud, there wasn't a single worker on the site who was unaware that the Dead Sea Scrolls had been discovered not all that far away, after a similar fall.

Thus, for the past three hours, Deirdre and Robin Karmo had been carefully working their way through the tunnels. Karmo had already published a paper, prior to the dig, in which he made a strong case for the site as Phoenician, and he was naturally inclined to interpret everything they saw in that light. Deirdre inclined toward the Crusaders, not just to counter Karmo, but because she felt the evidence pointed that way. However, nothing they had yet found in the tunnels supported either position — except possibly the three hieroglyphs. If they were indeed hieroglyphs.

"You remember," Karmo was saying, "when we took the right tunnel at the second arch, that tunnel, too, turned twice, the first time ninety degrees, the second time forty-five, but this time *opposite* in direction to the section after the first arch. Now this is why I think we should take the *left* tunnel this time."

Deirdre couldn't be quiet any longer. *"Don't you see it!"* She was surprised at her own vehemence. "We *must* go right again! It's the only logical path to take! In fact, I'll even show you what we're going to see over the *next* arch!"

"Just a minute." Karmo was completely taken aback by her force. He was not used to yielding control. "What makes —"

"No, no. *You* wait a minute." Deirdre was wound up now. "I'll tell you what. If I'm in error, you can be listed first on the paper we publish after this. If I'm right..." She let that hang in the air for a bit before adding, "By the way, I'm going to prove to you that this is a piece of Crusader work, too. Frederick II would be my guess!"

You would have to be a medieval history buff or a trivia nut to appreciate why Deirdre Breton believes the tunnels — and the symbols — to be from the time of Frederick II. But you don't need any historical knowledge to follow her logic. What symbol does she expect to see over the next arch they encounter, assuming that Karmo will agree to turn right?

21

The Fuchsia Track Suit Kidnapping

IT OCCURRED TO GEOFF DILLEY as he slowed the car to a stop that the girl acting as flagman — flag*person*, he corrected himself — didn't really need the big STOP sign she was holding. Most drivers, the male ones, anyway, would have slowed way down at the very least, just to stare. She wasn't just pretty, Geoff thought; she was, well, *outstanding!*

And it wasn't just that. It was the getup. Her construction hard hat along with the incongruous steel-toed boots were the only parts of her attire that even hinted at fulfilling their job description. Whatever the purpose of the rest of her clothes — the denim shorts and the tank top — it certainly wasn't for protection from sun, wind and rain!

Geoff waited until she walked closer before opening the driver's side window. Pretty sight or not, she was out in the heat, and he had no intention of giving up the luxury of air conditioning. Not today, anyway.

He flashed his badge. "This going to be long? I've got a call just ahead."

Her answer was drowned in the roar of a huge earth mover as it accelerated into and out of the ditch to get around them. The torrent of dust covered the girl and made Geoff crank the window shut quickly.

When he opened it again, she peered at the badge closely, then said, "I'll get you through. Otherwise you'll be here awhile. We're crossing equipment right now."

"Can I drive on that up there?" Geoff asked, nodding at the road ahead.

The girl bent even closer. Geoff began to think it might not be so bad to be trapped here, after all.

"It's torn up right through to the intersection, but you can drive it. Just take it easy. If you go right now, I'll hold up the next mover. You should be okay."

Geoff nodded in thanks and rolled up the window again just ahead of another blast of dust. The wind took this one and carried it ahead of him down the road and high into the air.

"Must make people around here real happy," he said out loud as he started the car forward.

The "people around here" were residents of a rural estate subdivision, big homes on big lots spread out to ensure privacy. It was called Deer Trail Estates and it was where Geoff was heading in response to a call. A possible kidnapping, although the duty sergeant had classified it only Code One, so Geoff was in no great hurry.

Within minutes he reached White Tail Boulevard, the main road into the subdivision. As he slowed to turn, his own dust cloud caught up to swarm over the car. Even with the windows tightly closed there was now a film on the dash and along the steering column. He regretted going through the car wash that morning.

Number 3 White Tail was the very first house and the address where the call had originated about half an hour ago. Although the caller had implied a kidnap, he'd not actually used the word. Geoff's sergeant was not treating it urgently for that reason.

"Sounds more to me like a domestic," the sergeant had said to Geoff, "but there's no question we've got to respond. Guy said his wife saw their daughter get into a car on that hill up behind the Estates. That was early this morning, but he didn't call till now. You figure it. Kid's sixteen apparently, so that could mean anything. Too late for roadblocks, anyway, so no need to rush."

The house had double front doors and a portico with impossibly large pillars, one of those designs, Geoff thought, that couldn't make up its mind whether to be Greek or Spanish. When the doors opened in response to his knock, he could see the same ambiguity continued into the interior.

"Officer Dilley." Geoff flashed his badge. "Mr. Potish? Vincent Potish?"

The man was dressed in a three-piece suit, the tie tight to the neck. There was nothing unusual in that for a Thursday at noon, but it did seem rather stiffly formal to Geoff — unless maybe this was not Potish.

It was.

"Yes. Thank you for coming. This way, please. To the study. My wife's there."

Vincent Potish led Geoff down a short hallway and into a booklined room where in front of the single, large window sat a lady in her midforties. She was wearing a pink track suit that was either brand-new or else entirely unaccustomed to perspiration.

"Dear, this is Officer Dilley. My wife, Stasia."

Stasia Potish held out a carefully manicured hand. She did not get up.

"Thank you for coming, Officer. This is so... so *upsetting!*"

For just an instant, a fleeting instant, Stasia Potish's elegant composure collapsed. Had Geoff not been vaguely aware of a kind of unease about the place, he might not have noticed.

"Our daughter, you see. She went jogging up there this morning." Mrs. Potish waved a perfect hand vaguely at the window. Geoff glanced up at the heavily wooded hill that loomed over

Deer Trail Estates. This was one of the few houses in the sub-division, he saw, where the end of the lot butted directly onto the base of the hill. That had to mean money, he knew. There was a premium for that view. Close to the main road, though. In the few seconds of silence he was sure he heard the machines he'd met only shortly before.

"She got into a car," Mrs. Potish continued. "Well, not a car; it was a jeep. A *sports vehicle.*"

The last phrase came out with such vehemence — and for no apparent reason — that Geoff was entirely taken aback.

"It was blue and white. Well, blue and *cream.* Navy blue and cream. These distinctions are important, aren't they? It was a Nissan Pathfinder."

Geoff was surprised — and impressed — by the amount of detail. But he didn't show it. He stepped closer to the window and peered out.

"I'm sorry." Stasia Potish was still talking. "I should have offered you a seat. It's just that everything is so filthy with dust. That terrible road work. They've been out there every day now for over a week. We can't sit anywhere without dusting first."

Geoff looked around. The place *was* dusty. Dust on the mantel over the fireplace, and dust on the ceramic tile in front of it. He could even see his footprints. There was an even, almost neat layer on the lamp beside Mrs. Potish; another covered the windowsill; the bookshelves were particularly dirty. Geoff could see where someone had wiped the back of Stasia Potish's chair and missed the corner.

"I'd rather stand, anyway," he said. "Perhaps…" He was trying to be tactful. "Perhaps you can go through the sequence of events from the beginning for me, please."

Mrs. Potish took a deep breath.

"Start with the argument, dear." It was the voice of Vincent Potish. He had retreated to the doorway after introducing Geoff and stayed there, hovering at the edge of the room.

"Yes, the argument." Mrs. Potish sighed. "Teenagers. They're so difficult. Do you have children, Officer?" She didn't wait for Geoff to respond. "Serena is sixteen. We had a disagreement this morning. Over... well, it was trivial. Aren't these things always trivial, Officer?"

As she spoke the last sentence it occurred to Geoff she had yet to use his name, but that point was obscured by the look she gave her husband. It was clear now that Vincent Potish was not a bystander in this situation.

"Serena left the house in a huff," Stasia Potish continued. "She was going jogging, anyway, so I didn't think too much of it. Typical teenage behavior. She was gone almost an hour. And that's when I saw her get into the car — the jeep. Up there."

She turned to look up at the hill. "That's another thing. She never jogs up there."

Geoff looked out the window at the hill. "You're positive it was your daughter? It's quite a distance from here up to the road there."

"She has a pink track suit like mine. Fuchsia, actually. And blond hair. Besides —"

"These, Officer Dilley," Vincent Potish interrupted. He was holding a large pair of binoculars. "My wife is the J.J. Audubon of Deer Trail Estates."

Any doubt of the tension between the couple was dispelled entirely now, for he had made no attempt to disguise the sarcasm.

"I sit here, Officer." Mrs. Potish said wearily. "In front of the window. This is where I watch the birds. It's my hobby. Early morning is the best time, you know. There's a rumor that a European finch has been seen... uh... I've never recorded one you see..." Her voice drifted into silence.

"And you had the glasses — the binoculars — when you saw your daughter get into the... uh... Nissan Pathfinder?"

"There's no question it was she," Mrs. Potish replied. "I watched the whole thing from here — through the glasses, yes."

"I see," Geoff said, and then lapsed into silence. He spoke again after a minute. "Excuse me," he said. "I'm going to talk to my sergeant. Perhaps we should organize more personnel for a search."

He moved quickly to the door, then paused." Ah... I'm sorry. This sounds so... so chauvinistic... but... you're sure it was a Nissan Pathfinder? My experience is that... uh... women tend not to pay much attention to details like that."

"Vincent has dealerships, Officer. We live and breathe cars here."

Sarcasm again. No veiling it, either. Geoff could tell there was discomfort in this house. Or else he was being set up.

An instant later, he offered just that observation to the duty sergeant on his car radio.

"They sure don't like each other," he said. "Or else they're darn good actors. That's a possibility," he pointed out to the sergeant. "Because their story breaks down."

What does Geoff Dilley mean by "their story breaks down"?

22

An Almost Perfect Spot

FROM THE AIR, THE TOWN looked like a child's drawing. The streets were a grid pattern: cookie-cutter perfect little squares outlined with a ruler. The buildings looked stamped out: everything the same size. No industrial monsters or warehouses or other outsized structures to offend the eye. Any differences in proportion seemed accidental more than deliberate, the kind of thing that results when uncertain juvenile muscles draw freehand.

But more than anything else, what made the aerial view unique was that in every direction, the town just stopped. On each side, the edge of town really was the edge of town! There were no strip shopping malls, no crowded little bunches of commercial ugliness to blunt the juxtaposition of urban and rural. Not even gas stations! On all four sides the town of Azure simply came to an abrupt halt at the last line of the grid.

On the ground, the symmetry continued. Azure looked like a Disney feature from the 1940s. Not quite *Cinderella*; just a bit too much regal fantasy in that one. And not *Snow White*. It was *too* bucolic. More like what *Hansel and Gretel* would have been if the wicked witch had undergone therapy in her adolescence and learned macramé. That was what Azure was all about. Boutiques. Craft madness.

And that was why the town looked so — well — *perfect!* Azure existed solely to feed tourists' insatiable desire to buy anything unusual, any kind of thing they would never, ever buy within an hour's drive of their own homes, the only stipulation being that it had to come from one of those little places that no one ever went into. Except on vacation.

That's why in Azure, stores like The Almost Sober Judge ("innovative bar accessories") and Contrary Mary ("not just silver bells!") stood pastel shoulder to enamel shutter with Wind in the Wisteria and Things Being Various and The Watched Pot. No ordinary enterprise dared raise its mercantile head in this town. No hardware stores. And definitely no auto parts. The supermarket — Azure's *only* supermarket — bore the humiliation of membership in a national chain, but since it was stuck away at the end of a street, and separated from Not Your Average Bookstore by a parking lot (demarcated in grids with potted junipers) its affiliation with A & P could only be seen if one peered directly through an artful whorl of tubelighting that said "FreshorFreezer."

Only one supermarket, but two drugstores, on the quite reasonable premise that tourists, either before or after a day of boutiquing, would need remedial help more than sustenance. Neither deigned to call itself a drugstore or even an "apothecary shop." Rather, in the very center of town stood The Pharmacopoeia, while at the outer edge of both community and cutesie-poo stood Nostrum.

Azure was — well, again — *perfect!* That it was also unreal was beside the point. Perhaps that *was* the point. In any case, the town served two purposes exceptionally well: one, of course, was tourism. It had become the kind of tourist stop that was now a reference point: (*"And what did you think of Azure?"*) The other was a natural outgrowth: espionage.

Experts estimated that Azure at the height of the tourist season held more spies than Vienna in 1948. Tourism made this possible. Because practically everyone in Azure came from somewhere else, usually very far away, the polyglot that flowed from places like Interjacence ("limited edition jigsaw puzzles") across the street to Tintinnabulation ("original design wind chimes") was so thoroughly international that any face, any costume, any style was, frankly, unremarkable. A sari drew no more or less attention than a John Deere hat.

Still, the popularity of Azure with "operatives" had its own drawback: they sometimes recognized each other! Already this morning Cecile King was certain she had seen MaryClare McInerney of CSIS. That the two of them were more or less on the same side — Cecile was CIA — didn't reduce her discomfort any. If there was one familiar person, she knew there could well be others.

Cecile was sitting at La Bonne Bouche, a delicatessen ideally situated for her purpose on this warm June morning. She had a very tiny package for Dorothy Elliott, and expected one in return. The little deli was almost enveloped in its own shutters, and hidden by a carefully pruned sycamore, surrounded to near shoulder height by the mandatory iron fence. Next door, The Pharmacopoeia was just slightly set back, so that from her table Cecile had a surveyor's sweep of Appleton Street as well as the intersection with Nairn. That in turn gave her a vantage point from which to watch the tour buses make their "dumps" before pulling away to park discreetly out of sight.

The only problem was that she couldn't sit too long without risk. For one thing, the impossibly uncomfortable little chairs were designed to keep customers moving. And why not? People didn't come to Azure to sit. For another, what if it really was MaryClare McInerney she'd seen? Who else might be around today?

Cecile leaned over an inky espresso so her eyes could make a quick unobtrusive scan of the street. So far so good. Nothing suspicious for the moment. At first, she'd thought the business at the bus dump a few minutes ago was a setup. Normally, two buses unloaded simultaneously at this special spot, but when she'd first sat down, the lead space had been occupied by Eternal Spring Tours, a load of seniors who took so long to disembark that the line of waiting buses was stacked south on Nairn farther than she could see.

By the time Cecile had finished her cruller, however, Eternal Spring was able to pull out and the dumping speeded up. During the first few sips of espresso, she'd watched a matched pair of Silverliners discharge their happy loads. She'd half expected Dorothy Elliott to be on one of these buses, but everyone who got off wore either a jacket or a T-shirt that said Cobbleton Pin Busters over a triangular logo of bowling balls. No way Dorothy was part of that! In their business you didn't want to stand out.

As she began a second espresso — Cecile knew it had to be the last — another set of buses pulled up. Still no sign of Dorothy Elliott. Cecile knew now she was going to have to —

There she was!

They'd worked together only once before: a quick exchange in a poorly lit café back on the east coast, but she knew it was Dorothy.

Cecile watched her thread down the street, working her way around the Eternal Spring seniors, who were managing to knot up the pedestrian traffic pretty badly. For a second she lost her, then picked her up again. Dorothy was a pace or two behind one of the Cobbleton Pin Busters, a big man with a rather slouching gait. Cecile watched as the two of them strode past The Espadrille, around the little crowd in front of Diaphany, where the resident glassblower was presenting a demonstration of his art, then directly across the street into La Bonne Bouche.

Even before Dorothy turned abruptly right at the doorway

and up the sidewalk, Cecile had left for the washrooms in the rear and the fire exit.

Cecile King and Dorothy Elliott caught a warning at about the same time. What made them simultaneously decide against the exchange at La Bonne Bouche?

23

An Interrupted Patrol

GARY ELLESMERE HAD TWO EXCUSES for being on the road on a hot August morning. The first was simply to get "field time." A reasonable enough explanation — on the surface, at least. After all, one of the first policy changes Gary had made when he became chief was to decree that everyone — and he meant *everyone* — who carried a badge would spend a certain amount of time in the field. So in effect he was simply following his own orders. "Leadership by example": it was a phrase he used often with the staff sergeants.

Gary's other excuse was to road-test — just one more time — the patrol car borrowed from the Tottenham City force. Another reasonable enough excuse, for his second move as the new chief was to convince the county treasury department that the force needed six new custom-built sedans to replace the highway patrol fleet. It was a coup on Gary's part. Tottenham City already had these new machines and he knew his people drooled every time one of the powerful vehicles was anywhere near.

Two sound and sensible excuses, then. And Gary Ellesmere knew his staff didn't believe either one of them. The plain truth was the Chief had a smashing hangover!

His fiftieth birthday the night before had been an occasion of such fanfare and hoopla that Gary allowed himself, in his words, "to be overserved." That was the real reason he was on the road this morning. He had forsaken an air-conditioned office for a very warm car, but the relative isolation had made it a fair trade. No telephones, no irate citizens, none of what he liked to call the "dilemmas of leadership." And even for a fifty-year-old this machine wasn't such a bad item to be spinning around in.

The sun made Gary squint as he turned off the highway onto a side road. Just about five minutes down the road was the purest and coldest drinking water in the whole county. It came from a spring that fed from underneath a long-abandoned, one-room schoolhouse and ran out a rusty pipe with enough force to make a permanent drinking fountain. Not even the exceptionally hot dry weather they were having this summer could slow it down. Local farmers called it the Tap. The little stream to which it gave birth they called the Creek. Either source would serve Gary right now. His dry throat was pushing upward to join a pounding headache.

It was when he pulled out of a careless wander across the yellow line that Gary saw the figure out on the road. In fact, his eyes took in the scene for a full second before his brain told him to brace up. Something was wrong!

The figure was a boy — no, a man. Short, though. He was running hard toward the patrol car.

In the few seconds it took to close the gap, Gary could see it was indeed a man. His policeman's mind went automatically through a checklist: adult male, white, maybe mid-thirties, about five-six, 165 or so, big muscles, mustache, brown and brown, balding on the peaks, denim shorts — cutoffs. Someone had lopped the legs off a pair of jeans. Green basketball jersey with 60 on it. No team name. Sneakers really worn and dirty.

The man was puffing very hard.

"Back — ba — oh, God! Back there!" He pointed vaguely behind him and leaned heavily on the driver's side door. "My wife. Back there. In the kitchen. She's dead! I know it! She's dead!"

Gary shrank back a little in spite of himself. The pungent smell of the man's sweat overlay the morning heat. He didn't like the guy leaning on the door, either. It hemmed him in.

"Back off. Lemme out." Gary spoke with calmness but authority. He didn't even notice that his headache was gone.

The man moved to lean over the fender. Runs of sweat rolled down his arms and whorled over the thin film of road dust. His breathing began to slow as Gary got out.

"No. No. Get back in! We gotta go…" The man waved at a spot farther down the road. He was obviously weak from the run and what appeared to Gary to be the onset of hysteria.

"My wife! She's dead! Blood all over. She's not breathing, she's — God! — *chopped up!*"

Gary could see the man was about to lose control.

"Okay, get in."

The man ran around the front of the car and got into the passenger seat. From the edge of his concentration Gary couldn't quite push away the impression that his passenger was going to stink up Tottenham City's new patrol car, and it was due to be returned that afternoon!

Maybe it was being ordered into the car, or the sense that someone was now taking charge, but something seemed to calm the man a bit.

"Down there." He pointed with more specific emphasis this time as Gary pulled back on to the road. "Just past the creek. Red brick house. How did — I mean, how come — I mean, a *cop!* I didn't expect a cop! I was running for help. My wife's dead. I'm sure of it. See, I was checking fence. Right there. That field. See?"

Gary could see a large pasture that had obviously not been grazed for some time.

"I couldn't a' been gone more than half an hour. Checking fence, I mean. Only one wire down and the field's not that big to go all the way round. I went back to th' house for a drink of water and there she was on the floor by the sink — turn there, the gate's open — and the phone's out! I ran out to the road. Nobody! I was running up to the Purdleys' for their phone. That's when I saw you."

The front right tire settled in a pothole as Gary stopped by the house. The man bolted out immediately and ran to a screen door that didn't seem to be quite closed.

"Hold it!" Gary shouted. "We go in together!" In one motion he stepped out the driver's side door and pulled his communicator out of its cradle.

The response at the other end was immediate. "Go ahead, Chief."

For a moment Gary paused to wonder just how the dispatcher knew who it was, but then he realized that the fancy new patrol car had a transmit code.

"I've got a possible homicide here." He could almost hear the attention double. "I'm three klicks east of Number 10 on County 22. Red brick farmhouse. Name Haspen, H-A-S-P-E-N, on the mailbox. I want an ambulance and a backup right away. For the present I'm calling this a domestic, but if you don't hear from me again in three minutes — mark, that's *three* — treat this as an 'officer down.' I'm going in now. Acknowledge."

The "ten-four" was instant. Gary dropped the communicator and flipped the switch on the light bar so that arriving vehicles could key in on the location more easily. As he ran up to the screen door he could see that on the wall just above some trampled flowers, the telephone line had been neatly severed.

"Okay. Stay just ahead of me," he said, and motioned to the man to go through the doorway.

Gary is being prudently cautious, but it's apparent he doesn't expect a trap. Why is he "calling this a domestic"? What makes him suspicious of the man he's supposedly helping?

24

The View from the Second-floor Promenade

AT THE INTERSECTION OF THE north and west walls of the Greater Wellington Shopping Center, the railing that surrounded the promenade on the second floor traced its way around an extension that jutted out over the main floor mall just enough to accommodate a pair of areca palms on either side of an incredibly uncomfortable plastic bench. At the grand opening ten years ago, some copywriter, in a burst of excess typical of the species, had labeled this spot "The Promontory." The name, however unmerited by the tiny space, had stuck.

"The Promontory" was D.U. ("Herbie") Michael's preferred observation post. From it, he could see the front entrances to sixty-two of the mall's ninety-three stores. He'd counted them several times. Herbie liked numbers. Equally important — perhaps more important — he could look right down on "The Green." Another pretentious label, this time identifying the mall's focal point and main meeting area.

The name was supposed to imply *village* green. Its principal attraction was the "Dancing Waters Fountain," in which arcing jets of water leaped from one little pool to another in random order. When it worked, the Dancing Waters Fountain was a delight. Unfortunately, its ambitions in the direction of terpsichorean splendour were regularly marred by breakdowns caused partly by lousy design, but mostly by one of the banes of Herbie's working life: teenagers who came down to The Green to hang out.

These kids who met at the mall to cruise and, from time to time, boost whatever goods they could from unwary merchants, were one of the main reasons Herbie appeared regularly on The Promontory with walkie-talkie in hand, ready to call in his patrols from all points in the mall when they were needed to thin out the crowd below. Herbie hated doing it. His people were supposed to spend most of their time on the alert to prevent shoplifting. D.U. ("Herbie") Michael was head of security for Wellington Center. He considered himself a professional, and found the traffic-and-rowdyism role offensive.

"What you see right now —" he was talking to a very attentive young man beside him, but at no point did he cease to sweep the mall with his gaze "— is typical Wednesday morning traffic."

He made a rainbow sweep with his right hand. "You'd think the whole city had nothing to do so it comes here."

The young man agreed. "It's hard to believe this many people go shopping on a Wednesday at 11:00 A.M."

"They don't." Herbie said grimly. "That's why we're here. Oh, most of them are shoppers, all right, and some of them are sitters. Like the old guys down at the fountain." He pointed at three old men sitting immobile on benches just as formidable as the one in The Promontory. They were staring straight ahead, apparently at nothing.

"I feel sorry for them, actually," Herbie continued. "I'm sure they'd rather be sitting in some sunny piazza or be out playing *bocce* somewhere, but they have nowhere to go, so they come here and sit and stare. When they're awake."

His young companion edged closer to the railing and raised himself on tiptoe to look at the old men. Indeed, one of them was sound asleep.

"Now, those two —" Herbie's tone changed "— are more the type you have to keep your eye on." He pointed at two teenage boys. Both wore baseball hats — backward — and large padded running shoes with the laces untied.

"They should be in school... those poor teachers. Yet at least kids like that are obvious. Most of the time they're just a pain. Noisy. Not too often you have to do anything about them until the numbers get big. Herd instinct takes over then. Still, they don't boost all that much except maybe in the record stores. Cassettes. And cigarettes. Watch them in the smoke shops."

Herbie's protégé nodded. For him it was orientation day. He was willing to take in all he heard.

"Where you get trouble is with the weirdos and the professional lifters. Now they... ah... see that guy down there, the one with the green windbreaker? I've been noticing him for about five minutes now. Strange."

The object of Herbie's attention had just walked up to the entrance door of Lambton Florists and was standing almost against it. He stood there for about ten seconds, seeming to stare straight at the door, then put his hand on it — tentatively — for a few seconds, and pushed. No result. Finally he pulled. The door opened and he went into the store.

"That's the third time he's done that," Herbie said. "First over there at Computer Age, then at Kinetic Sports and now Lambton's."

"Maybe he's doing research on doors?" the young man offered with a chuckle.

"Could be." Herbie smiled. "Could be a nutcase, too. Either way, he's one you've got to watch. There, too! There's another. That really fat guy. I've never seen him before. That counts. Somebody that big you'd remember so this one's a stranger."

Herbie was focusing on a very large man in the promenade

below, walking slowly, looking at each of the stores, but not going in.

"You'll soon learn." Herbie put his hands together. "There's a way that fat people walk, so you know they're real. Sometimes that large tummy is full of boosted goods. Would you believe last year we caught a guy with a *microwave oven* where his stomach was supposed to be! And his partner... she had a whole set of microwave dishes! Just like they were going into business. They..."

Herbie paused, his attention drawn to the front of Neve's Smoke and Variety on the other side of The Green. The young trainee's attention had gone there even before his. Neve's Smoke and Variety was clerked until 3:00 P.M. each day by a young lady whose name was Daisy, and whose two most notable characteristics were an ever-present wad of gum so big it completely precluded intelligible speech, and skirts so short they didn't come even close to earning their keep. Every morning at eleven, when Daisy came out and bent over to pile out the afternoon edition of the *Daily Telegram*, she drew a crowd. Starting with the old guys at the Dancing Waters Fountain. They were smiling now, completely awake and enjoying the morning.

The *Telegram*'s headline shouted up to the Promontory: LONGTIME LIFER ESCAPES! The radio and TV news that morning had been full of an escape the previous night from the penitentiary at the outskirts of the city. The *Telegram*'s lusty, tabloid competitor had doubled its normal headline size and screamed KILLER LOOSE! No subtlety there. On the other hand, the city's third daily, the sober and somewhat arch *Empire* aimed its headline at the disconcerting certainty of an economic slowdown.

As Daisy retreated to the Neve's counter, to the universal disappointment of the denizens of The Green, Herbie continued his instruction. "Pregnant women. Watch for them. It's such an old trick you don't see it much anymore, but never shut your eyes to it. A woman who's genuinely pregnant is going to sit down and rest once in a while. Most of the time they seem pretty uncomfortable, too. And — now there's something — those two guys in suits. When you see that you have to ask yourself what's normal. Two guys in suits in a shopping mall on a Wednesday morning? If they're here to do business they'll show it by the way they act. With purpose. If they're hustling — then it's different. It's all behavior. Just watch behavior. Sooner or later the boosters give themselves away."

The young trainee watched the two men carefully. They appeared to be lingering — waiting for something. His attention was diverted briefly by the two teenagers in baseball caps. They had suddenly emerged from Jazzy Records and one of them appeared to be walking abnormally fast. He raised his hand to point, but Herbie nodded. He'd seen them, too. Meanwhile the man in the green jacket had come out of Lambton Florists carrying a small, neatly wrapped bouquet — it looked like the $4.98 carnation special — and walked over to Dave Seglins Photography, where he repeated his strange behavior at the door there. The fat man, too, had now come back up the mall, and was standing by the Dancing Waters Fountain, arms akimbo, staring intently into Computer Age.

"For heaven's sake!" Herbie shook himself. "Behavior! I must be slipping! You stay here," he said to his protégé. "Keep an eye on everything and everyone out there. I'm going to call the police."

What has led D.U. ("Herbie") Michael to believe he has reason to call the police?

25

Death in the
Bide-a-Wee Motel

TO DETECTIVE FIRST CLASS DOLORES Dexel, the dead man on
the floor in front of her was hardly an example of what a big
drug operator was supposed to look like. There was no flash to
him, no evidence of heavy money, nothing that said "big time."
On the contrary, everything about him ranged from mild all
the way to even milder.

Starting with the brown slacks. Nothing approaching Italian
silk here; these were strictly off the rack. So was the tweed jacket, the kind made to last ten years before leather patches are called upon to adorn the elbows. Dolores couldn't see the shirt or
the tie, but she knew what they'd be like. From where she stood,
though, she could see the man's sturdy Oxfords had recently
been resoled. The heels were new, too; she could read CAT'S PAW
semicircled in the center of each. Even the man's wedding ring
said "reliable, ordinary, *solid* citizen." His fingers were curled
around the edge of an open Bible — the ultimate touch, Dolores

thought — and the ring reflected light from a cheap lamp beside the bed. It was a gold ring, not too wide, not too narrow, no adornment or stones or etched design. Just plain. Solid.

What was most emphatically unordinary, however, was the way he had died. No murder was ever run-of-the-mill, but this one was a step into the unusual. It was an execution. There was a small-caliber bullet wound in the back of the head at close range. Another in the middle of the back and one more at the base of the spine. Insurance shots, Dolores knew. Certainty that the victim was dispatched. The killing shot had been to the front, close range into the heart. At least that's what Dolores thought because of all the blood. She wasn't about to turn him over until the forensic guys got here. She needed photos, too.

That reminded her. What was taking the photographer so long? And the light bar she'd called for? The light especially. The seedy little motel room had a single bedside lamp to supplement the wan glow that tried to reach the floor from the overhead fixture. She needed to be able to see better.

"Forensic just called. They're on their way."

Dolores looked up to see her partner, Paul Provoto, in the doorway. The rattle of the Coke machine just down the hallway was so loud she hadn't heard him approach.

"The lights'll come with the photographer," Paul continued. "And I've got a blue sitting with the night clerk that called in. You can probably talk to her again now. She's not so cranked anymore."

He took a step into the room, then thought better of it. "Gawd. Did this guy bleed or what!"

Paul was right. It was one of the first things Dolores had noted. The blood was not spattered all over as she'd seen so often before (too often — only six months in homicide and already she wanted out). Rather, the blood had flowed — poured! It had run around the outline of the body on the beige tile floor all the way down to the sensible shoes, and in the other direction, along both outstretched arms. It was in the victim's hair (short, getting quite thin. And brown! Dolores had noticed that on the way in). The trail of blood had even curled around the open Bible, as though it were seeking its own path, unhurried, uninterrupted, framing the book neatly so that the double column of text looked even denser from top to bottom. Only the victim's hand, lying on the opposite page, was free of the red substance that was still oozing from the body.

Dolores looked up at Paul. "I'm going to go talk to the clerk," she said. She had to get out of the room. It was suffocating her. "We'll talk in the lobby. Call me if the photographer comes in the back way."

She walked carefully around the body, out past her partner and down the hallway to where the night clerk was waiting. Through the grimy skylight she could see streaks of gray. Be morning soon, she thought. Another night with no sleep.

The night clerk hadn't slept, either, certainly not since she'd called in over an hour ago. For most of the time Dolores and Paul had been at the Bide-a-Wee Motel, the young woman had been drifting back and forth over the border of hysteria.

She was on the calmer side when Dolores entered the lobby, but not comfortably so. She sat scraping away at a gouge in the surface of an end table with an incredibly long, and patently false, thumbnail.

The officer sitting in the only other chair got up. Two chairs, the badly scarred end table, some outdated magazines and another cheap table lamp made up the "front desk." There was no counter, only a window, a thick Plexiglas one that slid back and forth to enable the duty clerk to accept cash in advance. Nobody used plastic at the Bide-a-Wee Motel.

Dolores sat down gingerly. She didn't want to push the clerk. The chair didn't appear to be up to any serious test, either.

"Miss —" For a second she'd forgotten. "Ah... Miss Duvet,"

she began. "Can you tell me again where you were when you heard the shots?"

The question nearly turned out to be a bad mistake. The night clerk flushed and tears started falling along an already well-worn channel in her makeup.

"I *didn't* hear a shot! I *told* you that! I went for a Coke and I *saw* him… the bod…" The tears began to flow faster.

"Yes, yes. That's right. I'm sorry." Dolores put her hand on the young clerk's arm. "Of course you did. My fault."

The soothing tone had effect, and Miss Duvet's tears retreated to snuffles. Dolores also retreated from her ploy to see if the woman's rendering of events had changed since their first encounter.

"Let's go through it one more time." She was going to try a softer tack. "You went down the hall for a Coke. Then what?"

Miss Duvet took a deep breath. It seemed as though she was going to hang together now.

"Then I saw him. The door was — like — open. Like, I mean, who'd leave their door open in a dump like this? And the light's on, too. So I, like, look in. And jeez! There he is!"

"Did you go in?" Dolores took a chance with that.

"*No way!* I mean — jeez! Would *you*? Like — the guy's *dead!* I mean, I *think* he's dead. Like, there's so much blood he's *got* to be dead, right? 'Sides. Even if he's not — like, this ain't Mercy Hospital, right? What do I know from first aid? So I run back here and call 911. I mean — like — so you're me. What would would *you* do?"

"What time was that?" Dolores asked.

"*I don't know!*" Miss Duvet's fuse was shortening. "I didn't keep track! This ain't a hockey game! They don't even have a crummy clock in here, anyways!"

Dolores noted that Miss Duvet did not wear a watch, either.

"Did you…" she decided to go on. "Did you go back to the room then?"

"*Are you nuts?* No way I'm goin' back there! Like, already I gotta full-time picture here. I mean watch this!"

She lifted her face and closed both eyes with emphasis. In the poor light Dolores hadn't noticed till now that Miss Duvet's eyelashes were almost as long as her nails.

"Like, I gotta pair of three-by-fives here. Full-color glossy. You wanna picture? I got it, like every time I close my eyes!"

"It must have been terrible for you." Dolores had decided that the sympathetic approach was definitely going to get better results.

"Terrible. Like — try *mind-blowin'!* I mean, like, this guy. Mr. Straight. Mr. *Brown Clothes!* What's a straight guy like that doin' here, anyways? Like he's even got the Gid out!"

"The 'Gid'?" Dolores thought she knew, but she wanted to be sure.

"Yeah, the Gid. The Gideon. Like — yuh know — the Bible. He's holding it on one side: 'Gospel according to Matthew.' Like have I gotta picture or *what?* Yuh work in a fleabag like this yuh learn to read upside down. I mean — it's like fun to watch them make up addresses for the reg card. Anyways, I seen the Gid — the Bible. He's got it open. Matthew, right? And the guy's gettin' bald. I seen that, too. I mean I gotta picture. What else yuh wanna know?"

Dolores fumbled in her shoulder bag, ostensibly for a tissue but actually making sure her tape recorder was still running. She was about to ask when Miss Duvet had come on duty, but Paul came in.

"Kodak's here." He pointed out the front door. "And the lighting guys are just pulling in."

Dolores stood. "Tell the photographer to wait," she said. "I want some special shots from the doorway. Also from the feet up." She paused. "And Paul... come on out here a minute."

Paul led the way out the door to the parking lot.

Dolores had her notebook out. "I want you to call in some backup teams. Now! As many as the captain will give us for a neighborhood search. And post the blues around the circumference. It's probably too late, but I don't want *anyone* leaving here. Unless Miss Glamorous in there is lying through her teeth, somebody was in that room between the time *she* saw the body and *we* did."

Why does Dolores Dexel think that?

26

Bailing Out the Navy
— for a Price

Shifted to one side in the sagging easy chair, an ankle resting on the opposite knee, and slouched way down in the sinking comfort the old chair invited, Bob Ashby conveyed a sense of easygoing acceptance. It was a posture that said, "Okay, take your time. I'm here to listen."

He was dressed casually, too: cords, a knitted sweater. The only hint that he might not be just another employee of Ashburn Engineering, on a break here in the office, was the polish on his loafers. That and the fine leather document case on his lap.

In the flotsam of esoteric, machined parts that filled every conceivable cranny of the office of Ashburn Engineering, so many in fact that at first glance they almost hid the collage of outdated girlie calendars, these two items stood out. The leather of the document case particularly, for its elegant finish picked up the wan glow from a single naked light bulb in the ceiling, where it played forlorn host to a crusty coat of fly specks.

It took courage for Bob Ashby to sit with such apparent ease in the old chair. As with the rest of the office, "clean" was not an adjective the mind would admit in describing it. Nevertheless, Bob was not at all uncomfortable as he sat there, chin cupped in his hand, conveying a sense of complete, professional neutrality. A major point in his favor was that the chair faced the window behind Thurm Elliott, and Bob knew that any light from the setting sun that managed to struggle through the scum on the panes would reflect off his glasses and conceal his eyes. They were the only characters in his role-playing that he couldn't control. And since he flat distrusted Thurman Elliott, Jr. (with good reason), he knew his eyes would say so. Clearly.

For another thing, Bob Ashby had been in so-called offices like this many times before. As an independent consultant in industrial design, with a specialty in deep-sea salvage, he'd encountered operations like this one almost daily for more years than he wanted to think about. Although in regard to this particular visit, Thurm Elliott's reputation as a crook was an exception in the industry, rather than the rule.

"They're all in threes, the pieces —"(*cough, cough, harrumph!*)
"— every wuh — every wuh —" (*cough, cough, hack, ah-hack!*)
"— jus' a minute." Thurm Elliott stood up to hawk and spit into a cardboard box in the corner. He missed and the phlegm stuck to the side of the box.

For a second Bob's facade came unhinged as his gaze was irresistibly drawn to the gob of yellow dangling incongruously over the 4 in the stencil that said "Pineapple Juice 48 oz." This was the third time Elliott had stood up to spit into the box. The first two times he'd succeeded.

"Every one of them —" he seemed in control now, "— three links. So that means —" (*cough*) "— we're gonna hafta…" Another fit of coughing began. This one started as a rapid series of *huh-huh-huhs* and grew through a series of *harrumphs* into a veritable blizzard of belly coughs so hard Bob found himself trying to breathe on Elliott's behalf.

"Cold." He said, turning over a blackened palm in explanation. As though Bob Ashby really needed to be told. "Can't get rid of it." Thurman Elliott took a rag out of the back pocket of his coveralls and blew wet and vigorously, then wrenched his nose as though he were shutting off a balky faucet.

Bob's posture of casual ease was on very thin ice now. He had dealt many times in his business with people who had become brutalized over years of working with rusty, dirty, recalcitrant machinery in impossible conditions. Thurman Elliott, however, was one of the worst. Not just in manners, in ethics, too. The man had been forced out of business four times that Bob knew of, twice by bankruptcy, once running from a civil suit and the last time by government investigators. Still, he was the only one on the Pacific coast that anyone knew of who was capable of doing the job Bob had come to approve.

The steam-driven catapults on the *Whitby*, the navy's oldest aircraft carrier, had been sabotaged. How, or by whom, no one knew, but that wasn't Bob's concern, anyway. The binding chains had been cut into pieces — no simple task. That was another element of mystery in the case — who *could* have cut them? — for each link was forged of an alloy of steel, platinum and titanium. They were incredibly hard, and certainly impervious to the attack of ordinary tools. Yet the chains lay in pieces. Twenty pieces. And until they were restored to four separate chains of equal length, the catapults were useless and so, for all intents and purposes, was the *Whitby*. She could sail, and she could land planes. But she couldn't launch them.

That's why this particular job was so crucial and, for political reasons, so urgent. On the deck of the *Whitby* sat her full complement of aircraft. The press had not yet learned of it, and likely wouldn't unless the carrier had to sail down the coast, through the Panama Canal and up the Atlantic coast in turn, to either Norfolk, Virginia, or Halifax, Nova Scotia, where the repairs could be effected. A lot of navy reputation, therefore, hung on the skills of Thurman Elliott, Jr. and Ashburn Engineering.

That aside, past experiences with him had made the base commander turn to Bob Ashby just to be sure. Getting stung could be just as embarrassing as having to sail around to the Atlantic.

"Piece work —" (*cough, cough*) "— 's only way to bid this stuff. Yuh gotta open a link 'n' then close it 'round 'nother —" (*har, har, HAR!*) "— 's only way —" (*HAR!*).

Bob braced himself for another hawk and turned away from the pineapple juice box. It didn't come. Instead, he watched in disbelief as Elliott, with a single hand in practiced motion, snapped the filter off a cigarette as he put it in his mouth, and began to lift the papers on his desk in search of a match.

"'S' if they need four equal lengths, I make it sixteen cuts 'n' welds. Ten thousand per. 'At's one-sixty total. 'Suming I have no trouble. Now that's not outa line. 'Sides, they got nobody else. Ah, there!"

Thurm Elliott reached under a precariously balanced box of envelopes for a small metal container, opened it and took out a wooden match. He looked for a bare spot on the surface of his desk, gave up and then out of long habit stood halfway and scraped the match alive on the seat of his coveralls.

Bob Ashby took off his glasses. He was finished listening now. He let himself stare at the unshaven face on the other side of the desk. Interestingly, it was Elliott now who, behind the cloud of cigarette smoke, had adopted a neutral stance.

What irritated Bob, as a taxpayer and as a professional, was not the fee rate, although he'd come in with an upper limit of $7,000 or $8,000 in mind. It was the patent make-work fraudulence. Only $40,000. A pittance in military budget terms. A mote. A speck. But it was still a case of someone taking unfair advantage.

"Ten per is high, Thurm." Bob spoke for the first time since he'd sat in the easy chair. "But I guess I can get the navy to go along with *one-twenty* total. No advance, though. Not at ten thousand per."

The hard glint in Thurman Elliott's eyes lasted only for a few seconds before it washed away in another fit of coughing. This time when Elliott stood to face the pineapple juice box, Bob turned his head. Easygoing acceptance time was over. Elliott had got the message, so if Bob wanted to turn away to keep his stomach under control, there was no reason not to now.

It is clear that Bob Ashby has a different view of how the chains should be repaired, and his idea will apparently take less work than Thurman's Elliott's proposal. Elliott's way will cost $160,000; Bob Ashby's will be only $120,000. What is the difference in their strategies?

27

The Case of the Missing .38 Smith and Wesson

GARY WESTLAKE MADE A MENTAL note to find out who had been the last to use Number 9119. The car had literally come to life when he turned on the ignition, and he hated that. One by one he turned off the radio, the windshield wipers, the fan, the rear defrost, while he waited for the engine to warm. Whoever it was, he noted with even more annoyance, had even left the glove compartment door hanging open. All this, along with an accumulation of junk on the passenger seat: gum wrappers, a ratty toque (certainly not a regulation item but sometimes the highway patrol used them), a flashlight that should have been returned to its holder under the dash and what appeared to be a forgotten, half-completed accident report.

With one hand, Gary scooped up the mess and tossed it into the back seat. "There's one slob in this department," he said out loud, "who's going to be very sorry the Chief had to use a patrol car today!"

Gary had a fully developed passion for order and neatness. He began to plan, even enjoy, the substance of the anticipated chewout as he clamped the transmitter switch twice.

"Go ahead." Central Dispatch, at least, was doing exactly what it was supposed to do.

"Westlake here. I'm exiting the lot right now. Expect to return by 3:00 P.M. If there's…"

"Chief! We were just going to all-call you. Lowinski wants you. Says it's urgent."

Gary toyed for a moment with ignoring the request. New people on patrol had a way of failing to separate true urgency from simple impatience. Besides, he had a throbbing toothache. "Patch her through," he replied tiredly. He knew he couldn't entertain the thought of ignoring a call from a rookie.

Almost instantly the young policewoman was in contact. "Sir? Chief Westlake?" Gary hated Lowinski's habit of speaking in the interrogative. It made her sound like a teenager, which, come to think of it, he realized, she almost was! She was only twenty-one. "This is Chief Westlake." He tried not to sound gruff, but his tooth really hurt.

"Ah! Chief? The Packers case? I think I have something? You know the gun? The missing gun? A .38 Smith and Wesson, right? I'm holding a guy here. You better… uh… do you want to see for yourself?"

The Packers case was an unsolved murder, the first murder, solved or unsolved, in the seven years since Gary had become chief. One of the missing links was the murder weapon. Ballistic information had told them what it was, but that was as far as anyone on the case had been able to get.

"Slow down, Lowinski," Gary said, as much to himself as to the young woman on patrol. He could feel excitement in spite of himself, in spite of his aching tooth and the mess in 9119. "First of all, where are you?"

Lowinski was not about to slow down. "On King Road? East? I'm at… at…" The voice grew faint, then loud again. "At… in front of 414, okay? 414 King Road."

"All right. Hang on." Gary took a deep breath and thought

for a moment. A .38 Smith and Wesson was hardly something out of the ordinary. If it was only an unlicensed gun, then he'd be smarter to let Lowinski handle it herself. Good experience. But then...

"Lowinski. Are you all right? Do you need help?"

"No, sir, I'm fine. I have the susp — I mean, I have a possible arrest in the car. There's no trouble, okay? You want I should bring him in?"

"No. Yes! I mean... wait a minute, Lowinski."

Gary's toothache, which had been coming and going in waves, was gathering strength for another surge. He waited, but it didn't come.

"Uh... Lowinski? The Smith and Wesson? What's fishy about it?" Gary wondered if he, too, wasn't beginning to speak in the interrogative.

"No license."

Gary almost groaned.

"I stop him a few minutes ago, right? Tail light out. And I think I smell booze, right?"

Against his better judgment Gary answered, "Right."

"So. Routine check. I open the trunk. And there it is in the trunk. The gun?"

It occurred to Gary that Lowinski was not only interrogative in her style, she also spoke entirely in the present tense. "What makes you think it has anything to do with the Packers case?" he asked.

"Smith and Wesson, right?"

"Lowinski, we've been through that." The wave of ache had only been teasing before. Now it had arrived in force.

"Yeah, but that's it! The guy says he just found it! Like this morning?"

Were it anything but the Packers case, Gary would have made a second mental note: to have Lowinski take speech therapy. Instead he responded, "*Found* it? Where?"

"You know the construction on King Road? At the edge of

town? On the east? Toward Nobleton? Just at the bottom of the hill?"

"Lowinski, I know where it is!" One more question on top of the toothache would have tipped him over the edge.

"Well, the guy says he saw it lying in one of the big puddles there, right? Says he figures somebody ditched it. So he picks it up? Says he hasn't had time to turn it in. Okay?"

Gary heard himself say, "And you've, like, got him in your car now, right?" Whatever Lowinski's response, he didn't hear it. He was staring in shock at himself in the rearview mirror. "Lowinski, you've done well," he finally said. "Sit tight. I'll be there in two minutes."

He pulled the shift lever down into Drive, but before accelerating wiped a smudged fingerprint off the speedometer glass with a gloved hand. More dirt, he thought. "Lowinski! You still there?"

"Yes, Chief?"

"Lowinski, what car did you have yesterday?"

"Number 8228. The same one I always have. Why?"

"Never mind."

What has made Gary Westlake decide to endure toothache and discomfort to investigate Lowinski's potential arrest a little further?

28

On the Trail of the Stolen Horses

WITH THE NAKED EYE, ESPECIALLY from a standing position, it was impossible to tell for sure whether the stolen horses had been ridden along this particular trail. There were tracks, all right, hoofprints all over, almost all of them heading northeast, or else southwest, for that was the general direction of the trail. At a few points there were hoofprints that doubled on top of one another, rimming a semicircular pattern, showing that as a rider had reined up, the horse had done a bit of prancing. Most of the tracks snaked between two alder stumps that the farmer hadn't pulled yet, but there was nothing unusual in that.

Marv Chantler knelt to get a closer look, holding the reins of the rangy bay gelding with one hand. As he did so, the horse bent to nuzzle the back of his neck. It made Marv jump. "G'wan!" It was the first word he'd spoken since leaving the settler's grimy little yard at sunset the night before. The woman in the sod shanty had assured him in her laconic, distrustful manner that the horses had gone this way.

Marv ran his fingers over some of the prints on the trail. None of them was clearly fresh. They were more than a day old at the least. But from this close he could see the difference in the various horses: the size of the hoof, the ones that were shod and those that were not, the style of the smithies. He stood up and took a couple of steps toward the alder stumps, then knelt again. The bay followed without urging.

Here there was a different set of tracks. A wolf probably, or a large dog. With his eyes, Marv followed them across the trail. This animal had been in no great hurry. The tracks were straight for a few paces; they diverted in midtrail — likely to sniff some horse dung — straightened again, then diverted once more, almost certainly to sniff a varmint hole at one of the alder stumps. It was obviously abandoned, for dusty cobwebs stretched across the opening. The tracks then straightened once more and disappeared into the alder thicket. This was a fresh set, Marv could see. Last night, no doubt.

He stood up and rubbed the small of his back. The gelding came closer, expecting to be scratched. The hoofprints Marv was looking for — he just couldn't be sure. One of the stolen horses had thrown a shoe. Right foreleg. And there was a V-shaped chip out of her hoof. That had made the trail fairly easy to follow, and Special Constable Marvin Chantler of the Battleford detachment, North-West Mounted Police, had made steady progress for the past several days because of it.

There were three stolen horses, all of them, to the monumental embarrassment of the Battleford detachment, the Mounties' own! There was the huge jug-headed roan that Sergeant Gordon liked so much, a piebald mare of indeterminate ancestry — she was missing the shoe — and a bay gelding, full brother to the one Marv was riding now.

Their trail had led due north from Battleford and Marv had not lost it until just before he rode into the squatter's little farm last night at sunset. He thought about that moment as he pulled the bay round, put his foot in the stirrup and mounted.

The horse turned again, so that Marv had to redirect him to head back to the farm.

At first, last night, Marv had thought no one was there. But there were chickens scratching in the yard, and he'd heard at least one pig snuffling behind the sod shanty. Maybe *in* it, for all he knew. It was not uncommon for these little shacks to do double duty. Then the woman had appeared at the door: thin, worn, old way before her time, wearing a dress so faded from scrubbing it was hard to tell if it had ever had a pattern. Her hands were big and red and wrinkled from labor. A toddler clung to her leg, venturing to peer out at Marv only when he was sure he wouldn't be observed.

Marv had been at scenes like this many times since he'd come to the northwest. Settlers, squatters in the middle of nowhere, fulfilling the terms of their land grant by living on their quarter section. If it could be called living: ground down to the last ounce of resistance by poverty, hardship and total, absolute, isolation.

He'd brushed the dust off his tunic to be sure the red could be seen in the fading light. The reputation of the NWMP for honesty and fairness was known even to people like these. Maybe, he had thought, the sight of the red coat would allay some of the inevitable distrust.

It didn't. The woman never left the doorway. Getting her to speak was almost impossible. Still, she had acknowledged that yes, she'd seen three horses a couple of days or more ago. No, she couldn't remember much about them. One was very big. Gray. Another was patchy-colored. Two men. They didn't come near. Her man stood down by the fence with his shotgun. When Marv asked about where they'd gone she was a little more definite, pointing to the trail on which he was now returning.

This time as he approached the shanty there was more life: smoke from a hole in the corner of the roof, more chickens, and a dog that hadn't been there last night. It was barking furiously, running at the horse and backing away, making him dance nervously.

The woman appeared in the doorway again. In the morning light the dress was even more faded than the night before. The distrustful look was just the same, though. Nor was she any more forthcoming.

"You're sure those horses went up that way?" Marv smiled, attempting to break the ice.

She only nodded. Once.

"I know what I'm looking for," Marv said, "and I really couldn't see the tracks I want."

The woman lifted her face toward the sky and shrugged ever so slightly. "Rain," she said, barely opening her mouth.

Marv was silent for a long time. Then he sighed audibly. He had to let her know he didn't believe her now, but he didn't want to scare her, either. In a way he felt sorry. Not just that she was situated out here in the middle of empty space; it was more that she made him think of his mother back in Dorset. It was a lifetime since he'd seen his mother, since he'd answered the ad calling for young men seeking adventure doing police work in the colonies. There was nothing adventurous about his present situation, however, just uneasiness. Well, at least she didn't *look* the least bit like his mother. That was something, anyway.

What has convinced Marv Chantler that the woman in the sod shanty is misleading him — deliberately or otherwise?

29

The Royal Blue
Escort

"IF YOU ASK ME, THERE isn't a single blue Escort — uh, *royal* blue Escort — in the whole country, let alone Wythenshawe. I mean, how can we sit here for almost two hours and not see one up ahead there on — what's that street again — Brownlee? I mean, it's impossible! Likely the most popular car in the whole world and — Ow! *That's the third time!*"

Harvey Bottrell was slowly losing his customary good sense of humor. Whether he was right about the Ford Escorts or not, there was no mistake about the number of times he had banged his elbow on the parking meter. Sitting there in the nondescript, mud-colored Rover with Vin Murray, and with nothing to show for two hours of diligent watch, Harvey had begun to fidget. He had the feeling their stakeout was going to go sour, as so often happened. The thought disturbed him, and three times now he had bumped his elbow as he twisted round to look out the back window of the Rover.

Vin Murray, meanwhile, was concentrating on the task of relighting the bottom half of a cigarette. Earlier, he'd set a book of matches in front of him on the steering column. They'd fallen off and now he was looking for them.

To Harvey's further discomfort he simply responded, "Aye." Vin was not known for prattling.

"Well, at least —" Harvey was just the tiniest bit annoyed, "— at least can we back this thing up a bit into the proper parking space now that the car behind us is gone? So I don't have to sit nose-to-nose with this meter? I've got MANCHESTER PARKING AUTHORITY burned into my brain!"

"Aye." Vin had found the matches and lit up. His face was now completely obscured in a thick cloud of relit Player's Plain. It even moved with them, exactly in place, when Vin backed the Rover a few paces.

Harvey couldn't help himself. "Don't you think you should open your window, too?" he said.

The two men didn't know each other very well; they'd met for the first time only yesterday. Vin was a special assignment agent (antiterrorist) with Scotland Yard, working out of the Manchester office. Harvey, a Canadian, was with Interpol, working out of New York. The two were acting on a tip that the notorious Hans Keffer, of the Red Brigade, was in Wythenshawe, or possibly was coming to Wythenshawe, an eastern suburb of Manchester, for a meeting.

Keffer was famous among police forces in Europe, had been for years, because of his careful disguises and his obsession with "blending in," so he'd never be noticed. Neither Harvey nor Vin was surprised at the use of a Ford Escort. They knew it was a typical Keffer choice. The man knew England in great detail, and he'd know what car to pick. What did surprise them — and made them both dubious, though they'd not yet shared their doubts with each other — was the amount of information in the tip. Not just the car, the royal blue Escort, but the fact that the meeting was to take place on Robb Road in Wythenshawe. That was why the two were staked out here.

Vin nodded in agreement with Harvey about the window.

"Aye," he said yet again, then with careful deliberation transferred the cigarette stub to his other hand and rolled down the driver'-side window.

As the smoke swirled out, Harvey could see another No Parking sign on the pole opposite. Through the windshield — uh, wind*screen*, his inner voice reminded him — he could see the slashed red circle on every pole prohibiting parking all the way down to Brownlee Road. It intrigued him that the signs were so low.

"Y'know," he said, "in North America, the kids would be disappointed those No Parking signs aren't higher up the poles. Our kids like to make basketball jumps to see if they can touch signs like that."

Vin stared across at the signs for so long that Harvey wondered if it was possible he had never noticed this before. Vin took a final pull on the cigarette, then, with his thumb and forefinger, squeezed the glowing coal into the ashtray. Harvey waited for the "Aye."

Instead Vin said, "We play football." He put the cigarette butt into the Player's package. "It's closer to the ground."

Harvey's chuckle was swelling into a belly laugh, when it stopped in his throat. He and Vin stiffened into alertness in the same second. Coming down the street toward them was a Ford Escort. Royal blue. It wasn't new. Maybe two, three years old. Clean but not recently washed, certainly not shiny. Very Keffer. Nothing stood out.

The driver looked to be in his midforties. Everything seemed exactly right. But for one important thing. The two agents looked at each other.

This time Vin spoke first. "Nervy, that bloke. Or maybe he just doesn't know."

"I'd say he doesn't even know," Harvey replied. "But, then, maybe he saved our necks, too. We might have come down on him like a ton of bricks."

They both turned to watch as the car came abreast of them,

then passed on down the street until it topped a grade and dipped out of sight.

Harvey's shoulders drooped. "Looks like we're here for a while yet," he said, and then looked up at Vin. "That place where the other team is staked out? By the airport? What's it called again?"

Vin was looking around for the matches once more. "The Ship Inn."

"The Ship Inn," Harvey repeated. "It's a pub. Isn't it?"

Vin shook his head. "A right proper pub. Good ploughman's. Good place for a pint."

Harvey grimaced. "Some guys have all the luck."

"Aye," Vin said.

Why did Havey Bottrell and Vin Murray not stop or try to follow the royal blue Ford Escort that came toward them up Robb Road?

30

An Unlikely
Visitor — or Two

From the moment his office door swung open, Struan Ritchie knew this was not to be the kind of peaceful lunch break he always looked forward to. For one thing, Mrs. Bain, his exceptionally serious and exceedingly proper secretary, had not tapped the door first and then waited a discreet two or three seconds as was her custom. For another — Struan couldn't swear to it, for he didn't recall ever hearing it before — he was almost positive he'd heard Mrs. Bain suppress a giggle before she said, "Captain Ritchie, this gentleman has been here for the past three days to see you. All of the detectives... *hee...*" There it was again! Struan was sure of it this time. Mrs. Bain had giggled! "All the detectives feel you should handle this one."

For the moment, Struan couldn't see the gentleman Mrs. Bain was referring to, but through the open door he did get a sweeping glimpse of the squad room. Every single one of the detectives out there was watching — well, not just watching, they were staring, no, *gawking* — like a crowd at a fall fair. And they all had huge grins on their faces.

The detectives' expectations were bound up in the person of the little man who suddenly appeared from behind the ample Mrs. Bain, as though he had been hiding there.

"I'll be at my desk, Captain Ritchie." Mrs. Bain closed the door. Now Struan could hear loud guffaws out in the squad room. For a second he forgot his visitor. Only for a second.

"You're Captain Struan Ritchie, then. The medievalist, right? We're so pleased." As he spoke, the man stepped forward — minced forward, really — and sat in one of the two chairs in front of Struan's desk. He put an old-fashioned triangular-style briefcase on the other.

Struan tried not hard to stare. In spite of his years in police work he was inherently gracious. He'd never developed that suspicious weariness and confrontational pose so typical of police with long tenure on a big city force.

But his visitor invited staring. Provoked, it, in fact! The chairs in front of Struan's desk had over the past twelve years held con artists, wife-beaters, murderers, pickpockets, politicians, even — last week — a bishop. Today's guest, however, was like no other.

It wasn't just the unusual shape of the man; he had what appeared to be a normal torso on top of exceedingly short legs, so that sitting in the sturdy wooden chair, his feet — big feet — didn't quite reach the floor. Nor was it just his clothes. They were hardly a leading example of contemporary fashion, but that wasn't what distinguished them. It was more the combined effect of a vest, which did not quite match the suit, covered in turn by a cardigan that had no affinity whatever for the rest of the attire.

Still, it was not his appearance that attracted attention. It was the *manner* of the little fellow, Struan concluded. He had about him an aura of serenity, total serenity, the kind of at-peace-with-the-world that one imagines in cloistered nuns (Struan had met one or two of those) or successful graduates of prolonged therapy (Struan really wasn't sure whether he'd met any of those or not).

Whatever the source of calm in the man, he had made himself completely at home. In the brief instant when Struan was sizing him up, and trying to ignore the laughter in the squad room, the visitor opened the old briefcase and took out a book, which he set on the desk. The book appeared to be very old, written on what quite possibly was vellum. Struan got a rush at that. He really *was* a devotee of things medieval, a hobby that protected his mind and soul from the daily brutalities of urban police work, but not one that he could share with very many of his working colleagues.

The man then very calmly cleared a space on the desk. For more books Struan thought, but what appeared was a small, oval, beautifully crocheted doily followed by two Spode china luncheon plates perfectly matched. These were set out symmetrically on the doily. Now Struan really *was* staring!

"We are truly pleased you could see us." The voice was so calm, so gentle. Struan realized he hadn't been aware that the whole time the scene was being set, no one had spoken a word.

"Uh… it's… uh… not a problem. You…" Struan was stammering. He never stammered. His attention was being torn between the book, which he so desperately wanted to open, and the strange little man, who was now setting out carefully trimmed cocktail sandwiches on the Spode plates, along with — this was why Struan stammered, he was sure — tiny cocktail onions, individually wrapped!

"We hope you like tuna. These two have chopped walnuts." He nudged one plate slightly with a manicured hand. "These have celery. Surely you like tuna? Almost — *Of course he does!*"

Struan flinched at the latter outburst. It was so angry.

"Not necessarily." (Serenity again.) "Not everyone likes tuna. There are some people who — *Of course they do! Everyone does! You're doing it again!*"

This time Struan stole a glance into the briefcase. In spite of

151

himself he was looking for the source of the second voice. He shifted slightly in his chair so he could see behind the two chairs without turning his head.

The two voices continued. "*The book! Tell him about the book!* Yes, Captain Ritchie, the book. It's quite beautiful, isn't it? A 'Book of Hours' we're told. Mid-to-late fifteenth century, the agent said. Book of hours — that's like a prayer book, isn't it? It has prayers for special occasions and times of the day, doesn't it? Such a lovely thought. The wealthier classes — *Get on with it! Real or phony? That's why we're here!*"

That one made Struan jump. By now he was totally bewildered. The little man with the two voices and the beautiful book had sat throughout this entire exchange eating his elegant tuna sandwiches (one each of the chopped walnut and the celery) without a ripple in his peaceful demeanor.

With one hand Struan stroked the surface of the book's front cover. It certainly appeared to be calfskin, worn at the covers, but like so many pieces from medieval Europe, magnificently preserved. He opened it about midway to a beautiful spread. On one page, an illustration showed floating cherubs over what appeared to be children immersed in a bath, and surrounded by women, likely servants. Opposite, in rich ornamentation, with fine leaf work and a flower form motif in pink, blue, orange and green, was a single sentence in Latin: *Munditia pietam similis esse.* The M, in the style so typical of the era, took up over half the page, swirling in and around the sentence and finally enclosing it in an embrace of gold leaf.

Ever so gently, Struan drew the back of his hand over the letters to feel the irregularities of the scribe's delicate work. He was quite prepared to lose himself in its beauty, when suddenly his reverie was intruded upon by a loud guffaw from the outer office. With some reluctance, and also, he acknowledged later, because he didn't know what else to do, he took out an interview sheet.

"Uh… I'm sorry. This is standard procedure. I… uh… have

to have a record." He found he was still stammering.

"Of course. *Hurry up!* I understand. *Get on with it!*"

Struan put on his glasses. He never used them for close up, but it was another contact with reality.

"Your surname, please?"

"Miles."

"And your first name?"

"Miles."

"No, no. Uh… your given name."

"It's Miles."

"I think, maybe…" Struan took off his glasses and straightened his tie.

"*Miles Miles! Tell him! And not just that! Miles N. Miles! No middle name like everybody else — just N! Miles N. Miles. Our father didn't want a baby! We were a surprise! It's his idea of revenge! The book!* WILL YOU GET TO THE BOOK!"

For the first time, right in the middle of this outburst, Miles N. Miles looked directly at Struan. His expression was entirely benign, unmoved. Not a hint of annoyance. The only suggestion of anything out of the ordinary was a dollop of mayonnaise on the man's chin.

"Cleanliness is next to godliness, right?" Miles N. Miles said. "That's how the Latin on that page translates, doesn't it, Captain Ritchie? From the Bible, isn't it? The Old Testament?" The benign smile continued. "*For God's sake, I'll tell him! We'll be here forever! Look, we're rich, we're going to buy this for the museum! Now, is it real?*"

For the first time, the reason for the visit dawned on Struan. Also for the first time he felt he had a bit of control. "Ah, I see!" He was silent for a moment. He really wanted to linger over every page in the book, but at the same time he knew his busy precinct had no time for that.

"Why don't you gent — I mean… why don't you go to the university for an opinion? The medieval period is just a hobby with me, but they have experts. For instance, I can tell you that on this page here, with the sentence you're referring to, the Latin — it's not very good Latin. But, then, in a lot of monasteries the scribes themselves often didn't know Latin. A lot of the time they were just transcribers. Artists, too. Some of them. But, you see, if you went to the university…"

"*Not the university! Greedy! They're greedy! They want fees! They forget they're public servants!*"

"Wait… wait, Mr. Miles. The university — the range of expertise there is very wide, and you'll get better advice there. You see…" Struan took a deep breath; this was the part he didn't like to say. "You see, it's very unlikely that this is a book from the medieval period. It's generally agreed that medieval period ends around the year 1500, and I'm sure this book was produced well after that. Now, at the university, maybe there's someone who can tell you just when."

There was no reaction from Miles N. Miles. Just silence, which to Struan seemed quite prolonged, then a nod, as he began to return the luncheon plates to the briefcase. One of the sandwiches remained: a celery. For only the second time he looked straight at Struan. "*You don't like tuna, do you? Hah! I knew it!*"

What has led Struan to the conclusion that the book brought to him by Miles N. Miles is not likely to be a "Book of Hours" from the medieval period?

31

The Mission in
the Clearing

THEY HAD LEFT THE Land Rover in the bush and come in the last mile or so on foot. That had been the intent in any case, but because of the condition of the road they really had no choice. Curiously, instead of improving as they got closer to the little mission, the road had become worse, so that there was no question of proceeding without headlamps on. The moonless night was just too dark and the growth too thick. Even on foot they'd had trouble getting through quietly, but they'd made it without being discovered — or so they thought — and now the four of them were kneeling in the long grass at the edge of the clearing.

The squad was down to four, because the two Kikuyu "Home Guard" who normally rode on the roof of the Rover had disappeared shortly after the message came in on the wireless. Just melted away in the darkness. WO/I Ron Forrester had experienced this once before in an almost identical situation, and he wasn't really surprised. At bottom, he didn't blame them. These auxiliaries were called "government loyalists," but Ron knew that if their fellow Kikuyu in the Mau Mau ever caught them, they'd suffer a lot longer and a lot harder than the white soldiers in his squad.

What truly irritated Ron, however, and frightened him, too, was the loss of the wireless. Its battery pack, actually, for that was what the operator, Lance Corporal Haight-Windsor, had dropped under the rear wheel. The squad could do without Haight-Windsor. He was back with the Rover, nursing his broken arm, still drunk in all likelihood. Ron swore that when they got back to base, Haight-Windsor was going to be busted yet again, this time to private, but only after a nice long dryout in the stockade.

A message had come in two hours ago, the product of one of those radio wave flukes that amaze everyone and surprise no one. It was a call for help originating from St. Ignatius-in-the-Forest Mission, probably from one of the still smoldering huts in front of them. It had been picked up by a ham operator a continent away in Somerset. He managed to get the local police to believe him, and then, via a series of telephone calls, the message had been relayed to Nairobi and thence to Ron's base back in Nyeri. Major Bowman himself had called from there.

His booming voice over a burst of static had jerked them all awake. Good thing, too, for the last watch of the night was Haight-Windsor's and that was when he'd gotten drunk. It was during loadup that he dropped the battery pack.

The order was simple: "Divert from the patrol and proceed with all possible haste to St. Ignatius-in-the-Forest Mission. Use extreme caution. Under attack by Mau Mau terrorists."

An improbable name, St. Ignatius-in-the-Forest, but the mission was run by an equally improbable group of Jesuits from England. Against all advice they had refused to close it when the Mau Mau uprising had begun in earnest. On the contrary, the two fathers who ran the place had only just been relieved by two young seminary graduates fresh from Liverpool. Ron had never met them; he didn't even know their names. But he'd heard they were even more adamant than their predecessors about keeping the mission open. Now it seemed they were paying a price for their determination.

From where he knelt in the long grass, the light from the slowly rising sun told Ron that whatever had happened here, it was over, and the Mau Mau attackers were gone. Along with everyone else, it seemed. Or maybe they'd gotten out like the two Kikuyu auxiliaries. All but one of the buildings, the tiny schoolhouse, had been burned, destroyed. There was no sign of life anywhere, not even bodies. If there was anyone here, he (or she — Ron couldn't remember whether the nuns had finally left or not) would have to be in the schoolhouse.

Several yards to his left, PFC Willie Throckton shifted slightly to avoid a cramp. He looked over at Ron with eyebrows raised, and swung the barrel of his Lee Enfield Mark IV toward the schoolhouse. Ron signaled back "just hold on," then crawled to his right, where the two others, Barrow and Highland, were concealed behind the mission's upturned GMC pickup. From here, Ron reconnoitered once more, using the new perspective to confirm his strategy.

Without taking his eyes off the school, he spoke to Barrow. "S.O.P. I'm putting a grenade over there for diversion. Then Throckton's going in first. We cover. He shelters on the shadow side. When he's in, you go to the other side."

Barrow just nodded. They were an experienced team and had done this before. Even Haight-Windsor, like the rest of them, had done two tours in Korea only a few years before.

Ron leaned back to be sure Highland was listening. He was.

"You're staying," he said to Highland. "I'm pretty sure the place is empty. If there's no return fire, I'm going straight in the door."

Highland simply nodded and ran his index finger along the grenades in his belt.

No more than ten seconds passed between the time Warrant Officer I Ron Forrester threw the grenade and when he burst through the door of the schoolhouse. There had been no return fire.

Ron stood in the schoolhouse for a few seconds more, then called, "Looks clear! I'm okay! Stay alert!"

It was not Mau Mau style to stick around after an attack, but he was taking no chances.

The shambles in the schoolhouse was to be expected. Quickly Ron took in the scene. Benches and tables were piled in disarray along both side walls. With their *pangas* the attackers had chopped up the school's paltry few books and scattered them around. A huge gouge had been cut out of the already dilapidated chalkboard. Particular care had been taken with the crucifix. It was barely recognizable. What really held Ron's attention, though, was the two dead priests in the center of the room.

Strangely, there was no evidence of torture, but that might have been because the squad's approach had been heard or seen, after all. Both men lay facedown in a pool of their own blood. Their arms had been cut from elbow to wrist, ritually, and it appeared they had bled to death. The right leg of one priest was bound at the ankle to the left leg of his partner with a leather thong that must also have had ritual significance, for small animal bones dangled from it at precise intervals. Both men still wore their shoes and Ron couldn't help reflecting on the improbable contrast of the mystical thong and the sturdy, sensible black Oxfords. One was scuffed from top to bottom at the back of the heel, the other — in fact both shoes belonging to the other priest — sparkled with a fresh buffing. It almost seemed as if he, like his attackers, had done some ritual preparation, for his cassock, too, was clean and new, and his hair neatly combed, unlike the priest on the left, whose appearance was unkempt, disheveled.

Both men, however, lay in the same position on the floor, and when he saw the nails, Ron suddenly knew what the attackers had had in mind. He looked again at the chopped-up crucifix and shuddered. It was well the Mau Mau had heard the squad coming.

Taking a few steps, he picked up one of the nails, then, for the first time, noticed the key ring lying under the remains of a bench near the wall. With his foot he dragged it out and picked it up. It had an ignition key. That he recognized. Another key — he had no idea what it was for. There were two brass disks. Both said D.M. Vincent, S.J., on one side. On the opposite, one said, A+, and the other said, Dipth. W.C. Typhoid 12/07/54.

He put the ring in his shirt pocket, then looked around cursorily for more things like it. When he saw nothing, he reluctantly bent over the bodies and began to pat their pockets for belongings. Nothing. A white band on the wrist of one of them said there had once been a wristwatch there, but it was gone.

Ron rocked back on his heels for a minute, wrapping his arms around his legs at the knees. That was when the fly crawled up from inside the rather dirty Roman collar to settle on the nostril of the priest nearest him, and he saw the twitch. At first he thought it was his imagination, but when it happened again he yelled for Throckton. Throckton was the squad's medic.

The young PFC burst in immediately, his rifle at the ready.

"One of them's alive. I'm sure of it!" Ron realized he was still yelling.

Quickly Throckton took a pulse behind the jaw of each priest. "This one!" he said excitedly, indicating the one whose nose the fly had found. Then more slowly he added, "But not for long. It's thready. He's lost too much blood."

"No! No!" Ron was shouting again. "I'm A-positive! You can transfuse, can't you?"

"Yes, but... yes." Throckton could sense Ron's excitement. "But that's not enough!" He shook his index finger in a kind of maternal admonition. "To get enough, we'd kill you to save him! By the look of it he needs four, five pints! I can't take

159

more than one, maybe one and a half out of you, and that's dangerous, anyway!"

"Let me see!" Ron grabbed Throckton's identification tags. "No! You're A-negative!"

"So's Barrow," Throckton replied. "And Highland's AB something. Haight-Windsor's O-negative."

"O-negative!" Ron grabbed Throckton's arm. "That's universal donor, right? Can you get enough out of me and out of Haight-Windsor to keep the priest alive until we get to the airstrip at Rumuruti? That's an hour away in the Rover!"

Throckton pulled his arm away reluctantly. "But Colour Sergeant! It's not that simple! O-negative is okay, but... how do we know the priest's blood type matches yours? If we give him the wrong type, we'll kill him, anyway!"

"Trust me." Ron said. "Which arm? Let's get started." Then he shouted, "Barrow! Get out there and get the Rover and bring that fool wireless operator with you!"

What has made Ron Forrester confident that his A-positive blood is the same blood type as the priest who is still alive?

32

Trespassing on the MBA Property

THERE WAS NO WAY OF getting to the site without climbing up and then down a series of fairly steep knolls, and at the top of the fourth in a row, Jack Atkin paused once more to catch his breath. He leaned against a large maple, one arm extended as casually as he dared without falling over, and willed his lungs not to puff. Ron Minaker and Harold Bidigare were at least one knoll behind, and he knew they would both be breathing hard into the crisp autumn air when they caught up.

That would give Jack a bit of an edge, he knew; he wouldn't even have to say anything. In fact, the edge would be sharper that way, for he would hone it by initiating conversation in an entirely normal voice, while the other two would have to gasp for breath to respond. Jack had recovered from a serious coronary two years before and was now a committed distance walker. It did wonders for his condition and he couldn't help being just a bit born-again about fitness. Especially with Minaker and Bidigare, who were notoriously out of shape. The three old friends had been doing this to one another for years: one-upping

161

in a genial but very satisfying way.

The joshing wouldn't last long, though. This case was too serious for frivolity. Jack Atkin was a private investigator. Harold Bidigare was president of Rosseau Casualty Inc., a large insurance firm. And Ron Minaker was a senior partner in the law firm that handled all of Rousseau's litigation. They were here in what Bidigare called "absolute confounded nowhere" — Minaker called it "classic, post-Pleistocene terrain" — to look firsthand into a piece of evidence in the Dahlman case, a high-profile, potentially messy lawsuit that Bidigare's firm and its largest client, Mary Blair Associates, couldn't afford to lose.

Mary Blair Associates was a big land developer. For several years, in anticipation of urban sprawl from the city, MBA had been holding on to a big piece of hilly land that it planned to turn into an estate residential subdivision. The southwest corner of the piece, where the three men were now gathering, abutted a large tract of public land, destined one day to become a nature park.

For the present, the area had become a haven for young teenagers on ATVs, three- and four-wheeled, high-powered, all-terrain vehicles that Jack and many others privately referred to as kid-killers. MBA had posted No Trespassing signs and No Motorized Vehicles Allowed signs all along the property line, but the kids paid little attention to them, especially since this hilly part of the MBA property was dotted with mature maple and ash and a few oak trees, just sparse enough to make weaving through them at the highest possible speeds a real challenge to young ATV drivers.

Four months ago Sasha Dahlman, a fourteen-year-old and, to add to the complexity, second son of the city mayor, had piled up a Suzuki 230 and turned himself into a quadriplegic for life. Now the Dahlmans were suing MBA. Precedent in case law put MBA in a delicate spot despite the signs, for the property was not fenced. But the company did have a trump card to play: it was not clear whether the accident had occurred on the

MBA property or on the public land.

The Suzuki had been found, damaged but upright, precisely bisected by the property line, but in fourth gear and facing the public property. Searchers had found Sasha Dahlman about twenty meters inside the line on the public property side, but he swore that he'd flipped well back on the MBA side, that the machine had kept on going and that he'd crawled for some time before passing out. Both an orthopedic surgeon and a neurologist had testified that much of the spinal damage was likely due to "post-trauma aggravation," so the lad had indeed probably crawled after the crash. But from where?

This morning Ron Minaker had jolted both Jack and Harold with news he'd just received from Dahlman's lawyer. Yesterday, Sunday afternoon, Dahlman's elder brother had found Sasha's helmet in a hollow where several of the knolls lined up like a large pocky rash on the landscape. The spot was well inside the MBA property.

To Jack's immediate question, Ron replied that two other boys were with the older Dahlman and all three had already signed statements that they'd seen it clearly on MBA property from one of the hills and that they'd then brought out the local police to photograph it and take it in. Whether Sasha had been wearing the helmet or not, Ron pointed out, would be of no consequence. This was to be a jury trial, and in the hands of the very able Dahlman lawyer, Graeme Campbell, the location of the helmet would be damaging evidence, indeed.

The situation was urgent enough to bring the three men out here almost immediately, Jack in his hiking shoes, cords and a DiTrani hiking jacket, his two more sedentary buddies still wearing suits and ties, and both regretting it.

Jack pulled the zipper of his jacket up to the throat. It was chilly where he stood here on the hill. Indian summer had visited briefly and then left, about two weeks before. There was no snow yet, but winter wasn't far off. He ticked the zoom lever on his Canon Photura to get a better focus on Ron Minaker, laboring up the hill toward him. Minaker had found a pair of toe rubbers in his trunk and a red-and-black checked hunter's cap. At either end of his tailored suit, covered in turn by a rakish London Fog trenchcoat, Minaker was a caricature of himself, especially since somewhere back farther he'd undone the earflaps on the hat. By framing the look of discomfort on his face, the hat made him look like a very unhappy beagle.

Jack took two shots, one after the other. An intense, all-day wind the week before had cleared the trees of any remaining leaves, and he had a clear view. He could also see through the viewfinder that Ron wasn't puffing nearly as hard as Harold Bidigare, and Jack knew that would not go without comment.

"Tell... tell... tell the St. Bernard to pour! We're almost there!" Bidigare shouted. He really was breathing hard.

Ron Minaker was about to add something but checked himself and posed. Jack was taking a closeup. What Ron didn't realize was that one of the earflaps was now sticking out at a right angle. Jack would use that at a cocktail party sometime in the future.

"Sheesh!" Bidigare wasn't finished. "Can't you arrange a helicopter next time? Where are we, anyway? I bet there isn't a good restaurant within two hours! What time is it? I'm hungry!" Each sentence had come out in a rapid burst.

Ron Minaker looked at Jack and spoke with the deliberateness that results from very controlled breathing. "It really wasn't so bad. Frankly, I didn't realize this moraine had so many drumlin formations at this point. Back there we..."

"Is this... is this..." Harold Bidigare was fighting to slow his breath rate. "Is this dissertation going to be on your bill?" He turned to Jack. "I have heard more geology that I don't want to know in the past hour than..." He gave way to a fit of coughing.

Minaker chuckled. "I'm surprised you could hear, with the noise you make breathing!" He looked to Jack. "You don't have a resuscitator in that fancy jacket, do you? We've still got to walk back."

"No," Jack replied, " but I did bring Geritol, because I knew you two were coming." With his index finger he pushed up on his left breast pocket, exposing the top of a flask. "But here. First. While you've still got your eyesight…" He held out several large glossy photographs and a hand-drawn map. "You agree that's the spot down there? Where they supposedly found the helmet, I mean?"

His two companions took the material and studied it, sobered by the reminder of just how serious the situation really was.

"Not much doubt," Ron said. He looked back and forth from the photographs to the hollow below, then handed them to Harold Bidigare, who did the same.

"Good," Jack Atkin said with emphasis, and pulled out the flask. "You'd better fuel up, you two patsies. It was definitely worth coming out here, but now we've got to walk back."

The reason for coming out to this spot on the MBA property was to check the finding-of-the-helmet story and to find a flaw in it if there is one. It appears that Jack has done so. What is it?

33

When History
Becomes Math

WHAT JOHN FOGOLIN COULD NEVER reconcile, even from the informed perspective of the tenth grade, was how Sister Augustinetta could be so, well, so downright obnoxious and difficult, and still be a nun! All the other nuns he'd ever known, especially here at Quail Run Academy, were just what everybody thought nuns should be: helpful, kind — most of the time — and full of the peacefulness that spread to people near them.

Some of them were fun to be around. Like tiny little Sister Mary Theresa in the first grade. She wasn't much bigger than her students, but all she had to do was appear in the schoolyard and in seconds she looked like a queen bee in a swarm, with all the first graders clamoring around to hold her hand. Then there was Sister Anthony from the sixth grade, who was deeply admired by all the senior boys for the way she ripped the last possible ounce of power out of the convent's black Chrysler sedan. And Sister Mary Bernadette, who had a fastball that no one, not even Barney King in the senior school, could lay wood on.

But Sister Augustinetta? The only thing John could figure

was that she was a math teacher, and math teachers, he was convinced, just were sort of that way. Quail Run still reverberated from the short tenure of Ms. Thibodeau-Elmont, who'd taught math to the sixth, seventh and eighth grades two years ago. She became known immediately as "El Tigre" and in only three months was mysteriously replaced by the dramatically less efficient but infinitely more patient Sister Veronica.

Among other things, what bugged John — he looked down at the paper in front of him — was that Sister Augustinetta turned everything he liked into math lessons! Take this project here, in North American history. It was supposed to be *history*, for heaven's sake. And he *liked* history! But this…?

The tenth grade had been divided into "investigative trios." Each trio was given its own problem to solve, and each member in a trio held a distinct piece of information needed to solve the problem. The three parts, properly put together, along with a bit of very straightforward research, would supposedly yield the solution.

John Fogolin's trio had been given this problem:

Which of the firstborn children of Magdalene, Catherine and Korron, if any, would have been American citizens, or British citizens, when they were born?

All three held that question. John, in addition, was given this piece of information.

All three of Hezekiah Beame's daughters, Magdalene, Catherine and Korron, married at the age of twenty-two in Pawtucket. Each had her first child there, exactly two years after her wedding ceremony.

Magdalene celebrated her eighteenth birthday during the voyage from Bristol to St. John. At the time, Catherine was twice as old as Korron.

167

The door to study room 20 opened and closed gently, and a soft voice said, "I've got it, John. Found it right away."

John Fogolin's mood lifted measurably. One good thing — one very good thing — about this project was that Linda Sandness was in his trio. Because of that, he was almost grateful to Sister Augustinetta for the assignment, for although Linda didn't know it yet, she was going to be his date for the spring ball in two months.

Linda had returned from the resource center, where she had gone to look up details about the Seven Years' War. Her one-third of the trio's problem read:

> *Three years after the end of the Seven Years' War, Hezekiah and Martha Beame sailed with their three daughters from Bristol, England, to Saint John, New Brunswick, and a new life in the New World.*
>
> *Within two months of landing in Saint John, after a dispute with local authorities, Hezekiah Beame took the family to Boston, then shortly afterward to Rhode Island, where they settled permanently.*

"Listen," Linda said. "This really helps."

She moved immediately to the table where John sat, and began to read aloud from the book she carried. "The Seven Years' War," she read, "was fought in Europe, North America and India, between France, Austria, Russia and Sweden on one side, and England and Prussia on the other. It started when Prussia invaded Saxony in 1756 and —"

"Prepare yourselves, ye great unwashed! I have cut the Gordian knot!"

The downside of the project had arrived. The number three member of their "investigative trio" was Porky Schnarrfeldt, whose single but unforgettable claim to distinction at Quail Run Academy was that he had torched a fart in the boys' change room in the sixth grade, so successfully that he'd been hospitalized with second-degree burns. Moreover, his assistant in the act, Denny Walchuk, who was even more maladroit than Porky, had dropped the lit match into a wastebasket and started a fire that set off a smoke alarm, which in turn brought in the fire brigade and caused the entire school to be evacuated into a snowstorm.

Porky's venture was known ever after as the-Fart-that-Cleared-the-Academy, but, unfortunately for him and even more for his classmates, it had raised his profile to unofficial clown laureate, and there were times, like the present, when he was very hard to take.

His entrance had completely dissipated John's dreamy admiration of Linda's hair, and made him just a bit angry. "Where were you, anyway, Schnarrfeldt?" John barked. "We don't even know what your information is!"

"*Pax vobiscum*, faithful companions." Porky made a sign of blessing over the table. "Your dutiful complicitor has graced the triumvirate with this nubby tidbit." He spread his arms and cleared his throat, as John and Linda looked at each other in defeat. This was obviously a prepared speech.

"Hearken, peasants. I read. Ahem. The Treaty of Paris," Porky declaimed, holding an encyclopedia as though he were in a pulpit, "signed in 1783, signaled the conclusion of the American Revolutionary War and recognized the United States as a nation." He had pronounced "conclusion" *CON*-clusion, and when he said *NAY*-shun, John and Linda leaped in together before Porky got into his plantation-owner persona.

"What's the *first* part? The stuff you got from Sister?" John hadn't intended to, but he'd outshouted Linda.

Porky was undeterred. "I am not finished, peasant. You should also know that Rhode Island renounced allegiance to Great Britain in 1776, and that it signed the Constitution in 1790 and —"

"We know all that, Clarence," Linda said in a soft voice, using

Porky's real name. It had an instant effect. "What we need," she continued, "is your part of the trio information."

"I... yeah," Porky said. "Okay... uh... here."

He read:

> *When they landed at Saint John, Korron Beame was half as old as Magdalene had been when the Seven Years' War began.*

"That's all?" Linda asked.

"Yup." Porky nodded.

John's face broke into a huge grin. "You know," he said, I think it's enough!"

His smile broadened. Sister Augustinetta had overestimated how long it would take for them to get the answer, especially since it wasn't due till tomorrow morning. Now, if he could just find a way to get rid of Porky...

What is the answer to the problem Sister Augustinetta has given John, Linda and Porky?

34

Nothing Wrong with Helena, Montana

AS FAR AS STEVE FLECK was concerned, the one — the *only* — drawback to working here in Helena, Montana, was far outweighed by all the advantages. The drawback was that he never got to use his German, or his French, or his command of two Hungarian dialects. Nor was this considerable linguistic accomplishment recognized in his salary, or as a valuable asset in his department. Quite the opposite. Foreign languages, even here at the airport, only raised eyebrows. Just last month when Steve had taken a telephone call in the employees' lounge from his brother back in Uffenheim, and the two had nattered away, in German, about family gossip, his staff had gathered to stare in disbelief.

Still, Steve had dismissed this minor disadvantage years ago. Helena, he acknowledged, might be a bit of a backwater in the great international scheme of things, but being head of airport security here was a sight easier on the nerves than the same job in Frankfurt. He'd never gotten used to the sight of soldiers there, walking about in pairs, machine guns held crossways in front of their bodies. Nominally, these soldiers were under his charge, but he knew their first obedience was to the military hierarchy. And no one ever listened to him when he argued that their presence tantalized rather than deterred terrorists.

Charles de Gaulle in Paris was no better. There were even more soldiers in this airport, so he'd resigned after only a few months. As for Heathrow, he hadn't even bothered to go to the interview after walking through the terminal that served flights to the Middle East.

No, Helena, Montana, was just fine. Still a few too many guns for Steve's liking, but most of them were slung behind the cabs of pickup trucks. And they were hunting rifles, not machine guns. To boot, they weren't allowed into the airport, not even into the parking lot. That one had been Steve's most unpopular decree since becoming head of airport security some six years ago, but even that had faded as an issue when everyone got used to it.

In fact, Helena could well be the only airport in his considerable experience, Steve thought as he got to his feet to leave the office, where he could do precisely what he was doing right now and not feel guilty. That was to walk out while the fax machine — the one hooked into Immigration Security in Washington — was pushing out an incoming message. Messages to Helena never amounted to a pinch.

Besides, Steve was about to enjoy one of the pluses that had recently developed in this job. Two months ago he'd hired Meike Verwij to fill a vacancy in the floor staff. Not only was he able to use his smattering of Dutch now, but he also had designs on this attractive young lady, which she seemed to welcome. Meike had just buzzed him from the luggage area; the fax could wait.

The timing is perfect, he thought as he started down the wide staircase to the main floor. He could see Meike standing by the security barrier of the luggage area, and he knew that in five minutes she was due to have a break.

The anticipation faded, though, as he got closer. Meike had an anxious look on her face. And on the face of the man beside her was a look that, if anything, was ominous — and angry. He was expensively dressed and carefully manicured, his whole image pronounced by a head of elegant silver hair. He was being detained, and his aristocratic bearing made this affront to his dignity appear all the more ignominious.

There was no question of his stomping off, for behind him and Meike towered Jimmy Whitecloud, Meike's floor partner. Jimmy was reputed to be the biggest security guard in the business. Steve had to admit he'd never seen one bigger anywhere.

He put on his public-relations expression and walked toward them, but Meike darted forward and pulled him aside. She was apologetic.

"You said always to call you if we were suspicious, no matter what!" She was breathing very quickly and looking at Steve for confirmation.

He nodded, but his PR expression had now turned to a frown.

"And —" Meike was breathing even faster "— I hope I didn't do anything wrong here, but... see his luggage?"

Without being obvious, Steve shifted slightly to take in the two suitcases at the feet of the angry man. They were, like the man's clothes, top of the line and, while certainly not battered, seemed to be very much used. They'd seen travel — one of them in particular — with stickers, advertising such exotic locales as Jakarta, Dubai, Valparaiso and Buenos Aires.

Steve nodded again. He'd prepared a little Dutch expression on the way down, but somehow it didn't seem even remotely appropriate at the moment. That didn't matter; Meike wasn't interested in chitchat right now.

"You know how we're supposed to make people show their luggage ticket?" she said. "You know, match the ticket against the tag on the luggage?"

It was another one of the changes Steve had introduced. Most travelers were actually grateful. It precluded a lot of mixups.

"Yes, of course." He had spoken for the first time.

"Well, the man there — he couldn't find his. Oh, he did eventually. Had to go through all his pockets. His passport's Czechoslovakian. It must have a hundred stamps on it."

Steve was alarmed. "You surely didn't take his passport, did you? We're not authorized —"

"No, no. But what I do have is this."

For the first time Steve noticed the piece of paper in Meike's hand.

"You said if there's anything suspicious, we detain the person and call you, right?" Meike was breathing more comfortably now.

Again Steve just nodded. In spite of himself he was feeling a bit uneasy. There were times when he felt he overdid things. He knew that there were some on the airport board who thought so. However, after all those years in European airports — well, he just couldn't help it.

"So what is it you have?" he asked, reaching for the paper.

"His itinerary." Meike held it out, but he didn't take it from her. He could read it easily.

"He gave it to me to hold while he went through his pockets. His glasses, too, and the passport. That's before he got mad. It has to be an itinerary," Meike said. "See, the first date is yesterday. It shows a Pan Am flight to Chicago, then..." She put her finger on the second line. "Holiday Inn, 1-800-525-2242."

Steve could see the neat block lettering. The second date was today's, August 16, and it listed Northwest Airlines to Helena, Montana, then Best Western 1-800-528-1234. Tomorrow's was Northwest again, and it showed Calgary, Alberta: Hilton 1-800-268-9275. Then for August 18, Air Canada to Toronto, Ontario, Relax Inn 1-800-661-9563. The last was 19 August, United Airlines to Albany, New York: Howard Johnson 1-800-654-2000. Then at the bottom was a line, "Always call between 5:00 P.M. and 8:00 P.M. EST."

Steve looked at the man standing with his luggage under the shadow of Jimmy Whitecloud. Then he looked directly at Meike. "I wonder... Naw, it couldn't be. It's never in six years... I... Go stand with Jimmy. I'll be right back."

Taking the stairs two at a time, Steve dashed for his office and burst through the door. The fax was quiet now, but a two-page message dangled from the feeder gap. He tore it off.

"Level Two Alert," it said. "Detain for immigration authorities or local FBI." Then it went on to describe the suspected illegal entry into North America of Gert Neustadt, a.k.a Anton Dobrany, alleged 2IC of ODESSA. A second paragraph gave a brief summary of the man's alleged war crimes and a listing of procedures for contacting Immigration.

The second page had a computerized composite of Gert Neustadt's face. The fax, of course, couldn't illustrate silver hair, but the rest of the resemblance was unmistakable.

As he strode out the door, Steve felt a tingle of satisfaction at the realization he was going to be able to use his German, and this time the stares would be respectful ones. But what really gave him a charge was that he now had a very good reason to take Meike Varwij out to dinner!

No, there was surely nothing wrong at all with Helena, Montana. Nothing at all.

Obviously Meike found something suspicious about the silver-haired man that caused her to report to Steve Fleck. Exactly what was it?

175

SOLUTIONS

1
A Clean Place to Make an End of It

One of the very clear pieces of evidence is that the body has been dead for some time. The odor makes that certain, so it is quite likely that, as the coroner says, the victim has been dead for forty to fifty hours.

Therefore, if the woman backed the car into the garage that long ago, and left the motor running until she died, the car would have run out of fuel, and the battery would have been drained to powerlessness owing to the fact that the ignition was left on. Yet Bob was able to lower one of the windows by simply ticking the switch. He suspects that this car may not be the place where the person died.

2
Chasing the Bank Robbers

The cars are very similar, and Kay has willed herself not to attend to details like license numbers because she's on vacation. So there's probably nothing in the appearance of the cars to influence her choice.

It's possible that the robbers used two identical cars and one then became a decoy in the subdivision, but the chasing policeman didn't mention that. And there's still only one patrol car to follow two possible suspects.

However, the first car had its signal light going. That fact, at a T intersection that is apparently blind, would suggest the driver has some idea where he or she is going, or at the very least knows the T intersection is there. Since the officer in the chase car has indicated that the robbers are local, it's probable that Kay MacDuffee will therefore recommend following the first car to the left.

3
The Power of Chance

In all likelihood, Walter "Whispering" Hope has impaired hearing. He speaks very loudly, which is typical of people with diminished hearing capacity. Still, this may just be habit from trying to communicate on construction sites. The clincher is seeing Hope at work on a backhoe without hearing protection. It's very likely he has hearing damage if that's the way he works.

There is another element that may also prove to be pertinent. Whether Tom knows it or not (he'll certainly discover it if he looks into Walter Hope) on most construction sites the workers wear yellow hard hats and the bosses wear white ones. If Hope is a bossman, he's likely been around these noisy places for some time.

If it's going to be Hope's testimony that he overheard the defendants trying to deal goods on the patio of a bar, which itself is not an acoustically ideal location, there is good reason to suspect his credibility as a witness.

4
On Flight 701 from Hong Kong

Ralph Ransom has quite correctly found several of both men's actions suspicious, although they would be quite ordinary and everyday if the men weren't the subjects of a tip. There's no reason why Huan Lee, for example, should not make a telephone call from the lobby before going to his room. It's done all the time, and it's hardly suspicious. Also, the fact that the man has little luggage may well indicate his experience as a traveler. Similarly, what's wrong with Won Lee buying chocolate bars? Or what's suspicious about being hyper? Lots of people are, whatever their race or color or sex or...

The fact that both men are named Lee is a coincidence that should not raise any eyebrows. It's a very common result when a Chinese name is translated into English: a Smith or Jones equivalent.

But Ralph has picked up a discrepancy. Won Lee's passport does not show any trips to North America, and he told Turpin it was his first visit. Yet this hyper man bought Mars bars in seconds — literally "pumps out the change" according to Iggie Kavanagh. Someone who has never been to Canada will not be familiar enough with the coinage to do that. Canadian nickels, dimes, quarters — not to mention the loonie — are different from the coinage in Hong Kong. A stranger would have to take longer than Won Lee did to identify the coins needed to buy a thing "in seconds."

Anyone who has ever been in a foreign country for the first time knows that getting used to the money is one of the most awkward adjustments. Mr. Won Lee is not exactly what he purports to be.

5
Trying to Find Headquarters

The group is supposed to go to St-Aubert. Whether Montgomery's headquarters is still there, or even if it ever got there, is not Doug's concern, since he and his little squad aren't aware of what is going on around them beyond the awareness of combat.

Fortunately the road sign to St-Aubert is still attached to the post, even if it's pointing into the ground. So is the sign pointing to Bayeux, from which they have been traveling. For Doug, it was a reasonably simple procedure to mentally position the sign with the Bayeux piece pointing back along the road they have been traveling, then follow the sign to St-Aubert.

6
The Case of the Disappearing Credit Card

Julie Iseler has some advantages in this situation. One is that when she and Tammy Hayward deal with the Saint twins, the boys can be distinguished by their respective double and single crowns — although that's only useful if the top backs of their heads can be seen. Another advantage is that her experience as a hair stylist has made her more than usually adept in the physics of mirrors.

But this is not to take away from her powers of logical deduction.

While she was talking to Mrs. Saint, Julie saw one of the boys carefully decorating a tattoo with red felt marker. She also noted that the other twin had already completed his in a similar fashion. From the incident of the pinch, the previous spring, she knows that Paul is left-handed. Thus Paul's tattoo must be on the crook of his right arm and Peter's tattoo on the crook of his left.

With the redecorating in Hair Apparent, Julie can only see the cash and waiting areas via two mirrors when she's at her chair (where indeed she was, attending to George, when the telephone rang and she saw the VISA card being taken.) Under the old decoration system, she'd have looked into only one mirror to see the waiting and cash areas. She realizes that in that situation, every image is reversed. (Right arms appear left and vice versa). But in the new system, the second mirror — the one on the side wall — *re*-reverses the image, so that in the second mirror a right arm would actually appear as a right (and left as left).

To conclude that Paul has taken the credit card, she must have seen a right arm with a tattoo on it reflected in the second mirror. (By the same token, had she seen a left arm with a tattoo, she'd have concluded it was Peter.)

7
A Badly Planned Saturday?

Taken together, there are pieces of circumstantial evidence that might nudge Jeff Baldwin and others into being suspicious. Especially if it can be determined that Dan Turner and Jeannie Burnside have a relationship that is more than just friendly. Most especially if such a relationship existed before the Saturday trip.

It was Jeannie who packed the food, after all, and she whose snowmobile did not have a spare drive belt.

There's only the word of these two survivors, too, for what happened.

Jeff has twigged to a discrepancy between their story and what he has seen in his follow-up visit. Turner said they had used Mark Burnside's saw to cut trees for a shelter. And there is indeed a shelter made of pine trees. Jeff photographed it. And the trees had been cut for some time — several months at least, for the needles were dead — but not long enough for them to have fallen off. The real matter, however, is the stumps. The one Jeff was sitting against was only as tall as his ear, about the height of an adult's torso and head. So were all the others. Yet when these trees were supposedly cut, the freshly fallen snow was as deep as Dan Turner's height, and it had fallen on top of what was already a record winter fall. The stumps of trees cut at that point would be much taller than the height of an adult torso and head.

Why were the stumps short then, almost normal? Had someone cut them in advance late last fall? Or first thing this spring? And if so, why? Why is the shelter part of the story patently untrue?

8
From *Sine Timore*
(The official newsletter of the National Association of Security Services)

Since it was fairly certain that the cold-rolled steel parts were being carried out, first in duffle bags, then in the sealed cardboard boxes, it was a matter for Stephen of identifying which cardboard boxes they were concealed in.

Since the parts are heavy (cold-rolled steel is especially dense) they would add a considerable weight to what was supposed to be personal effects: clothing, for example. The obvious security method would have been to X-ray the boxes or simply heft them to find the heavy ones and open them. But that had already caused a strike. For reasons of labor peace, Stephen couldn't intervene in that way without very reasonable certainty of what he would find in a search.

By changing the "punch-out" procedures, Stephen devised a much subtler way of identifying boxes that were clearly heavier, and without touching them. Under his new system, the workers picked their individual time cards from the original wall rack, walked out the double doors to the lobby to stamp them and re-filed them in the rack there. In that process — at some point, if not all the time — the workers would have to carry their bread-box-sized cartons under one arm, resting on the hip. If the carton were heavy, the *other* arm would elevate; the body can't help it; the reaction is natural, and in the case of a very heavy weight, even necessary for balance.

Stephen waited till the third day. He was likely waiting until he was certain of a pattern.

(By the way, for Latin scholars: you were correct, *sine timore* means "without fear" or "without insecurity." Ablative case, of course.)

9
"Could Be the Biggest Thing Since Tutankhamen"

There are several questionable levels at which the rock climber's fraud might stumble, but not fall entirely. Isla de los Estados lies just off the eastern tip of Tierra del Fuego, and it *is* an unlikely spot to find a Stone Age tribe, principally because it's rather barren and subject to dreadful weather. Certainly there is no jungle there. Yet an inhospitable environment did not deter the aboriginal peoples in the very far northern latitudes. (And the tribe has established its quarters on the north of the mountain, away from prevailing winds at that latitude.)

Their food is mostly meat, which is logical given the climate, although one might be suspicious of the amount.

That there is no rear entrance/exit to the cave is cause for suspicion. Smoke from the fire might fill the cave. Still, the fire is at the entrance way; besides, early explorers in North America regularly reported the overwhelming smoke problem in the shelters of aboriginal peoples, so there's no reason for that to be an issue here, either.

What Thomas Arthur Jones probably noticed in many, if not all the photographs, was the neatness and the absence of garbage. Many of the shots revealed that areas surrounding the cave, and the cave itself, were very clean. Archaeologists look for garbage. The midden, or garbage heap, is a book in multiple volumes that tells them all about a people. This tribe, which had apparently been there awhile and planned to stay awhile, would by now have accumulated a goodly pile of refuse, and the rock climber, if he was "into archaeology in an amateur way," would have photographed it for sure. He'd have made a point of it. To Dr. Jones then, this is simply not the environment one could expect if the tribe were genuine.

10
A Report on Conditions at Scutari

Although the role of Bill Lacroix in this story is a fictional one, a real inspector during the Crimean War, like Bill, would have had much cause for frustration. That there was gross incompetence, not just in the field but in every facet of this war, has long been established by historians.

Many people know the war for the famous charge of Lord Cardigan's light brigade (which went in the wrong direction), or for the single most famous name from the conflict: Florence Nightingale, who did indeed cause dramatic changes in the administration and level of hygiene at the huge Barracks Hospital at Scutari. (Yet even Florence Nightingale's struggle went beyond the expected, for soon after her arrival in Scutari, she had to rule that she, and only she, could visit the wards after eight P.M., for some of her nurses had begun to take on duties with the men that had nothing to do with recuperative care!)

By reporting to the *Times* Fund (which raised £25,000 in 1854) Bill Lacroix would at least secure a willing ear. The "Russell chap" to whom the orderly refers — William Howard Russell, the first war correspondent ever* to actually write from the field — was vilified for his reports by the military, and called a "miserable scribbler" by the influential Prince Albert. No one in charge seemed to want to hear the truth about the Crimea, and it was only the courage of the editor at *The Times* that finally forced matters into the light.

By reporting to the *Times* Fund, Bill also would have had a clear chain of command, unlike the military in the Crimea. At the time, the British navy, responsible for moving the troops, had absolutely no connection with the army. Food and transport were actually the responsibility of the Department of the Treasury. The Medical Department reported to the Secretary for War (Sidney Herbert), while costs for the engagement were the responsibility of the Secretary for the Colonies!

In addition to all of the above, incredibly bad planning (Barracks Hospital was three hundred miles across the Black Sea from the Crimea and the fighting) and ill-disguised fraud were rife. It is an example of the latter that Bill Lacroix has noticed.

The "toff," the friend of Lord Raglan, in writing to Sidney Herbert, implies that Shed (or Ward) 14 has only sixteen patients, eight on each side. However, the beds in Shed 14 are arranged alternately, i.e., eight men lying with their feet toward the aisle and eight with their heads toward it, making sixteen on each side of the shed — thirty-two in all. When Bill stood at the side of the fusilier wounded with a bayonet, that soldier's head pointed to the outside. His head was right under the eave. The orderly, standing in the aisle at the bed behind Bill, was tapping the forehead of the soldier who had just died. When Bill asked the orderly to help pull beds farther into the aisle so the patients wouldn't be rained on, they pulled eight beds — every other one — in each row.

When the "toff" says that eight heads point out and eight pairs of feet point in, he's correct; but what he does not say is that there are eight heads and pairs of feet going the opposite way in each row, too. The intent is likely that Sidney Herbert will infer there is plenty of room in Shed 14, and since overcrowding was a major issue at Barracks Hospital, this report will surely mislead.

*The flamboyant Russell is often cited by trivia buffs as the *first* war correspondent. Although he was likely the first to report on-site truthfully, he was not the first correspondent. Media historians generally agree the first was Henry Crabb Robinson, hired by the *Times* in 1807 to report on the war against Napoleon in Central Europe. Robinson tended to use local newspapers as his source, rather than interviews or first-hand observation.

11
At the Scene of the Accident

There are two accounts of the accident here. Since the accounts are so widely different, at least one of them must be a fabrication. What Peterson missed is the time factor.

If the driver of the Corvette is telling the truth about where she has been, then the engine of her car will be cool to the touch. The Mercedes, of course, will be warm, but that's not the issue. If the Corvette is warm, then there is still a matter of working out who is telling the truth. But if it's cold, then clearly it was not on the road hitting a dog only a few minutes ago, as the Mercedes-Benz driver said.

12
The Midterm Exam:
Which Way Is Up?

The map seems to have picked up some printer's ink marks from the book in which it was stored for many years. That would account for the horizontal lines seen faintly over the H, and for the number 18, which appears in the bottom left-hand corner as the students view it on the screen. In this view (call it view 1) the treasured religious object is in the vertical shaft on the left. Now rotate the image 180 degrees (in your head or on paper). Call this view 2. In view 2, the treasured object is in the vertical shaft on the *right*. However, the number 18 is now in the upper right-hand corner, and has become the number 81.

Views 1 and 2 would be possible results if the map had been stored facing a left-hand page in the book. But that can't be. View 1 would mean that the number had rubbed off the page onto the map from the inside margin or bottom left-hand "gutter" (or call it the bottom of the right margin of the left-hand page if you prefer, or even the bottom right-hand corner). Books are not printed this way. Since medieval times, when monks were laboring away in their scriptoria, book pages have always been numbered in their upper or lower *outside* corners. Occasionally they will be numbered in the center of the page, top or bottom, but never in the inside margins or "gutters." (A very few reference books are rare exceptions to this.)

So, view 1 is not possible, or at best, highly improbable. View 2 is not possible because books are numbered with the even number on the left-hand page and odd on the right. If the map were facing the left-hand page in view 2, the number rubbing off would not be 81.

Therefore the map was stored facing a *right*-hand page.

Create view 3 by turning the page to view 2, then turning it over. Number 81, in this view, would again have rubbed off from the inside gutter: not very likely.

In view 4, which you get by rotating view 3 180 degrees, the number 81, an odd number, would have rubbed off from the bottom outside corner of the *right*-hand page — which is entirely possible and plausible. In fact, it is the only view that makes logical sense and must therefore be the correct one. In this view, the treasured object is in the left vertical shaft of the H, with the booby trap in the right.

Conceivably, Sean and MaryPat's students have a fifty-percent chance of guessing this, but the exam requires them to explain their reasoning. (Some students may reason that the number bled through the map from the other side, throwing off entirely the logic above. But that is not likely, for the text that appears only as vague lines on the H would then have been clearer, too. As well, thinner absorbent paper was not generally available until late in the nineteenth century.)

13
The Final Exam: Digging in the Right Place

The complications are several. For one thing, you don't know whether the treasured religious object is Salubrian or Egregian, so you may have to dig in both sites. Then, of course, you have to dig down the safe, *un*booby-trapped shaft in each case.

The key is first of all to find out in which country these shafts have been dug, and to do that you approach *either* of the two adults you see before you. It makes no difference which one you approach, if you ask the right question.

The question you ask is: "Are we standing, right now, in your country?" (or a variation that asks the same thing). You ask this because you can depend on Salubrians to be truthful and Egregians to prevaricate. Therefore, if you are standing in Salubria when you ask the question, a Salubrian will say "Yes" (the truth) and an Egregian will say "Yes" (a lie). On the other hand, if you are in Egregia, an Egregian will answer "No" to that question (a lie) and a Salubrian "No," as well (the truth). Therefore the answer "No" always means you're in Egregia; the answer "Yes" puts you in Salubria, no matter which of the two adults you ask and no matter what his or her nationality.

Armed with that information, you go back to your earlier research, from which you know that Salubrians perform all religious ceremonies facing south (and Egregians the opposite). If you get a "Yes" at one (or both) of the sites, then you put the setting sun on your right and make sure you are *facing* the shafts (south) before you dig. (If you passed the midterm exam, you'll dig down the shaft on the left.)

Should you find you're in Egregia, you'll put the setting sun on your left, and face the shafts before digging — the left one again.

14
A Double Assassination at "The Falls"

The two diplomats were of significantly different height. One was about the height of the sergeant, who is a head taller than Vince. The other was about Vince's height.

When Vince sat in the driver's seat of the car, waiting for clearance to tow it away, he adjusted the rearview mirror *down* so he could see out the back. Therefore it must have been adjusted for a taller person before: the taller of the two diplomats.

15
They Come in Threes, Don't They?

It isn't important to pin the date with exact precision here, only to realize the time is the late 1950s. At this time, telephone exchanges in North America — in fact, in most of the world — had names like *Walnut, Baker, Pennsylvania,* the first two letters of which were part of individual telephone numbers. Thus, Walnut 8-7425 (which today would be 928-7425) was usually written WA 8-7425. (And Pennsylvania 6-5000, was written PE 6-5000.)

It is R. David Sloan's telephone number that troubles Dale. Certainly his exchange would have had a name, but definitely not *Quaker.* That's because there was no letter *Q* on telephone dials. There is no *Q* today, either. Not on telephone dial wheels, and not on push-button phones (so being "too young" to solve this mystery is no excuse!).

Whatever Sloan's reason, he has given a phony number.

The precise date, incidentally, is 1958.

Ford Motor Company brought out two model years of its monumental flop, the Edsel: 1958 and 1959. Likely, the Dunns bought a 1958 Edsel (which would have come out in late 1957), since Mike refers to its purchase "last year."

The information about Castro makes the time 1958 instead of the other possibility, 1959, because it was in 1958 that Fidel Castro metamorphosed from gloriously welcomed liberator of Cuba (complete with a huge rally in New York's Central Park) into hated dictator (at least in the eyes of the U.S.). One of his first actions when he took over in 1958 was to nationalize most of the major industries, especially sugar.

16
Witness to a Hit-and-Run

The connection between the *black* Jimmy that Betty and her husband own, and the *blue* Jimmy that Betty describes as the hit-and-run vehicle, is at least as ominous as it is coincidental. Certainly Diane Van Hoof wants to talk to the husband, for Betty's story just doesn't wash.

The sun was in Diane's face as she sat in the café, so it was setting. (She'd just had a caribou burger from the luncheon menu, so it's not rising.) This makes the time of her meeting with Betty sometime after midday, likely early afternoon.

The time is winter, and Labrador, which ranges from approximately the 52nd parallel in the south to the 60th in the north, has very short days in winter. (January temperature range is minus 22 to minus 4 degrees Fahrenheit, or minus 20 to minus 30 degrees Celsius.)

If Betty has to get home from this meeting at the Two Seasons in order to set out a meal so that it will be ready for her husband when he gets home, it means that currently she's setting it out at a time when darkness prevails. If Betty, looking from the lit indoors to the dark outdoors, claims to have seen a *blue* Jimmy, there is reason for Diane to be doubtful.

It's also clear that the husband is working the day shift this week. This shift customarily ends around 3:00 or 4:00 P.M. (Next week he'll be on the swing shift, which is usually 3:00 or 4:00 P.M. to 11:00 P.M. or midnight; and he's not working the night shift right now.) This means he's driving home at approximately the time when the children have been dismissed from school and will be on the roads. And they would be on the roads, too. With enough snow to produce giant snowbanks on the airport runways, there's not going to be any sidewalk clearing. There's simply no place to put the snow!

Although Diane would not yet voice this suspicion, it's

possible that Betty's husband is engaging in a very hamhanded attempt at diverting attention in advance from a *black* Jimmy — just in case there is another witness. If the child was hit while Betty was setting out her husband's meal, the accident must have occurred at about the time when he was coming home.

17
The Plot at the Rockface

Trevor Hawkes needs the cooperation of his five fellow prisoners if his plan is going to work. However, he has reason to be positive in his outlook, especially since he is the only one who stands a chance of getting them safely down the mountains to Dubrovnik once they are on the other side — which is where they'll all want to be once Igor is dispatched.

There are two restrictions to Trevor's basket plan. One is that the royalists must never outnumber Nova's party. (He's counting on Nova, who is known to want to solve the Communist/ royalist dispute, and who therefore would not be party to, or permit, any murdering of royalists if the opposite should occur and the royalists be outnumbered at any point in the escape process.) The other is that the basket needs two people going over and at least one coming back.

For simplicity's sake, let the Communist three be identified as T (for Trevor), N (for Nova) and C3. The three royalists are R1, R2 and R3.

a) T and R1 go across. R1 is left there and T brings the basket back.

b) R2 and R3 cross. A tricky stage since all three royalists are now on the other side and may well decide to take off. Trevor is counting on their not knowing where to go or — since they are farmers and a civil servant — *how*. This is mountain wilderness. R3 brings the basket back.

c) N and C3 cross. R2 returns with the basket.

d) T and R2 cross. T returns for R3.

Given the isolation of their work post and the fog that Trevor is counting on, the escape should succeed.

As a matter of historical interest:

The British Special Air Service, the SAS, is so carefully shrouded in mystery that many people believe (because of its famous success during the hostage incident at the Iranian Embassy in London) that it was formed only in recent years as an antiterrorist force. The SAS was established in the Western Desert in 1941, the brainchild of Lieutenant David Stirling, a man with some unorthodox ideas about how to defeat Rommel. By 1944-45, when this story is set, the SAS was thoroughly established as an elite, lethal, behind-the-lines commando organization.

The only slight anomaly in Trevor Hawkes's situation is that SAS agents usually work in pairs that link together in various numbers to form "operational squads." Trevor seems to be working alone.

18
Regina Versus Kirk

On the most obvious point — that Devon Kirk's wedding ring was at the murder scene — Bill Seeley will no doubt argue Kirk's explanation of why Thorvald Heintzmann had it. As well, it seems almost ludicrous that Kirk would leave such clearly incriminating evidence lying about. A moot point is that none of Kirk's fingerprints were found in the study, although the two men obviously saw quite a bit of each other. If an argument is made that Kirk was careful to wipe away all his prints, it would hardly be consistent to leave the ring behind.

That the murder weapon probably belongs to Kirk is not in dispute. John Ford will very likely suggest to the jury that the fact it was reported stolen on April 9 is at best a clumsy setup, in preparation for murder. However, Bill Seeley has a point to make in the nature of the wounds. If Kirk is a marksman who belongs to a gun club, surely he would be able to shoot more accurately at close range, as suggested by Dr. Quinn's description of the body's wounds. And quite likely a marksman would have needed only one shot.

A discrepancy arises in the testimony of Royal Orchard, which possibly neither Ford nor Seeley expected. Inspector Regan says that her prints were found in Thorvald Heintzmann's study — the only prints besides Heintzmann's own. Yet in answer to Ford's question about phoning the police, Royal Orchard says she never went into the study.

Finally, the matches from the Olde Thornhill Bar suggest that Kirk may have been in Heintzmann's study. The deceased may or may not have been a smoker, but Kirk is. And he was at this bar shortly before the murder. However, as Inspector Regan has described the book of matches, they were used by a right-handed person, for the ones removed from under the Ls had to be taken off by a righthander. (Try to get a leftie to take off matches from the right side of a match book!) Kirk must be left-handed if the umpire wouldn't let him pitch with his wedding ring on, so these aren't his matches. Heintzmann, on the other hand, given Inspector Regan's analysis of the attempt to write a message, seems to have been right-handed, and since he frequented the Olde Thornhill Bar, the matches may well have been ones that he used. He or Royal Orchard.

19
Danger at the Border

The Fewsters and the Mounts had the van breakdown by the head of a valley as they were heading north. Now the road ahead of them forks as it enters the valley.

As Juan Tomas re-emerges from the right fork (which he had gone up earlier) he points to his right in hitchhiker thumb style and announces that the choice should be the left fork, the one that runs north or *norte*. Therefore the right fork, where he has been, must be more or less easterly, or at least northeasterly, if not due east. In any case, he would have been walking into the rising sun that morning (they had breakfast at first light) either directly, or if the direction is more northeasterly, then with the sun to his right.

At his return, Juan Tomas reports seeing the sun reflect off the lenses of binoculars, suggesting possibly soldiers or bandits. Gene and Frank — Ann and Connie would surely have seen through it, too — pick up that he is lying. Juan Tomas pointed up the valley wall. That's the sun side, and to look down at the road a binocular user would have his or her back to the sun. There would be no reflection off the lenses.

Is Juan Tomas a setup man for whoever is up there? The party can't be sure. All they know is that he's lying, and given present conditions, they have good reason to suspect an ambush if they go the way Juan Tomas wants.

20
The Case of the Strange Hieroglyphs

Deirdre has detected a mirror pattern in the symbols they have seen. The first symbol is the numeral one (1), with the numeral in its proper form on the right, and its mirror image on the left. At Karmo's suggestion, they took the tunnel to the right. They did the same thing at the second archway, where the numeral two (2) appeared (on the right, with its image mirrored to the left). Now at the third archway, they have seen the numeral three (3), with its mirror image on the left.

Each time they have taken the right fork, or the side on which the true or sponsoring image of the double pattern occurs. Deirdre believes that if they take the right tunnel again at the third arch, they will come to a fourth arch with this symbol over it, giving the numeral four (4) with its mirror image. *This time* they will take the left tunnel.

Whether the Crusaders are responsible for the tunnels and the symbols could well be the subject of lengthy debate. The numerals are Arabic, and Arabic numerals were introduced into Europe at the beginning of the thirteenth century (by Leonardo Pisano Fibonacci — if you want to impress your friends). In

1228, the aggressive and very successful Frederick II, king of Germany, king of Sicily, king of Jerusalem, launched the Sixth Crusade.

Frederick was certainly in Acre, and he was likely to have been a leader in the use of the Arabic numeral system, for he was a patron of art and science. More proof than that would be needed to attribute the tunnels and the symbols to him, but Deirdre can enjoy the satisfaction of knowing that it's highly unlikely they are Phoenician, or even remotely connected to that culture.

Deirdre's use of "off" to indicate direction is from cricket. It means "on the same side of the field as the batsman's bat." If Karmo's flashlight (his electric torch) is in his right hand, his "off" side is then his right side (thereby making the left his "near" side).

21
The Fuchsia Track Suit Kidnapping

It could well be that the Potishes are setting things up for Geoff. Mrs. Potish claims to be a bird watcher, a sufficiently serious bird watcher to be recording her sightings. It's fairly difficult to accomplish that in a fuchsia track suit that doesn't appear to have encountered dirt or perspiration. Bird watching, *true* bird watching, often involves a lot of crawling through awkward spots in both bush and field.

By itself that's not much, but it does go along with the manicured hands — hardly the style of an avid bird watcher. Not that bird watchers don't have manicures. However, they do get *out* to do much of their watching. Some of it may be done from chairs in front of windows, especially in the winter, but this is certainly not winter, if the flag person in the tank top and denim shorts is any indication.

Still, the most important clue to Geoff comes from the dust on the windowsill. It is in a neat layer. If Stasia Potish had spent some considerable time in the chair, at the window with the binoculars, it is reasonable to expect the dust on the sill to be disturbed or smudged. Whatever she was doing for some time this morning, it was likely not sitting in front of the window with binoculars, looking for a European finch.

22
An Almost Perfect Spot

Cecile King is already nervous because of her vague certainty that she saw MaryClare McInerney in Azure that morning, so she is understandably alert. The fact that she did not suspect anyone in the "Cobbleton Pin Busters" crowd suggests how clever that cover was for the man with the slouching gait. How he managed to draw attention to himself — which both Cecile and Dorothy picked up in time — was by failing to act like a tourist despite his very obvious tourist cover.

A real tourist would not have walked so purposefully past The Espadrille, and surely the glassblower would have merited a look. Also, tourists don't usually go directly into a difficult-to-see delicatessen — especially with the distractions of Azure — unless they already know where they are going.

Cecile and Dorothy may not know who the man is or what he is doing, but in their business, all they really need to know is that this very obvious tourist is probably not a tourist at all. Whatever he is, they don't want him near their exchange.

23
The Interrupted Patrol

Chief Gary Ellesmere has reason to be cautious. He's alone in an isolated area with only the word of an agitated man that a woman has been hurt or killed in the kitchen of the farmhouse. Extreme prudence would dictate that he wait for backup rather than go in alone, but Gary feels he has the perpetrator in front of him. It could be he is suspicious of the man for saying he was going back to the house for a drink of water. Why wouldn't he drink from the Tap or the Creek, since they're so close? Still, when the man said "Just past the creek," he might have simply meant "the creek" and not "the Creek."

More likely, Gary is uneasy about the man's alibi. He said he had been checking fences for the previous half hour, and pointed out the field. Gary could see the field had not been grazed for some time. Because the weather has been dry and hot, the vegetation, especially thistles and burdocks and similar weeds that thrive along fences, would be tall and hard and prickly. No one who knows he is going to walk the perimeter to check the fence would ever wear shorts. If the man's wife has been murdered, Gary will want a better explanation of his whereabouts before he went back to the house and discovered the body.

24
The View from the Second-floor Promenade

Despite the attention Daisy attracted, the newspapers she was piling made it quite plain that a prisoner from the nearby penitentiary was on the loose. Not just an everyday prisoner, either, but someone who had apparently killed, and who had been in jail a long time.

Prisoners don't open doors. Doors are opened for them, either electronically or manually by guards. Over time, prisoners become habituated to standing in front of doors, waiting for them to open — like the man in the green jacket.

25
Death in the Bide-a-Wee Motel

Dolores Dexel feels that the scene has been tampered with and that the person(s) who did it may still be around. Her deductions are based on the circumstances of the Gideon Bible. From where she stood at the victim's feet (she could read the brand name on his new heels) she was looking along the body and out to the doorway. And from that perspective she could see the victim's left hand (the wedding ring) grasping the edge of the book, with the palm over the page. On the uncovered page, Dolores could see a double column of text top to bottom.

Miss Duvet reported that in her "picture," she could see the Bible open to "The Gospel according to Matthew." Since she did not go into the room, Miss Duvet must have read that from the hallway or at best from the doorway. In this case, with the poor lighting, the only type large enough to actually read would have been the type from a title page.

A title page always appears on the *recto* (right-hand) side of a book. That's the way a book is laid out for printing. For an important or main title, or one indicating a major change in contents, it would be exceedingly rare to find it on the left or *verso* page. Matthew is the first of the four gospels of the New Testament — a major change in contents — and a Bible with the title page to the Matthew gospel on the left would be an extremely unusual one.

What all this means is that if Dolores saw a double column of text top to bottom on the exposed page when she was in the motel room with the body, then the title page (on the recto or right-hand side) is covered by the victim's hand. And the book, in that case, is turned *toward* the doorway. When Miss Duvet said she read "Gospel according to Matthew" upside down, it means the book was turned *away* from the doorway at the time. The recto side, the one with the title, would have been the uncovered page if this were the case.

Dolores is taking the position that Miss Duvet is telling the truth. There's no reason for her to have falsely added the bit about reading the title page upside down.

Finally, Dolores's deductions have determined that if someone moved the Bible, it must have happened fairly soon after the killing, because when she came to the scene the blood had framed the book neatly. It had flowed around after the book was moved; there would have been smudging otherwise. (It also means that Miss Duvet came upon the scene very shortly after the man was killed, which is why Dolores would like to know more about the time when she called.)

26
Bailing Out the Navy
— for a Price

Someone with Bob Ashby's long experience in industrial design, and with his innate distrust of Thurman Elliott, Jr., might be able to determine, without pen and paper, why the proposal from Ashburn Engineering is something of a "sting" of the navy. The rest of us will be better off with a diagram to help us visualize.

The broken chains are in pieces of three links each, and

there are twenty of these pieces. The navy wants all these pieces restored to four chains of equal length, so five of the broken pieces will be needed for each. One chain, therefore, would look like this prior to being restored.

Thurman Elliott's proposal, at $10,000 per cut-and-weld, would cost $40,000 for each chain. Times four such chains would make his proposed total of $160,000.

Reasonable enough. But Bob Ashby knows there is a less expensive way to do it, even if Thurm Elliott's high cut-and-weld rate is used. Bob's idea is to open all three links in *one* of the pieces, and use them to unite the remaining four pieces. This system requires only *three* cuts-and-welds per chain. At $10,000 per, that's $30,000 per chain. Times four chains is $120,000.

27
The Case of the Missing .38 Smith and Wesson

It is indeed conceivable that someone could have found a gun in a puddle created by construction. And, as Gary observes, the Smith and Wesson .38 is a fairly common weapon. But the potential suspect's story is flawed from two perspectives:

For one thing, the puddles created by road construction, or any construction for that matter, are rarely filled with clean or even translucent water. Usually it's very dirty, and it would be difficult for anyone to see a gun lying in it (unless he already knew it was there). For another — and this is probably the one that confirms Gary Westlake's suspicions — the puddle is quite likely to be ice-covered, frozen over.

Whoever last used Car 9119 had the fan rear defrost on. A toque, nonregulation, but sometimes used by the highway patrol, was lying on the front seat. The only reason to wear one would be to keep warm. Finally, Gary is wearing gloves. Taken together, the three clues should be sufficient to point to cold winter weather, and ice on still water.

28
On the Trail of the Stolen Horses

Marv Chantler was unable to see the hoofprints he was looking for on the trail to which the farm woman had directed him. That in itself is not enough to warrant serious suspicion. He was looking for the unshod right foreleg of the piebald mare, but he had, after all, lost the trail even before coming to the farm itself. It is entirely possible that the piebald, and the other two horses, have been taken up this trail but that their tracks are indistinguishable and Marv simply can't detect them.

What distresses Marv is the woman's implication that he can't see the prints he's looking for because rain has altered them. When Marv went up the trail this morning, he dismounted near the two alder stumps. There, following the tracks of the wolf or dog, he noticed a varmint hole covered by dusty cobwebs. The dust would have come partly from the breezes and partly — probably mostly — from the surface of the trail being stirred up by horses' hooves. Had sufficient rain fallen since the horses went up there, a couple of days or so ago, to alter or obliterate their tracks, it would also have drenched the cobwebs and washed the dust off, or quite likely have destroyed the cobwebs.

The farm woman acknowledged seeing three horses, two of which fitted the description of the stolen ones, so she knows what Marv is asking about. What he would like to know now is why she sent him up the wrong trail.

29
The Royal Blue Escort

Harvey and Vin are staked out on a one-way street. If Keffer is so obsessed with blending in and not being noticed, one of the elementary strategies he would surely follow is to avoid attracting attention with simpleminded traffic violations such as going the wrong way up a one-way street, as the driver of the blue Escort did.

By the same token, Harvey and Vin are on a stakeout and, in turn, don't want to attract attention, by "coming down," as Harvey put it, on someone unless they're sure of their mark. The driver of the Escort is so unlikely a suspect, because he drove the wrong way on Robb Road, that Vin and Harvey reached the same conclusion together, without discussion, and decided against pursuit or detention.

The two agents are in England, obviously; in Wythenshawe, a suburb of the city of Manchester. Traffic, as everyone knows, flows on the left side of the road; vehicles are operated from the front right seat. Vin is in the driver's seat. Harvey sits opposite. Because Harvey bumped his elbow on the parking meter, they are parked on the left side of Robb Road (as is customary). Harvey can see the front of No Parking signs all the way down

Robb Road, on the other side. The signs are thus facing their Rover. That means the signs are intended to be read by traffic moving along Robb Road in the same direction Harvey and Vin are facing. If two-way traffic were allowed, the signs would face the other way.

30
An Unlikely Visitor — or Two

Before Gutenberg and the popular use of movable type, most books of the medieval period were handwritten and beautifully decorated on *vellum*, parchment made of the skins of calves and lambs. But printers use paper, which is less suitable for gold decoration and painting. It may be reasonable to assume that the Book of Hours Miles N. Miles has brought to Struan is indeed from medieval Europe. (Struan himself, truly sensitive to the chemical effect of fingertips on the gold decoration, feels the text with the back of his hand.) The clue to the book's age, however, is in a phrase that is commonly known and equally commonly, and wrongly, attributed to the Bible.

"Cleanliness is next to godliness" is an admonition from the pen of John Wesley, the eighteenth-century British clergyman acknowledged as the founder of Methodism. (It's from one of Wesley's sermons, entitled "On Dress," and is based on a passage from the *New* Testament.) Thus the phrase, which Struan says is in poor Latin in any case, could not have been copied out by a medieval scribe in a monastery.

The Bible, incidentally, is wrongly attributed as the source for a number of popular sayings: "Fools rush in where angels fear to tread," for example, is from Alexander Pope's *Essay on Criticism*, written in 1711. "Spare the rod and spoil the child" is from English poet Samuel Butler's *Hudibras*, written in

1664. And the Bible itself gets altered. The famous "Pride goeth before a fall" is actually "Pride goeth before destruction, and an haughty spirit before a fall" (from *Proverbs*).

Given all this, and the other pressures on Miles N. Miles, it's understandable that he (they?) would seek advice.

31
The Mission in the Clearing

In the days before blood packs and refrigerated plasma supplies, or in conditions where these things were unavailable, it was not unusual to transfuse directly from one person to another in an emergency. Since Haight-Windsor is O-negative, the surviving priest will be able to receive his blood, because O-negative is a universal donor, as Ron Forrester says. (Other factors of course, would be taken into account in a modern hospital, but that's not where this is happening!)

Throckton believes that with enough blood, Haight-Windsor's and Ron's — if it's the right type — he can keep the priest alive until they get to the airstrip. The question is this: is the priest A-positive like Ron?

Using the following reasoning, he is, and given the emergency and the fact that he is *in extremis*, anyway, it's the best they have. Of the two priests who were bound together, the one on the left is somewhat unkempt and disheveled. He is the one who is alive (his Roman collar was dirty) and also the one whose right shoe is scuffed at the heel from top to bottom. That's the kind of scuff a right shoe gets if it is worn by a vehicle driver. The heel wears from the rotation at the accelerator. This particular priest must be the one who drives the mission's pickup truck then, and it must be his blood type disk (A+) on the ring with the ignition key.

32
Trespassing on the MBA Property

The solution here has much to do with the season, the terrain, the vegetation and the time sequence. Whether or not one needs the precision of Ron Minaker's apparent knowledge of geology, it is clear that the place where the helmet was allegedly found is in a hilly area, with many rises and hollows.

Jack Atkin, who seems to be in better shape for walking than his two friends, has arrived at the spot earlier than they, and has had time to look down from the top of a knoll into the hollow on the MBA property where the helmet is supposed to have been found. At this point, he has analyzed the time sequence and the seasonal factor.

If Indian summer has come and gone, this is October, possibly September or November, but no earlier or later. (Even without knowing when Indian summer arrives — and it doesn't always — it's still obvious that this is late autumn, for the leaves have gone and it's not yet winter.) The ATV accident must have occurred about July, or certainly in the summer. That's when the helmet, worn or not, would have come off there, if indeed the accident occurred there.

If Sasha Dahlman's elder brother and two friends reported seeing it from the top of the hill *yesterday*, and if the last of the leaves had been blown off the mature maple, ash and oak trees just under a week before, the fact is they couldn't have seen it as reported. In a treed area, with knolls and hollows, the wind will blow the dried leaves into the hollows, even filling them if there are enough trees. The helmet, deposited in the summer, would have been well covered by yesterday afternoon, so Jack has found an effective counter to use before the jury — if it comes to that.

33
When History Becomes Math

The Seven Years' War began in 1756, according to information Linda found in the resource center. If, as her part of the trio's information says, the Beame family went to the New World three years after the end of that war, they would have sailed from Bristol to Saint John in 1766. (1756 + 7 + 3 = 1766) During the voyage, Magdalene celebrated her eighteenth birthday, according to John's information. Therefore, if she married in Pawtucket at the age of twenty-two and had her firstborn two years later, Magdalene's firstborn would have arrived in 1772. (18 in 1766; 22 in 1770; baby born in 1772).

When the Seven Years' War began, Magdalene would have been eight years old. According to Porky's information, when the family landed in Saint John (in 1766) Korron was half as old as Magdalene had been at the beginning of the Seven Years' War. Therefore, Korron was four years old in 1766. She'd have been twenty-two in 1784 (1766 + 18) and her firstborn would then have seen the light for the first time in 1786.

From the information John has, Catherine was eight years old in 1766 (twice as old as Korron). She'd have married in Pawtucket then, in 1780, and given birth to her first in 1782.

From this point it becomes a matter of the trio's notion of what constitutes citizenship. Porky makes clear that Rhode Island, where all three married and had their firstborn, renounced allegiance to Great Britain in 1776. Quite likely, Magdalene's firstborn (1774) was born a British citizen. Korron's quite likely can be seen as an American citizen, since he or she was born after the Treaty of Paris in 1783.

Only the citizenship of Catherine's baby is debatable, since it was born after the beginning of the American Revolution (while Britain still regarded Rhode Island as its colony) but before 1783 when Britain recognized the U.S. as a nation. Quite likely, this is a debate John Fogolin would prefer to take up in private with Linda Sandness, assuming he can find something for Porky Schnarrfeldt to do elsewhere!

34
Nothing Wrong with Helena, Montana

Gert Neustadt (if indeed this is Gert Neustadt) is presenting the image of being a well-traveled individual, as the heavily stamped passport and the luggage with its stickers would suggest. An experienced traveler would not be likely to prepare an itinerary that lists the hotels where he is staying, using 800 telephone numbers. Anyone trying to contact him between 5:00 and 8:00 P.M., EST, would have a very difficult time doing so, because these are central reservation numbers for the hotel chain. He couldn't be reached at a specific hotel through an 800 number.

Not a big deal, but Meike has twigged to a discrepancy between the image and the reality and is simply following Steve's dictate that anything remotely suspicious gets reported. The fact that a general announcement about Neustadt has arrived by fax at just this moment is purely coincidence, but, then, this may show that the good guys do win sometimes.

Gert Neustadt, if he is second in command of ODESSA, is an officer in an organization of interesting, probably unsavory, characters. ODESSA is the "Organization der Ehemalige SS Angehöriger" — the Organization of Former Members of the SS.

Incidentally, some readers of *Nothing Wrong with Helena, Montana*, may put two and two together and come up with five by assuming that Meike may actually have recognized Gert Neustadt, for her name is quite clearly European. However, the fax machine, the computerized image, etc., put the time frame pretty much in the present. Since Meike is described as a "young lady," she would have been too young to have known Neustadt during or even after the Second World War.

FURTHER
FIVE-MINUTE
MYSTERIES

To Eric and Doris Cuddon,
from whom I learned a great deal

Contents

1

A Decision at
Rattlesnake Point

THE CABLE SCREAMED OVER THE large pulley at the end of the mobile crane, launching a massive assault on the morning quiet. The arm of the crane was fully extended to reach over the brow of Rattlesnake Point, for the body had to come up from two hundred feet below. It was the distance more than the weight that made the equipment work so hard.

As he talked to Trevor Hawkes, the young doctor from the medical examiner's office watched the big machine with a wary eye. Perry Provato had ridden down and then back up via the crane within the past hour, and he was not at all impressed by what he saw, now that he was watching from the top.

"It's like I said, Trevor," he pointed sideways with his thumb at the body that was now coming over the edge of the cliff. Trussed up in a rescue basket, it bounced and swayed at the end of the cable like some macabre yo-yo that had got stuck on the way to the spool. "Like I said, I might do a bit better at the morgue this afternoon, but I'll take bets that the death took place six to eight hours ago."

Trevor nodded and looked at his watch. "So . . . 'tween one and three A.M. Makes sense." He motioned to the crane operator

1

and then pointed to a clear spot beside the guard rail. "Highway patrol reported the car at, let's see, 4:46. Then . . ."

He waved frantically at the crane operator. "No! No! This side! Over here!" he yelled, pointing with both arms to the spot beside the rail.

"So," he said, his voice returning immediately to normal, "first light was 5:20. Patrol confirmed a body down in the scrub about ten minutes after that. And you went down, what? About eight o'clock. An hour ago, right?"

"Yeah, eight," Perry replied. "Never done that before. Go down on a cable, I mean. Can't say I want to again either! You just stand on the big grab hook and hang on! I mean, even the dead guy gets strapped into a basket.

"And what a mess when I got down there! He's a big guy. Not lanky like you, but a big one. Just think of the acceleration by the time he hit!"

Perry shook his head; his adrenalin was still pumping. "I remember this sicko physics teacher we had in high school. Liked to give us problems with falling bodies. She should try this one!"

Trevor looked at the body, lying finally where he had directed. Despite Perry's comment, it appeared remarkably intact. After a two-hundred-foot fall, all the parts were still there. In fact the face was almost unscathed. Only the big belly seemed pushed oddly to one side, and the suspenders on that side had come off. Trevor could see that the neck was broken, likely the spine, too, in several places.

"One thing, Perry, before you go. In your, uh, your uh, uh . . ." Trevor was trying to find the right word. Perry was so young. He settled on "*experience*" anyway. "In your experience, uh . . . well, there's a note on the driver's seat in the car there." He knew that Perry was looking at the silver-gray Lincoln Town Car behind them. It was parked in perfect parallel on the verge between the road and the guard rail. "Can't be sure, of course, till we go inside, but my guess is it's a suicide note. Now, what makes a guy do himself in like that when there's . . . ?"

"You mean," Perry took the lead, "why didn't he just let the car run and go to sleep? Or overdose? Or something softer like that? I dunno. I guess some of them just want to be more dramatic. I know that some jumpers do it because they really want to punish themselves. But it's a lot quicker the way he did it! Then there's always the . . ."

The rest of what Perry had to say was erased by the scream of the cable. Both men looked to see Trevor's rookie partner, Ashlynne Walmsley, on her way over the brow of Rattlesnake Point. Unlike the other passengers so far, it was clear she was enjoying herself completely. Ashlynne waved a camera at Trevor as soon as the operator set her down.

"Lots of shots," she said. "Covered everything."

Trevor pointed to the body. "Get a couple there," he said, "then the car from several angles. And . . . just a minute!" He knelt beside the body. "Make sure you witness this." He patted the dead man's pockets and then reached into one of them and extracted a small ring of keys. "Just in case some jackass lawyer ever wants to know in court where we got these."

"Trust me," Ashlynne said and began snapping shots of the car.

Trevor, meanwhile, waved goodbye to the retreating Perry and went to the driver's door of the Lincoln. He inserted a key and turned it sharply. All four door locks popped open simultaneously, along with — to his complete surprise — the trunk lid. He reached for the door handle, then shrugged and went to the back of the car instead. Except for a CD player and a small rack of discs, the cavernous trunk was empty and very clean. With his pen, Trevor spread the discs apart and craned his neck to read the titles only to bump into Ashlynne who was peering over his shoulder.

"George Strait, Randy Travis, Dolly Parton," she read aloud. "Reba McIntyre. All country. Well, he's consistent anyway. Kitty Wells! Who's Kitty Wells?"

The question made Trevor feel his age so he ignored it. "Time to go inside," he said. "There's nothing here. You go to the passenger side and open up. Just witness what I do. I got a funny feeling we're going to have to explain a lot about this one."

3

"You mean," Ashlynne asked, "you think it's fishy that a guy would park his car so neat if he's going to jump? And lock it, too? And take the keys?"

Trevor didn't answer. He simply walked around to the driver's door and opened it after Ashlynne had done as she was instructed. The paper on the seat was of a standard memo-pad size. Again using his pen, Trevor turned it over. It was a note. It said simply:

Try to get me *now.*

A.

"Want my flashlight?" Ashlynne asked when she saw Trevor tilt up the steering column and bend himself in to look under the seat.

He just shook his head.

"Then is it okay if I see where the radio stations are pre-set? And, uh, like, Trevor . . . shouldn't the fingerprint people be here?"

Trevor Hawkes maneuvered himself back out of the car and stretched his long frame. He looked over at the crane operator who had sidled as close as he dared to the body.

"Good thinking on the radio stations," he said finally. "And yeah, you're right. Let's give the forensic bunch their shot. There won't be any prints though. Whoever murdered this guy isn't that dumb."

What has finally convinced Trevor Hawkes that this is a murder case?

2

Something Suspicious
in the Harbor

SUE MEISNER BROUGHT BOTH OARS forward into the little rowboat and drifted until the boat bumped against the huge freighter. It was especially dark down here on the water between the two big ocean-going ships. She felt as though she were in a tunnel, with the superstructure of *The Christopher Thomas* looming over her and the even bigger Russian ship alongside, completing the arch. Still, there was enough light from the city to see the mark from early this morning, the little paint scrape where Sue had bumped against *The Christopher Thomas* the first time.

That had been with the police boat though, and Sue had been acting officially, as a constable with the Metropolitan Toronto Police marine unit. However, there was nothing official about this trip. It was anything but. She was in restricted waters to boot. Tiny, privately operated rowboats were not welcome in the main channel of Toronto harbor, and Sue knew if she were caught there, it would be hard to imagine what would be worse: her embarrassment or Inspector Braemore's wrath.

That was why, at sunset, she had taken the ferry from the city over to Ward's Island, collected the rowboat, and then pulled her way across the channel in the dark. By staying close to the piers along Cherry Street, she'd reached *The Christopher Thomas* undetected. So far anyway.

Sue shifted on the seat to relieve her sore back. The movement caused the little craft to rock, and it banged hard into the side of the freighter. The rowboat was aluminum, and to her, the sound in the tunnel between the two larger vessels was like a gunshot. But she knew it wouldn't be heard on deck. With the racket up there and in the hold, especially from the noisy diesels powering the loading winches, there wasn't a chance even for normal conversation, let alone picking up a sound from the surface of the water.

The crew of *The Christopher Thomas* had been loading big containers full of automobile engines for several hours already when Sue and her partner had made their official visit that morning. The two officers were responding to a tip. Sue had taken the call herself right after coming on duty.

"Something crooked in the harbor," the caller had said. "On *The Christopher Thomas* and maybe that Russian one beside her — the *Potemkin* something. You people should go check." Then the caller had hung up.

Inspector Braemore had not been very impressed. It was his opinion that some disgruntled sailor wanted to harass the shipowners and was using the police to do it. And Sue's visit this morning, if anything, seemed to confirm that, for they'd seen nothing amiss. She and her partner had circled the ship inside and outside. There were no safety violations, no evidence of contraband, not even a suggestion of drug use in the crew's quarters. *The Christopher Thomas* appeared to be just a freighter being filled with cargo by a busy crew that did not want two police officers getting in their way.

It was Inspector Braemore's I-told-you-so expression that had got Sue's dander up. It explained why, later in her shift, she had stood on the nearby ferry docks for half an hour and watched the loading through binoculars, and why she'd checked the ship's papers twice with the harbormaster. And it also explained — or so she told herself — why sore back and all, she was sitting in a tiny rowboat in the smelly darkness of Toronto harbor long after sunset.

"Well," she said out loud, "at least, it's paid off. At least now I *know* there is certainly something crooked going on. Tomorrow morning there's going to be another inspection so we can find out just what it is!"

What has led Sue Meisner to the conclusion that something crooked is going on aboard The Christopher Thomas?

3

In Search of Answers

EVERY WINDOW IN THE LITTLE studio was open as wide as possible in a vain attempt to catch whatever tired breeze might limp by from time to time. Inside, however, this arrangement produced no results. The air in the place had been hot, wet, and motionless all day. Still, at least one of Celeste Wyman's questions was answered: namely, why had Virgil Powys left every window — and the door, too — wide open when he supposedly dashed back to his house? In this heat wave, it made sense. No one was closing windows these days.

There was an answer, too, for another of Celeste's questions. Why wasn't the place air conditioned? By visiting the studio personally, by actually coming to the scene of the crime, so to speak, Celeste could see that an air conditioner would be intolerable. Too noisy. And it would box the place in. One of the studio's charms was that, despite the tight quarters, the number of windows created an impression of space. Powys claimed he had claustrophobia. Celeste certainly didn't, but she could sense what the effects would be if the sight lines were blocked.

She sat down at the table that served as a desk and looked out the large window across the room. Beyond it, over the alley and on the other side of a line of mature oak trees, traffic from Bronson Avenue superimposed its noise over the buzz and beep and chunter of the computers to her right. Side by side, on a counter that ran the length of the one wall without a window, sat a 486 tower, a Gateway 2000 4DX2, and beside it, a much more modest 386 desktop. Celeste leaned a little closer to the 486. Sixteen Meg RAM, she figured. Clockspeed of sixty-six megahertz. Powerful. A lot more powerful than its immediate neighbor.

The machinery made a sharp contrast to the Chippendale reproduction table at which she was sitting, but both the table and counter shared the disarray of the studio. Stashed in every available space on the counter was a flotsam of envelopes jammed with material, the lot held in place by a Gordian knot of wires and cables and power bars that only an original installer could ever untie. On the nearest edge of the table, pens spilled out of a pewter beer stein and trailed across to a pewter envelope holder lying empty on its side. On the left edge, irregular stacks of medical reference texts were interspersed with piles of dictionaries and manuals.

Celeste lifted a heavy metal stapler from the pile of papers on the crowded working surface in front of her. The first page, and then the second, the third, and then the fourth, when she looked further, answered yet another question. Powys was obviously one of those types who worked things out on paper first and only then went to the keyboard. It was not what she would have expected. Someone with his expertise, his passion for computers, seemed more likely to work "cold," right on the keyboard with no intermediate steps.

Virgil Powys had a reputation as a computer *wunderkind*. He'd started with IBM three years ago, and after two revolutionary patents, jumped to Apple for six months and then to Wang for two before going freelance. But he wasn't doing well at freelancing. He was brilliant but erratic; he needed the discipline of an organization around him, but with his reputation for instability no one would touch him anymore. Nevertheless, when Celeste's company, Hygiolic Incorporated, retained him six weeks ago, they thought they'd made a steal. This morning, "steal" suddenly had a whole new meaning.

Celeste Wyman was Director of Research at Hygiolic. It was a company specializing in the development and production of highly advanced and complicated drugs and medicines. For months the company had been on the verge of a historic medical breakthrough. By means of computer models, they had developed — theoretically — a vaccine to protect against common cold viruses. The trouble was no one could put all the strands together; there wasn't anybody in Celeste's department who could do it. And the board of directors had so severely limited access to the models for security reasons, that, in effect, Hygiolic had been going nowhere with what could be the biggest thing since the Salk vaccine.

Yesterday, Powys had called to say he'd done it. This morning he called again, this time to say he thought the work might have been pirated, that while he'd been out for just minutes, someone had been into the studio and into the program.

Celeste leaned back in the chair and stretched, idly running both index fingers against the flyscreen behind her. There were so many questions. Should she call the police? Not yet. Find out more first. Is it possible that Powys himself was stealing the program? That this whole break-in thing was a red herring? Not likely. It would be too hard for him to sell it. Oh, there were companies that would grab it first chance. But from Powys? No. Too easy to trace.

She leaned forward again, and put her elbows on the table. Did whoever had been into the system actually steal Hygiolic's big discovery? Yes. At the very least that had to be assumed. Espionage in medical research is as vicious as in warfare.

But then there were the truly niggling questions. Was Virgil Powys in cahoots with whoever did the pirating? Why, especially if he had put audit controls in the system that could tell him if someone had been into it, had he not encrypted the data? Used code? Powys's explanation was that Hygiolic was pushing so hard for results that using an encryption scheme good enough to protect against even a run-of-the-mill hacker would have slowed him right down. Reasonable enough, Celeste knew; she had been one of the ones pushing.

But then, at the very least, why hadn't he protected his system with a password? The answer to that was on the wall. For the third or fourth time in the past half hour, Celeste looked up at the wall above the 386. In large block letters she could see "HYGISNEEZE" written on the wallpaper with a felt-tipped pen. She shook her head. He had used a password all right! But then, hanging it out for all to see was something she did herself. So did others in her department. Not on the wallpaper though.

A noise from behind her made Celeste turn. Through the open door she could see Sean, her assistant, leaving the back door of the house and making his way across the lawn to the shed where Powys had built the studio. She counted Sean's steps: twenty-five. About twenty seconds, she calculated. Another ten to come up the stairs. Powys had said he'd gone back to the house to go to the bathroom, so that would be about thirty seconds each way. Allow, say, five minutes in the bathroom. Then he got a phone call. Long distance, he'd said, so that would be easy to verify. The call took about five minutes, supposedly, so according to Powys, he was out of the studio for ten or eleven minutes. Enough time for a pirate to dash in and copy everything? No, not at all, no matter how good. Not even if he knew where to go and how to get in.

So, was Virgil Powys out of the studio for longer than he had said he was? No doubt about it. And was he out for a longer time because he had arranged to be? Well, Celeste thought, maybe it is indeed time to involve the police. They're probably better at finding out that kind of information. At least she knew that Powys needed to be questioned.

Why is Celeste Wyman certain that Virgil Powys was out of the studio for longer than the time he claimed to be?

4

A Single Shot
in the Chest

BRIAN BRETON HELD HIS TONGUE as long as he could.

"For heaven's sake, Roly!" he finally blurted. "Doesn't it bother you to be playing with evidence like that?"

Roly Coyne lowered the binoculars for just a second, looked at them as though he were seeing them for the first time, and then put them back to his eyes.

"C'mon," he said. "What do you mean *evidence*? Who cares! This case is open and shut. At least as far as you're concerned. You got a body. You got a shooter. You got a confession. What more do you want? This case is, like, *closed.* I mean, *shut!* 'Sides, that's the ten o'clock class across the street there. I'll bet half the guys in our building are doing what I'm doing right now."

What Roly Coyne was doing, along with — according to him — half the guys in the building, was focusing a pair of binoculars on an aerobics class across the street from the morgue.

"You see, this ten o'clock bunch," Roly went on with unconcealed delight, "it's the one with all the chicks from the college up the street."

For the first time since Brian Breton had slipped into the office

12

five minutes ago, Roly turned his back to the window and faced him. "Here, see for yourself."

He handed the binoculars to Brian. "C'mon, take a look!" he insisted. "You never seen a spandex parade like this! Not over in the coroner's office anyway!"

"Aw, Roly, get off it!" Brian was annoyed. "It's bad enough being here without your juvenile nonsense." He used the opportunity to take the binoculars out of Roly's hand. "Besides, these are no good to someone like me, with glasses, without those little rubber cups on the eyepieces. Anyway, forget this and let's get down to the cooler. I want to get this over with."

Roly sighed. "Okay, Breton." He swiveled back to the window for one final, drooling stare. "You want to take any *terribly important evidence* down with us?" Without taking his eyes off the window he waved his hand vaguely at a table in the corner to his right. "It's all over there."

Brian had perused the evidence before, while Roly was studying aerobics. In addition to the binoculars Roly was using, there was a well-worn pocketknife with one of the blades broken off, a few coins, some wooden matches, a very dirty handkerchief, three fence staples, a bent nail, and — this one really caught Brian's eye — a World War I issue Ross rifle with the name MANOTIK burned crudely into the wooden butt.

"No," he said to Roly. "The evidence can stay here so you have something to play with when the aerobics class is over. Now let's go!"

Roly swiveled frontwards again. "All right, all right." Reluctantly he got to his feet. "Actually, this one shouldn't be so bad for you. Just your average dead body with a hole in the chest. I don't see why it always makes you sweat so. You don't have to kiss him! Anyway, you should have done this before I washed old Manotik. I bet he never had a bath in twenty years! Did he *stink* or what!"

"Roly! Just let's go." Already Brian was feeling sick to his stomach. After thirty years as an investigator with the coroner's office, he still had nightmares after a visit to the cooler, the refrigerated room full of slabs in sliding cabinet drawers where bodies were stored. Whenever he could, Brian ducked out of his obligation to examine cadavers, and in the case of old Manotik he was very tempted.

Manotik was a hermit who, for as long as anyone could remember, had lived in a swamp north of the city. The problem was, he was a squatter. Manotik had never owned the swamp. Three years ago, a company called Nucleonics Inc. had moved in, drained off all the water, built a complex of modern buildings, then surrounded the property with a huge chain-link fence and patrolled it twenty-four hours a day with armed guards. In a humanitarian gesture it soon regretted, Nucleonics granted Manotik a small piece of land next to the fence. It was from this base that the old man launched his campaign of harassment. At least the company *believed* it was the old man. His guilt had never been established.

At first, the problems were annoying but manageable. The Nucleonics property was plagued in turn by an infestation of snakes, then rats, and then skunks. But one night a section of fence was dynamited. A week later it happened again. Then the worst step of all: on six different occasions over the past two months, rifle bullets had winged through the windows of the Nucleonics executive suites. When a secretary was badly cut by flying glass, the company doubled the guard. It was one of the new guards who had shot the old man.

"His statement is pretty simple, isn't it? The guard's, I mean." Roly was repeating what Brian already knew as the elevator creaked its way down to the cooler. "He sees the old guy at the fence with the rifle poked through it, sorta hangin' there in the chain link. But shoulder level. And he's got those binoculars focused on the exec suite. The guard shouts at Manotik and the old guy grabs the rifle, so boom! The guard offs him. I'd say the plea'll be self-defense."

Brian wasn't listening. They had crossed the short hallway into the cooler and he was bracing himself. Roly, meanwhile, seemed to get cheerier.

"Number 42," he said, "right here." He rolled out the slab and grabbed a corner of the cover sheet. "And now! For your viewing pleasure . . . Ta-da!"

Brian gagged. "God, Roly," he muttered, then forced himself to look at the scrawny white form that had once been Xavier Manotik. Roly was right about the bullet wound, an almost harmless looking hole in the chest. The rest of the body looked so clean and untouched. So did the face. Well, almost. Roly may have scrubbed it, but years of dirt still marked the ridges on the old man's forehead and darkened the cleft in his chin. Only the nose seemed really clean. It was a long, thin nose with calloused indentations on both sides of the bridge, and creases leading down from it toward the mouth, the kind of creases that come from years of frowning.

Brian leaned closer to see the stubble on the old man's cheeks. Despite his distaste for this routine, he never failed to be fascinated by the fact that body hair continued to grow after death.

"Hey, you startin' to like this or something?" Roly's voice intruded. "Seen enough or what?" Roly wanted to get back to the aerobics class. "Let's go up and you can sign off."

"Not yet, Roly. Not yet." Brian replied. "There's something about that guard's story that smells as bad as this place does."

"What do you mean?" Roly asked.

What does Brian Breton mean? What's wrong with the guard's story?

5

The Case of the Stolen Stamp Collection

IN THE DOORWAY OF MIKA FLECK'S office stood a very nervous young man in a blue delivery uniform. Miles Bender was waiting to be summoned, and he wasn't the least bit comfortable about the idea.

Mika's opening statement didn't help either. "Come in here and sit down, young man," she said without looking up. "For heaven's sake you're going to wear out the rug with your fidgeting."

Miles shuffled across the floor to the only chair that was empty of books and files and all the paraphernalia of an extremely busy office. "It didn't get there, did it?" he said as he sat down. "The shipment. Like, the stamps?"

Mika looked over the top of her half-glasses, freezing Miles Bender in mid-squirm. "No," she said. "It did not. The first bonded shipment that Acceleration Courier Service has ever failed to deliver." She pushed up her glasses and looked through them. It didn't make Bender feel any more relaxed. "And I don't suppose you're surprised to know that collection is worth over half a million dollars. That's why we had a police escort."

"I know it was valuable." For the first time, Miles Bender

stopped squirming. "I know that. But how can you blame *me* if the cops stole it. I mean — they looked like cops anyway."

Mika spread her hands on the desk and spoke more softly. "Okay. Let's go through it again. You say two policemen took the stamps. Just like that."

"Not just like that." Miles was beginning to whine in spite of Mika's obvious attempt to be more gentle with him. "I mean, they were cops! Look, it was standard procedure. All the way to the border, like, there were these two Vancouver city cops, one in front and one in back just the way we're supposed to do it. And at the border the two American cops took over, the ones from Bellingham. Motorcycle cops."

Miles Bender was becoming more confident as he sensed his side of the story was finally being listened to. He leaned forward in the chair. "I mean, there was no reason to be suspicious; you wouldn't have been either. They had real police bikes. Real uniforms — the boots, the gloves, the sunglasses, everything!"

Mika opened her mouth to speak, but Miles kept talking. "I mean they even *acted* like motorcycle cops. You know, sort of strutty and cocky and . . ."

"According to this report," Mika broke in, "you got a good look at them."

Miles took a deep breath. "At *one* of them, yeah. When we stopped on the highway and they made me get out. The one that put his bike in the van and, like, got in to drive, he got pretty close."

"According to your description," Mika said, "he is about your height, but heavier. Bit of a beer belly. Blue eyes and a reddish moustache. Maybe 35 to 40 years old."

"Yeah!" Miles Bender was enthusiastic in his agreement. "And the cut, the nick on his cheek? They got that on the report there? Like maybe he cut himself shaving?"

Mika nodded and then looked up from the report. "And you say all this took only a couple of minutes. They stopped. You stopped. They ordered you out, and then one of them put his bike in the van, and they took off leaving you at the side of the road."

"Exactly! That's it exactly!" Miles was excited now. "I mean, like, by this time I know they're not cops but, I mean, like, what am I gonna do?"

Mika cleared her throat. She was looking over the top of her glasses again. "For one," she said, "you're going to tell us where they took the stamps. Depending on how well you do that, we'll work out the next steps later."

Why is Mika Fleck suspicious of Miles Bender?

6

Not Your Average Hardware Store

"SO YOU THINK THAT'S WHY we were handed this one?" Gordon Pape's question was rhetorical. He really didn't expect an answer but got one anyway.

"Figure it," Hugh Furneaux said. "Why else would the agency bring us this far north? It can't be any other reason. They've more than enough bodies up here for this kind of work."

"This kind of work," on this particular morning, was a repossession. Gordon Pape and Hugh Furneaux worked for SIMM Resolutions, a collection agency. "Field operatives," they were called in the agency's pretentious terminology, the ones who actually went out to face the locked doors, the insults, the angry dogs, the tears, even on occasion — and by far the most disturbing — sad, silent acceptance. All in order to repossess unpaid merchandise.

"My God. Look at it!" Hugh Furneaux exclaimed. "He must be a character all right."

The two operatives had pulled off the road to park in front of an ugly cement-block building. Its large yellow and black sign proclaimed it to be:

"A Real Man's Hardware Store."

Hugh scanned the shopworn banners in the display windows that flanked the front door. "Hard to believe there aren't some feminists out picketing here," he said. "I could see their point, too!"

The banners, all of them as dusty as the goods in the display windows, each supported Wilfrid Norman's idea of what a *real* hardware store must be, or a real *man's* hardware store at any rate.

"Real Men Don't Buy Teacups," one said.

Another offered:

"You Want *Seven* of Something? Ask Us!"

And directly underneath:

"No Pre-Packaging! We Sell You What You Want!"

Still another announced:

"If We Ain't Got It,
Then It Ain't Hardware!"

The "**ware**" had partly torn off from the end of the last banner and hung away from its host sentence at an awkward angle.

"You know," Hugh observed to his partner, "it may not just be that we're strangers. This guy could be very hard-nosed. Did you see the shepherd running loose out back in the storage area? I'll bet he didn't come with a 'Good with Children' guarantee. Wonder if there's any of those loose inside?"

Gordon Pape was about to reply but then paused. He was looking at the Christmas lights that hung from the fluorescent fixtures just behind the windows. In mid-July. Apparently Wilfrid

Norman's sole concession to the festive season was to plug and unplug an extension cord.

"I was here once," he said absently. "Needed a new handle for my splitting maul up at the cottage."

"Your *what?*" For the first time since they'd pulled in, Hugh took his eyes off the front of Norman's hardware store and looked directly at Gordon.

"A spli . . . Never mind. Not important," Gordon said. "The point is, the guy had one here. In stock. Actually he had about half a dozen! You just don't buy that kind of thing in a typical hardware store anymore. That's one of those crummy special orders that takes forever and gets surcharged to boot, all because some bean counter has told the owner his inventory has to roll over a certain number of times a year."

"And the whole place is like that," Gordon continued. "Full of everything you'd never get anywhere else. It's dirty and it's dusty and it's scattered all over the store. There's bins, barrels, shelves. Don't know how anybody can find anything, but they do. Well, anyway he does. Norman, I mean." He paused reflectively for a moment. "It's really your good old-fashioned hardware store. Everybody for miles around knows it."

"That's what I meant about why we were asked to do this," Hugh commented. "All the SIMM people up here must know him. That's why we're here to pick up — what is it anyway? It's a computer isn't it?" He reached into the back seat for a clipboard. "Yeah. Kirznet Cash Flow Control System."

He looked out at the display windows again. "Somehow it just doesn't seem to fit in there, does it?"

Gordon chuckled. "Probably why he hasn't paid for it."

"Well, pay or not," Hugh opened the car door, "let's get it over with." He was halfway out the door and then sat down again. "By the way, I make it 9:15. Is that what you've got? Awfully late for an old-fashioned hardware store to still be closed."

"That's true," Gordon replied, a note of concern in his voice.

The two men got out and stood beside their car to take in a

21

wider view. The area was very quiet. There was no one else around.

The "Real Man's Hardware Store" had no sidewalk in front of it, just a small parking lot, empty this morning. There were no adjacent stores either; the building was separated from the edge of town by a small field.

"This isn't a holiday or something, is it?" Hugh looked at Gordon as they approached the front door. "Don't they have a half-holiday or something like that in these little towns when everybody closes."

"Not in the morning," Gordon said, somewhat distractedly for they'd reached the door and it was definitely locked.

"Wow! Look at that latch!" Hugh said. "This has to be the last store in the country with a thumb la . . . Oh, oh! Look there."

"I see it — him," Gordon answered.

On the floor inside, just a few steps from the door, the body of a man lay face down at an angle slightly oblique to the door. Hugh and Gordon moved to the display windows on either side so they could peer in.

The body was that of a man at the far end of middle age. They could see white hair protruding over the edge of a baseball cap, some of the tufts leading to the back of his lined neck. He wore a red smock, the kind one might normally expect on a hardware store clerk.

The position of the body seemed peculiar. It lay in a very wide pool of blood that seemed to have congealed at the edges now. The man's legs were crossed at the ankles as though he had tripped himself and fallen that way. One hand, his left, was in the pocket of his shiny brown pants. The other was in the small of his back, palm upward. In the wan light from the fluorescents left on for nighttime security, both Hugh and Gordon noted its soft, clean, whiteness in contrast to the menace just above it. For there, inches above the hand, thrust deep into the man's back, was a black-handled knife, a multi-purpose sportsman's knife, probably one from the store. It appeared as though the victim's last living effort had been to try to pull it out.

Neither Hugh nor Gordon felt an urge to rush. There was no question the man was dead and had been for some time.

"I'll call," Hugh said, pulling himself back from the scene. "Do they have 911 here?"

"They must," Gordon replied. "Wouldn't matter anyway. Everybody knows Wilfrid Norman's place."

"Sure, but that's not Wilfrid Norman," Hugh said over his shoulder on the way to the car and the cellular phone.

Gordon Pape has been to Wilfrid Norman's store before, and might recognize the hardware man, but how does Hugh Furneaux know that the dead man is not Wilfrid Norman?

7

Murder at
249 Hanover Street

AS SHE PULLED OVER TO the curb, Janet Dexel cocked her head a little closer to the portable radio on the seat beside her.

"The wettest first day of October since records were started in 1826," the announcer was saying, "and the outlook for the next several days is more of the same."

Janet snapped off the radio and peered almost gloomily across the sidewalk at 249 Hanover Street. "A perfectly miserable day," she said out loud to herself, "and now a perfectly miserable night and a perfectly miserable place over there to go with it all."

Certainly, 249 Hanover Street was not inviting. Although the brick pillars supporting the heavy gates, together with the wrought iron fence, would never keep out any determined intruder, they said "You Are Not Welcome" in a most effective way. If the message failed here, at the edge of the property, then the double doors under the dimly lit portico at the house itself took a second stab at it, for their design repeated the warning that visitors to 249 Hanover Street would not be pleasantly received.

Janet groaned as she forced herself out of the car into the

pouring rain. She drew her heavy rain cloak tight around her shoulders and stared at the big house for a few seconds before walking back to an empty squad car parked at the curb behind her. She leaned in and switched off the flashing red lights, then made a note of the car's number before turning to walk quickly through the open gates. Staff Sergeant Janet Dexel hated fuss. She especially disliked police operations that attracted attention unnecessarily. Someone in her unit was going to get a dressing down as soon as she had the opportunity, and at the moment, the odds favored tonight.

Rain began to fall even harder so she broke into a run for the last few steps up to the double doors. Once inside, the sight of Chesley Barron-Ripple, or rather, what had been Chesley Barron-Ripple, quickly took her mind off the bad weather and the fool who had left the lights flashing. Two of her officers stood over the body. Neither was enjoying the assignment very much. One of them held a handkerchief over her nose.

Chesley Barron-Ripple was attracting the kind of attention that would have embarrassed him beyond measure had he been alive. An assistant from the medical examiner's office was snapping picture after picture of him where he lay on a priceless, silk-on-silk handwoven rug. Behind the police officers, a pair of ambulance attendants, looking far more at ease than anyone else at the scene, were holding a body bag like a pair of Boy Scouts about to fold the flag at the end of the ceremony.

One of the policemen, the younger one, almost stood at attention as he addressed his boss. "The lab people have all gone, Sergeant," he said. "Except for him." The policeman nodded at the photographer. "And he's almost finished — *Aren't you?*"

It was clear to Janet that everyone wanted to get this part of the investigation over and done with.

"We're waiting for you to give us the clear." It was the other officer. She was speaking through her handkerchief. "Detective Andrew is in the next room with the three . . . uh . . . I guess they're suspects, aren't they?"

25

"Oh? Suspects?" Another thing that bothered Janet was having her officers jump to conclusions. Especially if there were media people nearby. One positive outcome of the heavy rain, however, was that the situation was free of the press, at least so far.

"Well, I mean . . . I don't know if they're suspects. They're . . . they're . . . they've been *detained* by Detective Andrew."

The officer appeared relieved that she'd found the right word.

"There are three people," she continued with more confidence now. "There's the part-time handyman. And Barron-Ripple's daughter, and . . . and . . ." Her discomfort had returned. "And the *butler*, Sergeant Dexel."

Before Janet could reply, the younger policeman spoke again. "He said he was the butler, Sergeant, but I think he's really a kind of valet or personal servant. Anyway, he's got an alibi. He went to his sister's in Kennebunkport on the 30th. Been there for two days. Actually, all three have got alibis like that."

"I see," Janet Dexel said, searching her coat pockets for a tissue to pat the droplet of rain on her eyelash.

"Yeah, the daughter, Sergeant Dexel," the policewoman was still talking through her handkerchief. "She's . . . well . . . her alibi's pretty solid. She's been drying out in a clinic for the past month. Got back this morning. When she got home here she saw the butler . . . uh . . . valet, I guess, standing on the portico. Seems neither of them had a key so they sent for the handyman. He lives over in Lower Sackville.

"And what's *his* cover?" Janet wanted to know.

"Sounds reasonable enough," was the answer. "He comes once a week unless there's something special to do. Tomorrow's his day, and he missed last week. Says his wife and two neighbors can back it up."

"I see." Janet nodded at the body and then at the two ambulance attendants who still held the body bag stretched out. "I guess you can move him out of here now." To the police officers she said, "You two tell Andrew to advise that butler or valet or whatever he calls himself of his rights and then bring him downtown. I'll meet him there. Shouldn't be too hard to break up his story. You were right about 'suspect.' Just don't say it. Leave that kind of talk for the lawyers."

What is Janet Dexel's reason for suspecting the butler rather than the daughter or handyman?

8

Head-on in the Middle
of the Road

JUDGE ELMER GRIEB OF THE Superior Court sat on the edge of
an old wooden chair in his private office, elbows on his knees,
chin in his hands, staring at the brown medicine bottle on his
desk. *Karlsrhue Pharmacy*, the label said. *Take two tablespoons as
required. DO NOT EXCEED RECOMMENDED DOSAGE.*

Elmer had already exceeded the recommended dosage. Three
times. He was deep in thought, and whenever His Honor
pondered over a case, he invariably reached into the bottom
right-hand drawer for the helpful brown bottle from Karlsrhue
Pharmacy.

The stress of making decisions in civil law suits had taken its
toll on Elmer over the years. By his own admission, his nerves
just weren't what they used to be. But he had a very low opinion
of tranquilizers, indeed anything that came in the form of a pill.
And years of listening to the so-called expert testimony of
psychiatrists had entirely wiped away any faith he might have had
in their powers. So, every morning of a day when he was about
to endure the stress of handing down a decision, Judge Elmer
Grieb turned to his own, oft-proven therapy. He filled a brown
medicine bottle with homemade wine. Dandelion wine. His

mother had taught him how to make it. According to Elmer's theory, the powerful amber liquid not only calmed his nerves and cleared his head, it was even a cure for his troublesome arthritis. And if the truth were known, it probably explained why he suffered far fewer colds than the rest of the population! Still another plus was that the stuff actually looked like medicine and tasted even worse, useful qualities in case any of the court staff got curious.

Earlier this afternoon, for two long and uncomfortable hours, Elmer had been formally and officially perched on the Superior Court bench feeling very much in need of his medicine. Over this time he had listened to the testimony of four witnesses: the two plaintiffs, the defendant appearing on behalf of Carrick Township, and the driver of the Carrick Township road grader. The case was one of those percentage-of-blame lawsuits that always made His Honor uncomfortable because he did not like to play Solomon.

It was a car accident case. Both plaintiff and defendant admitted to some blame. At issue was what percentage for each. Cases like these sometimes took Elmer a whole bottle of medicine to think through.

Several months ago, the two plaintiffs, traveling in separate cars at midday with no other traffic nearby, had run head-on into each other at the crest of a hill out on the tenth side road of Carrick Township. At the scene of the accident the police had decided that since both drivers were smack in the middle of the road when they hit, they were mutually at fault. Hence no traffic charges were laid, and neither driver had been able to attack the other's insurance company. However, the two had now joined forces and, together, were suing Carrick Township and the township road foreman, Peter Hesch, on the grounds that it was road repairs to the hill in the week before their crash that had made it necessary for both of them to drive in the center. The two wore neck braces, and both produced medical certificates attesting to whiplash and other possible, as yet unknown, damage. They had managed to look seriously injured in the witness box.

When it was his turn to testify, Peter Hesch, the road foreman, acknowledged that yes, there had been road repairs on both sides of the hill the week before. It was a steep hill, he explained, and usually after a wet spring the hill was pretty rutted and full of potholes. It was a repair that the township carried out just about every year during a spell of nice dry weather, he said. But then Peter Hesch managed to get the plaintiff's lawyer all stirred up when he added, somewhat gratuitously, at the end of his testimony, that the two drivers had to be pretty stupid because "any damn fool should know you slow down and pull over when you get to the top of a blind hill."

At the reference to "blind hill" the plaintiff's lawyer had practically danced with glee and took almost an hour of court time establishing that on this particular hill on the tenth side road, it was impossible for a driver on either side to see a car on the other, until he reached the very top.

The fourth witness was Harvey Speelmacher, driver of the township road grader. To Elmer's considerable relief, Harvey's time in the witness box was brief and uneventful. Testifying in a case three years ago, Harvey had got very excited, and Elmer had had to adjourn for twenty minutes while the cleaning staff scrubbed wads of tobacco juice off the sides of the witness box.

This time it took Harvey barely a few minutes, a calm few minutes, to say that three days before the accident in question he had spent the morning with the township grader smoothing out the surface on both sides of the hill, the last step in the road repair. Then for no apparent reason at all, he added that he knew right well what day he had done it because it was his wife's birthday, August 9. He had booked off during the afternoon so he could take her fishing over on the South Saugeen, "bein' the weather'd been so nice and all."

After Harvey's testimony, the lawyers for both sides had summarized with surprising quickness, the plaintiff's counsel arguing strongly that because the hill was a "blind hill," Peter Hesch and Carrick Township were at least eighty percent responsible if not one hundred percent.

The gist of the argument from the defendant's counsel was that it was the two plaintiffs who were eighty percent responsible for what they had done to themselves, since common sense and safe driving obliged them to slow down and keep to the right in a situation where it might be a bit difficult to know what was coming from the opposite direction.

Elmer had recessed after that and directed everyone to return in one hour, at which time he would hand down his decision. That was eight tablespoons ago, and although he wasn't bothered by his arthritis anymore, he still had to go back into court and give his decision.

He reached for the bottle and the spoon one more time. This was definitely a ten-tablespoon case. What bothered Judge Elmer Grieb so much was the failure of the township side, the defendant, to bring up the most obvious counterpoint to the "blind hill" argument. And quite frankly, he didn't know what to do about it.

What is the important point that the township side has failed to bring up?

9

A 911 Call from
Whitby Towers

BEV ASHBY WAS SO DISTRACTED by the size of the crowd gathered
on the sidewalk that at first she didn't hear the concierge shouting
at her.

"They're up there!" He was bent over the driver's door, yelling
red-faced at the closed window and gesticulating wildly at the
building across the sidewalk. "Fourth floor! But you have to walk
'cause the elevator's been down since yesterday!"

It wasn't until several hours later that Bev ruefully
acknowledged, yet again, that maybe it's true what they say about
cops: they just stick out. For the life of her she had no idea how
the concierge had identified her, first as a police officer, and
second, as the detective sent to investigate the incident. She was
dressed in civvies, the car was unmarked, and she had used neither
siren nor light. And there were several other cars at the curb that
were clearly sent there by a police dispatcher. Yet the concierge
had run out the revolving doors of Whitby Towers directly to her.

"Your uniformed people are up there! Two of them!" Bev had
her window rolled down, but now he was yelling even louder.
"And the chauffeur that saw him do it!"

His shouting increased the size of the crowd and drew their

32

attention away from the incident that was entertaining them in the middle of the busy downtown street. A noontime fender bender had developed into a slugfest between the two drivers involved. Both were now draped over the hoods of their respective cars in handcuffs.

Bev had to push the concierge back to get out of the car. He was still waving his arms and sputtering.

"I'm the one that called 911," he said into her face. "The chauffeur saw him doing it from down here on the street! Hanging himself! Yelled at me to call and then ran for the stairs!" The young man wasn't shouting anymore, but he was still wound up enough to draw even more of the crowd toward them. Bev took him by the arm and forced her way through the gawkers toward the doors of Whitby Towers.

"Shouldn't this be *your* job?" she said over her shoulder. "I mean, you're the one supposed to be breaking trail, aren't you?"

"Yes, Omigod! Look, I'm sorry! This is only my second day And I . . . like . . . I've never called 911 before! And I . . ."

Bev pushed through to the revolving doors with the concierge in tow. Once inside, the plush quietness of the lobby calmed him with dramatic suddenness.

"Fourth floor," the concierge said with professional detachment. "Number 411. The stairs are over there behind that pillar. We're very sorry about the elevator problem."

Bev nodded. "I'll be back down in a while to talk to you. Just don't leave, please."

By the time she reached the fourth floor she was puffing a bit. She wondered how the occupants of Whitby Towers were tolerating a two-day elevator failure. It was an expensive building and even though "Towers" was an enormously pretentious title — the place had only six floors — a lot of money was needed for the rent here.

Suite 411 was easy enough to find, for a uniformed officer was standing in the hallway outside the door. He tipped his cap with his index finger as Bev approached. "Body's inside, Lieutenant. We have not cut him down; we've only been here," he looked at his watch, "seventeen minutes now. Chauffeur's in there with my partner."

He held the door open for Bev so she could see the entire tableau before taking a step. Suite 411 was a luxuriously appointed studio apartment. What marred the sight of the deep pile rug and highly polished reproduction furniture was the body of a silver-haired man, in excellent trim, hanging from a thin nylon rope, an overturned chair at his lifeless feet.

"His name is . . ." The patrolman started to speak, but Bev cut him off with a shake of her head. Twice she walked slowly around the body and then expanded the circle to walk around the room. Everything was in perfect order as one would expect at Whitby Towers. Well, not quite everything. The telephone wire was cut. Actually, not cut. Torn. That had taken strength. There was something else, too. Bev bent over in front of the balcony doors. What was it on the floor there, one end of a shoelace? No. Nylon rope. Looked like the same stuff that was around the dead man's neck. With a pen, she spread the drapes just enough to follow the rope to about knee level where the other end was clamped between the doors.

Nodding to herself, Bev looked up at the uniformed officer. "Now you can tell me his name," she said to him. "On second thought," she turned to the chauffeur, "you go first. Let's start with your name."

"Sandford Verity." No hesitation. He responded as though he'd anticipated her question. And he didn't talk the way Bev thought a chauffeur might, but then, she had to admit, she didn't really know any chauffeurs. Maybe they all talk this way! "What happened is very simple." He continued as though he were in charge. "My firm is Brock Livery Service. We pick up Mr. Seneca every day — that's his name: Audley Seneca — at 11:50 and take him to wherever he directs. It's a standing, daily order. Yesterday and today I came up here to his suite, because of the elevator situation, instead of meeting him in the lobby. You see, he has a prosthesis, an artificial leg actually, and the stairs are somewhat of a problem for him. This morning when I arrived I happened to look up. Thought maybe he might be watching that altercation on the street. That's when I saw him on the chair there, the rope around his neck. Of course I ran as fast as I could. Told the concierge to call 911. But I got here too late. The door was locked. What I should have done, I realize now, was get the concierge to come with me. With a master key. But then, after a crisis is over, one always thinks of things one should have done."

"Agreed, Mr. Verity," Bev said and turned to the uniformed officer. "Would you go down to the lobby," she said, "and bring the concierge up here? There's quite a big hole here in the story of Mr. Seneca's alleged suicide."

What is the "big hole" to which Bev Ashby refers?

10

The Case of the Kramer Collection

GEORGE FEWSTER WOULD NEVER HAVE admitted it to anyone, but had he learned how to use a modem and a fax machine when they first came on the market, he'd have taken early retirement even earlier.

It wasn't really early retirement in his case, as he was quick to explain to anyone who raised an eyebrow. It was more a second career. Instead of Professor of Archeology at Simon Fraser University, he was now George Fewster, Consultant in Archaeology. The change in job description may have introduced a tad of uncertainty into his cash flow, but that was more than compensated for by what he had done this morning, as he did each morning. That was to walk past his car, where it sat silently in the garage, pause to marvel at the birds squabbling busily around the feeder, and then go into the little office he'd built for himself some distance from the house. There, perched on the lip of a small mountain meadow with the town of Banff to his left, Mount Rundle to his right, and the Bow River down below, he could be warmed by some of the most beautiful scenery in the world. Or, especially in autumn after the leaves had fallen, he could peer around a corner of his house and feel sorry for the commuters heading out to the city. He could even work, if he was disposed to — and he was, most of the time.

This morning for example. During the night, his modem had brought in a report from the Museum of Civilization in Ottawa that he'd been awaiting for over a month. When he got his computer going and brought up the *KRAMER* file, he was rewarded with a screenful of information.

The top of the screen read: *Contents of Kramer Estate Collection.* A short personal note followed:

Dear George,

You're going to have fun with this one. It's a weird conglomeration all right. Some of it is just collectibles, hardly even rummage-sale quality. But every once in a while, as you'll see, there's a real gem. There's also some very interesting Arctic exploration stuff, if it's genuine. And quite a few coins. I think these might be very valuable. Anyway, have fun.

Sincerely,
Myrna.

The *Kramer Estate Collection* had been offered to the museum — for a price — some six months ago by a couple from a small town in the Eastern Townships of Quebec. George had the name written down somewhere. So far, the museum had been able to establish that the collection was put together quite a few years before by one Francis Kramer, a successful but extremely eccentric prospector whose final years had been spent in the Thirty Thousand Islands area of Georgian Bay, where he'd held a running battle with the local bylaw and health authorities because he insisted on living in a dry cistern.

But the Museum of Civilization didn't really care about Kramer's lifestyle; it wanted an evaluation of his collection, and that is what George now turned to on his monitor.

Under the personal note from Myrna, the screen said *Group One*, then it gave more information that went like this:

> *These items in Group One, George, will not appear to need your attention at first glance. They are mostly old magazines, some of them are nicely dated though. There's a* Reader's Digest *from 1922 and an 1890 edition of the* London Times. *A really exciting piece is a 1728 issue of the* Saturday Evening Post. *A genuine fraud, so to speak!*

George pressed PAGE DOWN on his keyboard. He wanted to get to the coins, but something in Group Two caught his attention. Group Two was a list of material that Myrna had called "Arctic exploration stuff." Most of it described artifacts from expeditions to the Arctic: items like the compass used by Robert Peary in 1906, Otto Sverdrup's toiletry kit, and a tin of brown beans retrieved from a cache set up by the Rae expedition in 1854. What twigged George, however, was the description of a tract. *On the Origins of the Blond Eskimo,* the title read. *By Vilhjalmur Stefansson.* George made a note to have that one couriered to him right away and then kept pressing PAGE DOWN until the screen finally showed *Group Three: Coins.* This is what he wanted to see above all. There was another note from Myrna:

> *Can't wait till you come to Ottawa to see these face-to-face. This is where the real value is, I think.*
>
> *There are two Washington half-dollars, 1792, in mint condition. Wait till you see them! And an Upper Canada halfpenny from 1883 that looks so good you'd swear it was never in circulation. There are several of this type. But probably the most valuable are the three really old coins in the collection. From some time B.C.*
>
> *There's a silver stater from Syria. It's fifth century B.C. The British Museum paid $4,000 for one of these last year and this one's in better condition, I'm told. The other two are Roman coins. They're both silver, too. One's from early in the reign of*

Caesar Augustus. Stamped 22 B.C., but unfortunately the profile of Augustus is not very good. The other one is about two hundred years later; you can't see the date, but the profile of Emperor Hadrian is as good as a contemporary issue!

There's more in the collection. A whole bunch of beaver nickels from the thirties with George VI on them, and some of those funny blackout nickels from World War II, but they're probably not of much interest to the museum.

George leaned back in his chair and stared at the screen for a few seconds. Then, impulsively, he turned the computer off without even getting out of the file. He was disappointed.

Before this report had come in, he had looked forward to a trip to Ottawa, even if it meant he would have to join the commuters on a drive to the city. Now he knew the trip would likely be unnecessary.

What is wrong in the Kramer Collection that has left George Fewster so disappointed?

11

Waiting Out the Rain

MICHELLE LINK SAT IN ONE of the two window booths at Kline's Soda Shoppe with Julie Varughese and two of their classmates from Memorial Junior School. All four stared gloomily at the rain pelting down on the street outside. They had headed straight for Kline's right after school, beating the crowd so they could get their favorite booth. It was a perfect location. In the corner at the window, the booth gave them a sweeping view of everybody in the little restaurant — more important, they could see who came in *with* whom and not be too obvious about it. As well, if the patrons failed to stir up any interest, they could usually find something diverting out on the street.

Not today, though. Except for two older ladies who had come in for tea, Kline's was unusually empty. So was the street. The rain had begun to fall the instant they arrived, hard enough to discourage any of the regulars from Memorial Junior and, except for two pedestrians who had taken shelter in the doorway of Vex's Pharmacy across the way, hard enough to pretty much empty the street, too. Now, two Cherry Cokes apiece later, and having exhausted the day's school stories, the four friends were bored and quite ready to leave, but the rain was not yet prepared to let them.

The only distraction, and the only person who seemed to be enjoying the weather, was a little boy standing in the gutter just off the sidewalk a few feet away from Michelle. He couldn't be more than three, Michelle calculated, watching him stand there in the water that sluiced down the gutter around his bright blue rubber boots, splashing up against and almost over the toes where someone — an older sister, Michelle speculated — had painted a large "L" on top of one and an "R" on the other with pink fingernail polish.

Through Kline's screened door, Michelle could hear the boy's squeal of delight as a candy-bar wrapper floated up to the toes, then made a complete circle and carried on between the boots. She followed the progress of the wrapper for a few feet and for the first time noticed the woman on the edge of the sidewalk. Must be the kid's mother, her speculation continued.

The woman was not watching her son — if it really was her son. She was standing under the awning at Whippany Appliances next door, listening transfixed to the radio bulletin booming from the store. Whippany Appliances was advertising Motorola, their new franchise brand, and a big cabinet model standing just inside the door put the news out onto the street.

Michelle could hear it from the restaurant:

" . . . from General Eisenhower's headquarters in England a confirmation that five divisions are involved: two American, two British, one Canadian. Early reports indicate that German troops have fallen back from the beaches at all five landing areas. Pockets of resistance are still strong, however, at Omaha Beach.

"The Columbia Broadcasting System's news service has also learned that . . ."

For the past two days the radio news had talked of nothing but the landings at Normandy, the biggest invasion, it was being described, in the history of warfare. Michelle watched the woman stare vaguely into the appliance store. She had not once turned around to look at her little boy. He had his rain hat off now and was filling it with water.

"Michelle! Earth to Michelle! Hey, get with it! The rain has stopped! Remember? The wet stuff? Let's go while we can!" Julie finally reached across the table and shook her friend's arm.

41

"I wonder if her husband's a soldier?" Michelle said, without looking at Julie. "The little boy's father. I'll bet he is."

"What *are* you talking about?" Julie shook Michelle's arm one more time. "C'mon! The rain's let up. We've got to leave now or we'll have to order another Cherry Coke. Either that or rent the booth."

Michelle and Julie said goodbye to their friends at the doorway to Kline's and headed up the street. For a few seconds, they, too, paused at Whippany Appliances and listened to the radio talk about Normandy. The woman and the little boy were gone. Somehow they had disappeared as the girls were getting out of the booth. The street began to fill with activity again, almost as if it had been waiting, pent up and hidden under shelter until the weather improved.

The two pedestrians from Vex's Pharmacy had crossed the street and were moving on ahead of the girls. Farther up they could see Mister Lum at Lum's Groceteria pushing carts of fruit and vegetables back into the sidewalk. Next to the appliance store two men got out of a truck belonging to Bitnik's Delivery Service and began to wrestle a soaking wet tarpaulin off a stack of cardboard boxes. Cars began to move up the street more quickly now, as though relieved by the prospect of drier progress.

Two minutes later, at the corner of Vine Street, Julie said goodbye, peeling off down Vine, leaving Michelle to continue on two more blocks to her home on Sanders Avenue. Michelle didn't expect to speak to Julie again until school the next day. For one thing, there was too much homework. More important, her parents had made one of those suggestions that parents tend to make about too much use of the phone on school nights.

The telephone rang anyway, about an hour after dinner, and it was Julie.

"Did you *hear* what happened? At Kline's?"

Michelle wanted to point out that obviously she had not, or why would Julie be calling, but she didn't get a chance.

"There was an accident! You know that truck? Bitnik's truck?" Julie was very wound up.

"It was right there when we passed. Remember? Those two guys unloading . . . uh . . . whatever it was? Anyway, *it rolled right into Kline's!* Right through the *window!* My dad says the brakes, no, no, the *emergency* brake probably failed."

"Julie . . ."

"I mean, right where we were sitting!"

"Julie . . ."

"Can you imagine? Like . . . if it hadn't stopped raining? We'd have been sitting right there! We could have been killed! Or really injured or something!"

"Not just us, Julie. But listen . . ."

"Don't tell your parents we were sitting right there in the window booth. I mean, I didn't tell *my* parents. You know what it's like. They'll get all worried and then they'll start thinking Kline's is dangerous and then . . . well . . . anyway. You know what parents are like. But isn't it *exciting?*"

"Julie!"

There was a pause followed by a soft and very tentative "What?"

"Julie, that was no accident."

Why is Michelle Link sure that what Julie Varughese has described was not an accident?

43

12

A Routine Check
in the Parking Lot

LOCAL LEGEND HAD IT THAT DINKS got its name in the 1920s
when it sported one of the first neon signs in the county and the
"R" in "DRINKS" refused to work. It didn't take a great deal of
entrepreneurial flash for the then owner to realize that this
fortuitous ellipsis had far more appeal to the passing public than
his own four-syllable name, so DINKS the bar became, and
DINKS it remained.

The name held up through a number of metamorphoses as the
bar changed from a jazz cocktail lounge with upscale pretensions
in its early days, to a dance hall catering to the army base nearby,
to a juke box *cum* hamburger joint, to its present phase: a cocktail
bar again. It had a live trio on weekends, deep, ruby-red decor,
cheap drinks, and a reputation that struggled hard to stay just this
side of sleaze.

The other constant in the history of the place was trouble with
the police. Over the decades, the local force had learned to factor
in DINKS as a normal part of their planning and projections.
Situated on the edge of town, DINKS was where locals came to
howl. So there were fights. Lots of fights. Most were the

cracked-head, broken-tooth variety typical of a confrontation between drunks, but occasionally the brawls were serious.

DINKS was held up, too, with tedious regularity, almost always by strangers passing through who never knew where the real cash was kept. In the fifties, the huge parking lot had served as a track for post-midnight drag races, and in the sixties, as a spot for civil-rights sit-ins. Not long after the Vietnam War, it became known as a drug-exchange campus.

However, until this morning, there had never been a murder at DINKS. But now, even that marker had finally been achieved. In typical DINKS style as well. There was not just one body, but two. As it was, had Ron Forrester not been a veteran of some considerable experience on the police force, he might easily have bought into the murderer's ploy, for the bodies had been set up to look like the victims of accidental death.

It had been cleverly done. DINKS, quite naturally, was a choice rendezvous for illicit affairs. The bar was big, it was dark, it was on the highway, nobody asked questions, and no one would ever, ever, dare to bring a camera into the place. Therefore, when Ron cruised into the parking lot at 4:55 A.M., he was not particularly surprised to note that the large sedan, backed into the far corner of the parking lot, under the protective branches of an old elm tree, was occupied. There were two people in the front seat. For all he knew, there could have been two in the back as well. Not likely though.

Out of habit and not a little curiosity, Ron drove slowly toward the car for a look, leaving his high beams on to warn the two he was coming. After all, it was really no concern of his what two consenting adults were doing in a car at 4:55 A.M., even in the parking lot at DINKS. He just wanted to make sure they were consenting and that the consent was mutual.

The veteran policeman's first suspicion that something was wrong came when he saw no reaction to his high beams. Usually in situations like this, the guilty parties tried to hide, or at the very least, turned around out of curiosity or annoyance. Then as he got closer and saw both heads lolling on the back of the front seat, he knew immediately that something was seriously amiss.

Ron accelerated the last hundred feet, then stopped. In a hurry now, he got out, ran to the car and pulled open the driver's door. It was too late. Without even taking a pulse, Ron Forrester knew from experience that both bodies had been dead for some time. He left the door open and went back to the patrol car, moving it perpendicular to the sedan so that the headlights would shine directly into the front seat.

On the other side of the man behind the steering wheel, a woman lay against the back of the seat, turned to one side, with her knees drawn up. Her shoes were off and her blouse unbuttoned. Her right hand dangled into the garbage carrier that straddled the center hump, and two fingers of her left were hooked into the man's belt. Ron couldn't see her face; it was tilted downward.

He could see the man's face, however. He'd been trying to ignore it all along, for the man sat leaning against the seat, his head turned to the left, eyes wide and lifeless, staring right at Ron, the whites gleaming in the lights of the patrol car. The pupils were tiny dots and the irises a washed out blue. The man's mouth was open, his tongue sticking out through lips that formed a perfect "O" as though he'd died in mild surprise. Like his companion in death, his shoes were off and his shirt unbuttoned. One hand lay on the seat beside him, the other, for what reason Ron could not figure, was stuck through the steering wheel, dangling at the wrist.

Ron turned on his flashlight and shone it around the interior of the car, even though the act seemed redundant in view of the powerful headlights behind him. The motor was still running, and there was about a quarter tank of gas left. The heater was on, too, set to "medium" with the fan set to "low." The radio played softly, an all-night station that Ron didn't recognize. In the back seat lay both headrests, a box of tissues, and a blue purse. Probably the woman's for it matched the blue shoes on the floor beside her lifeless feet.

A Routine Check in the Parking Lot

The veteran policeman reached across the dead man's body with great care to turn off the motor, then stopped, hardly believing what he'd almost done. Fingerprints! On the keys! This wasn't a case of two lovers forgetting about the potential danger of carbon monoxide. This was murder!

Slowly, and with even more care than he had used when reaching in, Ron withdrew his arm. The action brought his arm against the dead man's cheek, and in the morning silence he could hear the stubble rasp against his uniform. It made him shiver.

He shivered again just outside the patrol car and blew in his hands to warm them, as much because of the shock of what he had just seen as from the December cold. He looked up at the sky. No sunrise for an hour or more yet, he calculated, but then for the two in the car, no sunrise ever again.

How does Ron Forrester know that at least one and probably both of the victims have been murdered?

13

An Answer for Kirby's Important New Client

"HERE'S THAT GUY AGAIN! THAT Smythe-Boliver!" Mara Silverberg was excited enough by her discovery to be shouting. "Listen!" She held up one of the faxed pages and read:

"'Major-General G. Smythe-Boliver, Royal Fusilliers: born 1708, at Ross-on-Wye; died 1779, at Chipping Sodbury; battles of Fort William Henry, 1757; Fort Carillon, 1758; Plains of Abraham, 1759. Fluent French and Spanish; signing delegate, Treaty of Paris, 1763.'"

"Yes, but," the voice belonged to her sister Krista, "the diary here is written by a *Major* Gerard Smythe-Boliver."

"So?" Mara was sure of her ground. "That doesn't have to mean he was a major forever, does it? Besides, how many officers in one war could possibly be named *Smythe-Boliver?*"

"You're probably right," Krista acknowledged. "In a war he'd get promoted faster. And he's upper class, so that means he gets to be a general, too, I guess."

Kirby Silverberg had been waiting patiently and finally broke in. This was, after all, her show. "Read that diary passage one more time, Krista," she said. "Remember it's *Fitzwall* we're interested in. More so than this Smythe-Boliver character."

Krista responded by lifting a page slightly and pushing her glasses to the bridge of her nose. "'Tuesday, 21 October,'" she read aloud, then put the paper down. "See?" she said. "Just like all the others. No year given." She shrugged and picked up the paper again. "Anyway." She cleared her throat. "'Only two months since the beginning of hostilities and I have just lost my batman, Fitzwall.'"

"What's a batman again?" Mara wanted to know.

"Personal servant. Sort of a valet," Kirby said. "Officers all had one then."

Krista started again "'. . . just lost my batman, Fitzwall. Poor chap; exactly half my age. Cannonball took his leg just below the knee, and three fingers. Not likely he'll survive. His wife died last year. One child. A girl born when the wife was but fourteen and he only four years her senior! One finds it difficult to understand the lower classes.'"

Krista looked up at her sisters. "There's a bunch of blather next about the need for more trained troops, and a piece about the amount of drinking going on. Stuff like that. Most of the rest is about the problem of having to train another batman. Nice guy this Smythe-Boliver! No more about Fitzwall."

She turned to Kirby. "I've gone back twenty entries and ahead twenty. There's not one other mention of Fitzwall. You want me to keep going?"

Kirby put her elbow on the huge volume of case-law summaries she had been wading through to keep the pages from fanning out.

"Please?" she said, pointing to the stack of photocopies in front of Krista and then to the pile in front of Mara. "There's so little time. You have everything there that the Imperial War Museum was willing to send from their Seven Years War collection. Mom's got the stuff from Halifax and Dad's got the memoirs. The answer's got to be somewhere here in all this stuff, and I need it by eight o'clock tomorrow morning or I lose the commission. Worse, I could lose the first big client I've ever had."

Kirby was referring to the Boston law firm of Tory, Wigan, and Best. She had been hired by the firm to uncover the year of birth of one Simon Fitzwall, first born of Ethan Fitzwall who had come to Boston with his father from England via Halifax, some time before the American Revolution. What was crucial was whether Simon had been born before or after 1788, the year the state of Massachusetts signed the U.S. Constitution. The date was important in a dispute over public versus private ownership of some land in the Boston area.

In their own search, the lawyers had been able to follow a straight track backward in time for almost two hundred years. Then the string broke. They had all kinds of data: personal histories, memoirs, diaries, photocopies of eighteenth-century newspapers, but the writers of the material, as was fairly customary for the time, seemed to have either a cavalier disregard for dates or simply felt they were unnecessary. Kirby Silverberg, P.I., had been hired to complete the paper chase. She had been given less than twenty-four hours to do it and had turned to her family for help.

As her sisters dug back into the material from the Imperial War Museum, Kirby turned to her mother. "Anything from Halifax yet, Mom?"

"I've been waiting for my chance!" the girls' mother replied. She had been poring over documents from the provincial archives of Nova Scotia.

"Listen to this." She took up the huge magnifying glass she had been using to decipher the barely legible print and held it with both hands. "It's from the harbormaster's report. 'Ship arrivals for the week.'" She looked up. "I guess I don't need to say it doesn't tell us what week. Or month or year either. In any case. 'Ship arrivals for the week: the *Endurance* and the *Titan* out of Portsmouth.' There's a long list like that. Must have been a real busy place! But get this." She shifted in her chair and rotated the magnifying glass. "The *Earl of Shannon* out of Southhampton. Now . . ."

She flipped over several pages to one with the corner pulled down. "Here. 'Harbormaster's report to the Governor General.' It says:

'To Your Excellency's attention: with regard to the loss of the *Earl of Shannon* in Halifax Harbor on Sunday last, this ship until five years ago was the *Arquemada* out of Madrid. She was ceded to His Majesty's Navy under terms of the Treaty of Paris, along with . . .' Then there's a list of other ships and stuff like that."

"But Mom," Kirby tried to keep the exasperation out of her voice. "That doesn't . . ."

"I'm not finished. Listen. The report goes on to list the passengers from the *Earl of Shannon* who require passage on to Boston and who now await His Excellency's pleasure — he must have had to give them clearance or something, or maybe it was his responsibility after the ship sank. Anyway. Guess who's on the list? Fitzwall, Ambrose Esq., and three children, Abigail, Rachel, and Ethan!" She looked up triumphantly, blinking to clear the fuzz left by the magnifying glass.

"*All right Mom!*" This time it was Kirby doing the shouting. "Now all we need is . . . Dad's got Ambrose's personal history thing. That's got to have the rest of what we need. Where is he? Where's Dad?"

"He's asleep," Krista said. "You know what happens. Soon as you mention lawyers he either goes to the bathroom or falls asleep."

"Take it easy. I'm here!" A male voice came from the corner of the room. "What do you need to know about Ambrose Fitzwall? I've become an expert interpreter of his memoirs."

"Memoirs, Dad?" It was Mara. "There's only three pages."

"Not quite that simple," Laurie Silverberg replied. He got out of the big easy chair and joined his family at the table. "The man was self-taught. Had to be. It takes some figuring to get past his spelling. And the sentence structure!" Laurie shook his head. "Listen to this. 'This here is the story of my family after my first wife Etta died and I lost the leg and my fingers with the major and I married Solomon Lesham's second daughter Nattie what was already a widow with one child Rachel we had Ethan right away and come to America with my Abigail.' Now that's all one sentence. You should try . . ."

"Keep going!"

"Yeah, don't stop now!"

Laurie peered over his glasses and smoothed the curling edges of the photocopies with deliberate care before beginning again.

"'Nattie she died of the flux I never married again. We come to America on the *Earl of Shannon* a wormy tub she sank off Halifax good riddance.'

"You should see — he spells that R-I-D-N-E-S."

"Dad, c'mon!"

"Yeah, don't tell us the spelling. What happened!"

"All right, all right, all right. Let's see. Okay, yeah, '. . . good riddance. Abigail she had a hard crossing young Ethan being only half the age of her when I lost the leg and Rachel only twice that but it don't rain forever four years later Abigail married and two years after comes a baby girl then three more all girls. Then Rachel she got married and Ethan too at the same age Abigail was and all had the first babies two years after. Simon the only boy though . . .'"

"Chauvinist!" Mara was indignant.

"Why doesn't he tell the girls' names?" Krista asked her mother who, in turn, raised her eyebrows at her husband.

"He doesn't," Laurie acknowledged almost sheepishly.

At first, none of them noticed Kirby waving her arms.

"It doesn't matter! It doesn't matter! I don't care if he's a chauvinist pig, we've got the answer! We know when Simon was born!"

How has the Silverberg family found the answer for Kirby's client? In what year was Simon Fitzwall born?

14

Two Shots Were Fired

THE YOUNG POLICEMAN AT THE gate stiffened when he recognized the senior officer getting out of the car that had just pulled up. Instinctively, a hand went to his throat where his tie hung loosely around an open top button. Inspector Vince Pogor was a stickler for proper dress no matter what the weather, and the young constable knew it was too late now to rebutton his collar.

"You look like that when the media was here?" Vince was also known for getting right to the point.

"No. No, sir!" The young man's face, already soaking from the heat of the sun, began sweating even harder.

Vince lifted his hands to his hips. The gesture reminded him that he himself wasn't in uniform at all, that in fact he was in a T-shirt and shorts — kind of ratty ones to boot.

"Okay. Okay." he said. "Just . . . Look, you know the regulation. Tie on or tie off. Not that half-way stuff. Now. Where's the shooting site? That it up there?"

"Yes sir!" The officer was so relieved he absently brought out a none-too-clean handkerchief to wipe his face. "Just around the corner of the building there. You'll see the yellow tape."

For a second or two, Vince toyed with the idea of going back to division headquarters to change clothes. The incident with the

53

constable's tie had made him self-conscious about his own dress. In the end he decided not to. The media had been and gone, especially the TV cameras. Besides — he looked at his watch — the incident was already six hours old.

Vince was calling it an incident, not a *crime,* for the time being anyway. The evidence so far pointed in that direction. It was an accidental shooting, but a dicey one because of the victim. The dead man, Big Dino, was well-known to Vince, in fact to just about everyone on the police force, especially the anti-racket squad which Vince headed up. Big Dino had roots deep in organized crime. Until this morning. This morning Big Dino had gone down with two bullets in the middle of his chest just outside the rear entrance to Galahad Storage. He'd been shot from inside the building by a security guard.

"Ah . . . sir?" It was the constable. He'd taken his tie off. "Up there? Around the corner? Sergeant King . . . ah . . . he's waiting for you."

Vince grunted, just a wee bit embarrassed, then began to walk toward the rear of the building. He was glad to stretch his legs for he'd had a long drive. Officially, Vince was on vacation. The first two weeks of August were always his. That morning before anyone else in the family was awake, he'd taken a giant plate of bacon and perogies out to the deck of his cottage, despite the threat of rain, and had just snapped on the portable to listen to *The World at Eight* when the telephone rang, summoning him away from his beloved Lake Muskoka.

He'd headed down to the city right away, but changing out of the shorts and T-shirt did not even cross his mind. The heat wave that stretched from the American Midwest right up to the Arctic was so fierce that even the thought of full-length trousers made him sweat. And the heat was getting worse, too. On his way south, the dull sky that had covered most of Eastern North America that morning reneged on its promise of rain and cooler weather, completely contradicting the weather forecasters. By the time Vince could see Toronto in the distance, the sky had turned blue and cloudless and the day was flatiron hot.

Not a day to spend walking on confounded asphalt, he thought, turning the corner where yellow boundary tape squared off a section of empty lot. He hardly noticed the tape at first, or even how much hotter it was on this side of the building. What caught his attention instead was the overwhelming, relentless noise from the traffic on the Queen Elizabeth Way. Ten lanes of speeding, bumper-to-bumper racket so loud he didn't hear Jack King until the third yell.

"Vinny! Vince! In here! Outa the sun!"

Vince ducked under the tape, stepped carefully over the chalk outline of a body, and walked through the only open door. It had a small sign that said "EMPLOYEES ONLY." Jack King was standing inside. His tie was pulled down and he had two buttons undone. Jack began to speak immediately.

"It was like this," he said. Vince realized that Jack had been waiting in the heat for some time and had no intention of dawdling through his report. He wanted to get back to headquarters and air conditioning.

"The guard sat here, his back to the door you just came through." He pointed to a battered metal chair and an old wooden table with a deck of greasy playing cards on top. "Says he was watching the front. That makes sense 'cause that's where all the break-ins have been coming through. Especially the one two days ago where one a' the other guards got beat up so bad."

Vince raised his eyebrows but said nothing. Jack went on. "Then all of a sudden, he says there's this dark shadow over him. From behind. From the doorway. He whips around. The sun's in his face. There's an awful big guy there so . . . *Boom! Boom!* Two in the chest."

"Sounds a bit trigger happy, don't you think?" Vince spoke for the first time.

"Yeah. But don't forget the guy was scared," Jack answered. "I mean, there's been so much trouble here. All the break-ins. They had that fire where the guy was trapped in a room. Then there's that guard who was beat up. Word is he'll never walk again. Can't say I really blame the guard for shooting. And Dino. He's a big guy. 'Sides, he had no business back here. We think he's a renter here. Least he had a key in his pocket. We're checkin' that right now. Anyway, how's the guard supposed to know? As it is, the place doesn't open to customers till nine o'clock. And not through this door." Jack was pointing out the door to the east. Through the opening Vince could see the skyline of the city in the distance and the surface of Lake Ontario shimmering in the brightness of midday.

"I don't know, Jack," he said. "It's still too neat. This door was open then?"

"Propped open," Jack answered. "Just like it is now. Haven't you noticed how hot it is in here? I can believe the guard when he says the door had to be open. And that means he couldn't hear anything either. With the highway traffic at that time of the morning."

Vince nodded. "Yeah, I guess so. Sounds like accidental shooting all right. There's only one thing that's not right."

"Yeah? What's that?" Jack King wanted to know.

What is the flaw in the security guard's story that Vince Pogor is referring to?

15

Northern Farms Ltd. Versus Dominion Spraying Company

TRANSCRIPT: Docket #432

COURT IS NOW IN SESSION, the Honorable Mary-Joan Westlake presiding. First case is Docket Number 432: Northern Farms Limited, plaintiff, versus Dominion Spraying Company, respondent.

WESTLAKE: Thank you bailiff. Who is acting for the plaintiff?

DOYLE: I am, Your Honor. Douglas Doyle.

WESTLAKE: Ah yes, Mr. Doyle. We've met before. The Palgrave Poker case wasn't it? Well, never mind that. Would you summarize your claim, please?

DOYLE: Thank you, Your Honor. My client owns a farm bordering on the Bolton Canal and Regional Road 7. On the morning of 27 June last year, Dominion Spraying Company conducted an aerial spraying, in error, of a field in that farm. There were fifteen registered Holstein dairy cows in the field, nine of which subsequently died of the effects of the spray. My client is claiming damages of $147,000, plus costs.

WESTLAKE: I have your statement of claim here, Counsellor. You have one of the dead animals valued at $122,000?

DOYLE: Yes, Your Honor; that's Molly's Arch Dream III. I will be introducing evidence showing that figure as representative of an offer made for her on 16 May last year.

WESTLAKE: All right, Mr. Doyle. Mr. T. A. Jones, you're appearing for the respondent?

JONES: Indeed, Your Honor. In the interest of saving time, may I state that Dominion Spraying Company acknowledges that spraying took place over the field in question instead of over Bolton Canal on June 27, and that some cattle in the field died subsequent to that event. My client does not acknowledge that the deaths of the animals are connected in a direct way to the effects of the spraying. For the record, my client has offered Northern Farms damages of $25,000 for inconvenience. The offer has been declined.

WESTLAKE: Unless my mathematics is suspect, $25,000 is precisely the amount of the total claim, less the value of — what's her name — Molly's Arch Dream III?

JONES: That's correct, Your Honor.

WESTLAKE: Very well. Okay, is the plaintiff ready to proceed?

DOYLE: Yes. Plaintiff calls Mr. Fenton Purge.

(*Purge sworn.*)

Mr. Purge, you are the manager of Northern Farms Limited?

PURGE: That's right. We have a total of seven operating farms specializing in Holstein cattle and Landrace swine.

DOYLE: The property where the spraying took place on 27 June: would you describe it for the court?

PURGE: It's . . . well, a one-hundred-acre parcel bordered by a conservation area on two sides and by Bolton Canal and Regional Road 7 on the other two. We refer to it as Farm Number 3.

DOYLE: Specifically, I meant the field that was sprayed.

PURGE: Oh. Well, that's a . . . a . . . well, a square field about twenty-five acres in the southwest corner of the farm. It's about . . .

WESTLAKE: Mr. Doyle, what's this for? The respondent isn't denying that the spraying took place. Or where.

DOYLE: Background, Your Honor; I'll be brief. Mr. Purge, tell us what happened at this field on the morning of 27 June.

JONES: Your Honor, it hasn't been established that this witness was present at the field on the morning of June 27!

WESTLAKE: Mr. Doyle?

DOYLE: Very well . . . uh . . . Mr. Purge, what happ . . . rather, were you summoned to the, to Farm 3 on 27 June?

PURGE: Yes, in the early afternoon, when it was discovered that cattle were down in the field — collapsed. I moved fast 'cause that where we'd pastured Molly's Arch.

DOYLE: Surely you called a veterinarian?

PURGE: Indeed. Doctor Logan confirmed the cause of the collapse as reaction to a chemical used in insect control.

JONES: Objection!

WESTLAKE: Oh, really? On what grounds, Mr. Jones?

JONES: I think the court would prefer to hear expert testimony from the expert, not secondhand.

DOYLE: We'll be calling Dr. Logan, Your Honor. No more questions.

WESTLAKE: Any cross, Mr. Jones?

JONES: Yes, thank you. Mr. Purge, is it customary to let an animal that is supposedly worth $122,000 wander around a pasture field?

PURGE: Entirely. Happens all the time when the rest of its herd is pastured. Cows are very social animals. It's not unusual for them to go into decline if they're isolated. You just need good fences, and we have that. Well, not from above though!

WESTLAKE: Confine yourself to the questions, Mr. Purge.

JONES: No more for this witness.

(*No re-examination; plaintiff calls Eulalia Bean; sworn.*)

DOYLE: Ms. Bean, you are an employee of Northern Farms Limited?

BEAN: Summer help. I'm a university student, but I work summers at the Canal Farm . . . we call it Canal Farm.

DOYLE: And you were responsible for the care of the cattle in the field in question?

BEAN: I put them in there on June 21. Fifteen black and whites. Including Molly.

DOYLE: Molly's Arch Dream III?

BEAN: Yes. We call her Molly.

DOYLE: What do you normally do to care for the cattle?

BEAN: When they're pastured like that it's mostly supplement feeding and water checks. And of course you keep an eye on them.

DOYLE: Supplement feeding and water checks?

BEAN: Pasture's not good this year so I take hay out with the tractor twice a day. To a feeding trough. And there's no water in that field so we pipe it out from the barn. Water trough's right beside the feed trough at the fence. I always check that the float valve's working right.

DOYLE: And did you take out hay and do a water check on the morning of 27 June of last year?

BEAN: Yes, about 5:30. Sun was just coming up.

DOYLE: Did you check on Molly's Arch . . . uh, Molly?

BEAN: That's even more automatic than checking the water!

DOYLE: And she was well and healthy?

BEAN: Standing orders are that if she's not, we call the vet, then the manager, in that order.

DOYLE: Thank you. That's all I have. Mr. Jones?

JONES: Ms. Bean. On the morning of June 27, did you actually see the airplane spray the field and the cattle?

BEAN: Actually, no. I was just turning back into the barn when I heard a plane in the distance, but there's nothing unusual about that. Besides, I had machinery running in the barn.

JONES: Well then, just when did you become aware that there might be a problem with the cattle in your care?

BEAN: When Mrs. Organ phoned about two o' clock to tell me.

JONES: That's all I have of this witness, Your Honor.

(*No re-examination; plaintiff calls Parthenon Andreikos; sworn.*)

DOYLE: Mr. Andreikos. Where were you at approximately 5:30 A.M. on 27 June of last year?

ANDREIKOS: In my truck on Road 7. Goin' south toward the canal to . . . uh, you want me to say what I saw?

DOYLE: Go ahead.

ANDREIKOS: So. I waved at Eulie . . . uh, Eulalia. Miss Bean. She'd just come out of the barn with the tractor. Then I drove past the herd. So. You want to know where I was going?

DOYLE: It won't be necessary. Are you familiar with a Holstein dairy cow called Molly's Arch Dream III?

ANDREIKOS: Oh sure.

DOYLE: And you saw her in the herd there?

ANDREIKOS: She's awfully hard to miss. Really big. And she has — well, *had* anyway — this most unusual mark on her right side. A perfect triangle. Takes up her whole side. Never saw anything like that, ever. Mostly on Holsteins, it's blotches.

DOYLE: For you to see that, the animal had to be broadside to you.

ANDREIKOS: So. They were lined up at the feed trough. You see, soon as they hear the tractor they know Eulie's coming and they get ready. Cows aren't as stupid as people think.

DOYLE: Molly's Arch Dream was at the end of the line then?

ANDREIKOS: Cattle always feed at the same spot. Same way they always go to the same stall in the barn. Every time. So. The end of the trough pointing to the road must have been her spot.

DOYLE: Mr. Jones?

JONES: Mr. Andreikos, are you usually driving around in your truck at 5:30 in the morning?

ANDREIKOS: In the summer. I'm in the feed business. My customers are up even before then. So.

JONES: I gather Northern Farms is a customer of yours.

ANDREIKOS: Oh, yes.

JONES: Seven farms. They must be quite a customer!

DOYLE: Objection! Your Honor, my friend here is very close to making allegations!

WESTLAKE: You know better, Mr. Jones!

JONES: No more questions.

(*Plaintiff calls Daphne Organ; sworn.*)

DOYLE: Mrs. Organ, you are a neighbor of Northern Farms Limited Number 3?

ORGAN: Right across the road. Born in that house. Lived there seventy-eight years now.

DOYLE: Where were you at approximately 5:30 A.M. on 27 June?

ORGAN: On my front porch. That's where I have my tea.

DOYLE: Could you tell the court what you saw that morning?

ORGAN: I saw young Eulie take hay to those cattle.

DOYLE: What else?

ORGAN: Then I saw her go back to the barn.

DOYLE: After that.

ORGAN: I saw the airplane come. It flew — it was almost touching the ground! Spraying this terrible-smelling stuff. All over the cattle, too! It's a disgrace!

DOYLE: You saw the spray hitting the cattle?

ORGAN: Of course! And all over the field, too.

DOYLE: Then what did you do?

ORGAN: I went inside. I told you, it smelled!

DOYLE: We have heard from other witnesses that it was you who first noticed the cattle in trouble, and that you then telephoned Ms. Bean. Is that right?

ORGAN: Don't know if I was first. I only know what I saw. Those poor cattle staggered like drunks! When two o' them fell I got on the phone.

DOYLE: What time was that?

ORGAN: After my lunch. I have my lunch on the porch at one o'clock. Nice and shady then on hot days.

DOYLE: Your witness.

JONES: Are you familiar with a dairy cow called Molly's . . .

ORGAN: Of course I am. Who wouldn't know about a cow worth more than a hundred thousand dollars? Then she's got that funny triangle. Never heard of anything like that on a Holstein before.

JONES: Did you see this particular cow that morning?

ORGAN: I can't say for sure I saw her specifically. There's more to my life than watching cows, you know. I go out on my porch to have tea and watch the sunrise.

JONES: I understand. No more questions. Well, yes, one more. Mrs. Organ, didn't the terrible smell keep you from having your lunch on the porch?

ORGAN: The wind. Nice breeze blowing the other way. I wouldn't have gone out otherwise. I may be old but I'm not a fool, you know.

DOYLE: I have some re-examination, Your Honor. Mrs. Organ, could you pick out Molly's Arch Dream in a herd?

ORGAN: I already said I could.

DOYLE: Did you see her in the field from time to time prior to 27 June?

ORGAN: I surely did.

(*Plaintiff calls Dr. Robert Logan; sworn.*)

DOYLE: Would you describe your professional work, Dr. Logan?

LOGAN: I am a veterinarian in private practice.

DOYLE: Your Honor, I have here an autopsy report on the nine cattle in question, dated 28 June and signed by Dr. Logan. Mr. Jones has a copy. I would like to enter it as an exhibit.

WESTLAKE: Very well.

DOYLE: Dr. Logan, you describe the cause of death for the nine cattle as respiratory failure in reaction to a chemical substance. Does this apply to Molly's Arch Dream as well?

LOGAN: It does.

DOYLE: All yours.

JONES: Dr. Logan, would you explain the phenomenon "hardware disease" to the court?

WESTLAKE: Hardware disease? This better be relevant, Mr. Jones.

JONES: With respect, Your Honor, it's crucial to our response.

WESTLAKE: Very well. Let's hear about hardware disease then.

LOGAN: Indeed. Now, mammals of the suborder *Ruminantia,* which includes the *Typloda* . . . uh, camels, and the *Pecoran:*

deer, giraffe and so on, and of course the *Bovidae,* your cows —
all these have multi-chambered stomachs. Now . . .

WESTLAKE: Maybe a briefer approach is in order, Dr. Logan;
I'm not sure we need a whole anatomy course.

LOGAN: Yes, I see. All right then. Now . . . now . . . a cow's
stomach has four chambers. Most of what a cow eats is swallowed
whole, goes to one of the chambers, comes back up again to be
chewed as cud, and is reswallowed to another chamber. You see,
when they graze they tend to scoop and tear, often picking up
stones and bits of metal and garbage from the ground. It collects
in one of the chambers. Usually stays there for life. Sometimes a
beast will swallow something that just can't be stored and it can
cause problems.

JONES: Are the symptoms obvious? Of hardware disease, I mean?

LOGAN: It's not all that common a thing. When it happens
though, the problems can develop very fast.

JONES: Your autopsy report states that Molly's Arch Dream III
had hardware disease at the time of her death. Is that right?

LOGAN: Yes, but that's not unusual. You notice in the report
that several of the other cows had it, too.

JONES: But Molly's case was advanced.

LOGAN: It was serious.

JONES: Quite possibly fatal? In fairness, by the way, I should tell
you that I will be calling an expert in animal anatomy to
comment on your report.

LOGAN: It might have been fatal.

JONES: In fact, is it not possible that Molly's Arch Dream III was
already dead when the airplane sprayed the field on June 27?

DOYLE: Objection! The witness has already testified as to the
cause of the death!

WESTLAKE: I think I'd like to hear his answer, Mr. Doyle. It
might clear up some of the fuzziness we've been listening to from
previous witnesses.

What is the "fuzziness" Judge Mary-Joan Westlake is referring to?

16

An Unlikely Place to Die

BECAUSE OF THE TRAFFIC, MOSTLY the snarl at the underpass on
Wolfe Road, Brad Matchett got to the scene an hour later than
he'd said he would. A late afternoon thunderstorm yesterday, with
high winds and heavy rain, had caused so many power outages
that some traffic lights were still out, making the morning rush
hour worse than usual. Normally, Brad would have slapped the
red flasher on the roof and driven around the line of cars, but
because of the underpass, he couldn't do that. To make matters
worse, he'd then made a wrong turn. The big estates in Cedar
Springs were set in a maze of crescents and cul-de-sacs and
one-way streets designed to discourage all but the most
committed drivers. He'd become so lost he was forced to call the
dispatcher to find out where he was.

The only upside in this case so far, it occurred to Brad, if indeed
there can be upsides for the head of a homicide division, was that
being late wasn't really a disaster because an accidental death, even
if drugs are involved, is not usually a light-flashing, siren-blaring
matter. Unless of course the victim happens to be a *somebody.*

In this case, it was close. The victim was almost a somebody.
Not quite, but almost. Mme Marie-Claude de Bouvère appeared
from time to time on the social pages of *The Enterprise.* Not so
much because she was the wife of the former Haitian ambassador;

more because she was a one-time tennis star. Good enough for two cracks at Wimbledon in her teens. That made her status too close to call, so Brad had gone out himself just to be on the safe side.

Mme de Bouvère had been discovered shortly after sunrise by her gardener. The body lay in a gazebo set between the de Bouvères' huge house and their tennis court. On a table in the gazebo, along with her tennis racket, were all the appropriate paraphernalia for preparing and injecting a substance. Her tennis bag held three small bags of white powder. Brad knew all this from Sergeant Willy Peeverdale who, until Brad managed to get there, was the investigating officer in charge. For now, that was the extent of his information because the underpass on Wolfe Road had cut off radio communication. Now, almost an hour later, Brad was finally turning into a circular drive that looped the huge property at 23 Serene Crescent.

The property was very private. So were all the estates in Cedar Springs. A screen of sycamores and magnolias lined Serene Crescent so that even the most intrepidly curious driver would never see the house. Just to be sure, another screen, Colorado blue spruce this time, duplicated the effort about fifty paces behind the other trees. Interesting, Brad noted. Not one cedar.

Had it not been for the yellow crime-scene tape on the south side of the house, he would have spent yet more time looking for the gazebo, but the tape led him through a grove of honey locust and along a path of brick chips to the back of the house. The property here was even larger than the front. The gazebo, big as it was — to Brad it looked more like the band shell in Misty Meadows Park — appeared almost lonely and curiously out of place. It sat precisely midway between the house and the tennis court, completely surrounded by a perfectly manicured lawn.

"Nothing's touched, but we gotta move fast 'cordin' to the coroner." The voice behind him made Brad jump. He would never get used to Peeverdale's habits. The sergeant made no small talk, ever. He never said "hello"; he never said "excuse me." And if he was aware that he made people nervous by suddenly appearing behind them, he'd never made any effort to change. Peeverdale pressed on. "Says she can confirm the drug thing better the sooner she gets into the postmortem. Figures death occurred between ten and eleven last night. Sure looks like they OD'd. The guy died first she thinks, but only by a bit."

"The guy? They?" Brad realized he was sounding excited.

"Yeah." Peeverdale was never flapped either. "Guess that didn't come through on your radio. Y'see, the gardener, he saw Maa-daam de . . . de . . . whatever . . . lyin' there in that thing, that gay-zee-bo, and he split for the phone. Waited for us in the driveway. We found the guy. Figure it's Mister . . . Mon-*soor* de Boov . . . Boo . . . I can't get the doggone name right! Anyway we found him on the ground on the other side. Looks like he was sittin' on the rail and went over. For sure it's the missus on the floor, 'cordin' to the gardener. The guy's got no ID on him."

Sergeant Peeverdale dropped a pace behind Brad as they approached the gazebo, but continued talking. "Looks like the two of them were gonna play a little tennis last night. Or maybe they already played, it's hard to tell. And then they figured they'd get a little buzz on. My guess is they got some hot stuff they weren't expectin' and it did them in."

There were two steps up into the gazebo, and Brad stopped on the first one to study the body of Mme de Bouvère lying flat on the floor. Well, not really flat. Reclining was more like it. The woman appeared so composed, so much an elegant study in white. Not a mark or a smudge or a speck on the white blouse or the white tennis skirt or the white sneakers. Except for the slight pinch to her eyes, it looked as though she had known she would be seen like this and had prepared for it.

Peeverdale, meanwhile, had not interrupted his monologue. "Gardener found her there at about 7 A.M. Comes every other day to mow the lawn. S'pose that's why it looks like a billiard table. Mine sure don't look like this. Anyway, he came to get some equipment he left yesterday and noticed the lights on over the tennis court. That's when he saw Maa . . . her. He didn't see the guy. You gotta look over the rail to see him. Uh . . . the coroner, she wants us to hustle, Captain. It's the drug thing. Says the sooner the better."

"Tell you what, Peev," Brad said. "You give her a call. Tell her we'll be a while. We've got to figure out first where this lady died. And maybe the guy, too."

"You mean," Sergeant Peeverdale reached inside his tunic and scratched absently, "you don't think she died right here?

"No," Brad replied. "I don't."

Why does Brad Matchett think that Mme de Bouvère did not die at the gazebo?

17

To Catch a Mannerly Thief

AS SHE STEPPED OVER THE potholes in the street and leaned hard into a fierce east wind, Agnes Skeehan made a promise to herself: never again was she going to attend a conference in November unless it was within walking distance of the equator. Actually, for Agnes, anywhere warmer than Liverpool would do. Liverpool may have produced the Beatles, and it could point with pride at its importance to the Industrial Revolution, but to Agnes that was hardly enough to make up for the miserable weather.

She mounted the curb, trotted across the sidewalk, and pulled hard at the entrance door of her hotel. Three days at the Birkenhead Arms had taught Agnes to yank with both hands at the ancient portal.

"Ah, young missy!" It was the hotel porter. He made a contribution all his own to Agnes's opinion of Liverpool. "You've got a telephone message here, young missy. All the way from Canada! A Deputy Commissioner Mowat. Sounds important, missy. Talked to him myself, I did. Told him you were out, I did."

Agnes mumbled a thank you as she grabbed the message and ran for the creaky old elevator. As things stood at the moment, she was only three hours away from her flight home, but she had a feeling this call was going to change her schedule.

It did.

"I want you to stay over there in Liverpool and help them with this case." Deputy Commissioner Mowat's voice crackled and sputtered across the Atlantic only minutes later. "As a favor from us, you know, international police cooperation and all that." He paused, but then jumped in again as though to head off the objection he was expecting. "You're simply the best there is on handwriting. They don't have anybody that comes close to you. Now what I want you to do right away is go to their headquarters — it's right by your hotel there — and report to Superintendent Anthony Opilis. He's the head of their CID: their Criminal Investigation Department. Now what I want you to do is consider yourself on temporary assignment there. Indefinite. As long as it takes."

Agnes struggled so hard to keep from telling Deputy Commissioner Mowat where he could stuff the international cooperation and the temporary assignment that she barely heard the rest. She didn't really need to though. The tabloids were full of the case that prompted his call. "The Friendly Filcher" one daily called it. "The Case of the Courteous Cat Burglar" another dubbed it. Whatever he — or she — deserved to be called, the case involved an amazingly successful thief who was breaking into homes and stealing jewelry. He seemed to have a peculiar respect for his victims, and this, in addition to the size of the take, was what the papers found so interesting. At each theft — there had been seven now — the thief left behind a neatly handwritten note of apology and an assurance that the stolen pieces would find their way only into the hands of people who would appreciate their beauty and value.

These notes, Agnes knew, were the reason she was being loaned to the Liverpool CID. Mowat was right when he called her the best. Agnes Skeehan, *Corporal* Agnes Skeehan, fourteen-year veteran of the Royal Canadian Mounted Police, had a special interest and an even more special knack in handwriting analysis. At graduation from the police training college in Regina, circumstances had presented her with a choice of more study, or assignment to a mounted patrol at the Parliament Buildings in

Ottawa. Since race-track betting windows were as close to horses as Agnes ever cared to be, she picked the study and had never looked back. Eight months ago, her article in the *Journal of Forensic Science* had led to an invitation to address a conference in Liverpool. Little did she realize when she came down from the podium there, to a huge round of applause, that the next move would be, not to the airport, but into the superintendent's office at the Liverpool CID.

Superintendent Opilis, a long-time acquaintance of Deputy Commissioner Mowat as it turned out, was a plodder. His explanation of the jewelry thefts to Agnes was so detailed and so slow that she had to fight to pay attention. She kept turning her head toward the grimy office window to yawn, covering the move with a phoney cough.

The superintendent must have sensed her mood for suddenly Agnes became aware of annoyance in his voice.

"Withenshawe?" he said, or rather, asked. "I say, Corporal Skeehan. You heard me? Withenshawe Purveyors?"

Agnes blushed. She had indeed been drifting. The problem was, she just didn't want to be in Liverpool.

"Yes, Superintendent, I'm sorry." She got up and walked to the window, trying to appear alert by focusing on a weathervane pointing at her from atop a pub across the street.

"Withenshawe Purveyors of Speke Street." She cleared her throat. "Every one of the notes was written on Withenshawe's letterhead. I'm aware of that. And your people have definitely established that they were all written by the same left-handed person. I'm aware of that, too. But don't you think the Withenshawe Purveyors stationery is a most clumsy red herring? After all, who . . ."

"Indeed, indeed Corporal Skeehan." Opilis got up and joined Agnes at the window. "But you see, there are other serious reasons why Alistair Withenshawe is a right handy suspect." He paused awkwardly. "We . . . er . . . we've summoned him. His office is just a short walk south of here. What we want you to do is . . . Why! That's him! Right there. Across the street."

"Him?" Agnes pointed at a tall, very nattily dressed gentleman holding down a bowler hat. "The dude with the hat? And the cane? Look at him!" Agnes was fully awake now. "Does he always walk like that in public?"

"Yes, well," Superintendent Opilis was almost apologetic. "Ah, we have dealt with him before. I'm afraid he's a bit of a showman."

To prove the policeman's point, Alistair Withenshawe, who had been bouncing his cane off the edge of the curb and catching it, now began to twirl it high in the air like a drum major, spinning it first over one parked car, then the next, and then a third, before he brought it down and made a crisp military turn off the walk and into the street toward the police station.

Opilis let a touch of admiration creep into his voice. "Snappy, what?"

Agnes looked at him. "Yes, I agree. Snappy. But I'll give you any odds you want he didn't write those notes."

Why is Agnes Skeehan so sure of that?

18

Tracing the Couriers from Departure to Arrival

"SEAMUS? DID I GET THAT right? *Seamus?*" Mary Clare McInerney realized she was shouting the instant she saw heads in the outer office turn in unison toward her. She didn't have a lot of choice, however. The connection was very poor.

"Is that a first name or a last name? A code name more likely. Which?" she wanted to know.

She waited for the unnerving pause so typical of trans-global telephone calls, particularly from places like Northern Africa, the delay that always made callers think they'd lost their call. But the answer came through. Struan Ritchie was at the other end of the conversation. He was in Addis Ababa and he was shouting even louder than Mary Clare.

"Yes, Seamus!" Struan's voice was buried in crackle and hiss. "It's the only name I have, so it's likely a code name. The other one I have is a single name, too: Rothsay."

"Rothsay!" This time Mary Clare really turned the heads in the outer office. To make it worse she had forgotten the transmission delay and had almost spoken over the rest of Struan's sentence. It was important information.

". . . say," Struan was saying, "is the one who is flying out of Dorval in Montreal. It's confirmed. But I don't know where she's going."

Mary Clare waited and then, as quietly as she could in her excitement, said, "She?" and waited again.

"Yes, *she*," was the reply. "Two of the four couriers, it would seem, are women. Rothsay is one of them."

"And 'Saint' is the other then." Mary Clare didn't wait this time. "We got that yesterday. So that means 'Seamus,' and the other one we got yesterday, 'Felipe,' are males. Well, that helps. Not much though if they are good at disguises. What we really need to know is where each of the four is going and what airport they're flying out of. The only way we can coordinate this bust is if each of the couriers is tailed from departure to destination and nailed when they arrive. That way we scoop the parties at both ends, too."

Struan's voice came in over top of Mary Clare's. "I've got to get off. There's a lineup behind me and there's something going on down the street. Listen. I've got two more pieces. Seamus is going to Brazil, to Rio. Got that? But I don't know where he is now or what airport he's going to use. The other is . . ."

At that point there was a fierce crackling on the line, followed by an electronic whirr, and finally a dial tone. This time, Mary Clare's shout of frustration brought the entire outer office to its feet. She chose the moment to wave Harvey Bottrell and Cecile King into her office.

Mary Clare McInerney was a member of the Drug Enforcement Administration working out of "E" Division in Seattle. For the past six months she had been coordinating a team investigation into an illegal narcotics ring. Over the last three days, things had come together at a rapid pace; the team was about to close in on the four key couriers and, through them, the leaders of the ring.

What her team had been able to put together was that each of the four couriers, within the next forty-eight hours (using GMT-9 as the reference point, because she was working out of Seattle), would be flying to separate destinations with major deliveries. Mary Clare was certain her team could break the ring if the four could be identified and followed from airport to airport. They now knew who the four were. At least their code names — that was enough.

"That was Struan Ritchie in Addis Ababa," she said to her two assistants after they had seated themselves at the coffee table in her office.

Harvey nodded. "We know."

"The whole office knows," Cecile King added.

Mary Clare reddened slightly. "It was an incredibly dirty line," she explained, "with all kinds of ambient noise from where he was phoning, too. Sounded like he was out in the street. Come to think of it, he could even have been on an off-shore phone. The real problem is I think he had more to give us before the line broke down."

"Maybe what we've got will make you feel better," Harvey said. "Just some little pieces, but we're definitely getting closer."

Mary Clare got up from her desk and joined the two at the coffee table. "Lay it out," she said.

"We have three of the destinations," Harvey took three pens from his jacket pocket and set them on the table. "At the very least we can put a blanket surveillance on the airports." He held up both hands, palms out, before Mary Clare could say the obvious. "I know that's not what we want, but . . . anyway, one of the couriers is going to Hong Kong. That information is just five minutes old. It came in while you were talking to Struan. Another is going to Hawaii, to Oahu."

Cecile leaned forward. "And one is going to Bermuda. Better than that, we also know this one will be flying out of Orly, in Paris, to get there." She leaned back again. "What we don't have is who any of them are. We only know that three couriers are going to these three places."

Mary Clare picked up one of Harvey's pens from the table and began to play with it, bending it with both hands into a bow shape. "What did you come up with in the call to Chicago?"

Harvey made a face. "According to our contact there, uh . . . uh . . . do you think I could have my pen back?"

Cecile finished for him. "One of the couriers is definitely leaving from O'Hare there. But we had the destination wrong before. Originally, we thought it was Hawaii, but it's not, and we don't know what it is, either."

Mary Clare was sufficiently distracted by this information for Harvey to surreptitiously retrieve his pens, all three, and stuff them back into the safety of his jacket pocket.

"So." Mary Clare was speaking to no one in particular. "So. We are this close." She made a tiny space with her thumb and forefinger. "If only the time wasn't so short. If . . ."

"Mary Clare!" Cecile King was pointing at the winking light on her desk. "Your telephone. Wonder if that's . . ."

It was Struan Ritchie again.

"Sorry about that cutoff before." The line was very clear this time. "Just down the street, these two guys on a camel . . . Why am I telling you this? You'd have to be here. Listen. This is what I didn't give you. You know that Felipe, the one you said you got yesterday?"

Mary nodded as though he were sitting in the office.

"Well, I've had that one for a little while but couldn't confirm it. Guess if you got it from a different source, it must be right. Anyway, Felipe is at Heathrow right now, according to my information. In the departures lounge. Where he's going, I don't know. It's not Hong Kong, if that helps. Wish I could tell you, but I can't."

"No need." Mary Clare McInerney had a huge smile on her face. "That's the last piece of the puzzle." She held back the receiver so her grin could include the two assistants. "Let's call out the dogs," she said, "the chase is on!"

How has Mary Clare McInerney figured out where each courier is going and where each is flying from?

19

Not All Lottery Winners Are Lucky

FOR AT LEAST THE TENTH time that day, Captain Frank Ricketts pulled his head down turtle-like into his coat and wondered how on earth his parents could possibly have left Jamaica for a climate like this.

He pulled his hat down, too, so it would fit tighter over his head. The business of headgear was another issue. Just inside the back door of his home there was an array of hats and caps and toques of every possible weight and design, and never once did he seem to pick the right one as he left in the morning.

Chinooks. That's what everyone called the extreme, almost instant changes in weather here in Calgary. Abrupt rises in temperature of up to twenty degrees, sometimes in less than an hour. "It's what you get for building a city on the east side of the Rocky Mountains," everyone in Calgary said, as though the first pioneers had planned it that way. "You just have to get used to it," was always the next comment. Frank had never gotten used to it.

He took a step toward the body, trying to put chinooks out of his mind and being careful to put his feet down flat in the snow.

He also had the wrong shoes on for these conditions and didn't want to slip and fall.

It had been a typical Calgary winter so far. Two days ago, right in the morning rush hour, a sudden chinook had turned the snow into slush. Then before noon, the temperature had plunged to Arctic levels and stayed that way until earlier this morning when it warmed up just enough for snow to fall for an hour. Frank knew that one careless step on a layer of snow over ice would put him on his backside. That was an indignity he didn't need in front of the whole crime-scene crew, so he was very cautious as he approached the body and squatted down beside it.

"His name is Archie Deschamps-Lebeau, Captain. Or was anyway." Frank looked up to see Nick Andropolous, the oldest member of the homicide unit. Nick secretly fascinated Frank, for even though he had been born and raised in Crete, he always dressed like a typical urban Canadian, with no hat, no gloves, boots undone, and coat open.

"Seventy-three years old. Widower," Nick went on, reading from a ragged spiral-bound notebook pinched between his thumb and index finger. "Lived alone in the house over there. Stinking rich."

Nick closed the notebook and hunkered down across from Frank. "This is the guy, Captain," he said in almost a whisper, "the guy that won that giant lottery. It was — how many millions? — eighteen or something? Lotta good it does him now! You remember that don't you? He fired a shotgun at some reporters not long after to chase 'em away."

Frank remembered all right. Everyone did. Archie Deschamps-Lebeau had won the biggest lottery prize in history and had spent the time since trying to avoid the limelight that went with it.

"Yeah, I remember, Nick." Frank spoke softly, staring at the outline in the ice and snow where the body had lain face down. Two paramedics had carefully pried it up and rolled it over so that the lifeless eyes of Archie Deschamps-Lebeau were now staring at the gray afternoon sky.

"And I don't have to ask, do I, if you got all the pictures, since you decided to roll him over before I got here?" The annoyance in Frank's voice was clear. "And the measurements? What's the distance there between those indentations where his feet were in the ice? And what about that button over there? Is it his?"

"Hey, hey, Captain! Wait a minute!" Nick squatted down beside Frank, self-consciously waving his notebook. "We got everything. Anyway, we don't even know this is a homicide. There's no marks on the body. No signs of violence. Anybody else but this guy, we probably wouldn't even be here! The coroner's been and gone — by the way she says there's no way she can do time of death for sure 'cause the old guy's been frozen." Nick lowered his voice. "And some of the guys here are freezing, Captain. Er . . . you know what it's like. Some of them can't take the weather. They want to get going."

Frank looked up at the detective and grinned. "How come you never wear a hat, Nick? No! Don't answer that! I don't want to know!" He stood up and pulled down his own hat again. "Okay, let's get out of here. Incidentally," he nodded at the body, "who found him here?"

"His two daughters." Nick relaxed a bit and opened his notebook again as they walked toward their cars. "They dropped in on him every second day to see that he was Okay. He had a bad heart. But that's as much company as he put up with. Apparently they came and made him lunch and then cooked things for him and put it in a freezer. Cleaned the place a bit. Stuff like that. They're the only ones he ever let into the house. The neighbors confirm that. The daughters were here last time and everything was all right. Today they show up and he's nowhere around. They go looking, figuring he's caught the big one. Sure enough, here he was out at the end of the backyard."

The two policemen had reached their cars as Nick finished talking. Frank got into his, started it, and turned the heater on full blast before getting out again. "Nick," he said, "these two daughters. They in pretty good shape?"

"What do you mean?" Nick wanted to know.

"Like, husky," Frank said, "strong. Do you think they could have carried the old guy out here by themselves and dumped him, say if he were dead, or maybe if he had a heart attack but wasn't quite dead and they wanted the weather to finish him off?"

Nick looked surprised. "Well, yeah, one of them in fact probably could do it all by herself. Why? You think they did it?"

Frank nodded. "Sure looks that way," he said.

What has led Captain Frank Ricketts to suspect the two daughters of Archie Deschamps-Lebeau of murder?

20

Spy Versus Spy

"IN COUNTERESPIONAGE, HAUPTMANN AUGUST, we are not interested in spies as much as we are in spy *networks*."

"I understand, Herr Oberst, but . . ." Ernst August tried to break in, but it was Oberst Dietrich Staat's favorite lecture, and he was not about to have its delivery interrupted by an officer of inferior rank.

"So if we act upon your suggestion, Hauptmann," he continued, "we will succeed in doing what? We will arrest this . . . this Kopenick of yours, and what will we have? Nothing but another foot soldier, another pair of eyes and ears that can be replaced just like that!" Oberst Staat snapped his fingers. It was a constant habit of his, one he indulged in almost as frequently as asking himself rhetorical questions.

Hauptmann Ernst August yielded to the defeat that crept from the back of his brain, ran over his skull, and fixed his face in an immobile, neutral expression. There was no other way but to endure it. He had been through this lecture before: the same words, the same intonations, the same gestures. The same stinking cloud of cigarette smoke. It made him wonder yet again what devious gremlin of fate had conspired to have him transferred from the Abwehr, the military intelligence service led by his hero, Admiral Canaris, to the Sicherheitdienst, the infamous SD. It was bad enough that he had to admit to his fellow career officers in the Wermacht that he was now working for that madman, Heydrich. Worse was that his superior officer was Dietrich Staat, the most short-sighted drone in the service.

Staat's lecture went on. "Stuttgart is full of little traitors like your Kopenick, full of closet communists. I understand your enthusiasm and I commend it. Your skill, too, in identifying Kopenick. But what does he mean to us?" The colonel paused to squash out his Gauloise and insert another into the end of his ivory cigarette holder. He did not offer one to August. "It may mean one less instrument in the network for a very short while. But before long, he will be replaced. No, in counterespionage we must ask ourselves . . ."

Staat made an elaborate show of lighting the fresh cigarette with a table lighter on his desk. "You realize of course, Hauptmann, what would be of interest, what would be most useful . . ." Staat had forgotten the question he was going to ask and inadvertently, almost got right to the point, ". . . what would be most useful would be to find out who Kopenick's *cutout* is. Now. What would that do for us?"

Ernst August swallowed noisily. He was struggling to keep his mouth shut. The last time he'd endured this lecture, which was during the second time he had reported Kopenick's activities, Staat had laboriously explained "cutout" to him, as though both did not already know well that a cutout's role was to act as a protective connection between an agent and various subagents. The practice preserved security for the agent since, most of the time, a subagent never even learned the identity of his or her agent.

"If we knew who the cutout is, we could follow him. And then! And *then!*" Staat was reaching a plateau in his monologue. Ernst knew that either he would end it here, or God forbid, branch out in another direction. Before either could happen, Hauptmann Ernst August jumped in.

"Most astute as usual, Herr Oberst. You see, I know who the cutout is. Also, I know how they communicate. If you want to see them together and see how Kopenick passes the messages, we will have to go now while it is raining. If their pattern remains as consistent as it has been, they will rendezvous shortly near the Stiftskirche. At 1730 hours."

Luckily for Ernst August, his outburst coincided with one of Staat's elaborate inhalings. The officer core had been very much influenced in its smoking habits of late by French movies. But what Staat had just heard stopped all the mannerisms. And the lecture.

"You have his cutout?" The Oberst did not realize his mouth was agape.

"Yes, Oberst Staat. His name is Traugott Waechter. Swiss. At least he has a Swiss passport."

"Aha, a Swiss passport! Now what does that mean? It means . . ."

"Yes, Herr Oberst. He travels back and forth once a week. Stuttgart to Bern. I suspect that it is because of this Waechter that you — that *we* have not been successful with the radio location equipment. I believe that in Stuttgart, at least, *Rote Kapelle* makes very little use of radios. With Waechter available as a courier, there is no need."

For the very first time, Oberst Dietrich Staat was silent. His mouth stayed open, but there were no words. His cigarette burned away unnoticed at the end of the holder. The mention of *Rote Kapelle* often had that effect on German intelligence.

To the SD and the Abwehr, and the Gestapo, too, the *Rote Kapelle* or "Red Orchestra" was a cause of profound embarrassment. It was a highly successful Soviet operation, a network that especially in the first years of the war, sent amazingly accurate, thorough, and extensive reports to Moscow on German war production, military maneuvers, and even some of the long-range planning of the general staff. Many of the agents at the bottom of the chain — subagents — were ideological communists, a great number of them German, some Swiss, and some, like Kopenick, Czechs from the Sudetenland.

On two previous occasions, Ernst August's reports about Kopenick to Staat had stirred no response, a result he attributed to the continuing jealousy between the Abwehr and the SD. This time, what he offered Staat stimulated commitment to the common cause.

The commitment, or else the irresistible pleasure of wounding the Red network, boosted August over another hurdle with Staat, too. The two men were now sitting outside the Stiftskirche in August's somewhat battered, three-year-old Volkswagen. Staat had wanted to use his chauffeured Mercedes-Benz, but the captain had convinced him of the need for a small car, because to score their coup with Waechter and Kopenick they would likely have to maneuver through the medieval section of the city with its narrow streets and alleys.

They had arrived in the square in front of the Stiftskirche at 1728 hours and were lucky enough to be able to back into a parking space that concealed them from the street. Kopenick appeared at 1729 hours, making August look very good indeed. He stopped in front of the main entrance to the church for about thirty seconds, then drove off.

"Good! Where's the cutout? Why aren't we following?" Staat said through a thick cloud of cigarette smoke.

"He will be back." It occurred to Ernst for only the first time that Staat probably had no street experience at all. He was just an administrator. "They communicate with their cars," he added.

"Their cars?" Staat was asking questions to which he did not have a ready answer planned. Real questions. Ernst liked that.

"Do you see the little truck across the square? The plumber?" Ernst deliberately pressed on before Staat could answer. He knew the colonel had not noticed the truck. "That's Waechter. He uses different vehicles, but I've seen this one twice before. He also uses a . . . ah, here's Kopenick again!"

Both men watched as the *Rote Kapelle* subagent drove into the square in his tiny, black Renault. This time he did not even stop but drove straight through.

"He's waiting for the traffic to pick up just a bit more," Ernst explained. "The more traffic, the more vehicles, the better for them. But they're running out of time, I think. Waechter can't sit there much longer without attracting attention."

Almost on top of his words, Kopenick reappeared. This time, Waechter pulled out into traffic ahead of him. August accelerated out of the parking space and over the next block slipped the

Volkswagen in behind Waechter's truck. Within a few seconds, in what to anyone else would appear to have been natural traffic flow and interchange, the Renault was directly in front of Waechter. The three vehicles moved in single file that way for the next block.

"At the stop ahead," Ernst said. "That's where it'll start." Staat said nothing but smoked furiously as the line of cars slowed.

"Now! See!" Ernst August could not suppress his excitement. Or his righteousness. "See the message being sent? In Morse! Clumsy, but right in front of our noses! There!"

He translated excitedly.

"Bomb site — No! — *sight* . . . man . . . man . . . must be manufacture — Yes! *manufacture* — moved to Ess . . . Ess . . . *Esslingen!* What did I tell you! 'Bombsight manufacture moved to Esslingen.' They get . . ."

"Hauptmann! They're moving!"

In his excitement, Ernst had almost forgotten he was driving.

"Now wait till we stop again, Herr Oberst, and you'll see more! At this one, perhaps you will read the message for us. I can't stay right behind Waechter too long. He's a careful one!"

Dietrich Staat was exuding extreme discomfort and Hauptmann Ernst August basked in it. He knew the colonel had no idea what was going on.

"What's the matter, Oberst, is it the Morse?"

"Of course not!" the commanding officer snapped. "I know Morse! It's . . . I don't . . . I'm not . . . *How do you know it's Morse?*"

The Abwehr captain rolled his window down slightly to let some of the smoke out, then took even more time in an elaborate assessment of whether the ensuing draft caused any discomfort for his superior. Only after he'd stretched the situation to the fringes of bad manners did he reply.

"Under the truck, Oberst Staat. Look under the truck."

What has Hauptmann Ernst August discovered? How are Kopenick and Traugott Waechter communicating in Morse code?

21

The Search for Olie Jorgensson

THE INSTANT DETECTIVE-SERGEANT CONNIE MOUNT signaled the little team behind her to halt and take a short break, they all turned to a patch of wild raspberries that grew in profusion at the edge of the trail and began to eat greedily. It was just one more thing that upset her about this search and rescue mission. The searchers were supposed to lie flat and relax totally to conserve their strength; there might be many miles to cover yet and there was plenty of daylight left.

Connie's uneasiness had been growing steadily from the very second this whole affair had started. That was at 7:03 A.M. this morning, when she walked into the Healey Lake detachment office where she was commanding officer. The night dispatcher, "Lefty" Shaw, still had a half hour left on his shift. He was standing at his desk with his finger on the PLAY button of the answering machine. Connie heard only the very last part of the tape, but she recognized the voice in spite of the panic in it.

". . . don't know how long ago but he isn't anywhere on the campsite! We've looked everywhere! Won't you please hurry! He's so little!"

"That was Svena Jorgensson, wasn't it Norman?" Connie said.

She was the only one in the detachment — in the entire community — who didn't call him "Lefty"; she felt it kept him on his toes. Police work — his job — became secondary in Lefty's life whenever he was able to lay his hands on a new, or rather, new *old* car. Lefty was a collector of classics and two days ago a 1912 Reo had made him completely forget why he was being paid a salary.

"Before you tell me all about it, *Norman,* why is her call on the answering machine instead of on your backup tape? This means you weren't at your desk, were you?"

Lefty's normally ruddy countenance glowed a notch brighter at Connie's challenge. "I had to go to the can!" he said indignantly. "It happens from time to time, you know!"

Connie nodded. "I suppose so. Nature, right?" She took a step forward and pressed REWIND on the answering machine. "You know, that reminds me. It's certainly time those washrooms were cleaned. Especially if we've got to get rid of that Number 90 gear grease you managed to get all over yourself when you were in there."

Lefty turned full red this time but Connie didn't notice. By now she'd punched PLAY and was listening to Svena Jorgensson tell the detachment that her little Olie was missing from their campsite at the lake. As far as she, Svena, knew, he'd gotten up while she was still asleep and wandered off and out into the bush. Olie was only four years old.

That had happened six hours ago, and although Connie had put together a full search and rescue response within forty-five minutes, she still felt that the whole thing might be just a wild goose chase; there were so many things that weren't right to begin with, and so many things that turned out wrong as they went along.

For one, the armed forces helicopter she'd called in to fly over the area with a heat sensor turned out to be a waste of time. There were simply too many wild animals in the area and their body heat made the sensor work like a popcorn machine. The system worked better as the helicopter flew some miles farther from the lake, but there was no point to that because it would have been impossible for a child Olie's age to get that far away in six hours.

The tracking dogs caused another problem. One was a Shepherd, the other a Blue Tick hound that Connie had worked with once before. Both dogs led their handlers directly to an abandoned railway line several hundred yards from the Jorgensson's campsite. At that point, the animals disagreed. The Shepherd circled and circled and then simply sat down as if to say, "That's it. End of Trail." The Blue Tick bounded down the former railway line in complete confidence, enthusiastically dragging the handler and the search team after him. But then he stopped, too, and like the Shepherd, circled a few times and sat down.

By this time, it was eleven A.M., and the August sun was heating up everyone's nerves, not least Connie's. It was at that point that, against her better judgement, certainly against her best instincts, she let Willy Stefan take over. Not that Willy was incompetent. On the contrary, he was regarded — and rightly so — as the best tracker the area had ever seen. Local wags loved to explain to tourists how Willy could track a mosquito through a swamp. But Willy was not exactly a neutral party in this case. He was Olie's uncle, Svena's brother-in-law, and in the Jorgensson family, that meant complications. Svena and her former husband were involved in a frightfully bitter and ongoing custody dispute over little Olie. That's why Connie had immediately recognized the voice on the answering machine. Olie's father regularly failed to bring him back after "visit" times. Once, the father, with the help of his sister and her husband, Willy, had snatched Olie out of the backyard of the Jorgensson home and had taken him away for two weeks.

These contradictions and complications had been rumbling away in the back of Connie's mind as the search team followed Willy Stefan at a respectable distance down the railway line. Now he stood, after she had called a halt, waiting for her to catch up.

Willy wiped the back of his neck with a peach-colored cloth that said Dunn & Dunn Service. "Slow going," he commented, giving expression to yet another burr that Connie was feeling. They had been moving at a snail's pace all along.

"Tourist season," Willy added as though that explained everything. He held the cloth at the corners and made it flap before wiping his face with it. "There's just so many people hiking along here this time of year," he said through the cloth. "Makes it so hard to read the signs. No wonder the dogs got mixed up."

Connie's reaction was instant. "That does it!"

She turned and yelled back to the others. "You people! I want you to go back a bit. Back up. Go around the curve and wait there till I call."

"Now, Willy," she lowered her voice. "You and I are going to talk. No. Strike that! *You* are going to talk. Talk a lot and talk fast! I want to know where that little boy is!"

Why does Connie Mount believe that Willy Stefan has something to tell her?

22

Murder at the David Winkler House

CHRIS BEADLE PAUSED IN THE narrow hallway and looked back at the doorway she'd just come through. Her height was average; yet she'd still had to duck.

"Atmosphere," she said out loud to no one in particular. "Anything for pioneer effect. But then . . . why not?"

There was more pioneer effect right in front of her, for the door into the inn's only public washroom was just as small and would be sure to make a patron stoop. In fact, everything about the David Winkler House was small: the rooms, the halls, the doorways, the windows. But with clever restorations, the place seemed far more dainty than cramped. The David Winkler House had been built in the late eighteenth century by David Winkler — no surprise there — to accommodate his large family at a time when people were smaller than they are today. The present owners, the four innkeepers who had turned it into an extremely successful country dining room and inn, had been careful to preserve everything they could to make the place as authentic as possible.

From the moment Chris had left the graveled parking lot, which was quite carefully and deliberately separated from the building by a row of lilac bushes and a profusion of hollyhocks in full bloom, she had felt herself slide backward in time. The owners had done such a good job. From the squeaky gate in the stockade fence to the milk paint on the shutters to the weathered cedar shingles on the roof, the David Winkler House spoke "authentic." And it spoke "charm."

They had succeeded inside, too. Only someone who looked carefully for them would ever find electrical outlets or switches or wires. There was no evidence of a telephone anywhere, not even where the hostess greeted the guests. Even the washroom, where Chris now stood, was hidden away from the dining area. It couldn't be found without asking. Not easily, anyway.

Chris ducked and stepped inside, remembering why she'd come back here in the first place. There wasn't much room. Not only was it a unisex facility, it barely accommodated one person at a time. She pushed the door open right to the wall. It just cleared a sink styled in antique porcelain that stood on a thin pedestal in the corner ahead of her and to the left. On the wall opposite the door hung a framed mirror, surrounded by dried roses, dried fern, and Queen Anne's Lace. To her right, the unavoidable stark modernity of the toilet was softened by an identical mirror on the wall above it, this one holding up a tangle of green foxtail. In a deliberate sequence, Chris flushed the toilet, turned each tap on, then off, and gently pushed the door closed.

"Not bad," she said, again out loud but to no one in particular. It was impossible to make a washroom look eighteenth century, certainly in what had been a pioneer home. But everything was designed for silence. The door did not squeak, and the plumbing was absolutely hushed. No modern noises to intrude on the atmosphere.

On the remaining wall hung the sampler that Kate Mistoe said she was nailing up when Menelaus Atko was shot. It was a delicately embroidered piece of work, set in a frame similar to that used for the mirrors. It didn't have the familiar proverb or Biblical quotation, however. This sampler held another oblique intrusion from the twentieth century. What it said, in very fine needlework, was:

O, Winkler patrons, please take heed,
These things our septic does not need.

A most unpoetic list of the jetsam of modern living followed: matches, cigarette butts, napkins, hairpins, aluminum foil. Chris counted nineteen items that Winkler patrons were not to throw into the toilet!

Kate Mistoe had been here in the washroom when Menelaus Atko was shot in the dining room earlier this morning. Or so she said. Her story was supported, though, by Sandy Sanchez. Sandy's account was that he was going past the washroom on his way to the propane tanks out back at the time the shots were fired. He and Kate had stared at each other for what seemed like forever, frozen in shock and fear. Then they wasted more precious time colliding with each other in the narrow hallway in their effort to get to the dining room where they found the body of Menelaus, bleeding but not breathing. Through the window, both swore they'd seen a blue car roar onto the road from the parking lot in a plume of gravel and exhaust.

That part of the story was verified in turn by Karl Schloss who had been driving up the road to the David Winkler House from the opposite direction. He'd seen the blue car turn to the right in a skid at the intersection a short distance away, and then disappear. The dust from the gravel, according to Schloss, along with the exhaust, hung like a trail over the parking lot and down the road. Schloss had run into the dining room to find Sanchez and Mistoe clinging to each other, as far from the late Menelaus Atko as they could get.

All three, Mistoe, Sanchez, and Schloss, were now sitting in the kitchen waiting for Chris to finish her walkabout. To her, they were still prime suspects, in spite of the story of the blue car and the fact that their alibis all dovetailed so neatly.

Chris had questioned them separately an hour before. Schloss's story would be the easiest to check. He said he'd been in town at a service station getting the oil changed in his car. Normally that would make his alibi entirely solid, but there was a hitch. He had not come directly back to the Winkler House but had detoured via one of the farms where the inn bought fresh produce each day. When he saw that there was no one home there, he'd left and arrived back at the David Winkler House just in time to see the blue car speed away.

Sandy Sanchez, during his interview, had been exceptionally animated. As he spoke, his hands were constantly on the move in sweeping, dramatic gestures. The fittings on the propane tanks needed tightening, he'd said, making big round clockwise circles at Chris with his fist, as though he were holding a wrench. It was while he was on his way to do that, when he and Kate heard the shots.

Chris felt the man's animated style was natural; he probably talked that way all the time. In any case it would be easy enough to verify. So would his knowledge of propane systems. What bothered her most was that his story supported Kate Mistoe's, and it meant then that both were lying. So then what about Schloss? Was there a three-way conspiracy here at Winkler House?

One thing she had to do right away was talk to Atko's lawyer. The three prime suspects each owned ten percent of the inn. Atko held the rest. What she wanted to know was what kind of in-the-event-of-death clause there was in their partnership agreement. If Mistoe, Schloss, and Sanchez stood to gain substantially from their late partner's death, then . . .

Why does Chris Beadle believe that Kate Mistoe and Sandy Sanchez are lying? Why does she want to find out what Sandy Sanchez knows about propane systems? And how can she check out Karl Schloss's story?

23

Incident on
the Picket Line

12 October
Memorandum
To: Yvonne Hawkins, Manager of Claims,
    Belwood Insurance Company
From: Eileen Cook, Claims Investigator

THIS IS MY PRELIMINARY REPORT on the claim by Mr. Roger Monk of Roger Monk Transport Limited, for damage to his tractor-trailer.*

Mr. Monk is the owner-driver of the following vehicle: a diesel-powered, cab-over-engine style Freightliner tractor with a rear tandem axle. The cab has a sleeper compartment attached. The trailer is a flatbed type, with a single rear axle. Complete specifications for the vehicle will be in the appendix to my final report.

---

*   Please note that Mr. Monk is British, and describes the vehicle in his own claim as an "articulated lorry." The police refer to it as a "semi."

Incident on the Picket Line

The police report states that ten days ago, on October 2, Mr. Monk drove his tractor-trailer to the entrance gate of the Agromax Farm Machinery Company. He acknowledges that he was aware of a strike at Agromax, and that there had been several incidents of violence on the picket line. However, he contends that because his trailer was empty, he felt that the picketers would let him through unchallenged.

As Mr. Monk drove to the gate, members of the picket line set upon his equipment, presumably causing the damage listed in his claim. The police report confirms that during the incident both exhaust stacks were damaged beyond repair, along with the windshield and both headlamps. It also confirms that every single tire was slashed, so that both tractor and trailer had to be towed away after order was restored. Also, a striker entered the sleeper compartment and had to be forcibly removed. A complete copy of the police report is being sent to your attention.

Roger Monk has listed the following in his claim:
— towing charges
— complete repainting of the tractor
— replacement of the windshield and two headlamps
— replacement of two exhaust stacks
— replacement of sixteen tires
— replacement of one set of bagpipes.

My recommendations are as follows:

One: that the towing charges be paid immediately.

Two: that the repainting of the tractor be negotiated. This tractor is four years old, and the need for painting is at least partly the result of normal wear and tear.

Three: that damaged parts be replaced only if confirmed in the police report.

Four: The bagpipes are a special problem. According to police, a striker did indeed enter the sleeping compartment during the incident, but there is no independent confirmation that it was the striker who damaged the bagpipes, or that the bagpipes were even in the sleeper.

My recommendation is that the company decline to pay for them in view of the fact that there is already an attempt at fraud in this claim.

My full report will follow in two days.

Respectfully,
Eileen Cook

What is the attempt at fraud that Eileen Cook refers to?

24

Footprints on the Trail

TORREY MAZER HAD MADE IT to the top of the Criminal Investigation Branch for one very simple reason. She was a darn good cop. She knew it, too, as did the people in her department, which explained why there was never a hint of resentment from inside the force. Even when she encountered the inevitable smart remarks from people on the outside, her self-confidence always helped her to ignore it. However, what Torrey did not deal with very well was the fact that she was short. So short that her personnel file carried the minutes of an appeal meeting on the matter of her height held when she was a cadet-in-training fifteen years before. A physical education instructor had made the mistake of refusing to graduate her from his course, claiming she was too tiny to meet his standards.

In fact, Torrey topped the height requirements with even a bit to spare. But her legs were abnormally short and made her appear small. This was one point on which the male officers in her department showed no mercy. Though she could never prove it, Torrey knew that none of them ever *walked* with her. They took strides. Big ones, stretched to the limit so that she had to almost canter to keep up. Yet she could never bring herself to say anything, so that "almost cantering" became her on-duty style.

At the moment, just behind and to the right of Constable

Wally Harris, Torrey Mazer was cantering as usual — and she was more than a little embarrassed about it, too. She wasn't helped at all by the terrain. The rough, frozen field they were crossing was covered with flattened weeds and scrub brush that snagged at her feet and at the edges of her bulky overcoat. It had been a cold but snowless winter, bleak and ugly. Everything in the field was gray and dirty brown.

"We're coming right up to it now, Inspector," Wally Harris said over his right shoulder. "You can see there's some smoke still rising on the other side of the hill just ahead. If the wind was in our faces, the smell would gag you. We're lucky today."

The smell Wally referred to came from the charred bodies of thousands of turkeys that had died in a barn fire two days before. The Criminal Investigation Branch was involved because it had been a clear case of arson. Clumsy arson, too, but successful because of a terrible coincidence. Just before the fire, in a first promise of spring, a day and night of mild thaw had prompted the turkey-farm owners to move extra stock into the barn from other buildings. Thus the number of turkeys burned was much larger than it might have been. By the time the alarm was called in just before dawn, Mother Nature had suddenly reversed herself. The temperature plunged so fast that when the fire trucks arrived, the hose connections at the farm had to be loosened with torches. The delay had been costly.

Torrey doubled her cantering speed and caught up to Wally Harris just as they crested the hill. Then both of them stopped abruptly. It wasn't so much the sight of the smoldering ruin below them as it was the odor. Vile, pungent, and penetrating. Neither officer made any pretense about covering their faces.

"Normally we could go down right here, Inspector," Wally said. "But the footprints we came to see are over there." He pointed to a very steep hill on their left that ran straight down to the edge of what had been the barn. "The path is on that hill," Wally continued. "It goes from the barn up over the hill to an equipment shed. The path is so steep, they only use it in summer. It's a shortcut. Anyway, the footprints are there. It's pretty obvious that whoever torched the barn came down that path and set up with a slow-burning fuse, but, uh, Inspector, I think you're gonna see it can't really be Tibor Nish who made those footprints."

Torrey had come to the site to see for herself a set of footprints that may or may not have belonged to Tibor Nish who, for the present, was the only suspect. On the path down the hill, investigators had found a set of footprints made by a pair of size twelve Kodiak work boots. Tibor Nish not only wore size twelve Kodiaks, he had been dismissed by the turkey farm for drunkenness only a week before the fire. Nor did Nish deny that his footprints might be on the trail. He said he had returned to pick up a pair of coveralls four days ago. When he couldn't find them in the equipment shed, he went to look in the barn. He had used the path down to the barn because he was in a hurry, knowing he was not welcome on the farm. He'd found the coveralls, then hurried out the front gate. Another farm worker had seen Tibor Nish at the barn. She did not think it was four days ago, but rather, on the day *before* the fire, in the late afternoon. When pressed, however, she admitted she couldn't be absolutely sure.

Torrey could see the footprints in question easily, even before she and Wally came up the path. A single set of tracks leading down the hill. They were from big shoes all right, stamped into the middle of the path. The indentations were clear, especially deep at the heel. Kodiaks without question.

"Well," Torrey began, straightening up after a close look at the prints, "it's going to be pretty hard for Tibor Nish to explain these. My guess is if we lean on him a little he'll admit his guilt. Lucky for him nobody died in that fire."

Wally's face reddened. His lips shaped a number of words before he finally spoke. "But inspector." He put his own feet beside the footprints and took a step down the hill. "Nish has got . . . Nish has got. . . ." Wally found this hard to say. "Nish has got long legs," he finally blurted. "Longer than me even. He's taller than me. These footprints. They're so close together. Watch." He took a step that easily covered two of the paces showing in the frozen ground. "Whoever made these prints must have, well, *really short legs!*"

By now, Wally's face was far redder than a cold winter's day could make it.

"Wally," Torrey was being very patient. "Trust me. I'll give you any odds you want, that it was Nish. Let's walk down to the barn, *slowly,* and I'll explain."

Why is Inspector Torrey Mazer so certain that the footprints have been made by the suspect, Tibor Nish?

25

A Very Brief
Non-Interview

THE OFFICE WAS ULTRA MODERN, a place of hums. A hum came through the air-conditioning grate above the door. A double bank of fluorescent lighting hummed in the ceiling. Over in one corner, a 386 AT desktop hummed in droning, flat counterpoint to the spectacular, silent flowerbursts that looped in random delight on the screen.

Sheila Lacroix stood quietly in the midst of the hums. She could hear them, but paid no attention. There were too many other things to take in. The desk, just a few steps in front of her, was bulky, silent, imposing, and impeccably neat. Bookshelves on the wall to her left were filled with leatherbound volumes standing in silent, parade-ground readiness against the time when a user might have need of them. Below the shelves, a selection of newspapers was arranged carefully across a table. Sheila made a quick estimate; there were twenty different issues at least.

Across from her, and beyond the desk, the wall was glass from floor to ceiling, the panes set in almost invisibly narrow frames. She might have been on the 22nd floor of any office building in New York, London, Geneva, or Toronto. . . . Except for the newspapers. The New York and London *Times* were in the lineup all right, and out of the corner of her eye Sheila could see *Zeitung* on one of the mastheads. But the majority of the headlines were in Arabic. The view through the window told her where she was, too. Without moving her head, Sheila could count five of the mosques in central Amman.

But most especially, what told her — what would tell anyone — she was not in a western country was the very tall man bending over a tiny table near the remaining wall. He was turned away from Sheila, and except for the hand resting on the back of his hip, an incredibly long index finger pointing at the windows, she could not see any part of him as he was entirely covered by his pristine white, flowing *thobe,* and over that a shorter *aba* in desert brown. The tall man, whose other hand was furiously signing documents, was Ibrahim Jamaa, leader of the Brotherhood of the Eternal Light of Allah. It was he whom Sheila Lacroix had come to see.

"Now don't stare at him, whatever you do!" Sheila could remember every one of the attaché's instructions clearly. "As a matter of fact, don't make eye contact at all, or for more than a second or two. He knows you're western so he'll forgive you a glance, but . . . ," he shrugged, "you're a woman. Hey, I don't make the rules! This is Jordan, not Saskatchewan."

It had struck Sheila at the time that the attaché was exceptionally world-weary for one so young. "I have no idea how you did this," the young man had said, shaking his head. "No one — like, literally *nobody* — from any of the embassies has ever seen this guy close up; his organization is fanatical about secrecy — probably about a few other things, too! We've tried to get in here for months with no success, and here he gives you an appointment just like that!" He lifted his hand to snap his fingers for emphasis but then decided such behavior would be undiplomatic.

Sheila wanted to point out quite firmly that a year of traveling and beating on doors and shouting and bribing and threatening was hardly "just like that." Fourteen months ago, her husband had been kidnapped, presumably for political reasons, somewhere in Haseke province in Syria, where the border meets Iraq and Turkey. Bill Lacroix was a doctor working there with Kurdish refugees. From the time of his disappearance until now, not a single one of the Middle Eastern groups known to use kidnapping for political purposes would acknowledge they held him.

Sheila had let the Canadian Department of External Affairs prove itself useless before striking out on her own. Since then, although she was only vaguely aware of it, she was probably the only western non-diplomat and non-journalist to speak personally to the leadership of Black September, Hamas, the PLO, even the PPK. All of them had denied any knowledge of Bill Lacroix. Now Sheila was about to score the most significant coup of all, in the eyes of the diplomats anyway; she was about to speak directly to Ibrahim Jamaa of the Eternal Light of Allah.

"Don't speak first under any circumstances." The attaché had been full of advice. "You let him initiate the conversation. Somehow you've got to make it seem like you're answering *his* questions rather than the other way around."

"And . . . and . . ." The flow stopped suddenly. ". . . Uh . . . there's one more thing, Mrs. Lacroix, if you would?" For a few seconds, the attaché's diplomatic mask came off. "We . . . we know nothing about this Ibrahim Jamaa. We're not even absolutely sure what he looks like. One thing we know is that he's very tall. Unusually so, like, really basketball-tall! He wears a patch over his right eye; we know that. Speaks perfect English. Italian and German, too."

"So I'm supposed to bring you his birth certificate and his wedding album?" Sheila had long ago lost patience with External Affairs.

"No, no, no!!" The attaché reddened. "You see — and I'm being very frank with you here — what we have about him comes from the CIA and Mossad." He looked over Sheila's shoulder. "We really don't have a lot of faith in them anymore. So if there's anything that you see that is, well, *interesting*, we would like to know. Please?"

Sheila had taken one step into the elevator when he rushed to her and pulled her back gently. "One more thing we know. I don't really believe it would have anything to do with the whereabouts of Dr. Lacroix, but . . . Jamaa professes to be *mujtahid.* Means he's sort of a freethinker, especially about religion. Now the Shiites generally go along with that, but the Sunnis don't, and since Jordan is about eighty percent Sunni, that could make him a bit unwelcome here."

Standing in the office only a few minutes later, while Ibrahim Jamaa continued to write, helped Sheila understand all too well what it felt like to be unwelcome. However, when the man finally turned to face her, she forgot the feeling altogether. It was replaced by a sense of overwhelming menace that she knew would stay with her for a long time.

He was tall, all right, possibly seven feet, but that could be, Sheila later reflected, because of his power, his presence. Ibrahim Jamaa would have been a tower of malevolence at only six feet. He turned to her in what seemed like slow motion. First the patch appeared. Black, set in deep creases on the cheekbone. It was so striking that the rest of his face, Sheila was convinced, followed with abnormal slowness.

Despite herself, she stared. First at the patch, then at the single dark eye that appraised her without a flicker of response. Only when he brought his fingertips together in front of his chest — the incredibly long index finger had a matching partner — in what was just barely a gesture of greeting, did Sheila take her eyes away.

Jamaa took a step, then another. It brought him to the edge of the desk.

"Mrs. Lacroix," he said. Then there was silence. Sheila was suddenly aware of the hums again. She dared to glance up at the face and then looked down. The single eye still revealed nothing.

"Mrs. Lacroix," he said again. The attaché was correct about the English. Not a trace of an accent.

Sheila watched a long index finger as it tapped, first the edge of the desk, then the shoulder cradle attached to the telephone.

He appeared to be searching for the right words. The finger traced the slim, arching neck of a desk lamp. The man was clearly used to commanding long silences while others waited for him to speak.

"Your husband . . ."

Finally! The reason she was there! She was surprised the subject was broached so quickly.

". . . Your husband," he repeated. "The doctor. We have no interest in him. Our organization does not interfere with the work of medical relief. We seek only justice for true believers, the people who are thwarted in their search by the Zionist aggressors. I do not know where your husband is. The Brotherhood does not know where your husband is." Jamaa brought his fingertips together again in front of his chest and inclined his head ever so slightly. The interview — the *non*-interview — was over. He turned, slowly, and went back to the table where he had stood before.

Sheila had to pull her feet off the floor in order to turn and go out the door and across the hall to the elevators. She wasn't in the least surprised that the attaché got to his feet far more eagerly when the elevator doors opened than he had when they first met.

"What did you find out? What's he like?" He pressed in most undiplomatic style.

Sheila shook her head. "Nothing you'd be interested in. But it's a step ahead for me. The Brotherhood of the Eternal Light of Allah knows about my husband. They must."

"What makes you say that?" The young attaché was subdued, but curious.

"Because that was not Ibrahim Jamaa. Or if it was — which I doubt — that was not his office."

What has led Sheila Lacroix to this conclusion?

26

Murder at 12 Carnavon

HONEY SPEHR WAS UPSET. And whenever she became upset, the color would rise in her face. It would start beneath the formal collars she always wore in court, and then flush up her neck until her cheeks fairly beamed with a crimson hue. Right now she could feel them burning.

"Mrs. Spehr?" Judge Ellesmere was speaking to her. "Mrs. Spehr? Do you wish to cross-examine?"

"Your Honor." Honey cleared her throat and willed her cheeks to dim.

The judge spoke again, "Would you like a few minutes first, Mrs. Spehr?"

"Thank you, your Honor." Honey was relieved. Now at least she didn't have to *ask* for a recess. "That would be helpful. Unless my friend here objects."

She forced herself to look at Gilbey Barnett's attorney, for she knew that Todd Roland could see her cheeks, too.

Gary Ellesmere peered over his half-glasses. "Mr. Roland has no objection, I'm sure. Do you, counsellor?"

It wasn't a question. His Honor was rather unsubtly re-clarifying the pecking order. Todd Roland had been occupying center stage very successfully all day, and Ellesmere didn't care for the performance. Still, because Roland knew he was winning, the judge's arbitrariness didn't bother him in the least. Why would it? The jury had been nodding in unison with him all morning.

"Of course not, Your Honor. I'd be happy to let Mrs. Spehr have as much time as she needs to . . . ah . . . as she needs."

"Very well." The judge jumped to his feet, causing all the court officers to scramble to theirs. "Fifteen minutes," he pronounced over his shoulder as he headed for his chambers.

From where she sat at the prosecuting attorney's table, Honey's law clerk, Marion Kent, wondered whether the real reason for the judge's unaccustomed sensitivity was that he had to go to the bathroom. She didn't have a chance to comment, however, for no sooner did she and Honey get to their own ready room when Honey let go.

"He's lying, that slime, and he's getting away with it! He killed that woman! I know it. You know it. Anybody who bothers to think knows it. But he and Roland have got that jury thinking he's Francis of Assisi!"

She began to pace, tapping the index and third fingers of one hand into the palm of the other with each step. The effect was calming.

"Somehow I've got to make that jury realize that Gilbey Barnett may be smooth all right, but underneath the enamel is a liar! The thing is . . ." Honey's voice grew quieter, more deliberate. The rosy color was gone altogether now. ". . . The thing is . . . *how?* We'll never swing that jury back to rational thinking now. Not with what we've got to offer!"

Marion wished Honey wouldn't use the first person plural. Like the jury, she had been quite impressed with Barnett's defense; she wasn't at all as convinced as Honey of the man's guilt. But then — she had often admitted this to herself — no one had Honey's, "nose for phonies." Was Gilbey Barnett a phoney? Was he lying? Did he kill his wife? If anybody was ever going to find out, it would be Honey Spehr.

Her case had begun with a building superintendent whose testimony showed that Barnett kept a mistress. Then there was the late Mrs. Barnett's sister, who described the fighting between her brother-in-law and his wife. This was reluctantly corroborated by a member of the Barnetts' cleaning service.

Mrs. Barnett had been shot in the back of the head at close range with a .22 caliber pistol. No weapon had ever been found, but a smug little clerk from Records and Registrations had stood in the box long enough to hold up a registration card for a Smith and Wesson of that caliber. The name on the card was W. Gilbey Barnett.

A combination of testimonies from a forensic pathologist and a neighbor, who had seen Mrs. Barnett pick up the morning paper on the porch, established the time of death at between 10:20 A.M. and 11:40 A.M.

Honey's ace was Constable First Class Jeff Baldwin. She had called him last. ("Responded to a dispatch at 11:44 A.M.; a shooting at the rear of 12 Carnavon Boulevard.") Baldwin's notes were always impeccably precise. He had entered the sunporch at 12 Carnavon to find "the defendant standing over the deceased."

Despite the fact that no weapon was found, the smoking-gun impression that Baldwin left with the jury was very powerful. It was Honey's intent to show in final summation that the time frames, no matter what Barnett's alibis, were such that given all the other evidence, Gilbey Barnett was a guilty man.

Todd Roland, however, had a few surprises and they were very effective. To begin with he didn't cross-examine a single prosecution witness. A very chancy strategy, but if it works, one that creates the impression that these witnesses and their testimony are not really very important. It can also make the prosecution case seem short. Roland's second surprise was to call Barnett first, not last, as everyone expected, and his third was to ask Judge Ellesmere to clear the courtroom of all the subsequent witnesses. By then Honey knew what he was going to do but was powerless to stop it. Any objection would have strengthened his ploy.

Roland's strategy was to draw out Gilbey Barnett's own account first, replete with detail upon detail, then corroborate it piece by piece, bit by bit, inexorably, with a parade of witnesses, until it became concrete in the collective psyche of the jurors that the defendant simply had to be telling the truth.

Barnett acknowledged that, yes, he had a mistress and that, yes, his marriage had been in difficulty ("You see, I suspected my late wife of being a drug user and we argued a lot about that.")

Honey had leapt in with an objection because there was absolutely no proof of that, and Ellesmere sustained but it was too late. The idea was already planted in the jury. Roland managed to slip it in again as a reason for having a license for a gun ("I was sure she'd been consorting with some very shady people: drug people and that like.")

On the day of the murder, Barnett testified, he left for his office at 7:40 A.M. and left there in turn at 9:20 A.M. to have some breakfast at First Came the Egg ("You understand, she just wouldn't make breakfast anymore, so to avoid conflict I simply ate out.") He left the restaurant at precisely 10:30 A.M. ("How do I know that, Mr. Roland? Well, the waitress — poor thing, I felt so sorry for her — she was so busy that she tripped right by my table and spilled ketchup on me!") As he said that he turned and held his left leg out of the witness box as though to show the jury the stain was still there. That was when Honey's color began to rise fast for the jurors turned as one to look at the pant leg. *And they were nodding!*

Barnett finally got around to explaining his precise 10:30 departure by saying that this particular waitress had left the restaurant at the same time he did, and she had told him she only worked the early morning shift and was now going home to change clothes for her other job.

Then he went to Harry's Men's Shop for a final fitting on a suit. And that call was memorable because the tailor, who was normally so adept, stuck him with a pin ("right in the ketchup on my sock!").

After the fitting he left. ("I left at 11:10 A.M. How do I know? Oh, because I was late now. I wanted to go home to change clothes before my luncheon meeting and I looked at my watch. I had to get from Harry's to home and then to Le Coq d'Or by noon. It was going to be very tight.")

Barnett went on to testify he'd arrived at 12 Carnavon at about 11:40 ("I looked at my watch again at the top of the street") and that while going up the walk, he heard a shot at the back of the house. By the time he ran through the house, whoever had fired it was gone ("and I was just frozen there until Constable Baldwin found me just like he described").

The rest of Barnett's testimony went just like that: precise, unhesitating, completely forthcoming. Every time Roland backed him up to fill in a blank, the response came through as though it was scripted. Which in Honey's opinion, it was. She knew that by this time there was not a single juror who wasn't thinking dismissal. All they needed was some reinforcement to tip them into absolute certainty. And with the next witnesses, Roland gave them that in a flood of verifying details. That the main point was left essentially untreated — namely, that Roland had not shown at all that Barnett was elsewhere when the shot was fired — didn't matter. All the jury heard was how exact Barnett's testimony had been.

It began with the security guard at his office. ("Certainly I know Mr. Barnett. Everyone does. He's so generous to all of us especially at Christmas. He . . .")

"*Objection!*" Honey's objection had been so vigorous that it didn't even seem necessary for Ellesmere to sustain.

The guard went on to say that he signed Barnett in at 8:16 A.M. The secretary, who was up next, verified that he left at 9:20. ("No. Mr. Barnett didn't use to go out for breakfast, but for the past year he did all the time.") The waitress followed the secretary then, with testimony that Honey knew she'd never poke through. ("Oh, it was so embarrassing when I fell, but he's such a nice man . . .")

Ellesmere looked at Honey. His face said: "Go ahead. Object. I'm getting sick of this, too!" But Honey knew it would turn the jury away from her even further.

The waitress went on to say that Barnett left with her at 10:30

("I always leave at 10:30. I have another job at Ruskin's department store. It's hard when you're raising two kids all on your own with no help. Anyway he . . .").

Roland shut her down quickly then and called the tailor. That's when Honey's hope sank altogether. The little tailor was right out of Central Casting! Short, bald, pudgy, the most benign face she had ever seen. The guy was a fairy godfather!

And he had an accent. No, not just an accent. A *cute* accent! ("I haf been thoaty yeeahs tailor. Harry's-a ma brother.) By now, Honey knew the jury was watching a movie. This was entertainment! That was when the color started to creep up her neck. The tailor pointed at Barnett. ("Yes. He's-a come . . . oh . . . ten-toaty, maybe ten-foaty.") Then he smiled. ("That's-a ma suit! Foaty-two tall. You like . . . eh, Mistah Bahnett?") *Now the jury was laughing!* ("Dat morning. I'm-a rememba de ketchup. On da floor I kneel. Mesha da cuff, and-a there's-a ketchup on da sock.")

Wisely, Roland stopped him there. Although the jury was enjoying every minute, he could see that Judge Ellesmere's sense of humor had reached its limit. It wouldn't do to have the jury's mood blown away by a tirade.

Honey, on the other hand, was nearly apoplectic. That's when Ellesmere, instead of getting angry as well, called the recess. Now, in the ready room, Honey was trying to prepare herself to go back out. But to what? She knew that the jury was entirely in Barnett's camp. She knew that without doubt, in their room right now, they were regaling themselves trying to imitate the little tailor or clucking in sympathy with the waitress.

She knew that logic would not win them back. No matter how relentlessly she focused on the time frame and showed that Barnett *could* have made it from Harry's Men's Shop to his home in time to shoot his wife, nothing was going to penetrate the web of certainty that Roland had woven.

"The only way," she said to Marion, "the only possible way to make them listen to me is to break up that perfect story. I've got to show them they're being misled. The story's a layer cake; it's *manufactured.* If I can only show them one single contradiction then they'll listen, and we can go to work on the *real* evidence. Now we . . . Oh! Marion! I almost missed it!"

The color began to rise again in Honey Spehr's cheeks, but this time there was a glint in her eye.

Honey has found the contradiction, she thinks, the crack in the carefully crafted defense that she needs to return the jury to rationality. What is it?

27

The Case of Queen Isabella's Gift

TWO MONOLOGUES WERE FIGHTING FOR attention in Geoff Dilley's brain. One was by Vicar Titteridge. He was talking about keys.

"Tourists would be entirely disappointed in these," he was saying as he took a pair of shiny brass keys from his pants pocket and inserted one into the padlock hanging from a hasp on the old church door.

"They much prefer this kind of thing, of course." He held up a worn leather thong in front of Geoff's face, dangling a huge, black iron key larger than his hand. "Interesting, what? Can't blame them, really, the tourists. A blacksmith made this quite some time before locksmiths and that sort of profession were ever heard of, you see."

Geoff wanted to point out that the Romans had padlocks, that the Chinese had used combination locks for centuries, and that in the Middle Ages locks were made that could count the number of times a key was inserted. But the vicar struck him as the type that was unaccustomed to contradiction.

"The key is almost two hundred years old, we think. Can't be proven, of course, but church records indicate the door here was replaced in the same year George IV became Prince Regent. You know, when his poor father went bonkers once and for all. At any rate, it's only logical to assume the key was made at the same time."

He rapped on the door firmly. "Solid oak this. From the New Forest. Very unusual that. Needed royal permission to cut the tree. Still, the door's a relative junior compared to the church itself: 1320 it was dedicated. Legend has it Edward II himself was here for the ceremony. Doesn't seem likely though, for it's sure that Queen Isabella was here. And you know about those two."

Geoff wanted to say that yes, he did know all about those two, but he didn't for the vicar had finally inserted the big key and turned it. The door opened easily and noiselessly, exposing the cool darkness inside. It occurred to Geoff that tourists would prefer some nice, authentic creaking, but he said nothing and waited in the doorway while the vicar stepped inside and turned on the lights.

"You'll have to come up to the altar," the vicar said. "The candelabra were up there."

"Candelabra" triggered the other monologue, the one Geoff Dilley had been trying to suppress. It came back again, though. Verbatim.

"*Candelabra!*" It was Chief Inspector Peddelley-Spens and he was shouting. "Bleedin' *candelabra?* We've got seven — count 'em, seven — homicide investigations going on at this precise moment. There's mad Irishman bombin' the country to bleedin' bits. I've got a bunch o' bleedin fox-kissers chained t' the fence at Marlborough Hunt. The bleedin' prime minister o' bleedin Portugal is comin' this afternoon. And *you!* You want to investigate the theft of a bleedin' pair o' candelabra?" Peddelley-Spens stopped to take in a huge breath. "I suppose that next you'll want the weekend off, too, so you can join hands with those frog-kissers that want a bleedin' tunnel under the bleedin' M5?"

Suddenly, the Chief Inspector had softened to half volume. "One!" he said. "You can make one call!" And then to normal volume altogether. "Look, Geoffrey. I know how much you like bleedin' old things. But you're a good investigator. I need you here! Now you can trot off to — where is it? — St. Dunstan's-by-the-Water? But I want you back today before tea. Somebody's got to mind the crime rate while the rest of us are guardin' his Portugese worship!"

Geoff's love of "bleedin' old things" — he had long ago despaired of instructing Peddelly-Spens in the use of "antiquarian" — made him more than anxious to visit St. Dunstan's-by-the-Water. He knew the ancient church but had never been in it. St. Dunstan's was a tiny but most unusual structure. A chapel really, rather than a church, but it was Norman and that made it special. Since it was built in the early fourteenth century, when Gothic architecture had wholly supplanted all other forms, St. Dunstan's lay claim to being the last piece of Norman architecture built in England.

In the hour it had taken him to drive there, Geoff came to realize he would never be able to make Peddelly-Spens appreciate just how valuable, how utterly priceless and irreplaceable the stolen candelabra really were.

"A gift of Queen Isabella," the vicar had said on the telephone. "You can still see her seal. Gold, of course. Each piece has some quite lovely stones, too."

Geoff knew that if the candelabra were not found right away, their fate would go one of two ways: they would either be fenced to a collector or, more likely, the stones would be pried out and the gold melted down. Either way, no one would ever see the ancient pieces again.

"Watch your step." The vicar's monologue returned just a shade too late to save Geoff from stumbling as they walked up the short aisle. "Original floors, you know. Even stone wears after six-and-a-half centuries."

Geoff had been following the vicar as slowly as possible so he could look around. He wanted to spend time in this church. It was Norman, all right. Thick walls, round arches, windows that looked more like arrow slits.

"Right there. Above the altar. They stood on those two pedestals."

Geoff stared at the altar.

"No, no. Higher. Up there." The vicar directed Geoffrey's gaze to a point well above the altar where two small stone platforms jutted out from the columns leading from the ends of the altar to the roof.

"I assume . . ." the vicar was still talking. Other than introducing himself, Geoffrey had yet to say a word. "I assume he, or she — maybe even *they.* There were several dozen strangers here last night. Isn't it curious how we automatically believe it is males who commit crime? I assume the perpetrator, or perpetrators, attended Evensong last night and then hid in the church until it was empty. The candelabra were definitely here, for they were lit. Everyone saw them. They're only lit for Evensong. Too much of a bother, even with a step stool and extended candlelighters. And I assume that since we lock the main door on the outside as you saw, that he or she or they went out here."

The vicar led Geoff to a door behind the altar. "It's the only other way in or out," he said. "A concession to the twentieth century. Fire regulations and all that, you see."

He leaned against the crash bar, covering the little red-and-silver sign that said "Emergency Exit Only" with his bottom, and opened the door. Geoff followed him outside and turned to watch the door close and lock automatically.

"When I'm alone, I normally enter this way." The vicar produced the pair of brass keys again and opened the door. "Less fuss. Did so this morning."

Geoff followed the vicar back inside.

"Really don't know what made me look up. At any rate they were gone, and straight away I rushed back out and telephoned you."

For the first time, Geoffrey opened his mouth and was actually going to speak, but the vicar anticipated his question and beat him to it. "You're going to ask me about the verger, aren't you?

Well, we don't have one at St. Dunstan's. Poor old Albert died over a year ago, and we never arranged for a replacement. This is only a chapel, really. A Sunday morning service and then Evensong, so there's no need. One of the parishioners comes every second Tuesday. I let her in and we clean together."

Geoff took a breath and got out "How . . ." before the vicar said, "There were between forty and fifty last night. About fifteen regulars. No, no. This way."

Geoff had turned to go out behind the altar.

"So we can turn the lights out and double lock the main door again. Pity we have to do that. House of God and all that, but then I certainly don't have to tell you about it. The crime rate, I mean."

The vicar paused to straighten a hymn book, and Geoffrey blurted, "No, Vicar. I know all about it." The voice of Peddelley-Spens rumbled like distant thunder in the back of his mind. "But it's even worse when a man of the cloth adds to it. The crime rate, I mean."

Why has Geoff Dilley concluded that Vicar Titteridge has stolen the pair of candelabra?

28

Quite Possibly, the Annual Meeting of the Ambiguity Society

NORMALLY, BEING ASSIGNED TO COVER a yearly dinner for *The Citizen's* society page would be an out-and-out drag for any reporter, let alone one whose passion was investigative journalism. Being sent to the annual May dinner meeting of the Ambiguity Society, however, was a bit of a coup for Bonnie Livingston, so she didn't mind the traffic she had to fight on Derry Road, or the downpour that hit while she was pulled up at a gas station.

The members of the Ambiguity Society were an incredibly strange bunch. The principle aim of the group was clearly stated in the motto that adorned its letterhead.

"Prevaricate! Obfuscate! Flummox!"

That the letterhead contained neither telephone number nor address, was, of course, entirely to be expected.

Although the abiding tenet of an Ambiguity Society member's existence was to live life without ever responding directly or communicating clearly, as individuals they were harmless enough, and they were certainly amusing to the few outsiders who had ever heard of them. But their relationship with the press, whose self-appointed guardianship of the truth was as passionate as the society's love of deception, had become a competition. To reporters, the members' evasive and misleading responses to their questions were such an irresistible red flag that they were invariably willing to wade through the most enigmatic conundrums to find even the tiniest kernel of factual information.

Bonnie's excitement stirred, therefore, as she pulled into the parking lot of the Mono Cliffs Inn. When she got out of her car, she walked right into Bruno Steubens, the society's outgoing president.

Bruno nodded without smiling. "You found us again this year, Mrs. Livingston." It was not a question, simply a greeting.

"This will be the third consecutive annual meeting of the Ambiguity Society for me, Mr. Steubens. Quite a feat you have to admit. Now, since nobody from the media has ever covered four . . . ah . . . you wouldn't care to tell me the date of next year's meeting, would you? So my record can continue intact?"

She hastened to add, "I've always been fair in my coverage, haven't I?"

Bruno Steubens stroked his chin slowly and nodded ever so slightly. "That you have, I suppose. Been fair, I mean."

"So," Bonnie pressed a bit harder. "It's not unreasonable to ask for next year's date is it?"

Bruno continued nodding. "I guess not. I guess not. All right, well. It's going to be like this year, in the middle of the month."

"Oh really, Bruno. You can do better than that. She's really such a nice young person. For a reporter." It was Sally Steubens. Bonnie had not seen her get out of the car. "It'll be after the thirteenth, dear," she said to Bonnie. "After the thirteenth."

"Just a minute there!" The incoming president, Karen Di Creche, suddenly appeared from the other side of the parking lot along with her husband Julio. "Are you discussing next year's meeting? That's my territory now! Look, we'll tell you this much. Next year's meeting will be on an odd-numbered date. Now does that help you?"

"Not only on an odd-numbered date," Julio contributed, but on a date that is not a perfect square."

"I think you're going to confuse her with that, Julio." Karen turned to Bonnie and smiled indulgently. "He does that, you know. Sometimes he's just so misleading. Now, you'll have to excuse us. The executive can't be late for dinner, can we?"

With that, the four brushed past Bonnie toward the inn. She was writing furiously, concentrating so intensely that she was unaware of Sally Steubens until she whispered in her ear.

"Before the thirteenth, okay? It's all so ambiguous dear, isn't it? You know none of us is supposed to tell you the exact truth, but I just did, so now you should have the answer." With that, Sally hurried after the others.

When will the next annual meeting be held?

29

The Case of the
Missing Body

FOR SOME REASON, EVEN BEFORE she picked up the telephone, Lesley Simpson knew she wasn't going to like this call. Then when the smarmy voice of Eddy Duane greeted her, she knew her instincts had been right on. Eddy Duane was a lawyer in the crown attorney's office. He was not on Lesley Simpson's list of favorite people.

"Hey Les! How are ya?" "Les" would have spoiled the day in any case. Lesley hated being called "Les." Her name was "Lesley," spelled with an E-Y. "The British way," her mother had explained.

"Better brace yourself, Les! We're finally gonna charge your favorite client with murder." That got Lesley's attention. "You see, Les, old kid, we found his wife's body. Well, her skeleton really. It's the late Mrs. Vincent Gene, all right. Absolutely no question. We'll need the dental records to confirm it, but there's no doubt it's her. The ring on the finger, the one earring, the clothes, the shoes. And you know where she was found? Right in the backyard! Your boy's not too bright, Les! Burying his wife in the backyard!"

Suddenly Eddy Duane's voice became more serious. "Look, Lesley," he said. "I'll meet you in, say, an hour or so out at Vincent Gene's house. Cops are there now. The coroner, too. We've agreed to leave everything till you get to see it. One hour. Okay?"

With that, Eddy Duane hung up. Lesley realized she hadn't said a single thing on the telephone other than answering with her own name. Still, conversation wasn't necessary. Not in this case. It was three years old, but Lesley knew every detail as though it had started only yesterday.

Three years ago, the wife of gentleman-farmer Vincent Gene had left her husband sitting at the breakfast table of their expensively renovated Caledon farmhouse and was never seen again. That there had been foul play was pretty certain. Her car was found only minutes away from the house on a barely passable, unmaintained sideroad. It was full of blood — the type matched hers; the front seat had been sliced, presumably with a knife; and a single earring was found on the floor of the passenger side. But her body, if indeed she was dead, had never been found.

Vincent Gene, the husband, was Lesley Simpson's longtime client, and although he insisted he was innocent, the police had focused on him from the beginning. Only the lack of a body, Lesley knew, kept them from laying a murder charge. Now, it seemed, the last hurdle may have been cleared.

It took Lesley only forty minutes to get to Vincent Gene's farm. She noted with relief that Eddy Duane wasn't there yet. Lots of activity though — several police cars, an ambulance, a growing knot of neighbors gathering around the forsythia bushes at the end of the laneway. Near the back of the property, standing beside a backhoe, Lesley recognized Sergeant Rodney Palmer. The recognition was mutual.

"Ah, Ms. Simpson. We've been expecting you," the sergeant said as Lesley approached. Rodney Palmer was as polite as Eddy Duane was pushy. "Over here, if you want to take a look." He took Lesley over to a narrow trench that began where the bucket of the backhoe rested on the ground and ran to a small barn some distance away. Two policemen in coveralls were standing in the trench, their heads just below the top edge.

"It's supposed to be for a water line running to the barn," Palmer said. "They've been digging here four or five days." He nodded at the backhoe. "Operator found the body — uh, the *skeleton,* rather — first thing this morning. Well, actually, he turned up a shoe first; then when he saw a bone, he stopped and called us. We've almost finished uncovering the whole skeleton now. Wasn't that difficult 'cause the clothes are still in good shape. You want to see?"

Lesley took a deep breath. Then another one. "Yes," she replied.

Rodney Palmer took a few steps and pointed down into the trench without speaking. When Lesley followed and looked down, she knew the sight would stay with her forever. Whatever she had expected, it certainly wasn't color, yet that's what she noticed most of all. Color. The green grass at the top of the trench. Trampled but still green. Then the neat, precise layer of dark brown top soil. And under that, almost as if someone had drawn a line, a band of yellow. Sand, Lesley figured. Then below that, right to the bottom, blue clay. Maybe it was the blue, she thought, that made the clothing on the skeleton look so, well, so elegantly crimson, dirty as it was.

"See the one earring inside the skull, Les?" The sudden intrusion of Eddy Duane almost made Lesley stumble into the trench. "Quite a sight, huh? One your client never expected to see again, I'll bet. And you know what, it almost worked, too. You see the trench? It was supposed to go over there." He pointed to a spot several yards away. "But there's too much rock, so without even asking, the backhoe guy dug this way and *voilà!* The late Mrs. Vincent Gene. Right in her own backyard!"

Lesley Simpson looked straight at Eddy Duane. "Mrs. Gene," she said, "if indeed that is Mrs. Gene, was not buried here. Not when she died anyway." She shifted her gaze to Sergeant Rodney Palmer. "My guess is that if you can find out who dumped the skeleton into this trench last night and covered it up, you'll have the person who did the killing, too."

How does Lesley Simpson know that the skeleton was dumped into the trench last night?

30

The Case of the
Marigold Trophy

JANICE SANT BIT INTO A fresh wedge of orange and concluded that at least one of her five senses was working normally. The other four had slid into that never-never land the body finds when it has been doing the same thing in the same place for too long.

Since five o'clock, when the Palgrave Community Library opened for its Tuesday hours, Janice had been sitting in front of a microfilm viewer, slowly winding her way through back issues of *The Daily Enterprise.* Her sense of touch had long since disappeared into the hard wooden chair on which she sat. Only her right hand, which slowly cranked the microfilm across the screen, gave assurance that she could feel anything. She knew her eyes were still working for they continued to refocus after each movement of the old-fashioned type. But whether the focusing was a conscious act or simply a reflex after hours at the screen, she couldn't be sure.

Before she could assess the two remaining senses, Eugene Weller's cologne told her that at least one of them was still working.

"I'll be closing in about five minutes, Miss Sant." The gentle, elderly librarian beamed down at her. "It's actually five past nine already."

Janice looked over the viewer at the portly little man. He was compulsively arranging the little boxes of microfilm into three separate piles: 1903, 1904, and 1905.

"How have you done?" He walked around the table and put his face very close to the screen. The cologne was even stronger now. Janice knew he must be one of those types who dab it on all day long. "Goodness!" He straightened slightly, leaving a wave of scent behind. "March 3 already! You've done quite well, haven't you? Still think you should have taken a break though. Young people like you shouldn't skip meals." He walked around to the other side of the table again and tapped one of the piles of little boxes to make it absolutely symmetrical. "Just turn off the switch when we close. I'll put things away tomorrow. Sorry again about the missing October. No one knows why that month was never filmed. Don't forget now," he said as he walked away. "Five minutes."

Janice sighed and then sighed again when she tried unsuccessfully to wind the film along, for her hand had gone to sleep. What made her weariness and discomfort even worse was that this job was a freebie. Normally, she charged between $50 and $75 an hour plus expenses for an investigation, but this job she had volunteered for. On the surface it had seemed very simple. Ownership of the Palgrave Horticultural Society's proudest and by far most valuable — and beautiful — possession was being challenged. It was a trophy, a marigold, about the size of a teacup, set in a cluster of natural Baffin Island graphite on a base of local black walnut. The flower itself was twenty-four carat solid gold. On a rectangular plate set into the walnut were etched the words:

M. TOOCH
Grand Champion Marigolds
Albion Agricultural Exhibition
10 July 1904

125

When Miss Maribeth Tooch died in 1960, well into her nineties, her will had bequeathed this most unusual trophy — work of art, really — to the society. Unfortunately, it was tainted with an unresolved controversy. Maribeth's twin sister, Maribel, until her death in 1959, had steadfastly claimed that she had been the rightful winner and not the runner-up as the records indicated, because Maribeth had broken the rules.

Undaunted, since 1960 the Palgrave Horticultural Society had proudly displayed the Tooch trophy until two weeks ago, when its ownership was challenged in court by Rachel Tooch-Rothman, a grand-niece of Maribel, and her late husband, Denison. Janice's task, if it could be done, was to find out the truth once and for all.

So far, from *The Daily Enterprise,* she had learned that Maribeth had indeed been awarded the grand championship with Maribel coming second and that this most valuable and unusual trophy was a one-time gift of an anonymous benefactor. She had also learned that there were indeed rules for the marigold contest: requirements governing the type of seed that could be used (Stratus or Givern); specifications regarding exactly when the seeds could be sown (on February 23); instructions that the flowers had to be cut on the day before the Exhibition (on July 9); and a rule that winners were ineligible the following year. Janice had also discovered that she could wind her way through about five months of newspaper every hour, and although she had worked through the issues of *The Daily Enterprise* carefully and in sequence, she had still not found anything to help her clear up the controversy itself.

Not until Eugene Weller and his cologne had intruded to tell her it was closing time. That had woken her up, and later, she acknowledged she'd have missed it otherwise. Really, there had been no logical reason to pay attention to the story on the screen at the time. The headline was at best curious, and the story itself, similar to the stuff she had been skimming over with steadily decreasing attention as time wore on.

TWO TIME RUNAWAY

For the second time in only a very brief period, a horse owned by Mr. Curragh O'Malley has run away and injured a citizen. In yesterday afternoon's incident, the horse made contact with Mr. Ezra Templeton of Gibson Street while he was standing in his front-yard. Mr. Templeton has suffered a broken arm. Mr. O'Malley explained that the horse was tethered in front of the Dominion Hotel while he was conducting business inside, and it was frightened by some young boys playing hoop-and-stick. On the same day a week earlier, this horse broke its tether at the same hitching rack and struck down Miss Maribeth Tooch of Pine Street. Coincidence being what it is, Miss Tooch had only just stepped outside her solarium for a few seconds of fresh air after seeding marigolds for the annual exhibition in July. It was at this precise instant that the horse ran onto her property. Miss Tooch suffered bruises but no broken bones.

Her friends and acquaintances, and those of Mr. Templeton, will be pleased to know that both of these fine citizens are recovering nicely. Nevertheless *The Enterprise* believes that tethering by-laws in Palgrave must be more rigorously enforced if innocent people are to enjoy the simple privilege of standing in their own yards.

"I'm turning the lights out, Miss Sant. Oh, Miss Sant, I'm going to turn . . . Why Miss Sant! You look very upset! What's the matter?"

Eugene Weller rushed over to her in a cloud of concern and freshly applied cologne.

"Our beautiful trophy," Janice said. "We could lose it!"

Why does Janice Sant think the Palgrave Horticultural Society could lose its most prized possession?

31

The Coffee Break
That Wasn't

"RECEIVING AND DISPOSAL LOOK ALL right," Di Froggatt said as she came back from what had started out as a simple trip to the washroom. "As a matter of fact, not bad at all for a place like this, since they've got to share space with the deli next door." Having once been a health inspector, Di couldn't resist an opportunity to check things out. "Bit messy at the loading door," she went on, "but nothing that would warrant a charge. Normal really, for a Friday morning."

As she sat down, her knee bumped the single leg in the center of the table causing Lennie Strachan's cup of coffee to sway dangerously in its bright white plastic cup. Quickly Lennie put her spoon in the steaming brew to stop the swirling and without looking up said, "Don't apologize. I bumped it twice when you were out. There must be a special annex in hell for people who design furniture like this." She lay the spoon on the table and grinned at Di.

"Just try to sit up straight and be comfortable for more than three seconds. The seats are even worse!"

Lennie and Di were sitting — or at least were attempting to sit — in a small restaurant at the end of a shopping mall. The little restaurant was ultra modern. It's very name suggested what was expected of the clientele: *Eat 'n' Run* it was called. The place was exceptionally bright, almost painful to the eyes with its intense fluorescent glow, and in an antiseptic kind of way, it appeared to be squeaky clean.

To anyone who ate but failed to run immediately, it was soon obvious that the designer of the restaurant did not intend that customers should relax here. The tables were a study in flimsy molded plastic; so were the chairs. But it was their color that mounted the final assault: bright mauve with even brighter orange trim. As a result, most of the customers at *Eat 'n' Run* did exactly that, many of them without even realizing why. Except for, on this particular morning, Lennie Strachan and Di Froggatt.

Di took a deep breath and sighed. "Well, it sure isn't Lum's Café, is it?"

Lennie nodded. Di was referring to a comfy old diner, now long gone, that had stood on the site of this same shopping mall. The two friends had met regularly at Lum's Café years before. They had both been inspectors then with the city's Department of Health. Now retired, they got together once in a while for coffee and a chat. But there was something about getting together like this that always turned them back into inspectors again. Somehow they couldn't help it.

"Y'know, these things," Lennie said, changing the subject as she held up a tiny plastic container with the cream sealed inside, "imagine how much easier our job would have been if these had been around?"

Di smiled. "Yeah, if we had a free cup of coffee for every jug of cream we poked our noses into, we'd go into permanent caffeine surge!"

"Yes," Lennie replied, "but in one way these things have a serious drawback. Look at this." With her index finger she pushed four of the little containers one after the other. "Both of us drink it black, yet the waitress gave us two each. Had them in the pocket of her apron. I wonder how many of these get thrown out. Years ago it was hygiene. Now it's pollution."

Lennie kept on talking, but Di Froggatt wasn't listening. She was staring at Lennie's left hand as it came up to the edge of the cup of coffee. Clamped between her thumb and index finger was a fly. A *plastic* housefly!

Di was flabbergasted. "Have you still got some of those things?" Her tone indicated she didn't need an answer.

"Three more boxes at home," Lennie said without changing expression, and dumped the little black offender into her cup of coffee. It disappeared and then surfaced immediately, floating passively on top. "Never know when they'll come in handy. Ever want to get your grandchildren to leave the table? Oh Miss!" Lennie called the waitress. "Miss!"

The waitress appeared immediately.

"Miss. Look at this!" Lennie's indignation was quiet but unmistakable.

The waitress peered a little closer, saw the fly, then without a word took Lennie's cup away and disappeared with it behind the counter. She came right back and set the cup down in front of Lennie, mumbling, "Sorry," and then dug two more cream containers out of her apron pocket. "I'll tell the manager," she said.

"Yours okay?" the waitress said to Di.

Di just nodded her head. She was intent on Lennie's next move.

The waitress set down another two cream containers, this time in front of Di, and then moved away to another table.

"Well," Di said, "are you going to finish the test or not?"

Lennie's nostrils flared in mock indignation. "Watch me!" With a serviette she wiped the tip of her little finger and then touched the surface of the coffee twice. She licked the finger and looked at Di.

"I'll be darned," Lennie said.

Di leaned forward. "You mean you caught them?" she said.

This time Lennie Strachan's indignation was real. "Bet on it!" she replied.

What offence has Lennie detected at the Eat 'n' Run and how has she done it?

32

Who Shot the Clerk at Honest Orville's?

MARY CREMER LEANED BACK OUT of the doorway at 26 Division to see who had called her name.

"Here! Mary! Over here!"

This time Mary recognized the voice of her sister Caroline, but in the busy pre-Christmas bustle on the sidewalk, it took a few more seconds to locate her.

"All *right!*" Mary's enthusiasm when she finally saw her was genuine. "What are *you* doing here?"

Caroline pointed to the 26 Division lobby and gave a smile of chagrin. "Kee Park," she said.

"*What!*" Mary blurted, loud enough for a few passersby to pause in the crush and stare at the two young women.

"That . . . that . . . *jerk!* He's done it again! What is it that makes him think we're a package just because we're sisters?"

Caroline shrugged her shoulders. She tended to be just a bit calmer than Mary.

"It's just Baxter," she said. "I don't think he can help himself. Don't sweat about it. You've only got a few more weeks. Besides, this one's really interesting! Kee Park, I mean."

"I suppose," Mary replied. "At least . . . *Omigosh!*"

Both young women had forgotten they were blocking the doorway of the busiest police station in the downtown area, until two burly plainclothes types rapped on the inside of the glass simultaneously.

"Sorry," Mary said. She opened the door and slipped in quickly. Caroline came right after her.

"At least," she went back to her point, "it isn't support payments for a change, or crummy break-and-enter again."

"No!" Caroline was definitely excited. "Kee Park could be really big. They charged him this morning. Murder. I . . ."

"He's *charged?*" Mary grabbed her sister's coat sleeve. "I thought . . . "

"That's why I'm here." Caroline said. "Baxter got a call from Detective . . . Detective . . . let's see." She fished a piece of paper out of her coat pocket. "Blanchard! Yes, Blanchard. Didn't we deal with him once before? Kind of cute."

"*Charged?*" Mary was still absorbing the fact that her — *their* — client had been charged with murder.

She and Caroline were law students completing their one year of practicum before being admitted to the bar. Mary's time was to end in a month. Caroline was only midway through. Their firm, Baxter, Baxter, Quisling, Keele, and Wilson — only one, the second Baxter, was still alive — regularly took on a small number of legal-aid cases, all of which were with equal regularity turned over to students. "Freebies," the surviving Baxter called them, although both Mary and Caroline had been shocked when they saw the number of hours the firm billed the government for services.

Most of the cases were single parents chasing delinquent support payments or juveniles on break-and-enter charges or shoplifting. The case of Kee Park was different. Dramatically so. He had been picked up last night at a shooting in front of Honest Orville's, the biggest discount emporium in the city, perhaps even the whole country.

At first, Park was held as a material witness only, then on suspicion of manslaughter. That's when Mary came onto the case.

Now things had spun ahead by one more step during the time she traveled to the police station.

She pulled Caroline over to a bench in the lobby. "You had better fill me in."

Caroline opened her coat as she sat down. "Things have moved pretty fast in the past couple of hours." She stood up with a look of discomfort on her face and took her coat off. "I thought the city was supposed to be on a tight budget. They could save some money on the heating bill in this place. Anyway. You know all about Park claiming he was out on the sidewalk, just standing there when it happened." Caroline stopped to take off her scarf and paused to concentrate on a recalcitrant knot.

"For heaven's sake, what's the rest of it?" Mary insisted.

"Okay. Sorry. And he claims he didn't even know there was a robbery going on until these two guys burst out the door, chased by the clerk."

"Dumb." Mary shook her head. "The clerk I mean. What did the guy think? Chasing two people with a gun!"

"Yeah, but dumb or smart, he's dead," Caroline replied. "And our client is charged with his murder, and it doesn't look good."

Now Mary stood up and took off her coat. "You're right about the heat. But then, right now I guess it's got to be a lot hotter for Kee Park." She pursed her lips. "I just can't buy the murder charge. There's too much circumstantial stuff."

She sat down again. "Let's review what we've got. Two guys rob Honest Orville's about 8:30 P.M."

"8:40," Caroline inserted. "There's a time fix from the patrolman across the street."

"The witness?" Mary asked. She held up her hand. "Don't answer. It had to be him. Right?"

Caroline nodded. "Confirmed, too. He was calling in at the time."

Mary continued. "And the two guys — the robbers — run out onto the street, presumably to get lost in the Christmas shopping crowds. They're chased by the clerk. When he gets to the doorway, he gets shot."

"Not quite," Caroline said. "The patrolman had modified that a bit in his report. The shooting took place well out on the sidewalk. Under that great big huge sign. You know, the one with the fifty thousand bulbs or something like that."

Mary shook her head reflectively. "Okay. On the sidewalk, then." She paused again. "Then one of the two gets away, probably with the gun because no gun is found. That hasn't changed, too, has it?"

"No. Still no gun."

"Well, that's got to help our guy, doesn't it? So at this point our patrolman's partner comes out of the doughnut shop, and the two of them stop all the traffic and run across the street and arrest Kee Park and one other guy. The other guy's Asian, too, right?"

"Yes," Mary replied. "But Kee Park's Korean. The other one is Chinese. Name's Sung something. I've got the full name in here." She tapped her briefcase.

Mary frowned. "I still don't see how they can come up with a murder charge if they don't have the gun."

"Agreed," Caroline said. "They've vacuumed out the catch basins and gone over the sewers and picked through every garbage can for blocks and there's definitely no gun, but here's what you don't know. This morning the other guy, Sung . . . whatever, after holding out all night, confessed to the robbery *and* fingered Kee Park as his partner and the trigger man. His story is that he didn't even know Kee Park had a gun."

Mary got to her feet. "And our guy's story is that he was just standing there on the sidewalk when two guys — he said they were Chinese, didn't he? — burst out of the store. One of them shoots the clerk and walks away. *Walks!* Into the crowd. The next thing he knows is he's been collared and taken here to 26."

"And now," Caroline added, "charged with murder."

Mary began to pace. "I can't believe there isn't another witness. Only that patrolman."

"In that part of town?" Caroline raised one eyebrow. "You know what it's like down there. Hear no evil, see no evil." She grinned. "Speak it though. And for sure, *do* it!"

"So what does Baxter want us to do?" Mary asked, as much to herself as to her sister.

Caroline reached for her briefcase and stood up. "He's confident that getting the murder charge reduced as a first step will be pretty easy. Everything's so messy. No gun for instance. But what he wants us to do is to slow things down until we can get more time to assess what really happened. Also, to see if we can find any holes that will either reduce the charge further or maybe even blow it away. He said that once Kee Park is charged, then it becomes a case of our having to *dis*prove. It's easier if the burden of proof is on the other side."

"So we have to find reasonable doubt," Mary said.

"And the faster the better," Caroline replied.

Of the several elements in the case that Mary and Caroline can present to evoke "reasonable doubt," there is one that stands out just a bit. What is that one?

33

Speed Checked by Radar

"WHO'S THAT?" FRAN SINGLETON POINTED at a young man who had come out a side door and was now walking at a measured pace through the parkette toward a little annex building nearby. "And what's that building he's going to?"

"Dunno," Aaron Gold answered. "The guy, I mean. The building — it's for duplicating. Serves the whole complex here." He leaned closer to the steering wheel to get a better look at the young man without being too obvious. "No, I dunno," he repeated. "Could be what we're lookin' for. Maybe. Bit young though, don't you think? He's probably a grunt. Sure doesn't look like a terrorist, anyway. But then neither did that little old granny who carried in the bombs at Woodbridge, did she?"

"Grunt?" Fran thought she knew, but the young constable with her loved to use words that he knew she was unsure of. Aaron Gold did everything he could to make Fran think the generation gap was a chasm.

"Yeah, *grunt*. One of those career minimum-wage types. Room temperature IQ. Does all the donkey work. Nothing that takes any cells." He tapped his forehead. "Can't tell time at 9 A.M., but scorches the mat when it's 5 P.M. Lots of those types in there."

Fran watched the grunt — or terrorist — pause at the bottom of the steps to the windowless little building and look around, first to the left, then to the right. She saw the young man shift what appeared to be a bundle of file folders from under his right arm to under his left as he went up the steps. Then from a huge ring chained to his belt, he selected a key, and in a single motion, unlocked the door, opened it, and walked in. The grey metal slab closed automatically behind him.

"You see him look around like that?" Aaron Gold asked. "Before he went in?" When Fran didn't answer he kept on talking. "Could be checking things out. There's always duplicating to be done at this time of day, and they may have sent him out so things would seem normal. And so he could take a look, too." He paused. "Then on the other hand he could just be planning to sneak a smoke when he's in there and was just checking for supervisors. These are all non-smoking buildings now. That's hard on the grunts."

Fran didn't respond out loud; she just nodded. She was looking back at the main building again, looking for signs of anything unusual. If the building was under some kind of threat, there was nothing obvious. It was a small building by government standards, only two stories, easy to take in at a single glance. All of the windows had standard-issue vertical blinds and all of these were open, presumably to take advantage of the late afternoon sun. After a long, uncomfortable winter, this was the third day in a row of balmy spring weather.

Fran peered even harder. There was nothing unusual at all. A single fresh graffito made a cynical comment on the brass door plate that proclaimed the building to be the property of the Internal Revenue Service, Investigations Branch, but that certainly was not unusual. No, Fran could not see anything wrong at all. There was the expected amount of movement behind the blinds. Except, come to think of it, the corner offices on both floors. And the blinds on those two weren't as wide open as the others! Or was she overdoing it? Nothing says there *has* to be movement in every office, does it?

Ever since the bombing incident in Woodbridge last month, which had flattened still another IRS building, everybody was jumpy; the slightest suspicion was treated very seriously. Still, Fran thought, there is a limit.

"The thing is, the guy appeared normal enough, didn't he?" Aaron Gold was still speaking, and Fran realized she hadn't been paying attention. "But then they're not stupid; they're not gonna send somebody out to make things look cool and then have him draw attention to himself are they? Y'know, maybe we should . . ." *Beep beep beep beep beep beep beep . . .*

On the dash, the radar monitor lit up and started the incessant beeping that every officer hated with a passion. At the same time, it shut down Aaron Gold's continuing assessment of the subject's likely purpose and Fran Singleton's analysis of what was happening in the Revenue building.

"A live one! Good!" Fran began to talk fast in spite of herself. "Get out and pull him over," she instructed Aaron, "but just chew him out and then get him out of here! This has got to look normal, but no citations! I don't want you bogged down and I don't want any bodies between us and the building, so get rid of him as fast as you can."

Before she even finished, Aaron was on the street pointing a silver-gray Mercury Sable to the curb.

"Okay," Fran said, grabbing the transmitter, "if this is cover, then now we're covered."

She tapped the SEND button twice. From outside it would surely appear like a normal call-in. Possibly a check of the Mercury with a central computer.

But what she said was, "This is Command. This is Command. Stay put! Everybody stay in place! This is just a speeder. Everybody stay put."

Fran Singleton was speaking to eight heavily armed personnel in combat uniforms. They were deployed, well out of sight, around the IRS building but were ready to move on her signal.

About thirty minutes ago she had been sneaking a listen to the four o'clock news, waiting for the sports and the Stanley Cup commentary — the Flyers played the first of two weekend games tonight — when Sergeant Horowycz had interrupted.

"IRS building again, Inspector Singleton," he'd said. In their precinct that needed no elaboration.

"No response on the 4 P.M. check. Phone company says the line's okay, but we can't raise their switchboard. Probably we're all spooked by Woodbridge, but I don't like it. Thought I should tell you."

Horowycz was experienced. He didn't panic. And because he didn't like it, Fran took only about ten seconds to decide that the Emergency Response (E.R.) team was needed. She simply couldn't afford to fool around. The building was a regular for bomb threats. At income-tax time they cleared the place at least every second day on average; that's why her precinct made a telephone check every hour on the hour. After the Woodbridge incident last month — two fatalities in that one — everybody was understandably on edge.

What she didn't want to do, however, was turn on the crazies, and that was her dilemma. She knew that if the E.R. team rushed the building for a false alarm, the media would have a field day and every nutcase in the city would get the idea. That's why she and Constable Gold had set up a radar speed trap out front — a perfectly logical and, she hoped, unobtrusive way to case the place first.

In the few minutes they'd been out front, neither Fran nor Aaron Gold had seen cause for suspicion, except maybe those two quiet offices on the corners. The only activity they'd seen was the young man going to the annex.

He came out now — burst out actually — pushing the door open with his bottom, both arms loaded with paper, and sprinted down the steps.

As he hustled back to the main building, Fran tried to convince herself that he wasn't really moving a lot faster than he had when going the other way. The young man looked out at Aaron who still had the driver of the Mercury at the curb. Although Fran studied him closely, she couldn't be sure whether the young man had a smile or a sneer on his face. In any case, the tableau of Constable Gold and the speeder didn't appear to warrant more than a glance before he disappeared back into the IRS building.

She reached for the transmitter. For a few seconds she held it in front of her, evaluating her choices. Then she popped the SEND button twice.

"Command here. This is Command."

She paused again, just a bit longer than usual.

"Stand down. Repeat. The order is to stand down. Everyone stay in place, but I want nobody, I repeat, *nobody* visible." She looked at her watch. It said 4:28. "In about two minutes I expect a bunch of people to leave the building. . . ."

Fran slumped a bit behind the steering wheel, then adjusted the radio transmitter before tapping the SEND button several times. "This is Inspector Singleton for Sergeant Horowycz. Leshie, it's . . ." She looked at her watch again. "It's 4.29. At 4:35 I'm going into the IRS building with Constable Gold. No one else. I'm 99 percent sure things are normal. Just a check. If I don't get back to you by 4:40, assume there's trouble and send in the E.R. team."

What has made Fran Singleton 99 percent sure that things are normal in the Internal Revenue Service building?

34

Where to Send
"This Stuff Here"

BEFORE LUNCH ON HER VERY first day on the job, Sue Hageman realized why she was the third assistant to equipment manager Jurgen Nodl in as many months. By the end of the first week, she was not in the least surprised to learn that hers had also been the only application for the job. For the moment, however, how she got the job, or why, was not at issue.

What was at issue was that:

1. She was in the LAME Room (lost, abandoned, and misplaced equipment) of Meadowbanks Stadium in Edinburgh, Scotland.
2. She was standing in the midst of a pile of items which, except for a set of skis to go to Turin, were like Iago Cassini's photography bag and had nothing whatever to do with sports, especially football.
3. She had been handed a ratty brown envelope labeled: *Dispersal — Names & Addresses* by Nodl, who had apparently taken off for parts unknown.
4. He had told her to arrange for the immediate shipment of "this stuff here," to the "names and addresses in there."

"This stuff here," she was able to figure out, with the help of the equipment manager of the Glasgow Rangers, the only other person in the LAME Room when Nodl disappeared, was the personal belongings of the Veneto Thunderbolts. Well, not quite. "This stuff here" was only *certain* personal belongings of the Veneto Thunderbolts left over after Jurgen Nodl, in a rare fit of efficient performance, had trundled the rest of it, in fact all except these four open cartons, off to the shipping dock. The four cartons, each with items belonging to four different players from four different cities, had found their way into the LAME Room and into Sue Hageman's charge.

The Thunderbolts had celebrated long and hard last night after taking a week to win a soccer tournament (Sue was still having trouble getting used to calling it "football" here at Meadowbanks). Then except for Sue, Nodl, and one assistant coach, the players had run for the airport, leaving the team administration to send on their belongings and equipment.

"You just have to get it to the right airport." The manager of the Glasgow team was very helpful, in part, because he was one of the many former employees of the Thunderbolts and felt sorry for Sue. "It's the players' responsibility from that point. Half these fellows never go straight home anyway. Now you take those chess sets there." He half-waved at a carton Sue was straddling. "Belong to that fellow from Capri, I forget his name. Now, he won't go right home. Never does. I'll bet he'll be off to play for one of the South American teams. Season starts there real soon. They're all like that. Except maybe for the center-half from Milan. He and his wife got a business there."

He pointed to the brown envelope in Sue's left hand. "Jurgen's awfully unorthodox, but strangely enough he gets the job done. They say you just have to get used to his ways. I never could though. Not very many can. Still, I'm sure the four names and locations you need'll be in there."

After that, Sue dared to look in the envelope for the first time. There was nothing that even approached a manifest or an inventory or a list of names and addresses. Instead there were scraps and bits of paper. There were personal letters, one from Tino Savi declining Nodl's invitation to go skiing. Savi said that he did not ski, and that in any case, he and Giovanni Moro would be visiting in Naples at the time. Interestingly, there was an invoice for skis and ski boots; it was marked paid but the name had been torn off. Another invoice was addressed to Mrs. Gino Bellissime in Milan, but that was it. Just name and address. What was being invoiced was not included.

Sue sighed. This was not going to be easy, but at the very least, now she knew where to send the guitar.

Where and to whom will Sue Hageman send the guitar?

35

A Witness in the Park

AT THE BOTTOM OF A little knoll, Mary Blair paused and looked back at her footprints in the frosty grass. She was grateful she'd decided to wear flats at the last minute. With high heels she would never have been able to walk on the lawn like this for the ground was not yet frozen.

Mary turned a complete 360 degrees. There was no sign of Alicia Bell yet, but that didn't surprise her. It was still too early. She shaded her eyes against the sun as it rose over the top of the knoll, shortening its shadow and shortening hers, too.

Both the public park just to her left, surrounded by an imposing if somewhat ancient iron fence, and the unfenced section of lawn where she was standing had been landscaped years ago into a series of mounds or knolls. None of them were any higher than the average adult, but they gave the impression of rolling terrain, especially from far away. In the park itself, a series of gravel paths and beds of exotic flowers wound their way around the little knolls. Someone had once explained to Mary that the park had been landscaped this way in order to force people to walk through it slowly.

Indeed there was no other park like it in the city. Even its name was impressive: Rousseau Place Botanical Observatory. And it was also unique because it didn't cost the city a cent. Rousseau Place

Botanical Observatory was maintained — and very well, too — by a pair of wealthy but extremely eccentric flower growers. One of them, Jack Atkin, was Mary Blair's biggest client. The other, Ron Minaker, couldn't be for he was Jack Atkin's arch rival. It was yet another incident in the long-running feud between the two that had brought Mary to the park at a time of day when she preferred to be in bed, or at the very least, dawdling over breakfast. Mary was not an early riser.

"Here I am!" A voice disturbed Mary's reverie. "I say, Ms. Blair, good morning!" A rather stout lady in a tweed suit and an odd Victorian-looking hat was covering the closest knoll at a half trot. "You *are* Ms. Blair, the lawyer, aren't you? I hope I'm not late, am I? You did say eight o'clock. I had to walk all the way around the park because the gates are locked. They're not opened till ten."

"It's okay. It's okay. You're not late," Mary assured the newcomer. "And yes, I'm Mary Blair. If you know who I am, then you must be Alicia Bell, the witness." She shook Alicia's hand. "Thank you for coming. It's important that we go over what you saw Ron Minaker do before I initiate any formal legal action. You see, you're the only witness, and I want to get a handle on things right here at the scene of the crime so to speak." What Mary Blair did not add was that she also wanted to get a handle on Alicia Bell.

"I understand," Alicia replied. "I've been involved in this kind of thing before. As a witness, I mean. For Mr. Atkin, too, about ten years ago. It was the time that Mr. Atkin and Mr. Minaker got into that dispute over who had developed a blue azalea."

Mary's eyebrows went up at that one. It had been before her time. She had become Jack Atkin's lawyer five years ago, and in the period since, Atkin had sued Minaker — or vice versa — no less than six times. Every single one of the cases had been thrown out by the trial judge, who then proceeded to scold the two adversaries. And their lawyers! Mary was trying to avoid a repeat embarrassment, which was one of the reasons she had asked Alicia Bell to meet here.

"Now tell me one more time," Mary said, "what it is you saw Mr. Minaker do."

Alicia Bell cleared her throat. "It's quite simple really. As you know, inside the park there are twenty-six flower beds. Mr. Atkin has thirteen. Mr. Minaker has thirteen. The bed over in the far southeast corner is Mr. Atkin's. Has been since they took over the park. Two days ago, in the morning, I saw Mr. Minaker on his knees in that bed. He had a little shovel and he was digging flower bulbs. Digging them *out,* and putting them in a garbage bag."

Mary Blair's voice dropped a few tones as she slid into her cross-examination mode. "You're absolutely sure which flower bed it was?"

"Oh indeed!" was Alicia's reply, "the one in the southeast corner for sure. No doubt about that."

Mary pushed a little harder. "But surely Mr. Minaker saw you, and he wouldn't dig the bulbs out if he knew you were watching."

"Ah, but he couldn't see me!" Alicia Bell's eyes lit up. "Well, he *could* have, I suppose, if he tried real hard. But he didn't. You see, he didn't know I was there. I was behind the knoll in back of the flower bed, something like you and I are right now."

Mary pounced on that one. "But if you're behind one of these knolls," she said, "you can't see what's on the other side!"

Alicia Bell was waiting for it. "Of course not. But I wasn't all the way down at the bottom. More like halfway." She pulled at Mary's elbow and led her up the knoll a few steps. "See? Look! Here we are, only halfway up and you can see *everything* on the other side. They're only little mounds, these things."

Mary nodded but didn't say anything. She had to admit that it was really quite easy to be concealed and still see everything on the other side.

"If you doubt me," Alicia went on, "just wait until we can get into the park, and I'll show you precisely where I was standing. It was a day just like this. Sunny, but a real nip in the air. Leaves falling." She pointed to the frosty grass. "And you could see your tracks in the lawn just like ours here."

Mary nodded again, and again she didn't say anything. But she had heard enough. She was glad she'd got up so early, for she was convinced now that Alicia Bell was a professional witness. A witness available to the highest bidder.

What has led Mary Blair to this conviction?

36

An Urgent Security
Matter at the UN

IT HAD ALWAYS BEEN CHRIS FOGOLIN'S personal conviction that problems come in series of three. His brother Paul insisted that when you worked at the UN building, it was never quite that simple. Paul maintained that if diplomats were involved, there was always sure to be a fourth problem, which, given time, would turn out to be not the fourth, but the first of a new series of three. In the past half hour, the two brothers were already up to five problems and counting.

Chris and Paul Fogolin were members of the security branch at the UN building in New York. (Paul had once argued that just being in New York and working for the UN counted as problems one and two all by themselves!) At 8:45 A.M. their director had given them hands-on responsibility for a meeting to be held in the Singapore Room on the 22nd floor, at 10 o'clock. The security level was "Red AA." For the Fogolin brothers that meant problem number one, for Red Double A signified a situation involving antagonists. Usually, this meant diplomats from countries at war or about to go to war or just finished with a war. It was not at all unusual to have all three conditions at once.

The second and third problems were making the room entirely

secure and establishing an entrance/exit-pass system. Normally this would not be difficult, for there were laid-on procedures for both situations. But Chris and Paul had only an hour and fifteen minutes to activate them.

The fourth problem — or the first in a new series of three — was the seating arrangement. Diplomats sparring with each other over political issues often spent days, sometimes weeks, fighting furiously about protocol. One of the most intense, not to mention tedious and sustainable battles at a UN meeting was over just who would sit where. Fortunately for the Fogolin brothers, the chair of the meeting in this case was Ambassador Manamoto of Japan. Not only was he a neutral party in this conflict, he was a diplomat of long experience and a popular choice as chair because of his reputation for being utterly impartial. One of his unvarying conditions was that during face-to-face meetings between antagonistic parties, the delegations had to be intermingled.

He was also very astute. Manamoto had already sent Paul to replace the rectangular table in the Singapore Room with a large round table so there would be no dispute over who sat at the head or the foot. Then he sent both brothers to canvas the six participating diplomats in order to learn their seating preferences in advance.

"The vice-chair will be Mr. Bjarni Benediktsson, the attaché from Iceland," Manamoto had said to them just before they left. "Now I'm sure he will have no particular seating preference, but it would be an act of courtesy to consult him."

Even though the Fogolins thought there was no time for it, they knew all about the crucial importance of diplomatic courtesy, so they went immediately to the office of the attaché from Iceland. As it turned out, it was from him that they learned the problem count had gone up to five.

"I cannot verify this," Benediktsson intoned, "and I surely don't have to tell two such as you about the way rumors ricochet about this building. Nevertheless," he cleared his throat, "the information I have, the source of which, naturally, I cannot reveal, is of sufficient force and credibility that you should neither discard nor discount it."

Paul chanced a sidelong glance at his brother. The two of them never failed to be impressed by the fact that the quality of English they heard in this building, from people who had had to learn the language, was always so much better than what they ever heard on the streets of New York.

"My information is that there may be an assassin among the delegates at the table today. Of course I don't know who it is, or I would tell you. However, I can tell you that based on my involvement in, and knowledge of, the conflict being discussed here today, it is my . . . my . . . my *gut feeling*," Benediktsson cleared his throat and made a face, "that the intended victim is Bishop Leoni, if only because he is a most vociferous exponent of his cause and certainly, as a result, has the most visible profile of anyone on that negotiating team. Even more than General Nardone."

Chris raced back to Ambassador Manamoto with that information while Paul went off to Bishop Leoni's office. Manamoto expressed mild surprise, mostly at the thought that he had not heard the rumor by now, but agreed that if it were true, Bishop Leoni was certainly a likely target. Before Chris was able to suggest a postponement, however, the ambassador went on to say that if meetings at the UN were canceled every time such a rumor floated to the surface, absolutely nothing would get done in the place.

"Just get on with the task, young man," he said, ushering Chris into the hall. "Ten A.M. As planned and scheduled." He placed his right palm over the back of his left hand and held them in front of his chest. "This does indeed make the seating arrangements more important, as I'm sure you realize?"

With that, Chris double-timed it down the hall to the elevators. There were six diplomats to speak to in — he looked at his watch — fifty-five minutes! Luckily, his first stop was productive. Dr. Perez was not in her office, but her secretary, a frowsy gum chewer in a sweater that was way too tight, told him in classic in-your-face Bronx style that "If Dr. Perez has to sit beside that Gestido witch from the other side, she walks. Is that clear?"

Chris was almost out the door before she could shift the wad of gum around to add, "And she won't sit beside Leoni. Or her creep boss, Nardone, either. They're grabbers!"

Chris turned and ran, as much to get away from the gum as to find Paul, but first he had to stop at Ambassador Haruna's suite. Haruna was head of his delegation and had a reputation for arrogance that was fully sustained when Chris was ushered to his desk. Without even looking up, Haruna motioned "just stand there" with his index finger and then continued to read the front section of *The New York Times*.

He still hadn't looked up or even acknowledged Chris's presence when he started to speak. "As head of the delegation I expect to be seated next to the chairperson, naturally. And I would like to arrange that . . ." A door in the wall to Chris's left opened, and the ambassador looked up for the first time, an expression of extreme annoyance on his face. It stayed that way while an aide tiptoed to the edge of the desk, turned the intercom to "Off" and then disappeared as quickly as possible through the same door. The silence continued for a few more long seconds.

"I understand the table will be a round one. Very well. I would like one of my delegation directly beside me — Ms. Gestido. That should be no problem for you? She's essential to me for translation. You know what happens to General Nardone's English when he gets excited. Now, of course she won't want to sit beside the bishop, so I expect you to take care of that, too."

The ambassador had looked up at Chris only briefly. He was concentrating now on preparing a large Cuban cigar. "I trust you have been told by my aides that I have a need for ample supplies of fresh water because of some medication I am taking." Chris hadn't been told, but he had no intention of getting an aide in trouble by saying so. "So I would appreciate it if you would see to that. Those are all our requirements. You may seat our new delegate, Mr. Cresawana, wherever you wish. One must cooperate in these affairs, after all." Haruna looked up again and delivered Chris an entirely insincere smile. "I imagine you have already had enough instructions from Dr. Perez to keep you busy, haven't you?"

With that, Haruna returned abruptly to *The Times,* and in seconds, Chris was moving down the hall as fast as decorum would permit. Paul was coming from the opposite direction at the same pace.

"I can't find the bishop anywhere," Paul said as soon as they were close enough to talk. "His staff says he'll be at the Singapore Room all right, but they don't know where he is. Nardone was in though."

"Anything unusual?" Chris asked.

"Strangely, no." Paul replied. "I really thought he'd want something awkward, maybe to take Leoni down a peg — you'd almost think Leoni and not Nardone was the head of the delegation — but no, he had nothing. So are we set?"

"Well, yeah," Chris said. "We're not only set, we're being set *up!*"

"What do you mean?"

"You know your theory about the fourth problem being the first of a new series of three? Well, it's right. We've got problem number six now!"

"I don't get it."

"Wait till I tell you about the seating arrangement that Haruna wants. It's manipulation, plain and simple. He's got everybody sitting exactly where he wants them. I don't know why or what for, but he's done it. Have we got time to check the security clearance of that Cresawana guy?"

Chris turned and watched as an aide bustled past them down the hall. "Who knows?" he went on. "Maybe Benediktsson's assassination rumor is true."

How has Ambassador Haruna manipulated the seating arrangement? And why does Chris want to check the security clearance for delegate Cresawana?

SOLUTIONS

1

A Decision at Rattlesnake Point

Without doubt, Perry Provato will examine the body at the morgue, looking for possible causes of death other than trauma from the two-hundred-foot drop. Trevor, however, has drawn some preliminary conclusions because of the size of the dead person and the position of the steering column.

From Perry, and from Trevor's observation, it is clear that the dead person is big. Most particularly, he has a very big belly. If he had driven the Lincoln Town Car to the edge of Rattlesnake Point, parked it, and then jumped over in an apparent suicide, he would surely have tilted up the steering column and wheel in order to get out of the car. This is automatic behavior in large people whose cars have this feature (as all newer model luxury cars do). The fact that Trevor had to tilt up the steering column in order to get his own large frame in to peer under the seat suggests to him that someone else drove the car to Rattlesnake Point. That can only mean the victim was already dead when the car was parked there, or that he was thrown over the cliff.

This conclusion may or may not be strengthened when Ashlynne checks the pre-set radio stations. The owner surely prefers country music. If when she turns the radio on, it is not tuned to a country station, that would reinforce the contention that the driver was someone other than the owner. If the pre-set stations do not include country music stations, this may suggest further discrepancy.

Why the car was parked so carefully and locked is an issue. However, the open trunk revealed the neatness with which the vehicle was kept, likely a characteristic of the victim. It is probable that Trevor's investigation of "A." will reveal that he was an orderly person. The murderer, no doubt aware of that, must have deliberately parked and locked the car in the way that A. would have done.

2

Something Suspicious
in the Harbor

On this second trip to the big freighter, Sue was able to see from her rowboat the paint scrape, where that morning the police boat had bumped into the side. Yet *The Christopher Thomas* had been receiving heavy cargo for several hours before the first visit, it was being loaded all day, and it was still being loaded when she made her unofficial trip. A freighter receiving cargo like this settles into the water as it is being loaded. Therefore, Sue should not have been able to see the paint scrape from the morning visit. By now, it should have been under water. Tomorrow morning she is going to have a careful look at the cargo, probably to see whether it is really automobile engines, or maybe to see if there is any cargo at all.

3

In Search of Answers

It is understandable that Celeste would be suspicious of Virgil Powys. After all, he has been having difficulties with his freelance business, so a cleverly arranged theft might make it possible for him to garner two or even more fees for Hygiolic's medical discovery. But Celeste needs more than suspicion; she needs good grounds for suspecting that Powys intended to be out of the studio longer than the ten or eleven minutes he claims.

Her suspicions arise out of what she observed on the reproduction Chippendale table. The weather has been very hot so all the windows are wide open. Even though Powys's studio has windows on three walls and is on the second floor (or is, at least, elevated), there is still no movement of air for there is no breeze.

Why, then, would someone who intends to be out for only about five or six minutes (he didn't know he was going to get a phone call — or did he?) place a heavy metal stapler on his working papers unless he expected that they might be blown around? And they would be blown around only if a wind were to rise. Given the conditions at the time Powys left the studio, this was not going to be an immediate possibility, or at least not a possibility in five or six minutes. Powys apparently intended to be out of the studio for longer than he claimed, which, in Celeste's opinion, is worth probing further.

4

A Single Shot in the Chest

Brian Breton turned down an opportunity to use what were supposedly Manotik's binoculars to have a look at the ten o'clock aerobics class. His probable reason was that he did not share Roly Coyne's idea of what constitutes a good time. But what he told Roly was that he couldn't really use the binoculars because they did not have the little rubber cups on the eyepieces that are needed for people who wear glasses.

Even though there are no eyeglasses in the collection of evidence and personal effects on the table up in Roly's office, Brian realizes that Xavier Manotik wore glasses, and had for a long time, because of the calloused indentations on either side of the bridge of his nose.

These two facts indicate that Manotik was not looking through binoculars at the Nucleonics executive suites. At least not *those* binoculars. Obviously Brian wonders what else in the guard's account does not hang together.

5

The Case of the
Stolen Stamp Collection

Miles Bender described one of the "police officers" as having blue eyes and a reddish moustache. He also said the officers had real uniforms and genuinely appeared to be motorcycle police personnel, complete with the sunglasses they typically wear. But if they had sunglasses on, how would Miles Bender have known the eye color of the one who got close to him?

6

Not Your Average Hardware Store

In a hardware store where customers can buy "real" hardware from bins and barrels and shelves, where things are not prepackaged in a cosmetic sort of way, the clerks get dirty hands, for obvious reasons. Over time, the hands naturally become somewhat marked by years of digging into barrels of oil-covered nails and shelves of greasy bolts. This victim had a soft white hand showing in the small of his back. Therefore, it surely is not Wilfrid Norman, a long-time hardware store owner.

7

Murder at 249 Hanover Street

The butler is the only one with a careless alibi. He said he went to his sister's in Kennebunkport on the 30th for two days. Even though his sister may prevaricate on his behalf, he has still made the mistake of saying the "30th." The day is October 1 (as the radio announcer said), so if he was in Kennebunkport for two days, he could not have gone there on September 30. There are only thirty days in September.

8
Head-on in the Middle of the Road

Dust. Road dust from what must be an unpaved surface (or else why would a grader be used, and why would the rutting and potholing recur just about every year?). The accident happened at midday on August 9. In August, at midday, after the weather has been so nice and dry (according to Peter Hesch's testimony), and after a road has been repaired and graded, any car going along it will throw billows of dust into the air. The two plaintiffs would have had to be extremely inattentive — and therefore dangerous drivers — not to have noticed each other's dust, blind hill or not, and so to have been unaware of oncoming traffic.

9
A 911 Call from Whitby Towers

Sandford Verity said that he looked up when he arrived at Whitby Towers to see if Mr. Seneca was watching the incident out on the street. That's when Verity allegedly saw him on the chair, which implies he was about to attempt to hang himself with a nylon rope. However, when Bev Ashby noticed the end of a piece of nylon rope and followed the rope to where it was clamped between the balcony doors, she had to part the drapes with her pen to do so. From the street, Verity could not have seen through the drapes.

10

The Case of the Kramer Collection

Issue number one of *Reader's Digest,* is dated February 1922, so that part of the Kramer Collection may be authentic. The *Times* was begun in 1785, so the collection could quite easily have an 1890 edition. The 1728 edition of the *Saturday Evening Post* may indeed be a "genuine fraud." The magazine began publishing in 1821. In 1899, the publishers fabricated the claim that it had actually been started in 1728 by Ben Franklin. Even after the claim was proved patently false, it was never fully abandoned.

The Arctic items are quite possibly genuine for the explorers mentioned did sally forth in the years given. (And the practice of storing food in cans was developed in England for the Royal Navy in 1810, so the can of beans is okay.) The Canadian — later American — explorer Stefansson stirred up an international controversy after his "discovery" in 1910 of a group of native people on Victoria Island with fair, European features by theorizing that they had intermingled with Scandinavian colonizers years before. Stefansson called them "blond Eskimos." Thus it could be that the material in the Kramer Collection is authentic. However, it is for the coins that George is needed, and if one of them is clearly fraudulent, it's quite possible that everything else is, too.

The George Washington coins are surely legitimate. Coins were still being issued with the label *Upper Canada* well after Upper Canada became the Province of Ontario in 1867, so a half-penny dated 1883 and designated "Upper Canada" is real enough. In World War II, nickels without nickel were issued so that the valuable mineral could be used in the war effort. Coins from Hadrian's reign are common enough. But no coin produced in the B.C. era was ever labelled *B.C.* The notion of B.C. did not come into being until well after Christ was born.

11
Waiting Out the Rain

While Michelle sat at Kline's Soda Shoppe with her friends from Memorial Junior School, she watched a little boy standing in the gutter, enjoying the rainfall. He had boots on and the runoff was rushing up against the toes of the boots. This is confirmed by the candy wrapper which flowed up to his toes and then floated between the boots. The flow of the water therefore defines the slope of the street.

Behind the little boy (and downstream) is a woman, quite likely, his mother. She is standing at Whippany Appliances, next door to Kline's, listening to the news about the D-Day landing in France.

When Michelle and Julie leave Kline's, they walk past Whippany Appliances and see the two men unloading a truck belonging to Bitnik's Delivery Service. The truck is still further "downstream" from Kline's. If its emergency brake failed, it would not have rolled toward Kline's Soda Shoppe, but the other way. To cause the damage it did, the truck would have had to smash into Kline's window while under power. It was obviously not an accident.

12
A Routine Check in the Parking Lot

The victims have been arranged in the car as though they were lovers in a tryst. Because it is December, the motor is running to make the heater operative, and to a casual investigator that would suggest that they were overcome by carbon monoxide gas.

However, Ron notes the face of the male victim. The eyes are wide open, and most important, the pupils are very small. If the male victim had been sitting in the dark car with the lady for long enough for carbon monoxide to do its deadly work, his eyes would have adjusted to the darkness and his pupils would have been large.

Ron Forrester concludes, probably correctly, that the man was murdered elsewhere (in bright light) and then put in the car afterward. He concludes that if the man died that way, the lady probably did, too. It would have been easy to attribute their deaths to accidental carbon-monoxide poisoning if he had not noticed this detail.

13
An Answer for Kirby's Important New Client

Simon Fitzwall was born in 1789.

Ambrose Fitzwall lost his leg and three fingers two months after the Seven Years War began. Since the war ended with the Treaty of Paris in 1763, he therefore lost the leg in 1756. Smythe-Boliver was 48 then (born in 1708) and Fitzwall was half his age, or 24. Fitzwall had a daughter (Abigail, according to his personal history) who, Smythe-Boliver says, was born when Fitzwall was 18, making her 6 years old in 1756.

Fitzwall came to Halifax, and then Boston, with Abigail and Ethan and Nattie's child Rachel in 1768. (The *Earl of Shannon*, on which they sailed, sank in Halifax five years after the Treaty of Paris in 1763, under the terms of which she became a British ship.)

At the time of the crossing, Abigail would have been 18 years old. She married four years later (at the age of 22) and had a first child two years after that.

At the time of the crossing in 1768, Ethan was 3 years old (half the age Abigail was when Ambrose lost the leg) and Rachel was twice that, or 6 years old. Both Rachel and Ethan married at the same age Abigail married (22). Thus Rachel married in 1784 and Ethan in 1787. And both, like Abigail, had their first-born two years after that. Simon was Ethan's first born in 1789.

14
Two Shots Were Fired

Because of the heat wave, it is reasonable to believe that the door was indeed propped open as the guard said. And it may well be that the guard faced the front if that's where previous break-ins occurred. Therefore, his back would have been to the open door. However, even though the open door faced east, and what would therefore have been the rising sun, the fact is there was no rising sun at the time of the shooting. The area was covered with gray cloud when the shooting took place, between six A.M. and seven A.M. (When Vince Pogor arrived, it was noon and the crime was already six hours old.) The sun did not come out until Vince was driving to Toronto, some time after he was about to listen to the eight o'clock news while eating his breakfast.

Given these conditions, the security guard's statement that he was startled by a dark *shadow* from the doorway behind him is highly suspect.

15
Northern Farms Ltd. Versus Dominion Spraying Company

Quite possibly Judge Westlake is bothered by the fact that not one of the witnesses has said, specifically and unequivocally, that he or she saw Molly's Arch Dream III in the field in question around the time that the spraying took place. Fenton Purge was not there at the time. Daphne Organ, although she is specific about having seen Molly *prior* to June 27 from time to time, says she did not pay particular attention on that morning. Eulalia Bean and Parthenon Andreikos are evasive. Their answers only imply that the cow was there at the time.

In combination, the answers become even fuzzier. Fenton Purge tells us the field is in the southwest corner of the farm. Daphne Organ, who lives right across the road from the farm, watches the sunrise from her porch while having tea (and then has lunch there because it is in the shade). Thus Daphne must face east. Regional Road 7, then, one of the borders of Farm Number 3, runs north-south. Since Parthenon Andreikos first waved to Eulalia Bean then, a few seconds later, saw the herd as he went toward the canal (south), the barn from which Eulie exits with hay is north of the field.

Eulie takes hay to a feed trough at the fence. Beside it is a water trough to which water is piped. Logically, the troughs are going to be at the fence nearest the barn.

Andreikos says the ends of the troughs pointed to the road. Therefore, the troughs were set up at the north end of this square field, perpendicular to the road. If he saw Molly broadside at her spot at the end of the trough, as he implies (having noted the triangle), then Molly would have to be facing north. The problem with his testimony is that he says the triangle was on her right side. If she was facing north, waiting for Eulie to arrive with the hay, Molly's right side would have been facing away from Road 7. Andreikos may have been able to see her broadside all right, but not the side that has the triangle. Judge Westlake has figured this out and probably wants to find out if this valuable animal might have died of hardware disease prior to or around the same time that the spraying took place. It could be that Northern Farms is simply taking advantage of a coincidence.

16

An Unlikely Place to Die

The time of day is early morning because Brad got trapped in rush-hour traffic. The gardener discovered Mme de Bouvère's body just after sunrise and turned on the alarm. The coroner estimates the time of death at between ten and eleven the night before. Therefore, if Mme de Bouvère and the man lying outside the gazebo had gone out to play tennis and indulge in some drugs the evening before, they would have walked over the lawn that surrounded the gazebo while it was still wet or at least damp from the rain that accompanied the late afternoon thunderstorm the day before. Because the gardener cuts the lawn every second day, and because he cut it yesterday, *before* they walked to the gazebo, Mme de Bouvère would surely have picked up a blade of grass (likely several) on her white sneakers. Yet Brad noticed that her sneakers, like the rest of her clothing, were pristine: entirely free of any specks. It appears to him that she somehow got to the gazebo without making contact with the lawn. Whether or not she died of a drug overdose, it is likely that someone carried her there after she was already dead.

17

To Catch a Mannerly Thief

Agnes Skeehan walks into her hotel leaning into a strong east wind. She responds to Deputy Commissioner Mowat's phone call and he tells her to go right to the office of the Liverpool CID, specifically to Superintendent Opilis. Through the window of the superintendent's office, Agnes notices a weathervane on a pub across the street pointing right at her. Since the wind is from the east (blowing *toward* the west) the superintendent's office must therefore be on the east side of a street that runs north-south.

Both Agnes and the superintendent then see Alistair Withenshawe across the street, walking to the police station because he was summoned there. Opilis told Agnes that Withenshawe Purveyors has an office just a short walk to the south. Therefore, this "dude" as Agnes called him, is walking toward the north, on the west side of the street. His cane must be in his street-side hand, or *right* hand, for he first bounces it off the curb, then twirls it over parked cars.

Agnes concludes that to engage in such adept cane work, Alistair Withenshawe must be using his preferred hand, his right hand, the same hand he would use to write notes. Since the jewel thief's notes are written by a left-handed person, Agnes is willing to give odds that Withenshawe didn't write them.

18

Tracing the Couriers from Departure to Arrival

Mary Clare McInerney and her investigating team need to find out from which airports the drug couriers code-named — or *possibly* code-named — Seamus, Rothsay, Saint, and Felipe are flying out, and their respective destinations as well.

The team has put together the facts that the couriers are leaving from Dorval airport in Montreal, Orly airport in Paris, O'Hare airport in Chicago, and Heathrow airport in London. The destinations that the team have discovered are Brazil (Rio), Bermuda, Hawaii (Oahu), and Hong Kong. The problem is to put the information together so that it can be determined who is flying where, and from where, so that they can be followed and the appropriate arrests made.

From Struan Ritchie, Mary Clare first learns that Rothsay is flying out of Dorval airport in Montreal, and that Seamus is going to Brazil.

Cecile King reveals that the one flying to Bermuda is flying out of Orly in Paris. That cannot be Seamus then, since he is going to Brazil. And Rothsay cannot be going to Bermuda, because she is flying out of Dorval.

When Struan Ritchie calls back he reveals that Felipe is flying out of Heathrow, which means he, too, is not going to Bermuda. When Struan says that Felipe is not going to Hong Kong, it is apparent that Felipe must be the one going to Hawaii. Rothsay, then, is going to Hong Kong. The courier code-named Saint must be the one going to Bermuda.

Once the team works out where the couriers are going, it is fairly easy to work out where they are flying from. They already know that Felipe is at Heathrow and Rothsay is leaving from Dorval. Saint (the one destined for Bermuda) is leaving from Orly, so Seamus must be going to Brazil from O'Hare.

19

Not All Lottery Winners Are Lucky

Two days before Frank Ricketts visited the body of Archie Deschamps-Lebeau there had been a chinook. In the morning rush hour, the snow had melted to slush, and then before noon the temperature had dropped to way below freezing and stayed that way. On that day, the two daughters had supposedly visited Archie and made him lunch — this is *after* the quick thaw then freeze — and reported that he was okay. They say they found him today when they came on their regular call.

However, Archie's body had been impressed into the ice. Frank wanted to know whether Nick and the crew had measured the distance between the indentations made by his feet. He also noted that the paramedics had pried the body loose carefully and rolled him over onto his back. Frank has concluded that Archie's body was out there *before* the chinook of two days ago. (It had lain on the ice, then sank into it during the thaw, and then was frozen in when the temperature plunged.) Yet according to the daughters, the old man was all right during their visit two days ago.

20

Spy Versus Spy

Because the *Rote Kapelle* did not use radios in Stuttgart to any great extent (at least in our story) the counterespionage service of German intelligence did not have great success with the direction-finding equipment used to locate clandestine radios — and thereby spies — in World War II. It is reasonable to assume, therefore, that Kopenick is not sending Morse code messages to Traugott Waechter by means of special equipment they have had installed in their vehicles. (Besides, Waechter shows up in a variety of vehicles; that would have been too much of a technical challenge had they been using such equipment.)

For obvious reasons, they would not be communicating with written signs or hand signals, not in the midst of traffic in a German city in the middle of World War II.

Then there's the fact that Hauptmann August can read the code while he is *behind* Waechter's little truck and cannot see Kopenick at all. The only way that the Morse can be used, therefore, is through the brake lights. When the vehicle stops (Kopenick's) he taps out the code to Waechter right behind him. Ernst August told Oberst Staat they had to see the two spies rendezvous while it was still raining. Either by luck or persistence, August had no doubt learned that by driving behind Waechter when the pavement was wet, he could see the brake lights of the car in front (Kopenick's) reflected off the pavement beneath the following vehicle (Waechter's). By that means August could see and translate the Morse message.

This apparently naive method of communication (Ernst August called it "clumsy") was actually used from time to time, especially in World War II. It is highly likely that real spies would not have communicated in open Morse, however, but would have had a code developed for the purpose.

The use of Morse code had declined dramatically by World War II in favor of the far more economical Baudot Code devised by a French engineer (named Baudot, what else!) in 1874. Still, who has ever heard of Baudot Code?

The *Rote Kapelle* was exceptionally successful as a Soviet network in the early years of the war, but careless use of their radios, along with increasing sophistication in radio location techniques and technology on the part of German intelligence, reduced their effectiveness by 1943. Post-war analysis, incidentally, attributes the network's downfall largely to the fact that too many agents knew one another. They did not use "cutouts" sufficiently or effectively so that when one was caught, the domino effect was very damaging.

21

The Search for Olie Jorgensson

Willy Stefan, as Connie knew, is not a neutral party in this case, being Olie's uncle, Svena's brother-in-law, and perhaps most important, being married to the sister of Olie's father.

Willy has been leading the search team down the abandoned railway line at a very slow pace. He explained to Connie that the slowness was owing to the fact that signs along the trail were hard to read, there being so many tourists hiking down the line at this time of year. His mistake was in giving that as his excuse. If there were enough tourists walking along this line to disrupt the tracking process, those same hikers would have cleaned out the wild raspberries, too. Yet they grew in abundance at the edge of the trail. For reasons that Connie wants to uncover, Willy has lied to her.

22

Murder at the David Winkler House

Chris Beadle walked into the tiny washroom pushing the door open wide. The door barely cleared the sink in the corner ahead and to the left. The sampler is hanging on the wall behind this door. If Kate Mistoe had been nailing up this sampler when the shots were fired, she would have had to close the door. Otherwise she would not have been able to get at the wall.

The problem with her alibi arises out of the fact that Sandy Sanchez says he saw her as he passed, at the time the shots were fired. (They stared at each other in shock and fear.) If the door had been closed, he obviously would not have seen her.

When Sandy spoke to Chris and animatedly made clockwise motions with his fist to describe the tightening of the fitting on the propane system, he may have been inadvertently revealing ignorance about propane systems. Threaded fittings throughout the world are tightened clockwise and loosened counterclockwise. By international agreement, threaded fittings used in gas systems (e.g., propane) are tightened and loosened in the opposite way.

Karl Schloss had the oil changed in his car. The service station would have noted the odometer reading at the time of this oil change. By checking the odometer reading right now, Chris can calculate how far he drove after leaving the service station. By having him retrace the route he said he covered on the way back to Winkler House, Chris would be able to verify whether or not he actually did so.

23

Incident on the Picket Line

You don't need to be a trucking expert to know that Roger Monk is claiming an incorrect number of tires. The police confirm that all his tires were slashed, but no tractor-trailer combination has sixteen tires.

Casual observation as you drive along the highway confirms that on the very front axle of the tractor portion of a tractor-trailer, there are two tires, one at each end. On all other axles, whether they be tandem or single or center air-lift (the type you often see retracted up off the road surface), there are always four tires, two at each end.

A little bit of logic added to this observation tells you that the least number of tires possible on a tractor-trailer combination is ten. The next largest tractor-trailer has fourteen, then eighteen, twenty-two, twenty-six, and so on. Never sixteen.

In Roger's case, he is trying for two extra tires. His tractor has a tandem axle on the rear. "Tandem" means "one behind the other." That means a total of two axles at the rear then, each with four tires (making eight), which along with the two on the very front makes ten tires on the tractor. A single axle on the trailer adds four more tires, which makes a grand total of fourteen.

24

Footprints on the Trail

Tibor Nish does not deny using the path to get to the barn. And there is a witness who saw him there. But Nish said he came *four* days ago, which is two days before the fire. The witness thinks he came on the *day before* the fire but cannot be absolutely sure.

Then there is the matter of Tibor Nish's long legs versus the fact that the footprints are close together, implying a short-legged person. On the day before the fire, there was a thaw, a day and night of mild weather. Anyone walking down a steep hill on frozen ground, during a thaw, would necessarily take short steps, with special care to dig in the heel as much as possible to keep from falling. This is because the top few inches of earth in these conditions melts and becomes soft. This layer of soft mud on top of the frozen ground makes the surface impossibly slippery. Anyone walking on it has to be very careful and must take short deliberate steps, especially on a hill. Since the only tracks on the path are from size twelve Kodiak work boots, and since Tibor Nish does not deny using the path, the only day on which those tracks could have been imprinted was on the day before the fire: the day on which the witness thinks she saw him at the barn.

25

A Very Brief Non-Interview

When Sheila Lacroix entered the office, the office door was behind her, and the wall to her left held books and newspapers. Ahead of her (the third wall) was glass through which she could see central Amman. On the remaining wall, Ibrahim Jamaa, or rather, his substitute, was signing documents.

He had his back to Sheila and he was covered with thobe and aba so that only one hand was exposed. Since the hand rested on the back of his hip and the index finger pointed to the windowed wall, the hand therefore must have been his right. He was signing documents with his left hand, and so he must be left-handed.

When Ibrahim Jamaa's substitute took two steps to the edge of his desk and spoke to Sheila, he ran one of his long index fingers over the shoulder cradle of the telephone and along the thin neck of a desk lamp. For a left-handed person, those items are on the wrong side of the desk.

If he prefers to speak on the telephone and write while doing so (hence the shoulder cradle), the telephone would be on the other side of the desk so that the receiver could rest on his right shoulder while he wrote with his left hand. If there is any doubt about this logic, it is dispelled by the position of the desk lamp. It's on the same, or wrong, side of the desk.

26

Murder at 12 Carnavon

As Honey states, to herself and to Marion, the task she has is to point out a discrepancy in the seemingly precise case that Roland has built, so that the jury will focus on the issue at hand. If she can show that at least one of these ever-so-carefully verified details is inconsistent, then perhaps the jurors will reconsider their position.

There's no compelling reason to suspect the waitress of collusion in spilling the ketchup to give Barnett a reason to go home at midday. After all, waitresses do spill things. Besides, if it were a contrived spill, it would more likely have been coffee. Still, the weakness is in the spilled ketchup. During his testimony, Barnett held out his left leg to show where the ketchup had fallen. He then very carefully told the jury that he remembered being stuck with the pin by the tailor, right where the ketchup was still on his sock.

Anyone who has ever paid attention when pant cuffs are being measured and marked, especially by a professional tailor, would notice that the tailor always measures just one leg — the *right* leg. The little tailor, who would of course have been performing professionally, must have seen the ketchup on the right sock, whether or not he really stuck it with a pin.

This tiny point is precisely what Honey needs as a wedge.

27

The Case of Queen Isabella's Gift

Even though the vicar is a clear suspect, his story that a visitor to Evensong hid in the church is entirely plausible. But the story breaks down over the electric lights. Geoffrey's visit to St. Dunstan's-by-the-Water takes place during the day. Chief Inspector Peddelley-Spens, during his tirade, said that the prime minister of Portugal was coming in "this afternoon" and that he wanted Geoff back "before tea." It took Geoff an hour to get to St. Dunstan's, so it is daylight when he and the vicar enter the church.

They unlock the main door and enter. The church is dark and the vicar turns on the lights, so lighting is necessary at all times, even daytime, to function in the church. Because the vicar asks Geoff to exit by the main door so they can turn the lights out and lock up, the only light switches must be at that door.

If the vicar entered that morning by the back emergency door (as usual) and looked up (which was unusual), would he have been able to see that the candelabra were missing without first going to the back of the church and turning on the lights? The candelabra, after all, were placed so high that even with a step stool and an extended candlelighter they were difficult to light. It is far more likely that the vicar already knew they were missing.

It is interesting to note that Geoffrey was also very much aware that the conflict between Edward II and his queen, Isabella, was so intense that by 1326, six years after the dedication of St. Dunstan's, it had degenerated into civil war or, depending on one's point of view, a legitimate revolution. It's quite possible that in 1320 they may not have attended a dedication together.

George IV became Prince Regent in 1810. His father, by this time, was reported to be having animated conversations with a tree in the Great Park at Windsor, thinking it was Frederick the Great.

28

Quite Possibly, the Annual Meeting of the Ambiguity Society

Bonnie must assume that none of the members are telling her the exact truth; yet she must take their answers at face value for her calculations. If she does that, she will find that every date but one in the month of May appears at least two, sometimes three times, when all the answers are considered, thus representing the nature of the Ambiguity Society.

Sally's first answer specifies a date *after* the thirteenth of the month. Her second specifies a date *before* the thirteenth. Thus every day is accounted for at least once except the thirteenth.

Karen Di Cresce's answer adds the thirteenth along with every other odd-numbered date, and Julio's answer specifies every date of the month except May 4, 9, 16, and 25. Thus, every date in the month is mentioned at least two or three times (thereby establishing further ambiguity), except for May 4 and 16.

The very first response, the one from Bruno Steubens, specifies that the meeting will be held on the middle of the month just like this year. The middle of the month of May is the sixteenth, which means that date, too, has two answers. Therefore the only single, unambiguous choice of date is May 4.

29

The Case of the Missing Body

Lesley Simpson could see that at the point in the trench where the skeleton was found, the earth was being excavated for the very first time as the trench was being dug. Had someone buried the body of Mrs. Vincent Gene there three years ago, the earth would have been disturbed by that excavation. However, what Sergeant Palmer pointed out to Lesley was a skeleton lying in earth that was still in its natural layers. It is entirely likely that this earth hadn't been disturbed since the last glacier passed through.

Therefore, the skeleton of Mrs. Gene must have been brought to the trench from elsewhere, dropped in, and then covered with loose earth for the backhoe operator to find the next day. If Vincent Gene is charged, it will likely be Lesley Simpson's argument that he is being framed by someone who put the body in the trench in an attempt to make it appear as though she had been buried there some time before.

30
The Case of the Marigold Trophy

Janice has been reading back issues of *The Daily Enterprise* on microfilm. She has available issues from 1903, 1904, and 1905. When Eugene Weller tells her it is closing time she is looking at a date in March. Since she has been reading carefully and in sequence for four hours (from five to nine without taking a break) and since she can cover five months of issues in an hour, the March she is looking at must be March 1904, the year the trophy was awarded to Maribeth Tooch. (She has covered twenty months; all of 1905 plus nine months of 1904 minus an October for either year. This would not work out if she had started with 1903 and worked forward in sequence.)

The date she is looking at is March 3. According to the article, Curragh O'Malley's horse ran down Ezra Templeton on March 2. On the same day a week earlier, it struck Maribeth Tooch just after she had seeded her marigolds. In three out of four years, the date of the same day a week earlier would have been February 23, the planting date for marigold seeds according to the contest rules, but 1904 is a leap year (any year divisible by four); therefore the date she was struck, *and* the date on which she seeded her marigolds for the contest, was February 24. The Grand Champion Marigold exhibitor of the 1904 Albion Agricultural Exhibition broke the rules!

31

The Coffee Break That Wasn't

What Lennie is attempting to determine is whether she got a fresh cup of coffee or whether the waitress simply took out the plastic housefly and returned with the same cup of coffee. That's why she tasted the coffee with her little finger. She must have put sugar in the original cupful. When she tasted coffee from the "new" cup it must have been sweet, causing her to conclude the worst.

32

Who Shot the Clerk at

Honest Orville's?

Certainly the missing weapon is one element on which Mary and Caroline will undoubtedly lean, but their strongest point is likely a simple matter of physics. The time is pre-Christmas, close enough to the day itself for the Christmas shopping rush. The two young ladies were wearing coats, and Caroline made note of the overheated police station. Therefore, this is Christmas time in the northern hemisphere, so that by 8:40 P.M. it will be fully dark outside. If Honest Abe's sign has around fifty thousand bulbs, as the discussion reveals, then the area where the shooting took place will have a great deal of bright artificial light. However, if the shooting took place well out on the sidewalk, under the big sign, Kee Park would have been *backlit*. It would have been extremely difficult, therefore, to make out his face, if not impossible. Given that the patrolman-witness had to run across a wide busy street to nab Kee Park and Mr. Sung, who were in a crowd, and had to stop traffic to do so (which would inevitably mean taking his eyes off the suspects), the two law students may well choose to press the witness on the issue of making a positive identification in, say, a lineup. He's not likely to succeed without reasonable doubt.

33

Speed Checked by Radar

This was certainly not an easy decision for Fran to make. If there is something wrong, some threat in the building, then she will be held liable for failing to act. Yet to rush the building with the E.R. team could be disastrous for several reasons. Even for her to go in, with or without Constable Gold, could complicate things, too. And both choices attract lots of attention and would alert the crazies.

It behooved Fran to weigh the situation carefully, which is just what she did. Given what she learned from Constable Gold about the likely type of individual it was who was walking to and from the annex building, and given that it was very close to 4:30 P.M. on a Friday afternoon, she believes that in moving quickly, this possible "grunt" was behaving normally.

If it were likely that he was returning to a difficult situation, at least one that he couldn't leave by 4:30 P.M., he would probably have moved more slowly or deliberately. Quite likely the sight of a speeder being caught would have merited a longer look, too.

He might even have tried to send a signal of some sort to the two police officers.

All this, however, is meaningless if the young man walking to the annex building is not a regular employee, but one of a group that has taken over the building, and who has been sent to the annex to further the appearance of normality. But one action of his signaled to Fran that he is a regular employee, and one familiar with the place. He not only anticipated the locked slab door while walking up the steps, he selected the right key from a large ring of keys and unlocked the door in a single motion. All his actions indicated that he has done this many times before. A "plant" would have been less automatic at some point in the procedure.

34

Where to Send "This Stuff Here"

In the LAME Room, there are four cartons, each with items to go to four different players. Sue has to identify which item goes to which player and then arrange to send it to the airport of the appropriate city.

The former holder of Sue's job (now with the Glasgow Rangers) says that Nodl will have the names and addresses in the brown envelope she is carrying, however unorthodox they may seem. The names are Tino Savi, Giovanni Moro, and Gino Bellissime. Iago Cassini's name must be on one of the items already: the photography bag. The four cities are Turin (where the skis go), Naples, Milan, and Capri (where the chess sets go).

Iago Cassini gets the photography bag. Tino Savi does not ski, so he gets neither the skis nor the photography bag. Tino Savi does not live in Naples (he visited there) or Turin (where the skis are being sent). Since he does not live in Milan (where Gino

Bellissime has a business with his wife), Tino Savi is from Capri and therefore gets the chess sets.

Giovanni Moro does not live in Naples or Milan (or Capri), so he must be from Turin, where the skis go. Since Gino lives in Milan, Iago Cassini must be from Naples. The remaining item of the four must be the guitar, which then goes to Gino Bellissime, or to his wife, in Milan.

35
A Witness in the Park

The season must be autumn, for Mary Blair's shoes leave prints in the frosty grass. Alicia Bell says there are leaves falling. Yet it must still be early autumn, for Mary notes that the ground was still too soft to walk on in high heels.

Anyone who gets up early enough on crisp but sunny autumn days, when the temperature is close to freezing, has seen the frost on the grass sparkling in the sunlight. However, particularly in early fall, that sparkle disappears within two to three hours of sunrise at the latest as the earth warms.

Alicia Bell was doing fine with her story about Ron Minaker digging flower bulbs out of Jack Atkin's flower bed until she mentioned the footprints in the frosty grass. It's quite possible that two days ago when the alleged digging took place, the weather was identical to the weather on the day Mary and Alicia met. And it's quite possible that Alicia could have been concealed just over the brow of a knoll behind the flower bed in question. But she couldn't have stood there until at least ten o'clock for the park gates are locked until then. By that time, in early fall, the frost on the grass has long melted away in the sunlight.

It appears that Alicia Bell was enjoying her story so much that she went too far.

36

An Urgent Security Matter at the UN

There are to be eight people at the table in the Singapore Room: Ambassador Manamoto and Bjarni Benediktsson, who are chair and vice-chair; General Nardone, Bishop Leoni, and Dr. Perez from one delegation; Ambassador Haruna, Ms. Gestido, and Mr. Cresawana from the other. Chris and Paul Fogolin can begin the seating arrangements knowing that the delegations have to be intermingled, and knowing that the heads of delegations will sit beside the chair, Ambassador Manamoto.

However, Ambassador Haruna has manipulated the seating. He has accomplished this by requesting that Ms. Gestido, of his delegation, be immediately beside him. (It makes no difference whether she is on his right or his left; by extension, therefore, Haruna can be either on Manamoto's right or left; the manipulation works in either direction at this round table. For purposes of description here, assume that Haruna is on the left, with Ms. Gestido to the immediate left of him.) Because of Ambassador Manamoto's intermingling condition, Mr. Cresawana cannot sit to her left in turn, and she does not want to sit beside Bishop Leoni, so only Benediktsson or Dr. Perez can sit there.

Ambassador Haruna apparently knows that Dr. Perez will not sit beside Gestido, so Bjarni Benediktsson must then be the one next to Ms. Gestido. To Benediktsson's left will be Dr. Perez because Haruna knows she won't sit beside Leoni or Nardone. Then to her left, in order, will be Mr. Cresawana, then Bishop Leoni, then General Nardone, as the circle goes back to Ambassador Manamoto.

This is the only seating arrangement that is possible if all the diplomats' requests are to be honored. And it has been arranged

Solutions

principally by Ambassador Haruna. Whether or not he has help from others (like Dr. Perez) we cannot be sure. All we can be sure of is that he has manipulated the seating arrangement with only one simple request: that Ms. Gestido be seated beside him. And his reason for the request is entirely valid and reasonable, too.

What is achieved by the manipulation is getting Mr. Cresawana immediately beside Bishop Leoni. Since Leoni is the suspect target, and Cresawana is new, it is only natural for the Fogolin brothers to suspect him.